CW01638720

Simmer Do

THE EARLY WAILERS' STORY

John Masouri

Jook Joint Press

Copyright © 2015 John Masouri

The right of John Masouri to be identified as the author of this work has been asserted in accordance with the Copyright, Designs and Patents Act 1988.

First published in 2015 by Jook Joint Press

All rights reserved. No part of this book may be reproduced in any form or by any electronic or mechanical means, including information storage or retrieval systems, without permission in writing from the publisher, except by a reviewer who may quote brief passages.

ISBN: 978-0-9933759-0-3

Front cover illustration by Jerry Neville.

Jook Joint Press

41 St Nicholas Road

Brighton BN1 3LP

www.jookjointpress.com

Simmer Down

THE EARLY WAILERS' STORY

John Masouri

Also by John Masouri

Steppin' Razor: The Life Of Peter Tosh

Wailing Blues: The Story Of Bob Marley's Wailers

"The original Wailers with Bob, Bunny and Peter.
That's the first reggae I heard in late high school.
They were the Beatles of reggae music, no question.
That's the ceiling of the art form right there."

Actor Eddie Murphy, as told to the author.

Contents

PART THREE

High Tides, Low Tides

Introduction

Bob Marley's story is well documented. Films, books and websites celebrating his life abound and every track he recorded, released or not, is readily available online. He's a global treasure who's afforded the same kind of cultural importance as Bob Dylan or John Lennon, which is extraordinary considering where he's from and the genre he represents.

'Simmer Down' isn't another book about Bob Marley, but the vocal group he formed back in the early sixties with Peter Tosh and Bunny Livingston. These are the faces that deserve to be carved on reggae's Mount Rushmore. All three Wailers later became successful in their own right but the songs they recorded together are reggae music's crown jewels, akin to Elvis Presley's Sun recordings or Muddy Waters' early Chicago blues. It was this trio who led the evolution from ska to roots reggae. Like the Beatles, their music carried the hopes of a younger generation and would define an era. Members of both groups became figureheads, but whereas their British counterparts went from being lovable mop-tops to leaders of the hippy revolution, the Wailers made the transition from slickly dressed rude boys to dreadlocked Rastafarians. Their songs have since stood the test of time, and retain their relevance. They reflect the powerful cultural tides that were prevalent during the late sixties and as a music historian I found this hard to resist. The Wailers' lyrics weren't just shaped by life in the Kingston ghettos, but also the US Civil Rights movement and African liberation struggle, the Bible, Rastafari and Black Power – influences that permeated much of their output from 1968 onwards.

That was the year I first heard them, in the wrap-around darkness of an illicit house party in the Meadows, a rundown area of Nottingham bordered by Arkwright Street and the Trent Embankment. These weekly gatherings were the equivalent of rent parties in the US. They were places where Caribbean migrants would socialise together and to the same musical backdrop they were accustomed to back home. Whoever organised them would charge a small admission fee, and then sell drinks and occasionally food inside. No one had a license, or gave any thought to health and safety. There would be security on the door, but you never knew what might happen. Fights weren't uncommon, and the police had to be bought off if the same address was used for more than a few weeks at a time. Locals called them shubeens but they were also known as "blues parties," since they'd been around since the days when rhythm and blues was the music of choice in the Caribbean.

The numbers of West Indian families living in the Meadows had risen sharply in recent years. Their neighbours were white, working-class people raised on austerity and hard work, and Enoch Powell's infamous 'Rivers Of Blood' speech was still ringing in their ears. Most of them weren't racist in a violent or organised sense, but felt threatened by dint of being poor and uneducated. We can see the same thing happening today, as Eastern Europeans bear the brunt of people's fears but then Nottingham always felt as if it was at least ten years behind the rest of the country.

London may have been swinging and Californians still groggy from their Summer Of Love, but my hometown's inner city communities had far slower cycles of change. The Meadows had streets of identical terraced houses, their red brick exteriors uniformly blackened with dirt. Each house was a "two up, two down" with a small back garden and outside toilet, and an alleyway snaking between them and next door. Inside, televisions the size of a wardrobe flickered in tiny front rooms filled with coal and tobacco smoke. I lived a couple of miles away in Carlton, but there was little difference in terms of lifestyle. No one I knew owned a telephone, and few people had cars or ventured much beyond the neighbourhood pubs where the occasional black regular would get called "Chalky," by way of acceptance.

My generation was the first to grow up and go to school with Caribbean people in England. Whereas our parents saw differences, we uncovered similarities and yet the inequalities were there for everyone to see. Multi-cultural Britain was in its infancy, and skinheads were its biggest threat. There was no Premiership back then, but lots of us at school shared the same passion for football. Nottingham Forest had Ian Storey-Moore and Jim Baxter playing for them but the team kept flirting with relegation and it wasn't just white kids wishing we could get rid of Johnny Carey and sign George Best. The difference was that I could go to the matches, whereas my black friends couldn't. That's because skinheads would stand outside the City Ground on match days, handing out National Front literature and threatening any black fans they came across, regardless of which team they supported. These right-wing thugs took the fun out of going to football matches and they didn't do reggae music any favours either. You'd have to keep an eye out for them and especially after dark when they'd roam the streets looking for trouble. Occasionally a group of them would burst into a rock hangout, causing longhaired hippies to scatter in every direction. They'd have to think carefully before gate-crashing a shubeen though, since some of the patrons carried knives or kept a machete or piece of lead pipe in the boot of their cars, and weren't afraid to use them. Some of these skinheads were genuinely into the music, but still went around beating up black people. I never could figure that one out, but was too fearful to ask.

At fifteen, I still wasn't old enough to get into clubs, even before the days of ID cards. Kids my age usually went to matinee shows, like when Jimi Hendrix played the Theatre Royal with Pink Floyd. That was my first-ever concert, and it changed my life. Hendrix was like an exotic traveller from another galaxy – living proof of a parallel dimension, peopled by the kind of free spirits who never ventured into the Toby Jug or local workingman's club near where I lived. At that time, the boundaries of my world were determined by family holidays in Skegness and the occasional school trip to London. I was driven by thoughts of escape and developed an insatiable hunger for music, art, books and drugs. I devoured these at every opportunity, thinking they would help me to spring the trap. Knowledge was key and yet music provided the bigger stimulus, and also the greater sense of belonging.

It's impossible to over-estimate the influence of the Beatles and Rolling Stones at that time but there was also a blues revival under way; soul music was at an exhilarating peak and a new generation of artists had begun to emerge from Britain's folk tradition. I thrived on such diversity and still do. My uncle Endel had started the ball rolling after introducing me to jazz and rock and roll, and I've my mother to thank for filling the house with the sounds of black American pop like Stax and Tamla Motown, as well as British bands like the Kinks, Small Faces and The Who. (The less said about Matt Munro and other crooners the better.) Tuning into John Peel's 'Night Ride' radio show led me to more esoteric wonders like Captain Beefheart and Frank Zappa but then Peel had integrity, and was fearless in his listening habits. Soon, Ravi Shankar and free jazz would enter my orbit, and John Coltrane's 'A Love Supreme' is still one of my favourite jazz albums.

My friends and I smoked lots of hash in those days. Black and sticky Nepalese Temple Balls, streaked with opium were our preferred choice. We'd also drop acid some weekends, which was an activity shrouded in ritual and even reverence until the giggles started and we settled into marvelling at an orange or pencil for a few hours. Drugs enhanced our appreciation of music in ways that we'd never believed possible. We felt as though we were pioneers, sailing into uncharted territory. What innocence! None of us had yet witnessed anyone struggling with mental problems as a result of taking psychedelic drugs. We were young and naïve, and hell-bent on opening the doors of perception, which we'd read about in the underground press and Carlos Castaneda's 'The Teachings Of Don Juan.' I, like many others of my generation, would never see things in quite the same way again. LSD revealed the absurdities of accepted truths and taught us to question everything we already knew, which meant whatever our parents and schoolteachers had drummed into us. We felt that society wasn't working for us, and it had outlived its purpose. We wanted to see change, and welcomed the influx of people from Britain's former colonies as a step in the right direction.

The first Jamaican single I bought was Prince Buster's 'Al Capone,' which had just returned to the charts a second time. We called this style of music "Blue Beat," since the word "reggae" wasn't in use yet. Buster was an electrifying performer but it was my first experience of sound-system that got me well and truly hooked. A friend called Lorna said she had an uncle who ran a shubeen and would I like to go? My take on race relations was about to undergo a severe examination. I wasn't feeling too confident before we left for the Meadows but the last vestiges of it drained from me completely just as soon as I saw the people milling about outside, and realised that I was out of my depth. A few minutes later we squeezed past the doorman and entered a maelstrom of pulsating sound, heat, ganja smoke, laughter and sexual energy that left me speechless. The next couple of hours would have a profound effect, and leave me eager to repeat the experience. It would be a while before I felt any kind of welcome but that first visit passed without incident and I couldn't wait to go back there. I was used to exams at school, but the tests that mattered now took place in semi-darkness as the music assaulted your senses and the bare walls glistened with sweat. I remember providing amusement for one or two large ladies, who backed into me as I was stood in a corner and slowly gyrated in time to the music. It was impossible not to feel aroused, even whilst looking around in wide-eyed terror to see where their boyfriends might be!

The music was the biggest draw however, and I loved hearing it in that environment. Over by a far wall the DJ would rock on his heels whilst stood over a single deck, the valves of his amplifier glowing in the murk as he played music so loud and bass-heavy, it made your whole body shake. For me, there was an aura around these people and what they did. I discovered that the best selectors were also storytellers who could fathom the mood of a gathering at will, as if by way of divine intuition. It was in reggae dances where I learnt how *serious* music could be although to be honest, I didn't know what I was listening to most of the time. No one ever announced the records, or at least not in a form I recognised. Also I was used to buying singles at Woolworths, and they only sold whatever was in the charts. I remember finding Johnny Nash's 'Hold Me Tight' there but other examples were few and far between, and I hadn't yet heard of any specialist shops. Soon I'd be able to recognise individual tracks and artists, but it seemed to take forever.

The first Wailers' tune to emerge from the mists of my great unknowing was 'Nice Time,' which came out on their own label. The production was almost ramshackle, but the melodies were enchanting. "Long time we no have no nice time. Do you think about that? This is my heart to rock you steady. I'll give you love any time you're ready..." Despite its title, there was nothing escapist about 'Nice Time.' Whoever was singing didn't shy away from the fact that life was hard, even as he created a safe haven for him and his girl to romance in, and I liked that. I'd never heard of Bob Marley at the time and wouldn't realise it was him singing 'Duppy Conqueror' either, which I remember hearing before I left Nottingham for good.

The London reggae scene had its share of racial tensions but the sound-systems were too powerful an attraction to miss, even if the crowds were unfriendly compared to those a hundred miles further north. 'The Harder They Come' was showing at art-house cinemas as I arrived. Several months later and the Wailers' 'Catch A Fire' proved pivotal in introducing roots reggae to rock audiences who warmed to the band's tales of love and revolution. Even reggae fans hadn't heard anything like it before and when they appeared on 'The Old Grey Whistle Test' singing 'Stir It Up' and 'Concrete Jungle,' my jaw literally dropped in amazement. It was a truly defining moment, but the memories of hearing 'Nice Time' bouncing off the walls of those crowded house parties in the Meadows would never fade.

Without realising it, I'd already begun my search to discover the essence of where such music came from and what it meant – not just musically, but to its core audience. That was more than forty years ago. Jamaican music has evolved out of all recognition since then and yet the magic of that original Wailers' line-up remains. In their relatively short time together, Bob Marley, Peter Tosh and Bunny Livingston recorded some of the best and most influential ska, rocksteady and early reggae sides ever made, yet their legacy has been diminished by the confusion surrounding the name "Wailers."

Coxsone Dodd had called them "the Wailing Wailers" when issuing their debut album but the original vocal trio always referred to themselves as "Wailers" and considered it a badge of honour, considering all the adversity they'd faced in keeping the group together. Since Bob sang lead on the majority of their songs, it was no surprise to find some of their early singles credited to "Bob Marley and the Wailers," including a few released on their own label. If the description was merited then the other two clearly didn't mind, since Peter was also awarded top billing on occasion. Significantly, all three signed the deal with Island Records that resulted in 'Catch A Fire' and 'Burnin'' as equal partners, which is why those albums were credited to "The Wailers." It was only after this original deal with Island had expired that disputes over the name surfaced.

In early 1974, prior to the release of 'Natty Dread,' Chris Blackwell invited Marley to sign with Island as a solo artist. This was inevitable, since Bob was prepared to work with Blackwell and Peter and Bunny weren't, but the manner of the split was to have far-reaching consequences for everyone in the Wailers' circle. Relations between them had already soured when Marley and Blackwell decided on the name "Bob Marley and the Wailers" for Bob's solo releases. In appropriating the name "Wailers" they obliterated the original group's legacy and handed it to Marley's backing band in one fell swoop.

In my opinion this was an act of wanton self-interest, and should never have happened. Blackwell wanted to promote the Barrett brothers as a crack rhythm section, which was fair enough. They'd already achieved fame in reggae circles as the Upsetters and merited recognition alongside the era's other great backing bands, including the Meters. The point is that Marley could have turned down Blackwell's suggestion or conferred with Peter and Bunny about it but did neither. Instead he assigned the title of "Wailers" to his hired sidemen but then left them off the revised Island deal whilst allowing them to believe they were stakeholders. They weren't, since there was no paperwork to back up such claims, despite Family Man acting as a surrogate producer on most of their records, and all of Bob's releases being credited to "Bob Marley and the Wailers."

I've often wondered about that conversation between Marley and Blackwell, on which so much ill feeling would come to rest. It was collusion at best and something more sinister at worse, because some would later claim that it brought a curse upon the Wailers. Dark mumblings told of Marley signing a devil's pact, which made him sound like Jamaica's answer to Robert Johnson, except instead of selling his soul to the devil in the moonlit glare of a Mississippi crossroads, Marley could have been stood under the mango tree at Island House as a fierce heat beat down beyond the shade. Either that or sat outside the rehearsal room at dusk, his treachery accompanied by a chorus of cicadas. Conversely, Peter and Bunny would get blamed for the Wailers' break-up, as Bob's misdeeds went unchallenged. Bunny felt so strongly about what happened that he changed his name to "Bunny Wailer" since at no point did he and Peter relinquish their identity as Wailers, irrespective of any solo projects. That would have meant severing their links to the past and all they had struggled to achieve, which is not something they would have done lightly. Years later, Bunny would attempt to sue "the impostors" who'd stolen his and Peter's mantle. He failed in this and Aston "Family Man" Barrett has continued to lead a band called the Wailers ever since, trading on the Marley repertoire.

'Simmer Down' belongs to a previous era – one that allowed room for dreams and even a little innocence amidst the bloody political upheavals. It completes a trilogy of books I've written about the Wailers, which can also be read separately. This one evolved from a surfeit of additional material and the desire to focus on that original trio without placing the emphasis on

Marley, or shoehorning the three principals into convenient stereotypes. The story of their development is inevitably bound up with that of post-colonial Jamaica, which is a country I've visited many times over the years. Its people have enriched my life in ways I could never have imagined, whilst the music continues to fire my enthusiasm long after casting its spell in those Nottingham blues parties.

PART ONE

Learning The Ropes, And Jumping Fences

CHAPTER ONE

Forward March

It was the advent of radio that made all the difference. Young people in the fifties wanted something that spoke directly to them, rather than the wartime generation. Salvation arrived in the shape of a sound and attitude that swept all before it. The impact of rock and roll – white folk's rhythm and blues – on American and European teenagers has been well documented. It was borne on a tide of euphoria that's refused to fade, but the Caribbean has its own musical stories to tell. Before the arrival of the first-ever state-owned radio station in 1959, Jamaicans would listen to American stations such as WINZ and WCKY broadcast direct from Miami, or Rediffusion – an early form of cable owned by the British. Songs by popular crooners like Frank Sinatra, Bing Crosby, Dean Martin and Nat King Cole would leave their imprint on the next generation of Jamaican singers almost by osmosis but rhythm and blues was the No. 1 choice of local teenagers, along with a smattering of Latin, country and western, jazz, gospel and calypso. Jamaica had its own form of native folk music called mento yet it sounded outdated next to the shuffling rhythms, infectious melodies and witticism of genuine calypso which enjoyed widespread popularity throughout the Caribbean, and not just Trinidad.

After the war, many Jamaicans had travelled to the States on short-term visas, cutting cane and doing farm work for more money than they could earn back home. Some returned with gramophones and records, whilst others bought them from seamen looking to make a bit of extra money. Kingston was a busy port and ships from the US, Panama, Russia, Canada, Britain and Germany regularly sailed into the harbour, inching their way through the flotillas of small fishing boats before regurgitating hundreds of sailors into the downtown nightclubs and whorehouses. Demand for new records was high and before long, the fifties' reputation for austerity was wilting under a tsunami of 45-rpm singles, jukeboxes and transistor radios.

Rivalry between the early Kingston sound-systems was fierce. Most played American rhythm and blues since there were few local recordings available at first, but then local record producers like Clement "Coxsone" Dodd and Arthur "Duke" Reid began to forge a distinctive sound that whilst influenced by New Orleans and America's Deep South, had a ragged excitement that could only come from Jamaica. These early recordings were intended as "specials" for their sound-systems, which they'd string up in small halls, on lawns and even street corners. In an era mercifully free of noise regulations, songs by Fats Domino, Louis Jordan, Lloyd Price, the Platters, Coasters and Drifters would ring out in the warm night air, interspersed with local variations some called "half blues."

Coxsone would become a major figure in the Wailers' story. He used the Blues Blasters, led by Cluett "Clue J" Johnson, on the majority of his early sessions. Aubrey Adams (piano) and Ernest Ranglin (guitar) were members of that band. These two musicians changed the rhythm around, and placed the emphasis on the second beat of each bar. The music now had a mento flavour, and sounded more Jamaican. The style they created that day was called "ska" and originally referred to a dance, as well as genre. Drummer Lloyd Knibb, who'd studied with the "burru" people, and Derrick Morgan were both primary architects of ska. The latter's early records for Prince Buster featured Jah Jerry Hines' clipped rhythm guitar, and helped shunt the music in a new direction. Like Ranglin, Jah Jerry brought a jazz sensibility to bear on these early recordings, but then he and his fellow band members were all keen jazz fans in any case.

All of the big-name American jazz and rhythm and blues artists loved to tour the Caribbean and news of their arrival in Jamaica travelled fast. Shows held at the Carib and Regal Theatres drew large crowds and were often talked about for weeks afterwards. Many featured local support acts and not just singers, but also dancers, comedians and even contortionists. In England they were called "variety shows." Those in Kingston were always well attended yet it was mainly working-class people who excitedly took their seats at weekends. The middle classes rarely ventured that far downtown, but preferred dancing to big bands led by Eric Deans, Redver Cook, Ivy Graydon, Ray Coburne, Roy White, Milton McPherson and Carlisle Demetrius, who played at places like the Silver Slipper in Crossroads. As Independence drew closer these bands began to scale down in size although a number of Jamaica's best jazz musicians had already left for America and Britain by then, leaving Kingston record stores like Bop City and the Royal Roost – both named after New York jazz clubs – looking emptier by the day.

By 1961, the raucous energy of rock and roll had dissipated and the British charts started to fill up with trad jazz and novelty records, yet there was still a lot of good music around. The

Miracles' 'Shop Around' became Motown's first million-seller and together with the Marvelettes' 'Please Mr. Postman,' heralded a landslide of hits from the label. Under Berry Gordy's direction, Motown was recording young, black unknowns from Detroit's housing projects and turning them into stars. Theirs was a fresh, new sound fusing pop, rhythm and blues, gospel and doo-wop, and whilst it was still a little raw around the edges, it possessed so much vitality. Sam Cooke, with current hit 'Cupid,' continued to set the benchmarks however. Cooke's melodies and phrasing took the breath away at times, although Ben E King ran him close with 'Spanish Harlem' and 'Stand By Me.' Such songs could be heard all over Kingston, just as in New York and London.

It was the era of Brook Benton, Jerry Butler and Gene Chandler, as well as Ricky Nelson, the Everly Brothers and Dion. 1961 was also the year Ray Charles topped the US charts with 'Hit The Road Jack' – a record steeped in country and western, and that found him challenging some deep-seated preconceptions about race and music. Ray Charles sang country like his forbears approached hymns. He brought a different range of sounds, nuance and emotion to the songs, and demonstrated how music itself has no boundaries, but only our imaginations. Jamaican teenagers knew instinctively that Charles had chosen to sing country because he'd grown up with it and felt its power as a storytelling medium, just like they had. Soon, they'll walk into a Kingston record shop and find Marty Robbins' 'Gunfighter Ballads' and Skeeter Davis' 'Greatest Hits' prominently displayed on the walls. It wasn't like that in England but considering the influence of Southern radio back in the fifties, its hardly surprising country music should be so popular in Jamaica. Patsy Cline's 'Crazy' was the reigning misty-eyed ballad, and Elvis Presley impossible to ignore. Just three years earlier, Elvis had returned from the US Army and been corralled into making desultory Hollywood films. Despite this, his popularity continued to grow and 'Are You Lonesome Tonight' and 'Wooden Heart' were both massive hits in 1961. Elvis also recorded his first-ever gospel album that year except Caribbean style gospel wasn't necessarily confined to church songs, or the Christian religion.

Inspired by the revival churches, Laurel Aitken, who was born in Cuba to a Jamaican father, had already issued songs with Biblical themes like 'Zion' and 'Judgment Time.' A true musical pioneer, he'd also sang about Ghana's Independence on the first Jamaican recording to feature African style drumming. Records like this opened the door for a more African expression in terms of lyrical and musical content. Marcus Garvey had long urged black people to acknowledge their shared African ancestry and his teachings, fired by Biblical rhetoric, would surface in any number of songs from the dawn of the sixties onwards, when the term "roots music" was virtually unheard of. It was around this same time, as Jamaica awaited Independence and was solidifying into a two-party state that the Rasta movement became a real presence in the ghettos.

The Rasta faith had first appeared in Kingston in the 1940s, preaching a back-to-Africa credo and proclaiming the divinity of Ras Tafari Makonnen, who'd been crowned Haile Selassie I, Emperor of Ethiopia, ten years earlier. Kingston's slum dwellers lived amongst both Rastas and burru people, who'd kept their

African traditions alive by drumming and chanting. Whilst burru people didn't necessarily share the same spiritual goals as the Rastafarians or "locksmen," there was a natural affinity between the two groups. For example, both smoked marijuana (or "herb" according to Rastafarians) and were scorned as outcasts. Many of them had been jailed, or forced to make a living hustling on the waterfront. The burru people were generally more lawless than the Rastafarians and every time one of them was released from prison, they'd celebrate long into the night with their frenzied drumming and incantations.

Count Ossie would become synonymous with Rasta drumming, and his appropriation of burru styles was a defining moment in the development of Jamaican music. At first he visited burru elders in Back O' Wall, otherwise known as the Dungle. The sessions then moved to Salt Lane, where master drummer Brother Job schooled him in the rhythmic arts. Ossie often practised at Brother Issie Boat's camp up in Warieka Hills, where a Rasta preacher, Brother Love, would read from the Bible as Ossie and his drummers played. This was around 1960, soon after the Count had moved to Adastra Road, near Rockfort. Rastafarians were intent on retracing and then reclaiming their African heritage, and for once the Jamaican government was prepared to listen. In the wake of the Claudius Henry debacle, Rasta spokesperson Mortimo Planno proposed the University of West Indies conduct an official study of Rastafari. The University duly assigned a team of scholars, including the late Rex Nettleford, to prepare a report. Their findings exposed appalling social conditions, and revealed that Rastafari brought hope to people who otherwise had none. Acting swiftly, the Jamaican government sent a delegation of

Rastafarians – including Planno – to Ethiopia in April 1961. The Emperor gave them a royal welcome, offered them land for resettlement and assured them of his support. This was a significant development and five years hence, will lead to the Emperor making a state visit to Jamaica. Before returning home, the delegation also visited Sierra Leone, Liberia, Ghana and Nigeria. Predictably, some people considered their mission a waste of time and resources, whilst others would revise their opinions and view Rastafarians in a different light.

According to Rachel Manley, a majority of Jamaicans had decided the Rastafarians were "simply dirty and lazy. The poorer people where they lived thought they were mad and laughed at them, whereas the more well to do resorted to their customary bigotry. When they could find no plausible reason for their fear and hatred, they made one up."

Many mistook the Rastafarians' red eyes – caused by smoking herb – for criminal intent or madness, but Rachel's grandfather Norman Manley deemed these Third World prophets "deeply religious," and remarked how "the minute a person takes off the traditional dress and habit of Britain, we all go into a state of shock." He also made reference to "middle class hysteria" but when told the Rastas wanted to go back to Africa he said this was nonsense, because "they'll find they can't be Jamaicans in Africa; they can best be Jamaicans right here." Having seen country people smoking ganja from he was a child, Manley was also tolerant of herb smoking. The English had their whisky and tobacco he said, whilst Jamaicans had white rum and ganja. "It's the same difference," he explained, "I say it's about time Jamaicans unshackle themselves and do whatever it is that comes more naturally to them or we'll never have true independence."

Whilst Laurel Aitken had got there first, it would be the Folkes Brothers' 'Oh Carolina,' produced by Prince Buster and featuring Count Ossie's drummers, that introduced the sounds of nyahbinghi or Rasta drumming to a wider audience. Buster had launched his own sound-system, Voice Of The People, after a stint working for Coxsone and had grown up around Rastafarians in Salt Lane. Count Ossie insisted that his music was for spiritual purposes when Buster first approached him, and took some persuading before venturing into JBC's studio for the session.

Buster recorded Bunny & Skitter's 'Chubby' the same day but it was another of their compositions, 'Lumumba,' which tapped into the zeitgeist more convincingly. Bunny & Skitter had written the song as a tribute to the Congo's first elected leader, Patrice Lumumba, who was assassinated in January. It was recorded at a time when Africa's liberation struggles were making headlines around the world and provoking serious debate in Trench Town, where no subject concerning black people went unnoticed for long.

Seventeen new African nations had formed in 1960, the same year that South African police had opened fire on black protestors in Sharpeville, killing sixty-nine people. It was the "Sharpeville Massacre" that first alerted foreigners to the problem of apartheid in South Africa and such injustices would be thrown in sharp relief by Harry Belafonte's latest discovery, singer Miriam Makeba. Alas, her words did little to appease South Africa's apartheid regime. The ANC and Pan-Africanist Congress were banned, and their leaders either imprisoned or driven into exile. By now, the struggles in Namibia, Zimbabwe, Guinea,

Mozambique and Angola were being decided by guerrilla warfare, prompting Dr. Martin Luther King to name Africa's bid for freedom as "the greatest single international influence on American Negro students." He, like Norman Manley and W. B Du Bois, rejected the panacea of repatriation. Instead, King described the American Negro as "neither totally African nor totally western. He is Afro-American, a true hybrid, a combination of two cultures."

This was the level of debate taking place in some of the Rasta camps dotted around Kingston, in amongst the shantytowns. The people from there may have been poor, but it would be a mistake to think they were ignorant too.

1962 would prove a momentous year. There were changes happening in the Caribbean region and Jamaica, like Trinidad, would soon be master of its own destiny. Independence was the brainchild of Norman Manley, who'd been voted Jamaica's first Prime Minister in 1959. A year later, his rival Alexander Bustamante demanded Jamaica leave the West Indies Federation and put up posters everywhere, asking "Federation. What Will It Really Cost Jamaica?" This led to a referendum in September 1961. The majority voted "No" and so Jamaica withdrew. Manley then asked Britain for Independence, which was duly scheduled for August 6th, 1962. The announcement was met with joy, and an outpouring of nationalistic fervour began. New businesses sprang up all over the island and improvements were made to factories and office blocks, as well as both airports. Manley however, became dispirited and called an early election, which he lost. On polling day, a Russian ship had entered Kingston harbour amidst rumours of a Communist takeover, and his cause seemed lost from that minute onwards. Bustamante's victory meant he was best placed to take credit as a number of Manley's projects came home to roost, such as building a National Stadium in Kingston and commissioning a new flag. Both political leaders were later offered knighthoods. Bustamante accepted his but not Manley, who grew old rueing how Jamaica's resources hadn't trickled down to the poor, and that he hadn't been able to implement more far-reaching reforms.

Bustamante was Prime Minister as midnight fell on August 5th 1962 and Jamaica became a free, independent nation within the British Commonwealth. People sang and danced in the streets whilst others crammed into the National Stadium, which quickly swelled to its 35,000 capacity. Princess Margaret and her husband, the Earl of Snowdon, watched as the Union Jack was lowered and the Jamaican flag hoisted in its place. Combined choirs then sang Jamaica's new National Anthem as hundreds of notable guests, including America's Vice President, Lyndon Johnson, paid tribute. The ceremony was followed by a magnificent fireworks display, which could be seen for miles. There were other firework displays and parties all over the island that night. Flags and bunting were everywhere and since the next two days were Public Holidays, there was plenty of time for revellers to recuperate.

No sooner were its colonial blinkers removed, than Jamaica began the task of re-examining its legacy. The George VI Memorial Park was renamed National Park, where a National Shrine was erected in memory of Marcus Garvey, Paul Bogle and George William Gordon. Jamaica was honouring its own in a move designed to instil pride in its citizens, and all three National Heroes were rebels. Two died as the result of a slave uprising, whilst the other preached black self-reliance before being toppled by the US government, who feared Garvey's influence over his two million followers.

Within a week of Independence, the ninth Central, American and Caribbean Games opened at the National Stadium. Jamaican athletes again distinguished themselves, winning many gold, silver and bronze medals. The excitement generated by these games proved infectious. Businesses flourished and nationalism took on a multitude of different forms. Jamaica now had its own television network for example, whilst ska was the national dance. The music had become celebratory, and it was infectious. Derrick Morgan had seven records on the Jamaican charts in 1962, including 'Forward March,' which summed up the mood of an entire nation. "Gather together, be brothers and sisters. We're independent, we're independent. Join hands to hands, children started to dance. We're independent, we're independent..."

Jamaica's new Minister for Culture, Mr. Edward Seaga, had been a record producer before committing himself to politics. He understood the importance of music and the arts, and encouraged Jamaican artists to reflect their own identity rather than conform to European tastes. In 1963, Seaga established the Jamaica Festival Of Arts and promoted the work of Louise Bennett – affectionately known as "Miss Lou" – who chose to write and perform her poetry in patois, rather than "proper" English. Miss Lou's use of patois would prove highly influential, and made Jamaican people feel good about themselves. Seaga had strong ties with revivalist churches and also backed Kingston's High Priestess of kumina, Mrs Imogene "Queenie" Kennedy's presence on the airwaves, courtesy of JBC. It was a rich and fertile period for the arts – even the new James Bond film, 'Dr. No,' had been filmed on the island the year before – but no sooner had the euphoria settled than an American Airways 707 crashed into the Caribbean Sea just off Jamaica's coastline, killing ninety-five people.

A year earlier, hot on the heels of Fidel Castro's revolution, a hijacked Cuban plane had landed in Kingston on its way to Miami, provoking US displeasure. Cuba was a near neighbour, and Castro a hero to many for having battled colonialism. Alas, his alliance with Soviet Russia would cause problems. John F Kennedy had only been in office a short while before trying to invade Cuba, after Castro allowed Russia to install nuclear missile bases there. A showdown resulted, and hostilities were only narrowly averted in late October. Impending nuclear war cast a long shadow over Jamaica and the world at large. Memories of Hiroshima and Nagasaki weren't too far in the past, and older folks shivered inwardly at the thought of further conflict. They really shouldn't have worried. Danger was averted and the only conflicts to involve Jamaica were internal ones as the country attempted to shake itself free from colonialism. It will be the youth who bring fresh hope, and search for ways to exert their own ideals.

CHAPTER TWO

Simmer Down

Anticipation had crackled in the air like electricity in the first few months after Independence. There was even a glow of expectancy in Kingston's ghetto neighbourhoods, as people allowed themselves to dream of brighter tomorrows. Trench Town was no different and took on a pastoral air at times – especially at sunset, when a reddish cast would envelope the huge tamarind tree at the corner of West Road and Third Street. During the day, children climbed in its branches, looking for ripe pods they could break open to get at the tasty morsels inside. Trench Town already had a tough reputation, but there still tracts of wasteland where fruit trees grew wild and local residents could help themselves to guineps, mangoes and ackee. Some would raise a little change by selling them to passers-by and then head for Fargo's shop, where they'd buy essential supplies such as rice and flour. Boys would sell peanuts on the kerb outside, or maybe play a game of marbles as they waited for customers. There was a park on First Street where the older youths played cricket and football after school but it was at nightfall when the area came alive and people gathered to talk and play music, or sit outside under the stars hunched over tables playing peck-a-pow – a game Chinese migrants had brought to Jamaica, and that occasionally erupted into violence if play got a little too heated.

It was under the tamarind tree, right outside Wempy's front yard where Bob Marley, Peter Tosh and Bunny Livingstone met for the first time, at one of the impromptu jam sessions that took place there most evenings. Bob and Bunny were already close friends. Bob's mother and Bunny's father were partners, and all four lived together on Second Street. The two boys immediately felt drawn to Peter's ready smile and good humour. He was strong, lean and handsome, and a year or two older than them. At six foot four, he was considerably taller as well, but it was his singing and playing that impressed them most. Peter's guitar may have been borrowed, yet he strummed it like a veteran. Surrounded by onlookers, he'd sung 'Go Tell It On The Mountain' and 'Sinner Man' with great purpose and not a trace of nerves. Before long, they'll discover he can also play piano and organ, as well as sing falsetto and baritone.

Bob and Bunny didn't play instruments yet and so they were fascinated by this newcomer's proficiency. Peter had grown up in Westmoreland, on Jamaica's western shoreline. He'd learnt to sing in church and school choirs in Savannah La Mar, and had even taken piano lessons for a while before leaving for Kingston aged seventeen. That was a year ago. Upon arrival he'd lived with his aunt Mary in Denham Town, although it wasn't long before he upped sticks and moved in with his maternal uncle at 19 West Road, in Trench Town. The Morris' had six children, ranging from Peter's age to six-year old Pauline, whom he baby-sat occasionally. His uncle was a cabinetmaker although the family also made syrup, which they'd sell to shops and restaurants all over Kingston. Peter wanted more than anything to be a singer, but was currently working for a dry cleaner called Mr. Tibbs on Fourth Street, where he pressed clothes and ran errands.

Like Bob, Peter barely knew his father and this had made him determined to make his own way in the world. He listened intently as they told him about auditions and in Bob's case, actually making records. These two youths had already tasted what he'd long dreamt of and the three became friends straightaway. Bob too, was from the country. He'd been born and raised in Nine Miles, a tiny hamlet just twenty miles from Jamaica's north coast in the parish of St. Ann's. His father, Norval Marley, was a white – or as some would have it, light-skinned – Jamaican from Clarendon, who'd worked in the parish for a time inspecting government property. It was there he met Bob's mother Cedella, who was a poor black teenager, and considerably younger than him. After she became pregnant he married her but then returned to Kingston soon afterwards, for treatment of a hernia. Cedella saw little of him after their wedding, although he did visit her for a week after the baby was born. It was her husband who chose the name Nesta Robert Marley – Robert after his brother and Nesta for reasons unknown, except he'd made sure Cedella could spell it properly before he left. Apparently, Norval Marley's mother was so distraught about her son's relationship with Cedella that she disinherited him. This was effectively the end of their marriage but when Bob was five, Norval wrote to his wife, offering to educate their son in Kingston. Cedella agreed, and sent him off alone in a bus to Kingston where his father met him, then dropped him off at the house of an elderly, infirm woman Bob had never met. The only education he received was in how to survive, alone and uncared for, in an alien environment. It would be nearly two years before friends of the family discovered him and took him back to Nine Miles, where life could be just as hard. His mother often left on trips to Kingston, whilst his grandfather Omeriah Malcolm was a real disciplinarian. In Bunny's words, Bob "had to earn every meal,' because it was tough on him as a mixed race kid. He says the young Marley was a wild child and very tough – that he never cried, never gave in and had incredible drive. He was also scrupulously honest, and people felt they could trust him.

Bob was eleven when his mother met Bunny's father, Thaddeus "Thaddy" Livingston, who was a builder. Bunny, who'd been raised in Kingston, was just nine and already showing signs of musical prowess. He'd been "stick drumming" from the age of four and like Peter, had made his own guitar from wire, wood and a sardine tin. Soon after Thaddy and Cedella got together, the new family left for St. Ann's except country living wasn't to Thaddy's liking and they made a U-turn back to Kingston within less than a year. Temporary accommodation at several different addresses in the downtown area followed until they eventually settled in Trench Town. Cedella's brother had recently left for England, and offered them his apartment in the government yard on Second Street. By that time there were two breadwinners in the family, since Cedella worked as a housekeeper and ran a cold supper shop, selling liquor and food at the corner of Beeston Street and Spanish Town Road. Money was coming in and whilst their new home was modest, it afforded a welcome degree of security.

Bob attended a handful of different schools (including Ebenezer and St. Aloysius) before leaving aged fifteen. He then worked as a welder until an accident almost blinded him. Music would be his main focus from thereon. It was around this time that he started entering talent shows at places like the Queen's Theatre, where in-between the main acts – Alton & Eddie or Higgs & Wilson say, backed by Kes Chin's band – members of the public would be invited on stage to sing a song or two. As at Harlem's famous Apollo Theatre, audiences would cheer for singers they liked, and boo the rest off stage. The winner would then get a pound, or maybe a guinea. Bob used to sing a song he wrote called 'Fancy Curls,' which was his first-ever composition. Occasionally he'd win, but mainly he'd practise at home or around the neighbourhood.

Ken Boothe remembers Saturday sessions in Back O' Wall, where young hopefuls like himself would wait their turn as more established names put them through their paces.

"These guys were older than us, so if we don't hear anything from them when we sing, like a compliment, then we don't feel like singing," he told the authors of Reggae: The Rough Guide. "Even Bob Marley, the first time I saw him was at Back O' Wall. He'd just come from the country, but everybody was just young and pursuing the music."

In March 1962, just days after his seventeenth birthday, Bob recorded a handful of songs for Leslie Kong, who'd recently launched the Beverley's label and was looking for new talent. Bob's on record as saying Desmond Dekker, who worked alongside him at the welding shop, introduced him to Kong. Another source suggests it was an aunt of his who recommended him to Derrick Morgan's girlfriend, Pat Stewart. Derrick was Kong's A & R man at the time as well as his lead act, which meant he'd certainly know about the two young hopefuls who'd turned up at Beverley's ice cream parlour on Orange Street. Bob and Bunny had auditioned together, and then arranged to meet Kong at Federal for the actual session. Bunny arrived late and so Kong sent him away, saying how studio time didn't come cheap. It wasn't Bunny's fault – he'd been delayed at school – and so you can imagine his disappointment. Shame, because Bunny had wanted to sing a song he'd written called 'Pass It On,' which he'd later record with the Wailers.

Bob's first session yielded a 7" single, 'Judge Not,' credited to Robert Marley. Bob's mother always used his first name, Nesta, but everyone else called him "Robbie," hence Robert. It was an auspicious start but probably didn't feel like it at the time as Kong got him to sign a release form, then pushed him out the door once the session was finished. 'Judge Not' was his second-ever composition, and a keenly wrought observation of how people spread gossip or "susu" 'pon each other," as they say in Jamaica. Whilst written about what he's seen in Trench Town, it carries a universal message. "Who are you to judge me and the life that I live?" he asks, before warning that "the road of life is rocky, and you may stumble too." Bob's delivery is a little shaky, but he's helped along by a simple melody played on a recorder, and that gives the song a mento air. Kong issued 'Do You Still Love Me' – another breezy, ska and rhythm and blues hybrid, sang in similarly naïve fashion – on the flipside. It's a basic lyric, written by a boy who's worried that his girl's found someone else. You can dance to it but it doesn't sound like a hit, despite the insistent beat and Charlie Organaire's wheezy harmonica.

Bob's second single was 'Terror.' Bunny was at the session and swears it was actually recorded although no one's found a copy of it yet – at least not at the time of writing. 'Terror' remains the reggae collectors' Holy Grail and was followed by 'One Cup Of

Coffee' – a cover of a 1961 hit by US country singer Claude Gray, credited to Bobby Martell. Either Kong chose to rename Bob, thinking Martell sounded hip, or the label printer messed up. No matter, because despite its' intriguing storyline and tighter production, 'One Cup Of Coffee' soon disappeared without trace. A few weeks later, country singer Patsy Cline was killed in a plane crash and Jamaicans paid tribute as only they knew how – by playing her songs incessantly. It was around this same time that Derrick Morgan invited Bob to perform with him. This was summer 1963, shortly before Derrick left for England. They did two shows – one at the Capri Theatre in May Pen, Clarendon, and the other in Montego Bay. At the first Bob was nervous, and danced better than he sang. When he'd launched into 'One Cup Of Coffee' the audience had booed him, so he quickly switched to 'Judge Not' instead. As soon as he started into the first verse the crowd started cheering wildly. It was his first real lesson in stagecraft, and he learnt it well. Leslie Kong had promoted these shows, but no other recording sessions were forthcoming. Shortly afterwards Bob and Bunny auditioned for Duke Reid and Prince Buster, who turned them down because of his rivalry with Derrick Morgan. Buster didn't like the fact that Morgan was recording for a Chinese producer instead of a black man like himself, and sent the youngsters on their way.

Bob and Bunny met Peter not long afterwards. They'd already befriended Alvin Patterson – affectionately known as "Seeco" – who lived across the road at No. 20. He was a few years older than them, and would become a father figure to Bob in due course. Seeco was a veteran from the days when calypso ruled the roost, and had known the likes of Lord Flea and Joe Harriott. He was quick to recognise the boys' talent, and encouraged them to practise every chance they got. Bob regularly sang in his yard after that, where the two of them worked on songs like 'Simmer Down.'

Trench Town was awash with talent at that time. Jamaican hit-makers Alton Ellis and Delroy Wilson lived nearby – also Delroy's brother Trevor, AKA "Batman" – whilst Junior Braithwaite was a neighbour of Joe Higgs, on Third Street. Music was all around except where Peter lived because in Bunny's own words, "nothing ever really happen on Fourth Street."

A lot was happening elsewhere though. In April, there had been clashes between Rastafarians and police in Montego Bay and several people ended up dead during what Jamaicans called "the Holy Thursday Massacre." Two months later, President John F. Kennedy talked of the moral crisis affecting America and promised action. In a televised speech, Kennedy said, "the Negro baby born in America today, regardless of where it's born, has about one-half as much chance of completing high school as a white baby born in the same place on the same day; one third as much chance of completing college; one third as much chance of becoming a professional man; twice as much chance of becoming unemployed; about one-seventh as much chance of earning $10,000 a year; a life expectancy which is seven years shorter; and the prospects of earning only half as much."

His words (and intentions) caused fierce debate. Soon afterwards, white racists killed Medgar Evans, a local secretary of the NAACP. The bid to change America and also attitudes towards the black race, was getting ever more serious. Action was called for and Dr. Martin Luther King rose to the occasion by announcing a march on Washington, due to take place in August. Just over a hundred years had passed since President Abraham Lincoln had signed the Emancipation Proclamation abolishing slavery, and it had taken that long for people to come together and demand their Constitutional rights with one voice. Two hundred and fifty thousand people gathered around the Lincoln Memorial in Washington that day listening to speakers like Dr. King, who gave his famous "I have a dream" speech.

Time magazine would vote him Man of the Year, even as Miriam Makeba urged the United Nations to use their influence in freeing the thousands of political prisoners held by South Africa's apartheid regime. Congress was still debating President John F. Kennedy's Civil Rights bill when he was assassinated on November 22nd. His successor, Lyndon Johnson, will take up the cause but this was shocking news. Every radio station throughout the world interrupted their schedules to report his death, and in Jamaica it was no different.

The Wailers' favourite station was WINZ, broadcast from Miami. The reception wasn't always so good, but the anticipation of knowing they were going to be hearing all the latest American hits more than made up for it. They'd gather round a big, old-fashioned Phillips radio owned by Bunny's father and then sing to their hearts content, even if there were other people around. Peter had always loved singing to the radio, and now had friends who felt the same the way. Any number of songs could set them off – especially 'My Prayer' by the Platters, Frankie Lymons' 'I'm Not A Juvenile Delinquent' and Gene Chandler's 'Duke Of Earl' – but then it all came together for Bob, Bunny and Peter during a verse of Little Anthony and the Imperials' 'Tears On My Pillow.'

"Bob is singing and me and Peter start harmonising without even planning what we're going to do," says Bunny. "Anywhere he turns, it's like we are pinned into each other. We're locked in..."

Harmony groups were all the rage and here were three teenagers, dreaming of musical careers and searching for ways to make it happen – not in hope alone, but with the steely determination of knowing their lives could depend upon it one day. In the meantime, the music continued to weave its irresistible spells. The Drifters' 'Up On The Roof' and 'On Broadway' were runaway hits that summer, as was the Miracles' 'You Really Got A Hold On Me' and Ray Charles' latest tearjerker, 'Take These Chains From My Heart.' Some talented new voices had emerged too – Motown acts Stevie Wonder and Marvin Gaye for example, and white groups such as the Beatles and Beach Boys. Folk music was on the rise as well. Peter, Paul & Mary had sang on the Washington march and their current hit 'Blowing In The Wind' was written by a young street poet called Bob Dylan.

Joe Higgs recalled it was Bob who introduced him to Peter, and who'd visualised bringing the Wailers together. Higgs' mother sold fruit at the corner of Third Street and West Road, and his sister was also a singer. He was a few years older than any of the Wailers, and had started out in a duo with Roy Wilson, who lived on the same street. The pair had been persuaded to sing together at a talent show in 1958, after entering separately. Joe was eighteen at the time. Shortly afterwards, Edward Seaga saw them perform at the Ward Theatre and became their manager. Higgs & Wilson's debut single 'Manny Oh' was a No. 1 hit in Jamaica, but then Seaga decided to concentrate on politics and so they went over to Coxsone.

It was around the time Bob, Bunny and Peter began rehearsing with him that Joe wrote 'There's A Reward,' which is still one of the most moving songs in the entire reggae canon. The Wailers' rehearsals took place in his kitchen and the first thing he taught them was to sing from their bellies, rather than up in their throats. "Harmony structure was basically what I taught them," he said, "precision, craft, technique, breath control and sound consciousness."

Bunny says as a harmony singer, you're supposed to be in harmony with all other sounds around you. That means you can have a hundred people all singing different harmonies at once, and yet they can still be in harmony with one another. Bunny likens it to running. A group of people can run together and yet not get in each other's way, even whilst heading in the same direction yet they've got to run in their own lanes otherwise they'll crash into other people around them. He says it gets confusing if you take too much notice of what others are doing around you. Instead, you have to concentrate on your own melodies and stay out of their way, knowing that the next person is harmonising around you.

Peter and Bunny both had great voices, but Bob struggled with harmony and therefore sang lead more often. He also had the most expressive voice and was the acknowledged leader of the group. Whilst Bob had always seen the Wailers as a trio, those three weren't the only youngsters passing through Higgs' ghetto academy. Although a strict taskmaster, Joe jokily referred to his students as "the Teenagers" or even "the Roosters" if they were acting cocky. He also called them the Juveniles for a time. It was a loose aggregate, with Bob, Bunny and Peter at its core, and they were close. Barrington Sayles, who lived just down the street, was a regular as were Junior Braithwaite, Garth Dennis, his sister Joan, Ras Cardo, Cherry Green and one or two others.

Virtually every day, Bob and Bunny would call round to the Morris's house for Peter, or meet him at the drycleaners and then head out to find a rehearsal spot. Sometimes they'd walk down Ebenezer Lane to Back O' Wall; other times they'd rehearse in a yard at the corner of Fifth Street, accompanied by friends like Sabu and Tabby. This worked fine for a while, until the neighbours complained about the noise and called the police. They also rehearsed at No. 8 First Street, where Bob's friend Vincent "Tatta" Ford lived, and at the corner of Second and Third Street – anywhere they could work on songs and practise harmonies.

Peter's guitar supplied rhythm and key for these early rehearsals. He'd have to borrow one – sometimes from Joe Higgs – until Bob "liberated" a beaten up box guitar from the Ebenezer Club, at the corner of Ebenezer Lane and Darling Street. Not long afterwards, they were due to play at Sheriff Brown's cold supper place in Greenwich Farm. (Sheriff "John" Brown would later have a cameo role in 'I Shot The Sheriff.') Already late and feeling the need for some exercise, the three of them raced each other down the street; Bob and Peter collided and Peter sprained his ankle, which remained swollen for days. Yet it was the loss of their instrument, now smashed beyond repair that hurt most. Their second guitar was bought from a Rastaman in Trench Town called Deacon, who'd kept it hanging on his wall unused. In time to come they'll fix a pick-up on it, so they can play it through an amplifier. Bunny will later use this same guitar on tracks from his

'Blackheart Man' album. He says Peter would get tired from playing it so much and hand it over to him or Bob for a while, so they could practise the chords he'd showed them. All three Wailers will become proficient guitarists in due course, but it was Peter who had the most natural ability.

That October, Hurricane Flora swept through Jamaica, causing widespread flooding as the island endured its heaviest rainfall for over sixty years. Damage to the island was estimated at over two million pounds, and many lost their homes. A month later Carol Joan Crawford was chosen Miss World, and became the first Jamaican to ever win the title. Her triumph was clouded by Kennedy's assassination but it had provided a ray of sunshine for Jamaica amidst all the tragedy.

In February, sports fans took note of a brash young boxer named Cassius Clay, who was due to fight heavyweight champion Sonny Liston. Clay taunted the older man mercilessly by calling him "an ugly bear" and then beat him in the seventh round. Not only did he win the fight against the odds; he did it with incomparable style and the Wailers became instant converts. Clay was a showman and full of confidence but the man was a soul brother too. People loved his ghetto style rhymes and humour and when Clay said, "I shook up the world!' after the fight, he wasn't joking.

The Wailers continued to rehearse during the early months of 1964 and to a backdrop of fresh hits on WINZ led by the Impressions' 'Keep On Pushing,' the Drifters' 'Under The Boardwalk' and Martha Reeves & the Vandella's 'Dancing in The Street.' British groups had begun to storm the American charts after the Beatles' appearance on the Ed Sullivan Show.

Beatlemania didn't extend to Jamaica, but people there certainly heard about it.

Back in England the BBC launched Top Of The Pops, a chart show that immediately commanded sizable television audiences. Soon afterwards, Millie Small became Jamaica's first-ever international singing star with 'My Boy Lollipop' – a near identical cover of the Barbie Gaye hit that was so catchy, people are still singing it now. People in England called the new sound "Blue Beat" (after the record label) but Millie's record featured the same driving rhythm and blues as heard in Jamaica, only with additional pop sheen and a dash of bluesy harmonica. 'My Boy Lollipop' flew to No. 2 on the UK charts in March, and was a hit the whole summer long. Its success would be a wake-up call for Jamaica, and the diminutive Millie's first appearance on British television – even in black and white – was a revelation. The craze for Jamaican music in England gained rapid momentum from there but it was Millie, aided by Chris Blackwell, who lit the blue touch paper.

In late July, news of Jim Reeves' death dominated the airwaves. The country singer was very popular on the island, and his songs would be played non-stop in the weeks ahead. Marley biographer Stephen Davis tells of Bob witnessing a horrendous incident he'll forever associate with "Gentleman" Jim's music. It happened when a jilted man dragged his girlfriend out into the street and then beat her to death with an iron pipe whilst people in the neighbourhood did nothing to help her. The man had been playing mournful ballads – including some Jim Reeves sides – at full blast whilst waiting for her to come home, and no one dared confront him when the violence started. That's how the pressure got to some people. It stripped them of all emotion except anger and despair, and then pushed them to the very limits of their endurance. People in Trench Town instinctively understood their pain, even whilst praying for strength.

As the Wailers continued to sing on street corners and in local parks, they gained small groups of admirers who followed them from place to place. Singing in the ghetto was different from busking, because no one had any money to give them. Instead it was a real test of their popularity, and a valuable one. When they weren't practising they might take in a film – 'A Fistful Of Dollars' maybe, starring Clint Eastwood – or follow the bus into Maxfield Avenue, since there were always lots of dances in that area.

By the summer of 1964, they were as well rehearsed as they possibly could be. The only thing missing was a name, since the Teenagers, Roosters or whatever else Joe called them just didn't sound right. They needed a name that said something about who they were, and where they were coming from. Living in Trench Town they identified themselves with the poorest members of the community - people who'd suffered, and struggled to make their voices heard. Somewhat inevitably, they reached for the Bible and decided on the name "Wailers" after reading Jeremiah Chapter 9, Verse 19, which begins, "For a voice of wailing is heard out of Zion…" Bob will later claim, 'we call ourselves Wailers because we started out crying…"

Once Joe Higgs had pronounced them ready, Seeco went to see Coxsone and told him about the youngsters he and Joe had been grooming. Coxsone asked to hear them so Seeco sent the Wailers for an audition, which didn't go too well. They returned to

Second Street feeling dejected after Coxsone said he couldn't use them, and to come back in six months' time.

"When they go there at first, I never go with them. I send them," Seeco told Wailers' fanzine Distant Drums. "I was cooking that day, so after him say they must come back in six months I get mad and say, 'No man. We have to do some recording now,' and I take them back up there, same time, explain some things to Coxsone and him say, 'Alright, let's try them.'"

This is where the Wailers' story becomes problematic. According to Seeco the group didn't play 'Simmer Down' during that first audition, whereas Bunny swears they did, albeit as an afterthought. What isn't in question is that no one deserves the title "Godfather of Jamaican music" more than Coxsone. Like Berry Gordy's, his empire started from humble beginnings, but the music of the sixties and seventies simply wouldn't have been the same without them. Coxsone's mother had a general store at the corner of Beeston Street and Love Lane, and discovered she could attract extra customers by playing music on an old gramophone by the front door. Does this make her one of Jamaica's earliest DJs? Well, yes except it was her husband, Mr. Darlington, who ran the family's first sound-system. When Coxsone was away working on farms in the American South, he'd collect rhythm and blues records and send them to his stepfather. Mr. Darlington played in a union hall affiliated to the JLP. His chief rival at the time was Lord Koos, who played for PNP supporters in the hall opposite. It wasn't until Coxsone returned to Jamaica that he took the sound out of Union Hall, renamed it Sir Coxsone's Downbeat and started playing at different locations around Kingston, competing against rival sounds like Sky Rocket, Duke Reid, V Rocket and Monarch. This was some time before he went into production, around 1958. After that there was no stopping him and it wasn't long before he had several sound-systems on the go at once, each staffed by a different crew and yet still called "Downbeat."

Ever the entrepreneur, Coxsone promoted shows at the Ward and Palace Theatres, as well as out-of-town venues such as Delmar Theatre in Port Antonio. He also ran Monday night sessions at Carnival Lawn on North Street and played every Friday night at the Barbecue Lawn on Fleet Street in Rae Town, with King Stitt at the controls. This was near where the PNP had their headquarters. As records became more readily available, he opened a shop at the corner of Orange and Charles Street.

One of his helpers was a bright, wiry youth from Hanover called Lee Perry who'd started out as a dancer, doing moves like "the Chicken Scratch." Perry would become Coxsone's right-hand man, helping out with the sound-system and also auditioning young hopefuls as the sixties got underway. He was good at it too, because Coxsone already had the beginnings of a decent stable before the Wailers turned up in the summer of 1964. Toots and the Maytals were there, and also Stranger (Cole) and Ken (Boothe.) His star turn however was Delroy Wilson, a former child prodigy whose early hits sold in droves – this during an era when island-wide sales of 50,000 weren't uncommon.

Wilson had recorded several jibes aimed at Prince Buster, allegedly written by Perry, and that had caused sparks to fly among Kingston's music fraternity. Jamaican audiences thrived on such rivalry and it meant Coxsone usually performed to big crowds – especially when he played in West Kingston, where several of his main acts lived.

According to Bunny, the Wailers auditioned for him at one of his regular Sunday afternoon sessions in early July. At thirty-two, Coxsone was younger than they'd expected. Peter played guitar and the group sang four songs – 'Straight And Narrow Way,' 'I'm Going Home,' 'Do You Remember' and 'I Don't Need Your Love.' The latter was Bob's latest composition, and the song he thought would please Coxsone most. It didn't, and he wasn't especially impressed with the others either. Having turned them down already (or so we're led to believe), his patience must have been wearing a little thin. Bunny then suggested 'Simmer Down' which Bob sang reluctantly, since he was writing songs like 'Destiny' at the time. Bunny loved it though and before Bob could protest, Peter struck up the chords and everyone else joined in. Coxsone was always listening out for songs he could play on his sound-system and knew he had a winner in 'Simmer Down.' Stopping them after just two verses, he expressed his delight and told them to return the next morning so he could record it.

This is where accounts again differ, since by the time the Wailers return to Studio One to voice 'Simmer Down,' their line-up will include Junior Braithwaite and Beverley Kelso, who'd been drafted into the group at short notice. Those early rehearsal sessions in Higgs' kitchen had involved girls like Cherry Green and Joan Dennis. Bob was convinced that the Wailers' sound could be improved with the addition of more voices and his thoughts had drifted towards Beverley Kelso – a fifteen year old girl who'd been singing with his friends Peter and Carlton Richards in a local youth club band. They'd heard Beverley sing in their school choir and had invited her along to the youth club where she soon made a reputation for herself. Bob went round to her house on Fifth Street and invited her along to a Wailers' practise session that evening. Beverley had told him to come back after five and to ask her mother's permission, which he did. She then accompanied Bob to Second Street, where she met Peter, Bunny and Junior for the first time. Beverley told Roger Steffens this took place the evening before they were due to record at Studio One and that Bob, who she said was leader of the group, taught her the parts they wanted her to sing.

"We rehearse 'Simmer Down' that same evening, and I didn't go to school the next morning because Bob said we were going to the studio. We were going to cut 'Simmer Down.' I don't know whether he'd made an arrangement with Coxsone or what."

Having his own studio saved Coxsone considerable time and money although in order to stay afloat, he had to keep the hits coming. Luckily there was no shortage of local talent or retail outlets, plus he'd already struck a deal with Chris Blackwell to distribute his records in England. Coxsone had bought the premises at 13 Brentford Road in 1962, but it had taken time for his studio to become fully operational. The building, and more importantly the *sound* made there will be forever known as "Studio One." His first tape recorder was an Ampex 350 – a heavy, mono machine Cosimo Matassa referred to as, "four guys and two hernias." It was only a one-track system, yet Coxsone had learnt to feed several microphones into two six-channel Lang soundboards, and then use a Neumann U-67 mic for the lead vocals. There were microphones for each instrument and the backing singers, plus maybe three or four around the drum kit. This set-up was very similar to the one Matassa used at his famous studio in New Orleans, where Dave Bartholomew, Fats Domino, Shirley & Lee, Lloyd Price and so many others recorded throughout the fifties and early sixties.

That first Wailers' session is said to have taken place on July 6th and we can just imagine the youngsters' excitement as they met by Peter's house on West Road, then walked as far as Fourteenth Street before following Greenwich Park Road round the lip of Calvary Cemetery and turning into Brentford Road. Once they got there, the group first had to convince the gateman they'd come on business, which couldn't have been easy. This man Boston will later have a minor screen role in 'The Harder They Come' as the preacher's handyman, and was no pushover. He eventually let Bob, Bunny, Peter, Junior Braithwaite and Beverley Kelso enter. Even Peter, who was normally so confident, felt a little nervous that day, as it was his first time in a studio. Coxsone had said to get there by nine except they would have a long wait before any recording took place. That's because the band members arrived separately or in small groups and weren't ready until twelve-thirty, which left just half an hour for the actual recording. Bunny sensed some of them were annoyed at having to back a bunch of unknown kids, and this made the Wailers feel even more uncomfortable.

Coxsone was his own engineer for the most part, and it was he who taped the Wailers' first session. 'Simmer Down' was recorded in two quick takes, after they'd rehearsed it in the studio all morning. Bob had written the song after Cedella warned him not to be so reckless, otherwise "the battle would get hotter" and when the hawk is circling, chickens better look out! The line "sweet goat run him belly" is pure Jamaican folklore. The sweetest part of any plant is the young green shoots, except they give goats diarrhoea. The moral of this story is don't be impatient and rush ahead, when you've time to think about what you're doing. Few youngsters want to hear a message like that and the way Bob sings 'Simmer Down,' it could never be mistaken for a deterrent. There's too much zeal in his voice for that. In fact the energy in this track is unbelievable, despite Bunny's fears that they'd over-rehearsed.

"You can rehearse the song so much that after a while it doesn't have any taste," he recalled. "You have to be searching for little hooks in the song to enjoy it because it's been rehearsed so much, but when you get into the studio and the Skatalites start warming up, everything becomes new again. The song sounds like it's just born."

The band's line-up that day was comprised of Roland Alphonso (alto sax), Tommy McCook (tenor), Johnny "Dizzy" Moore (trumpet), Jerome "Jah Jerry" Haines (guitar), Jackie Mittoo (piano), Don Drummond (trombone), Dennis "Ska" Campbell (baritone sax), drummer Lloyd Knibb and Lloyd Brevette, who played double bass. The Wailers heard them grumbling about low pay as Coxsone helped them set up the equipment, but thought no more of it. Bob already knew Roland, Jah Jerry and Lloyd Brevette from his Beverley's sessions. The trio had formed this new band after the owner of the Regal Theatre hired singer Lord Tanamo to organise some recordings for him. Tanamo brought in his favourite players and suggested they call themselves the Satellites, since America, the Soviet Union and Britain had all embarked on space programmes by then. "Satellite" was a current "buzz word" but Tommy McCook said,

"No, let's call ourselves the *Ska*talites." Everyone fell about laughing, and the name promptly stuck.

It was a band with a difference. For one thing, all the members were classically trained and could read, write and arrange music. Several of them had attended Alpha Boys School on South Camp Road – a Catholic institution run by Sister Mary Ignatius, and that was famous for turning out fine musicians. As young men they'd grasped what Charlie Parker and other bebop originators were doing and reveled in it, believing jazz to be black people's classical music. Whilst Alpha pupils were renowned for their technical abilities, most lacked stage and road experience at first. They'd have to learn such qualities from more established musicians yet these guys had been playing in various big bands all over town for some time, and were accustomed to backing a variety of singers.

Lord Tanamo and Tony Da Costa were their two regular front men. On Sundays they'd play at Bournemouth Gardens to mainly middle class audiences and the musicians would read from sheets, just like members of an orchestra. It was less formal in the hotels and nightclubs, where they'd play a mix of show tunes, jazz standards and calypso, as well popular British and American hits. The Skatalites played a lot of what Sonny Bradshaw refers to as "white" melodies, with subtle chord changes, but it was the rhythmic power of their performances and the brilliance of individual soloists that set them apart. All the horn players were established instrumental stars in their own right, and insisted upon the highest standards. If the Wailers felt intimidated, they had good cause to be.

Alphonso and McCook were Cubans, born in Havana but raised

mainly in Jamaica. Roland was fluent on both tenor and alto, and had recorded for Stanley Motta at the very dawn of Jamaica's music industry. He made his reputation playing in the Sonny Bradshaw Seven and was close friends with Coxsone. Back in the late fifties, he, Don Drummond and Tommy McCook had recorded straight jazz for Coxsone's label, before ska emerged. Jazz had once meant the big band swing of Duke Ellington, Glen Miller and Benny Goodman. That was before be-boppers like Charlie Parker and Dizzy Gillespie had rocked the jazz establishment to its foundations during the wartime years, paving the way for hard bop specialists such as Horace Silver, Lee Morgan and Art Blakey, as well as more commercial offerings by Dave Brubeck, Miles Davis and the Modern Jazz Quartet.

Like ska, jazz had also absorbed other styles, and especially from Latin and Caribbean countries. Stan Getz was busy championing a smooth form of Brazilian samba called bossa nova, whilst Sonny Rollins had already recorded calypso melodies – most notably 'St. Thomas' – around the same time as Harry Belafonte's mainstream hits. Mambo had lit up New York dance-floors back in the fifties too, but salsa music was the latest sensation thanks to Celia Cruz, Mongo Santamaria, Willie Colon, the Palmeira brothers and Tito Puente, who'd transplanted their Latin rhythms from Cuba and Puerto Rica with great success. Were it not for these other genres, Jamaican ska and reggae would have probably taken longer to gain international acceptance. Their popularity gave Jamaican musicians hope that they too, might carve out a reputation for themselves in New York one day.

Tommy McCook modelled his style on that of Sonny Rollins and had spent time playing in the Bahamas. He'd only been back on the island two years before joining the Skatalites, and bebop and Beat influences peppered his dress and speech. His playful take on words inspired Peter to make more expressive use of language, whilst Don Drummond was arguably the most talented Skatalite of all. Bunny describes him as "humble and meek" and says he was a fastidious person, always wiping his horn. He also recalls Don wearing Army issue crepe soled shoes and not being able to afford clothes, which is sad. Older heads in Jamaica still talked about Herman Wilson and Carl Masters, but all that changed once George Shearing voted Drummond one of the Top Five trombonists in the world.

Coxsone loved how the Skatalites' sounded, and knew they were an explosive combination. The group's full complement of horns harked back to the big band era yet there was something new and thrilling about them at the same time, and especially when they played ska. Their relentless, driving beat will power countless hits in Jamaica over the coming months, but the youthful exuberance that spills from their earliest recordings with the Wailers is undeniably special, and ska music will rarely sound so fresh and jubilant again. As Bunny tells it, "the Skatalites lick fire, and nah plug in nutten."

The group had made their stage debut at the Hi Hat Club in June, and those who there talked about it for months afterwards. Coxsone had provided the PA and equipment since it was a show promoting the band's first album 'Ska Authentic,' which he'd produced. Tracks like 'President Kennedy' and 'Lee Oswald' followed a precedent set by jazz musicians like Rollins and John Coltrane, who'd made their thoughts known by naming their instrumentals after current events, and especially those relating to the Civil Rights struggle.

Despite Kennedy's assassination, the Civil Rights Act went through Congress and made racial discrimination in public places such as theatres, restaurants and hotels illegal. For the first time, employers were required to provide equal employment opportunities, and those receiving federal funds could now be cut off if there was evidence of discrimination based on colour or race. The Act also attempted to deal with the problem of African-Americans being denied the vote in the Deep South, which met with considerable resistance. Within weeks of the Bill being passed in early July a series of civil uprisings and riots began, beginning with disturbances in Harlem, Rochester and Philadelphia. The local authorities responded by calling out the National Guard, which only made matters worse. There'd been outbreaks of violence in Panama too, at the beginning of the year, causing the deaths of twenty people and serious injury to hundreds more. Scuffles between Mods and Rockers on England's south coast seem trivial by comparison yet still mirrored a growing dissatisfaction with authority. Jamaica, with its turbulent history of slave rebellions, wouldn't be far behind.

The Wailers learnt a lot from being around the Skatalites, and listened intently whenever the band members talked among themselves. The Wailers were now in privileged company, and not just musically. These men had debated the Civil Rights Act, and absorbed the teachings of Dr. Martin Luther King and Malcolm X. They had religious feelings too, and headed for the Rasta camps when in need of spiritual sustenance, good company and strong ganja.

"Every man was Africa conscious and knew themselves," Bunny

said of the Skatalites. "They knew about Marcus Garvey and Emperor Haile Selassie I. They were serious people, and even more serious musicians."

None of the Skatalites had dreadlocks yet, but Rasta consciousness made them rebellious towards authority. Also, members of the band were all too aware of their elite status in Jamaica, and could prove difficult at times. For instance, if they didn't want to back a particular artist or play what they called "church keys," they'd refuse point blank and that was that. Brevette, who'd embraced Rastafari from early could be especially temperamental, whilst Dizzy Moore was arguably the most Africa conscious of all since he lived a life of seclusion way up in the Warieka hills. Generally speaking, society people looked down on the Skatalites because they were Rasta sympathisers and smoked herb. As a result, they didn't get a look in at Kingston's more prestigious venues and it may also explain why Edward Seaga didn't choose them to represent Jamaica at the 1964 World's Fair, which opened in New York during April. The Skatalites were red hot at the time but Seaga took Byron Lee and the Dragonnaires instead, who'd learnt to play ska from watching the Skatalites rehearse! The Jamaican delegation had included Prince Buster and Jimmy Cliff, who would both play an important role in popularising ska outside of the Caribbean. Even Jackie Kennedy, America's First Lady, had thrown her arms back and forth, dancing the ska to Lee's heady rhythms. The Dragonnaires were good, yet lacked the driving, jazz-powered virtuosity that characterised the Skatalites in full flight. Bunny thinks the reason why the Wailers didn't get a lot of exposure in the early days was because of their closeness with the Skatalites.

He says that the band's reputation rubbed off on them, although the Wailers would soon pose challenges of their own.

Four more songs were recorded during that first session. The same four in fact, they'd sung at the audition. Listening to them, it's clear the Wailers were far from being the finished article, despite Bob's earthy vivacity and the others' enthusiasm – especially during the gospel numbers 'I Am Going Home' and 'Straight And Narrow Way' (with Junior Braithwaite on lead vocals.) The Wailers' singing is still raw and largely untutored, but whenever Roland and Tommy step up and wax lyrical, their sax solos counterbalance the Wailers' feverish performances quite beautifully. 'I Am Going Home' marks the first time Peter's guitar is heard on record, except you'd never know it. 'Do You Remember' (later renamed 'How Many Times') then slows the pace a little except Bob's fervour is undiminished and by the time they finish the session, he and the rest of the group will have given it everything.

Coxsone was suitably impressed, despite his initial misgivings. As they wound down and prepared to leave he offered to pay them a weekly wage and provide them with clothes for stage performances, which they gladly accepted. Once the deal was struck, they were expected to attend the studio regularly and present new material for recording. Their new manager / producer was looking to establish Studio One along similar lines to Motown and turn it into a hits' factory. He'd even appropriated Motown's slogan of "The Young Sound Of America" and turned it around to read "The Sound Of Young Jamaica." 13 Brentford Road was already a place where young artists made friends, learnt their craft and mixed with more experienced singers and musicians. They learnt to approach music professionally, which is why so many of Coxsone's discoveries – despite lamenting the lack of proper accounting – refer to Studio One as "a musical college." For the majority, it was the first time they'd had a steady income and been given the opportunity to hone their talents. That's because in addition to recording them, Coxsone directed their careers. He taught them stagecraft, made instruments available, put them with songwriters and even hired choreographers like Sidney Brown and Clifford "Blackie" Ellis, "to show the guys some moves."

"Most of the artists who came to me were fresh and young, " he'll later recall. "They loved singing, but they had no musical background or experience, so the older, established artists had to help them. We had people like Delroy Wilson, the Gaylads and the Maytals who were all there before the Wailers, to show them the ropes. The most important thing was to get the guys accustomed to count the beats per bar, whether eight bars or whatever, then their harmonies and how you approach a song. Joe Higgs was of great assistance to them, and Delroy Wilson too. Delroy brought on all the youths because of his youthful voice. He set the trend for that time and without a doubt, when the Wailers came I was happy for that teen sound I was getting from them. It's just that I had to give them a sense of direction, because they came with a bunch of cover stuff and we had to show them how to approach writing songs."

Joe Higgs was always with them in the studio at first, listening carefully and making corrections as he saw fit. Each song would routinely require two or three attempts before they got it right and yet few of these alternate takes survive, since tapes were regularly erased and re-used. Whilst Higgs' input was invaluable, Coxsone also designated Roland Alphonso to tutor the Wailers and teach them the rudiments.

"Roland is the one to teach the Wailers, the beats per bar, to check where to come in and where to stop singing" he says in the liner notes to 'Destiny: Rare Ska Sides From Studio One.' At the back of the studio was a room stacked with singles and albums, which Coxsone called "study records." The most popular were by groups like the Caravans, Impressions, Highway QCs and the Drifters although visitors to the back room have said there was no shortage of New Orleans, jazz, country, rock, Latin and folk music, as well as soul, gospel and rhythm and blues. Coxsone would often point out songs he thought might suit a particular singer. Most of his charges couldn't afford records of their own and so he played a crucial role in exposing them to different genres, and broadening their musical education.

Along the way, in addition to acquiring professional skills, they came to appreciate the benefits of collaboration and teamwork. Some artists were more successful than others, except at Studio One everyone was encouraged to remain down-to-earth and to get on well with one another, no matter what job they performed. Whilst there was a darker side to his personality at times, Coxsone was proud of the family atmosphere he'd created around the studio, as illustrated by the following remarks made to Roger Steffens.

"Behind the studio there were lots of fruit trees – breadfruit, ackee, lime and orange, so during the days we'd be cooking ackee and breadfruit with dumplings. The singers and players did the cooking. Whenever a session got underway, whoever wasn't singing would "run the boat," and control the cooking. Each day we'd take a break about noon. Our regular studio hours during the weekdays were from around ten until four, and then we'd finish up about five or six. On Saturday and Sundays we'd lay the vocals and sometimes in the evenings too. We told most of the artists not to leave their day jobs, so we'd run the studio to fit their schedule. Sometimes a guy would ask his boss for two hours off, from noon to two so he could go and record, but the only other times we could get them would be evenings or weekends."

Coxsone has claimed 'It Hurts To Be Alone,' backed by 'Mr. Talkative' and issued on a maroon and silver label in late 1964 was the Wailers' first release, but the matrix numbers contradict this. 'Mr. Talkative' was certainly the Wailers' debut UK release but it was 'Simmer Down' that flew out the traps with hurricane force and topped the Jamaican charts for several weeks, selling a reputed 80,000 copies. This was during the annual Independence celebrations, in August. Legend has it that 'Simmer Down' was played twenty-five times in a row at one of Coxsone's dances in Skipper Land, shortly after they'd recorded it. Top ranking rude boys would go to his dances and request songs they liked, then buy a beer for whoever was selecting. Each time they requested the same song, it would play again and again... The night that happened with 'Simmer Down' Peter was taking a shower and got so excited, he ran out in the street with soap in his ears! No one in the neighbourhood knew it was the Wailers and they didn't let on either; they just soaked up the atmosphere and said nothing. People went around saying it was a new group from Second Street but soon the Wailers won't be able to go anywhere without being recognised, or singled out from the crowd.

CHAPTER THREE

Keep On Pushin'

The Wailers' stay at Studio One would last two years. During that time they'll voice more than a hundred ska and early rocksteady recordings, many of them hits in Jamaica. Some will even reach Caribbean audiences in England, although the band members will learn nothing of this until years later. Back in the summer of 1964, they were still caught up in the moment. The fact that their records were being played on local radio – let alone in dances halfway across the world – was cause enough for excitement but then anything seemed possible in newly independent Jamaica, and especially with Coxsone at the helm.

It was at Brentford Road where they served their apprenticeship and gained experience of the music business. 'Simmer Down' was an anthem right from the start, and Bob's lyrics – though written two years earlier – had undeniable relevance. Gangs of disaffected youths in Kingston's poorer communities now roamed the streets at night armed with ratchet knives, beer bottles, sticks and stones. Some even shared a cutlass or homemade gun (called a "one-pop)," which they kept hidden from prying eyes. The situation had turned volatile and it put ghetto people under more pressure than ever – this time from within. 'Simmer Down' spoke to these "rude boys" in a language they understood, and it was they formed the Wailers' core support. Coxsone wasn't best pleased and whilst welcoming the band's initial success, he was shrewd enough to steer them in other directions as well.

The Wailers soon fell into a regular routine of writing, recording and rehearsing. They didn't get to perform all that often but were always practicing, whether at the studio or back in their usual haunts. Recording sessions took place at least once a month. Coxsone would then test their new material on sound-system before releasing it on 45. This meant he rarely missed, since he'd created a demand for the songs in advance. His office was at the back of the premises. That's where he'd play records and educate his artists to what was happening in the worlds of gospel, folk, soul, country, pop, doo-wop, jazz and calypso. He'd expose them to anything he thought might suit their particular styles and help them to sell more records. Although not officially their manager – Bunny claims they effectively managed themselves at this juncture – he got the Wailers thinking about how they projected themselves and encouraged them to write more of their own material. In return, they were required to contribute to other artists' records as needed, and take pride in making Studio One the island's number one label. This is similar psychology to that used by Berry Gordy at Motown. It fosters team spirit and ensures there's always fresh, creative input close to hand.

Needless to say, the Wailers eagerly complied at first. That's how an early line-up of the group, including Braithwaite and Kelso, came to sing backing vocals on Lord Bryner's 'Where's Sammy Gone,' which Coxsone issued in early July. Their singing is ragged and naïve, yet hardly lacks enthusiasm. Given his past connections, this must have delighted Seeco. Lord Bryner was from Trinidad, and the topic a familiar one to fans of mento and calypso. Eric "Monty" Morris' had recently hit with 'Sammy's

Dead' and it's likely Lord Bryner's song was an "answer" version, designed to capitalise on that record's popularity. Other tracks of his featuring the Wailers are thought to exist, since he recorded a lot of material for Coxsone that hasn't surfaced as yet.

It wasn't long before the Wailers returned to the studio and cut three songs of their own, with Bob on lead vocals. 'Mr Talkative' was apparently Coxsone's idea, as someone – possibly Prince Buster – had been bad-mouthing him. Years later, Bob will sing it over for Bunny Lee as 'Mr. Chatterbox,' yet it's this first version that packs the bigger punch – literally, with Bob gleefully promising, "Biff baff buff, that's what you're going to get..." Essentially, 'Mr. Talkative' is another rude boy tune, albeit one sweetened with tight, repetitive harmonies and lyrical horn solos. It's full of energy, whilst 'Climb The Ladder' was considered "a throw-up song, for the sound-systems," according to Bunny. A precursor to 'Small Axe,' it would have made the perfect follow-up to 'Simmer Down' with its infectious chorus and spirited message. Not only that, but the line "The harder they come, the harder they fall. This is a lesson for one and all" may well have inspired Jimmy Cliff's 'The Harder They Come,' released several years later.

"The thing is, I never see Bob sit down with pen and paper or anything like that," Beverley Kelso recalled. "He and Peter would be playing the guitar, and then Bob would just start singing and tell us what to do. I never see him sit down and work things out. They'd just come up with a song and that's it, but everybody would come up with lines – Bob, Bunny, Peter and Junior. They all shared in writing the songs, then we just sing them for the band and rehearse. We used to go in the studio a little early, shortly before recording but it wasn't no long rehearsal. Sometimes I couldn't manage a harmony and I would just walk away. Bob used to say, 'she won't even try. She just walk away and leave people.' I never talk too much but one thing I know, and that's Bob brought a confidence to me."

'Climb The Ladder' will finally appear on 45 in time for Christmas backed with 'Straight And Narrow Way,' featuring Junior Braithwaite but not Beverley, who'll be gradually sidelined. The Wailers had three lead singers whose voices were all different and this made them unusual. Whereas the band saw this as being democratic, Coxsone may well have relished the idea of keeping three options open simultaneously. Either that, or he was undecided who should lead the group overall.

Joe Higgs sings baritone on 'Your Love' since Peter apparently couldn't manage it. "Who was taking too long to do that?" Higgs asked Roger Steffens. "Peter was very stubborn. I taught him a lot." Joe Higgs and Seeco were the two people closest to the Wailers and whilst Peter's relationship with Joe will survive such a rebuke, it's strange hearing someone else sing in his place. Marley's delivery betrays faint traces of Buddy Holly although the overall feel is gloriously uproarious, as on a number of other early Wailers' sides.

Bunny says most of their songs were written in G and E and they just played the chords that fitted with their melodies, since that's all they knew at the time. Members of the Skatalites, and especially Roland Alphonso and Jackie Mittoo, would then help them construct their songs properly.

"These are the people who should get the credit and these are the people who should be looked upon as the foundation of it all," he reminds us. "The Skatalites were the energy. They were the vibration of it all."

Bunny, aged seventeen, sampled his first draw of herb around this time. Coxsone didn't allow herb in the studio but had no objection to people smoking it out in the yard where one of Alton Ellis' backing singers did brisk business most days. All the Wailers smoked "hard" according to Bunny yet Beverley disputes this, and says they didn't develop the habit until a year or so later. Their next session took place in mid-July, and this one's different in that it will mark Peter's emergence as a songwriter. 'Maga Dog,' which he delivers with gusto, warns against feeling sympathy for skinny, "maga" dogs (both canine and human varieties), since they're liable to turn round and bite you. It's clearly inspired by calypso, whilst 'Hoot Nanny Hoot' is one of those nagging, instantly familiar tunes written about a dance craze. It's also Peter's first lead vocal with the Wailers and was even credited to Peter Touch and the Wailers on 45. In all likelihood, it was inspired by the US television show 'Hootenanny,' which aired in Jamaica just as the folk boom got underway. The show was filmed on different campuses and the students encouraged to sing-along with the performers, who played mainly acoustic folk music. 'Hootenanny' lost credibility after it banned Pete Seeger, which in turn sparked off a boycott led by Joan Baez. It folded soon afterwards, although not before gospel singers like Clara Ward, the Staple Singers and Alex Bradford, or country artists such as Flatt & Scruggs and Johnny Cash won themselves many new fans.

By late summer the Wailers were on a roll and revelling in the Skatalites' support, whether singing ska, calypso or gospel. The band's rhythms fizz and crackle behind them as new songs like 'Tell Them Lord,' 'Destiny' and 'Habits' add to their legacy. Joe Higgs' girlfriend, Blossom Johnson, sings harmonies on 'Destiny' and 'Tell Them Lord.' Higgs was always in the studio with them and filled in on vocals wherever necessary, which affords further proof of how unsettled the Wailers' line-up was back then. 'Tell Them Lord' is a sufferer's lament and there wasn't a ghetto man or woman on the island who couldn't relate to lines like, 'can't get no work, and can't get no food. Can't find no resting place, my belly's made of wood." 'Destiny' meanwhile, is an appeal for more brotherly love, and a reminder of how we'll never regret the good we do for others. Whereas Dizzy Moore's trumpet solo is full of pep and invention on 'Tell Them Lord' he's curiously lacklustre on 'Destiny,' even quoting from 'Pop Goes The Weasel' midway through. Peter's back singing baritone on 'Habits,' and that's him playing guitar as well. Junior sings lead but the song's once again written by Marley whose weave of influences – mainly drawn from the Bible and everyday life – results in another surprisingly mature effort by someone still in their teens. The band's talent is all too evident, even if they do lack consistency. The Wailers sang their first Christmas song that summer, and we can only imagine the effort involved in warbling 'Christmas Is Here' – later renamed 'Sound The Trumpet' – whilst the sun beats mercilessly overhead. Records like this speak volumes about their professionalism but then the Wailers were notoriously dedicated, and rehearsed constantly. Residents of Trench Town recall seeing them walking down the street on their way to Studio One, singing at the tops of their voices as they practiced the songs they were recording that day.

Peter's now getting increasingly proficient on guitar and proves as much on 'Amen,' which Coxsone again credited to Peter Touch and the Wailers. The group had two guitars now. The smaller one was left with Tartar for safekeeping. The larger one they called Betsy and kept with them at all times, since Bob, Bunny and Peter were rarely seen alone.

"If you can see one Wailer without the rest, then the others must be around the corner on their way there or something like that," recalls Bunny. "If Bob would go somewhere we go there too, and share with him. We are comfortable because we have each other. That's how Wailers used to think. We were brothers and never go about our business without worrying what's happening to a next man. No, the Wailers didn't live so. If anybody had an accident, then every man would be heading for where he was. We shared everything we had. If I knew one of the others didn't have any money and I came into some, then I go look for him. That's how Wailers lived."

Johnny Pate, who arranged much of the Impressions' material, wrote 'Amen' for the musical 'Lilies Of The Field,' but it was the Impressions' version that caught the Wailers' attention. Some time earlier, the Impressions had released their third album, 'Keep On Pushin',' which soon found its way into Coxsone's collection. It contained two songs that would forever define the Civil Rights movement, the title track and 'Amen,' as well as another Wailers' favourite, 'Long, Long Winter.' Peter's gospel training made him favourite to sing lead on 'Amen' and if he sounds a little like Toots Hibbert, well they're both coming from the same tradition. The arrangement couldn't be more different from the Impressions' version and yet the song's a triumph;

Peter's singing lends it authority, and there's none of the shrill naivety heard on other early Wailers' recordings.

Ermine "Cherry" Green says she sang on this track, although it's Bob's harmonies that stand out. Bunny describes her as "a nice radical, every man's little sister; every man's little friend. We all loved her or else she couldn't even come near Wailers' business. She had this little, high-pitched voice that is so fine. She can't use it so accurate but there were times when we Wailing Wailers just say, 'Cherry, sing on this song here. It sound nice.'"

Cherry's brother Georgie will one day achieve reggae immortality after a mention in Marley's 'No Woman No Cry,' where he's credited for keeping the "fire alight." In late July, the four male Wailers sang harmonies on Lee Perry's 'Hand To Hand' – a song that's also known as 'Man To Man' and sounds like a nursery rhyme. In addition to making records, Perry was Coxsone's general assistant. His first songs for the label (including 'Chicken Scratch' and 'Mother-In-Law') had been recorded at Federal a year earlier, shortly before Studio One opened. A small, scrawny figure, Perry was older than the Wailers by several years and had an oversize personality. His family were from Kendal in Hanover parish, not too far from where Peter was conceived. He'd been a domino shark, dancer and tractor driver before moving to Kingston and auditioning a song called 'Rough And Tough' for Duke Reid, who then gave it to Stranger Cole. When Perry complained, Duke became violent and that's when Coxsone "created a little job for him." Perry was soon a regular fixture at Downbeat dances. He ran errands for the sound-system and label, and then helped audition new talent once Coxsone opened for business. Over the next three years he would keep busy by helping out on sessions and recording a number of tracks under the guise of King Perry. He was amusing, but apparently not that popular with local audiences. Rita Marley's group the Soulettes recorded and performed with him, and she remembers him being booed off stage at the Ward Theatre one Christmas.

To the Wailers, this was all grist to the mill. Whilst they didn't have too many releases to their credit as yet, they continued to record at regular intervals. In early August they went into the studio without Junior and recorded 'Donna,' 'Dance With Me,' 'Wings Of A Dove' and 'Nobody Knows.' Bob sings lead vocals on all four songs, three of which are covers. Mahalia Jackson and Louis Armstrong both sang memorable versions of 'Nobody Knows (The Trouble I've Seen),' as did Big Bill Broonzy, although Marley's version is a rewrite and not a straight cover. It's remarkably free of pathos, although whether this is good or bad is a moot point! Peter's vocals dominate the harmonies, and that's Coxsone and his friend Blackie providing the handclaps. 'Dance With Me' borrows heavily from the Drifters' 'On Broadway' and is fairly superfluous, whereas 'Donna' and 'Wings Of A Dove' were both big hits for the Blues Busters – a fellow Jamaican group who'd made waves in America and recently accompanied Sam Cooke on his tour of the island. 'Wings Of A Dove' had been a staple of mento bands for years and was also covered by the Hiltonaires (for Coxsone), Prince Buster, Carlos Malcolm and Byron Lee & the Dragonaires, among others. The Wailers' cut is a little ramshackle, whilst 'Donna' marks the first and only time Beverley Kelso ever shared lead vocals on a Wailers' release.

Local competition at this time included songs by the Maytals ('Never You Change') Techniques and Alton Ellis ('Dance

Crasher'), as well the Blues Busters. The Skatalites were also rattling off hits like 'Ball Of Fire,' 'El Pussy Cat,' and 'Guns Of Navarone,' in-between backing most of Coxsone's other acts. Like certain members of that band the Wailers too, had a reputation for being standoffish. This was helped by the fact they'd huddle out of sight most days inside the shell of an old van stood on bricks in Coxsone's back yard, practising their harmonies and writing songs and then staring down anyone who tried to interfere. People used to laugh at the Wailers' van and liken it to a furnace since it got devilishly hot around mid-day, causing them all to sweat profusely.

One man who did get close to them was Jackie Opel. He invited Peter and Bunny to sing harmonies on his song 'The Mill Man' recorded in early August. Dizzy Moore rated Jackie Opel as "the best of the bunch," whereas Bunny describes him as "the greatest singer I ever hear. Jackie Opel sang anything – ballads, calypso, jazz, blues and ska. He was a little short guy with bowed legs, and fit. He sang the highest pitch that sounded as if he's whistling."

Jackie had arrived from Barbados during 1962, after being discovered by Byron Lee. He became a star in Jamaica on the strength of hits like 'Push Wood' and 'Cry Me A River,' which became huge sellers. The Wailers were possibly in awe of him a little, because Bunny recalls they were surprised and flattered when he began hanging out with them. His off-the-cuff methods must have been like a breath of fresh air after Joe Higgs' strict tutoring, since Jackie could write hits right there in the studio without recourse to either pen and paper or rehearsals. He was a showman too. 'Push Wood' and 'The Mill Man' were both rife with bawdy innuendos and quickly raced up the local charts. Some compared his stage act to that of James Brown, whilst others have described him as "the Caribbean's answer to Jackie Wilson."

The Wailers learnt a great deal from him, and soon developed an explosive stage act of their own. By now, they were performing most Mondays at the Jamaica Success Club on Wildman Street. It was a club night Coxsone promoted to showcase his artists, and with Jackie Opel and Delroy Wilson often topping the bill. The first time Seeco saw the Wailers perform on stage was at the Success Club and he was amazed! There was no room on the small stage for aerobatics, unfortunately. That would have to wait for when the Wailers played bigger venues such as the Palace Theatre, where they'd perform the routines they'd been practising on the beach. They were smartly turned out too, in their tight-fitting suits and black shirts with shiny spots. Peter called these suits "shiners," and took pride in pressing them at the dry cleaners where he still worked to earn extra money.

Beverley Kelso wore a white crinoline dress with sequins that night. Out on the sidewalk, dancers were entertaining the crowds waiting to get in. The best-known included Persian the Cat and Harry T, who'd use handkerchiefs and sticks for props as they whirled around in their top hats, demonstrating all the latest dance moves. It had all the makings of an unforgettable night, and yet the Wailers' first appearance at the Palace Theatre wouldn't be a happy one according to Beverley, who performed just three times with the group in total.

"The theatre was rammed packed. They get a good turnout that night," she told Roger Steffens, "but the audience end up stoning us with bottles, stones and whatever they could throw at us because the show start and the next thing there was a blackout. After about half an hour the lights come back on and when the show started again Bob come on from one side like he's flying, and Peter come on from the other side... They were flapping their arms like that because they couldn't dance! Bunny was the only one who could do those things but when we start to sing, the lights went out again and the place went up in arms, and bottles come down on us... We all have to run backstage and we were there for a long time. We couldn't come out until everybody had left the theatre.

"The second show was in Montego Bay and actually the same thing happen. We drive one whole day for that show but when we got there, they didn't have no music box; they didn't have no lights. It was like something was going on. Bob tried to calm down the crowd and tell them to simmer down but I think it was a set-up. I don't know whether it was because Coxsone want to get the money but it just break up like that. It was a disaster right there again!"

Beverley's mother had made her clothes for the first show, but told her daughter she wasn't prepared to keep buying material for stage wear out of her own money, and that she ought to ask Coxsone for some, which she did. After Beverley's mother bought the fabric she gave the change to her daughter, and that was the first money she'd seen from her singing career to date.

"When Peter and Junior see that I get money from Mr. Dodd, they go to see him as well. We didn't do too much shows after that because the group had begun drifting away from Mr. Dodd. I don't know whether there was a money problem because I never discuss it with anybody. I just go there and sing, then go home. The only time money was discussed with me was when Peter said there was something between Bob and Bunny, and they're keeping it in the family. I don't know whether Mr. Dodd give money to Junior before he leave for Jamaica but I doubt it. I don't think that Junior ever get anything but everything was going so fast... Every day we would be in the studio recording or doing something. If we weren't recording for ourselves, then we were backing up other people. Anyone who wanted a back up, we'd just come in and harmonise. We were in the studio most of the time. We were like Mr. Dodd's family because there were times when we didn't go home. When Junior was leaving us to go to America, we were recording an album and so we'd be there in the studio two, three days at a time! We didn't have any time for sleep. It was just fun. Sometimes I'd run home and come right back..."

Delroy Wilson was a neighbour of theirs and so they gladly helped out with harmonies on 'I Want Justice,' although in truth they do little but sing 'Yeah yeah,' on the chorus. Delroy was the same age as them, but had been singing a good while longer and it shows in his more measured approach. Meanwhile, the Wailers' own sessions continued in similar vein as before. 'Go Jimmy Go' is another dance track, nothing more, but enthusiasm again leaps from every groove. Coxsone will later include it on the album 'This Is Jamaica Ska,' whilst 'Teenager In Love' was originally a hit for Dion & The Belmonts during the hinterland between rock and roll and the Beatles. Dion Di Mucci had sang it straight, innocently almost, as feather-light doo-wop harmonies billow around him. Writer Doc Pomus had kept the lyric simple, and it had effortlessly tapped into the teenage mindset as the sixties dawned. The Wailers' version couldn't be more different and in spirit, as well as execution. The chorus (with Peter singing falsetto) may just pass for guileless, but Bob's lead vocal implies lust rather than romance and he's rewritten the verses so that the song's now accusatory instead of wistful. "You put me through your milling machine. I never thought you could act so mean..." This 'Teenager In Love' is an alpha, ghetto Jamaican male and definitely no clean-cut American kid wearing white socks and a nice sweater. And when Bob croons that he "doesn't know what to do," it's not because he's overcome with shyness or feelings of helplessness; it's because he's weighing the options. Alas, the rhythm track's disappointing. In fact it's leaden, and only redeemed when Roland Alphonso's fluttering sax arrives midway through. The Skatalites played plenty of hotel bars in their time and here's where they capture it on record, unfortunately.

This same line-up, with Trinidadian guitarist Lyn Taitt sitting in for Jah Jerry, play behind 'Love Won't Be Mine This Way.' It's a ballad and Bob sings it as if he's heartbroken, except slower material rarely suited the Wailers during this early part of their career. They used a different set of musicians on 'Where Will I Find,' which is also known as 'Lights In The Harbour' (and shouldn't be confused with the Platters' 'Harbour Lights.') This band featured Carl McCloud on drums, Lloyd Spence on bass and Richard Ace on piano, yet it's Ernest Ranglin's fluent guitar lines that standout. 'Love Won't Be Mine This Way' was a favourite of Bob's from those early Wailers' rehearsals in Skipper Layco's yard. It's not one of their best however, and sounds maudlin compared to their other hit ballad from the same period, 'It Hurts To Be Alone,' recorded in late August. Junior sings lead vocals, as he does on 'Don't Ever Leave Me' and 'True Confessions.' The latter wasn't discovered until 1991 and its authorship is still open to question although by virtue of words like "drugstore," it's clearly American in origin. Ranglin's choppy chords and a careering harmonica solo underpin this one, whilst 'Don't Ever Leave Me' took three takes to get right and is painfully overwrought. Both tracks remained unreleased, and may well have fared better as Ernest Ranglin instrumentals in truth. It's exquisite how he quotes from the Impressions' 'I'm So Proud' on 'It Hurts To Be Alone,' which Coxsone released in November. Four takes were recorded altogether and amazingly, Ranglin plays a different solo on each. Bunny Wailer told Roger Steffens that, "only Ernie Ranglin can play them kind of guitar. Ernie go into some jazz where you can't follow him. He was the father. Every Skatalite looked up to Ernie. They are all pupils who are trying but they never reach Ernie's standard."

Ranglin had lived in Trench Town during the late fifties and played on many of Clue J and the Blues Blasters' early hits for Coxsone. By the mid-sixties, he was living on the north coast and only playing the occasional session. He's arguably the greatest instrumentalist Jamaica has ever produced. His playing on 'It Hurts To Be Alone' is masterful, propelling it to No. 2 on the RJR charts over Christmas. Within weeks of this session, Junior Braithwaite left for America with hopes of becoming a doctor.

"It was Junior Braithwaite who had the voice and the drive," said Coxsone. "I loved how he delivered 'Don't Ever Leave Me' and 'It Hurts To Be Alone.' If he hadn't left for Chicago to join his parents, maybe he would have still been the lead singer of the Wailers. I appointed Bob as leader when he left."

No sooner had Junior left than Bob sang a duet with another of Coxsone's protégés, Marcia Griffiths. The sixteen year old had only started singing professionally earlier in the year but 'Oh My Darling' is a real tearjerker, and taken at snail's pace. Philip James, lead singer of the Blues Busters had been visiting his girlfriend when he heard Marcia sing from next door. At first he couldn't believe his ears, but quickly introduced her to Byron Lee and insisted she be included on a talent show at the Carib Theatre, which she won with a Carla Thomas song. She then joined Studio One, where she voiced her debut recording, 'Wall Of Love,' before singing with Marley. Marcia will later tour the world with him as part of the I-Three, and contribute backing vocals to a majority of his hit records for Island. Her performance on 'Oh My Darling' is remarkably assured for a sixteen year old.

It was around this time that another female entered Bob's life; a teenage unmarried mother called Rita Anderson who lived with her aunt Viola on Greenwich Park Road, in an area named "Ghost Town" on account of its proximity to Calvary cemetery. The Wailers would pass by aunt Viola's house on their way to Studio One, and it was Beverley who learnt that Rita wanted to make a record.

"Rita used to stand by her gate with her baby in her arms and she used to wave to us, like she's just waiting to see us" Beverley told Roger Steffens. "Bob, Peter and Bunny, they would burst out laughing when they see Rita. Bob would say, 'see that black gal? Who she a call to?' They'd call her "the monkey" and other names and it used to upset me so badly. I used to wave back to her until there came a time when I'd stop, and I'd play with the baby and t'ing. Then I'd run and catch them up and they'd say, 'what? You stop and talk to the black gal? Is it a pickney yuh want?' They carry on like that until one day Rita say she want to sing a song, and I tell her to sing a part for me which she did..."

Less than a week after Beverley recommending her to Mr. Dodd, Rita's group the Soulettes – shared with her cousin Constantine "Dream" Walker and friend Marlene "Precious" Gifford – were at Studio One recording their debut single 'Opportunity.' All three members will became closely linked with the Wailers. Bunny and Precious were soon to become an item whilst Peter had designs on Rita, who spurned his advances after he came on a little too strong one day. Whilst Bunny was aware of what had happened, Bob didn't appear to know about it, or at least pretended not to. Peter then had to swallow his pride for the sake of the group as Bob moved in on her. "She like the little red boy, so Bob start to look after her and say she was his gal now," explains Bunny. "Peter never loved Bob for that. You can't love that, but Bob was like that for his whole career. He was a very selfish youth, self-centred and full up so at times."

Rita, whose daughter Sharon had been born the previous November, sings harmonies on 'I Need You' and she's a far steadier influence than either Beverley or Cherry, despite her relative inexperience. Coxsone assigned Bob the task of coaching the Soulettes and he lost no time instilling discipline in his young charges, despite his budding romance with Rita. For the first time, there was a degree of uncertainty with the Wailers. Junior's departure and Peter's loss of face weren't exactly insurmountable yet the dynamics within the group had changed, leaving the door

open for something new to happen.
Seizing the initiative, Coxsone teamed the Wailers with the Mighty Vikings; a band comprised of Esmond Jarrett on drums, Desi Miles on bass, Hux Brown on guitar and Lloyd Delpratt on piano. Instead of the Skatalites' horns players, they were augmented by Bobby Ellis on trumpet, Tony Wilson on tenor sax and Seymour Walker on alto. It was in October that Bob, Bunny, Peter, Beverley and Cherry recorded 'Lonesome Feelings' and 'There She Goes' with this line-up, and the band's sound is noticeably different from that of the Skatalites. Their rhythms don't have the same drive to them, and the solos are nowhere near so inspired. 'Lonesome Feelings' is the standout. Joe Higgs and Sylvia Richards sing harmonies on that track, together with Cherry Green. The latter is more prominent than ever before, but only succeeds in sounding untutored.
"Bratty (Junior Braithwaite) was a very important loss to the group which made it difficult to cope with," admits Bunny. "It was a challenge which meant hard work and sticking together now that a key link was missing, and it proved to be a strenuous and bewildering task. After a few recording sessions, we decided to adopt Cherry who'd been interested in being a member since Junior's absence. She officially rehearsed with the group, then our next recording session was pre-arranged by Coxsone to revolutionise the Wailers' sound a bit, so the Vikings band was chosen for this one. The session proved fruitful for Coxsone because out of it came three smash hits – the Wailers' 'Lonesome Feelings,' a Vikings' instrumental and Higgs & Wilson's 'There's A Reward.' Cherry was not the ideal replacement so after putting in some more hard rehearsals and recording a few more tracks,

Cherry resigned from the group."

After she died in September 2008, Roger Steffens was moved to comment that, "her role in the Wailers has gone largely unnoticed." Cherry lived in Skipper Layco's yard and was well-liked by the band members, although it's said that she couldn't cut it live and so never performed with the Wailers. The changes in their line-up brought a different dynamic to the group's sound. It became more focussed, even as Jamaica continued to unravel. The unions had recently been on strike, complaining of government "oppression." This strike had lasted four months. At one point, workers gathered outside of the JBC offices where Michael Manley lay down in the street and made a speech mentioning the walls of Jericho. "Joshua!" someone shouted out in the crowd. The man had charisma as well as a social conscience, and the name would stick with him.

"The inequalities glared at us in the streets," wrote his daughter Rachel, some years later. "The rich were still rich and the poor were still abject, and there might as well have been an ocean between these two extremes."

It wasn't just black people in the Caribbean who felt aggrieved about lack of equal opportunities. Malcolm X, speaking at a rally organised by the Mississippi Freedom Democratic Party declared, "There's only one way to be a first-class citizen. There's only one way to be independent. There's only one way to be free. It's not something that someone gives to you. It's something that you take. Nobody can give you independence. Nobody can give you freedom. Nobody can give you equality or justice or anything. If you're a man you take it and if you can't take it, then you don't deserve it."

This was in December 1964. The contrast between him and Dr. Martin Luther King couldn't have been more pronounced although both shared the view that African-Americans should align themselves with the liberation struggles happening in Africa and elsewhere. Malcolm confirmed this during that same speech, delivered from the Hotel Theresa in Harlem.

"In my opinion, the greatest accomplishment made in the struggle of the black man in America in 1964 towards some kind of real progress was the successful linking together of our problem with the African problem," he told the assembly. "I wanted to point this out to you because it is important for you to know that when you're in Mississippi, you're not alone. As long as you think you're alone, then you take a stand as if you're a minority or as if you're outnumbered, and that kind of stand will never enable you to win a battle..."

Two months earlier, Nelson Mandela and other leaders of the now banned ANC were jailed in South Africa on terrorist offences, even as other African countries gained independence. In 1964, Northern Rhodesia had been renamed Zambia and Nyasaland became Malawi. Zanzibar also had a revolution, threw out their colonial rulers and joined forces with Tanganyika, creating a new nation called the Republic of Tanzania. Rebellions and uprisings were changing the world's political landscape at a rapid rate, and fuelling much discussion in Rasta camps and tenement yards throughout Kingston.

The talk soon switched to events closer to home after Don Drummond murdered his girlfriend, rhumba dancer Margarita Mahfoud, on January 1st. He'd stabbed her to death in a fit of jealousy, yet wasn't the violent type according to several former associates. Drummond was committed to Bellevue mental hospital within days of the murder and would die there four years later. Bunny Wailer and Vin Gordon insist he was occasionally let out to play sessions but other members of the Skatalites dispute this, saying he never played again. Whatever the truth of this, the trombonist's death aroused suspicion. Some say that Margarita's father, who hadn't liked the fact that his brown-skinned daughter had taken up with a poor black musician, had Drummond killed by hospital staff. It's difficult to understand why her father would wait that long to extract revenge but apparently the police never requested an autopsy, despite calls for them to do so. Drummer Hugh Malcolm wasn't alone in suspecting foul play and set out to prove it by pretending he was mad, and getting admitted to the same ward. Fellow inmates told him that Drummond had been gagged, tied and then beaten to death by four men, which led Malcolm to demand an inquiry with "one hell of a commotion" upon his release. Eventually the coroner did perform a post-mortem, which confirmed the rumours had been true.

We never did find out what had driven Drummond to murder the woman he loved. Maybe it was a crime of passion after all although some have suggested he was under financial pressures, despite his success. Coxsone is said to have paid him just fifteen shillings per side, despite the shy horn player having written and arranged a good many of them. Tommy McCook would later tell Leroy Pierson that he could "drink off" what Coxsone paid him "in half an hour." He and other musicians swear that Drummond never reacted violently or spoke out of turn about this, but say that it constantly played on his mind.

Less than two weeks after Drummond's arrest, Bob, Bunny, Peter and Beverley voiced a doleful cut of the Impressions' 'I Made A Mistake' with a slimmed down band comprised of Lloyds Knibb and Brevette on drums and bass, Lyn Taitt on guitar and Jackie Mittoo, who swaps piano for organ. It's a love song, full of regret and more than likely recorded in tribute to Drummond. The sentiments certainly suggest as much. It was released on 45 with Bunny and Rita's cut of 'The Vow' on the flipside – a song that Doreen & Jackie had already voiced for Coxsone, and had been a hit for Gene & Eunice on Aladdin several years earlier. Peter sang harmonies behind Bunny and Rita, and then joined Bob and Bunny in the chorus line for the Soulettes' 'One More Chance,' recorded in January. It's a relief to hear the Skatalites again, even without Don Drummond. They transform everything they play on and lift the singers, but even they can't prevent Rita straying off-key at times.

That same month, Bob, Bunny and Peter (but no other Wailers) recorded a bunch of songs including 'Diamond Baby,' 'Playboy,' 'Where's The Girl For Me,' 'Hooligans' and 'Jumbie Jamboree,' plus an alternate cut of 'Hooligans' called 'Hooligan Ska.' Lyn Taitt plays guitar instead of Jah Jerry, otherwise it's the same Skatalites' line-up as before. 'Where's The Girl For Me' isn't the Jerry Butler song, but another mournful ballad – one employing clever changes of tempo that prevent the song from becoming too mawkish, whilst Taitt's solo evokes memories of Ernest Ranglin's recent sides with the Wailers. 'Where's The Girl For Me' was coupled with 'Diamond Baby' on 45, and credited to Bob Marley and the Wailers. This belies Peter's claims – made almost a decade later – that it was Chris Blackwell who singled out Marley for star billing. In fact it was Coxsone who did that first, and also granted Peter his own share of the limelight.

'Diamond Baby' would remain a sought-after Wailers' rarity for years, and is loosely based on the Impressions' 'Talking About My Baby.' It's far from being a straight cover, although the influence is obvious. Bob's vocals are quite sloppy in places but the chorus is raucous as hell and the rhythm a king-size stomp that threatens to plough down everything in its path. 'Playboy' meanwhile, borrows from the Contours' 'Do You Love Me' – a song made (even more) popular by the Beatles. It's a knowing performance, but then the Wailers are stronger as a trio and continuing to grow in stature.

Peter sings lead on 'Jumbie Jamboree,' which all three Wailers wrote together. The melody and chorus have a carnival air, but the lyrics – like those of 'Hooligans' – tell of a disturbance that took place at the Palace Theatre over Christmas. The Wailers were due to perform on a bill promoted as "Battle Of The Giants," except a riot broke out after the lights had failed and the concert was cancelled. Jamaicans were used to power cuts but when the theatre was suddenly plunged into darkness, the mood became ugly. Bunny was sprayed by broken glass after youths began pelting the police with bottles, and then attacking them with lengths of wood they'd torn from the seats.

There's no mention of the blackout in Peter's account, and yet there's a reference to it in 'Jumbie Jamboree' – "jumbie" being another word for "duppy" or ghost. There's a swagger to Peter's delivery which leaves us unsure as to whether he really disapproved of what happened or not. Bob on the other hand, leaves us in no doubt on 'Hooligans,' which is the first Wailers' song to directly address their rude boy following. First he points out, "We were more than friends, yet the bottles were splintering all over the place..." He then takes off the gloves, telling them that, "Hurry come up is always rude, breaking things and smashing rules. Man, what do you think you are? A leggo beast for sure..."

Civil disturbances were now increasingly commonplace. For the past eighteen months there'd been squabbles over the allocation of work on government development projects, and matters were about to get a whole lot worse. It was a tradition in Jamaica to create temporary jobs before Christmas as a goodwill measure. Four hundred people had been employed as street sweepers in December, but more than seven hundred turned up at the KSAC (Kingston and St. Andrews Corporation) pay office, demanding their wages! The ensuing chaos led to running battles with police and numerous arrests and injuries.

Six weeks later, news arrived from New York that Malcolm X, America's most outspoken advocate of Black Nationalism, had been assassinated whilst giving a speech at the Audubon ballroom in Harlem. He'd been gunned down in front of his wife and children after previous attempts upon his life had failed. It was assumed his assailants were white, yet they turned out to be African-Americans with ties to the Nation Of Islam. Retribution seemed inevitable and before long, Muhammad Ali's apartment was set on fire and the Nation of Islam's New York headquarters firebombed. This was just before Ali's rematch with Sonny Liston – Ali having sided with the Nation of Islam against Malcolm. The Nation's leader, Elijah Muhammad had earlier courted controversy by describing Christianity as, "a religion organised by the enemies of the Black Nation to enslave us to the white race's rule." More to the point, he'd identified lack of self-regard as the greatest handicap to black advancement, and proclaimed it the root cause of black people's disunity.

Two weeks later, a Civil Rights march from Selma to Montgomery ended in violent clashes between the police and protestors. Dr. Martin Luther King had declined to endorse the march after meeting with President L. B. Johnson, who'd taken to using phrases like, 'We shall overcome.' A year earlier, Dr. King had been awarded the Nobel Peace Prize. In his acceptance speech he'd announced that, "the deep rumbling of discontent we hear today is the thunder of disinherited masses… All over the world, like a fever, the freedom movement is spreading. The great masses of people are determined to end the exploitation of their races and land. They are awake and moving forward toward their goal like a tidal wave. You can hear them rumbling in every village street, on the docks, in the houses, among the students, in the churches and at political meetings."

Within three months he will be in Jamaica, where the Gleaner reported that ten Rastafarians armed with machetes had stormed into a post office and then a school, causing teachers and pupils to flee for their lives. The article claimed riot squad officers had been forced to use tear gas on the Rastafarians, who wanted businesses to shut for Holy Week. This incident was entirely false. What really happened was that three Rastafarians had used abusive language over some trivial incident at their local post office, and the cult's fearful reputation had done the rest. Fears of a Rastafarian uprising had been fuelled by an incident in Coral Gardens, Montego Bay some eighteen months earlier, when a gang of six Rastafarians had robbed a petrol station. In the shoot-out that followed, two policemen were killed and three seriously injured. Two of the Rastafarians were also killed and three of them later hanged. It had been open season on Rastafarians for some time, ever since the Reverend Claudius Henry had attempted to launch an armed insurrection. In 1960, police raided Henry's training camp in the Red Hills area and arrested more than thirty people for treason, many of them dreadlocks. In total, more than a hundred Rastafarians were arrested between April and June of that year. Historian Terry Lacey has described the situation as "an ill conceived and poorly executed attempt" at organising an armed rebellion against the Jamaican government and security forces. "Yet in a sense, it was a pointer towards the future," he said.

A few years later and Jamaican audiences would embrace some of the key protest songs of the Civil Rights' era, like Curtis Mayfield's 'People Get Ready' - a soul-stirring continuation of the "train to glory" theme, steeped in Biblical reconciliation. It was the Impressions' latest hit and a favourite of the Wailers, who sang it in rehearsals. We can imagine their excitement as they headed to a downtown studio for publicity photos, dressed in matching suits and aiming to emulate their better-known American counterparts. Bob, Bunny and Peter look remarkably young and fresh-faced with their short, cropped hair and ready smiles. These shots will later appear on a number of album sleeves, beginning with the Studio One set, 'The Wailing Wailers.'

It was around this same time they joined Leonard Dillon in the studio for sessions that would launch the Ethiopians' career. Dillon was from Port Antonio, where he was known as "Jack

Sparrow." Soon after arriving in Kingston he met Peter, who strummed guitar as Dillon sang several of his own compositions. Tosh was impressed, and invited him to meet the other Wailers during a rehearsal in Second Street.

"I went down there and when I see that excitement, I get very timid because a lot of people is there," Leonard told Leroy Jode Pierson. "Well, they rehearse their songs and after they take a break, Peter look on them and say, 'Bunny, Bob, this brother have some nice tune. Mek we hear them.' And Bunny just look up at me and say, 'Sing now.' Peter started playing the guitar and I sing my songs. When I sing they say, 'Yeah man, them sound good,' and tell me they'll take me up by Coxsone in the morning."

The Wailers were good as their word; Coxsone liked what he heard and "Jack Sparrow" got to record four songs the next morning, three of which featured the Wailers. 'Ice Water' was the standout with its chugging backdrop and mento-style vocal arrangements. It's easy to hear what had attracted Peter's attention and his instincts would be proven right as Dillon went on to write a string of hits, including 'Train To Skaville' and 'Everything Crash.'

In Bunny's words, Leonard was "a good living brother, clean living. We never knew him too long, but we knew that about him in the short time we knew him." Leonard later formed the Ethiopians with Stephen Taylor. "All of my musical harmony ideas are coming from Wailers," he told Leroy.

A short time later, Bob, Bunny and Peter recorded a handful of songs with Beverley Kelso, who was now just an occasional member. They included 'Do It Right,' 'Love And Affection' and 'And I Love Her,' which must rank among the group's worse-ever recordings. In fact it's derisory compared to the Beatles' original, which Capitol Records had issued on 45 the year before. 'Do It Right' is likeable enough and a good dance record but 'Love And Affection' is one of the great ska classics, featuring an instantly memorable chorus and some fine, baritone harmonies from Peter. Dizzy Moore's trumpet solo is fabulous too, although Tommy McCook had grown increasingly weary of Coxsone's behaviour and left for Treasure Isle. Roland Alphonso switches to tenor and Lester Sterling the alto, whilst Vin Gordon had replaced Don Drummond on trombone.

'Love And Affection' will roar out of jukeboxes for the rest of that summer. The Wailers were now regular hit-makers in Jamaica, and rarely slipped off the charts for long. It had taken them just a year to reach this far and yet there was little cause for celebration. That's because Joe Higgs and Seeco were no longer part of the Wailers' inner circle after persuading Bob to keep a bigger share of monies owed the Wailers. Junior Braithwaite hadn't liked this and complained to Coxsone, who then used it as leverage in trying to convince Bob that the other members were troublemakers and he'd be better off without them. Bob was so embarrassed by this incident he didn't speak to either Joe Higgs or Seeco for about a year afterwards.

CHAPTER FOUR

Wantie Wantie

Dr. Martin Luther King addressed students at Kingston's University of the West Indies on June 20th, 1965. After denouncing South Africa's apartheid regime he spoke of a recent trip to India, where he'd studied Gandhi's ideas about non-violence firsthand. Dr. King's visit to Jamaica was widely reported in the local media, but ghetto youths like the Wailers were wary of anything that seemed weak or too conciliatory. It will be Black Power, and not passive resistance that comes closest to mirroring their aspirations in future.

Black Power founder Stokely Carmichael was head of the Student Non-Violent Co-ordinating Committee, or SNCC. He was Malcolm X's heir apparent and instigated reforms in the US county of Lowndes, which had "a reputation for brutality that made white as well as black Alabama shiver."

In March 1965, not one black person was registered to vote there. The arrival of SNCC members served as a catalyst and over the next eighteen months or so, nearly four thousand black people registered to vote and formed a political party called the Lowndes County Freedom Organisation, whose symbol was a black panther. Seven of its members would run for office in the county elections of 1966.

"SNCC had long understood that one of the major obstacles to helping black people organise structures which could effectively fight institutional racism was fear," declared Carmichael.

"History shows the black people could come together to do only three things – sing, pray and dance. Any time they came together to do anything else, they were threatened or intimidated."

His voice will resonate beyond the US to all parts of the Caribbean, including Jamaica and his native Trinidad. Yet it will take a while longer before the Wailers' music becomes more politicised, and especially with Coxsone vetoing their choice of material. In late summer they made their first recordings using the Ampex two-track machine he'd recently bought in London. It was a productive trip, since he'd also signed a UK distribution deal with Island Records, whose success with Mille Small's 'My Boy Lollipop' had opened important doors for ska and "Blue Beat" music over there.

It was Sid Bucknor who engineered these latest sessions. There were advantages in being able to record vocals on one track and the rhythm on another but the Wailers missed the adrenalin of singing with a band roaring behind them, and also the camaraderie with other musicians. From now on they will sing in headphones, and over pre-recorded backing tracks. This meant they could sing softer, and with more nuance. They didn't have to shout or strain, and it made their harmonies sound even sweeter. They could also afford to make mistakes if necessary, without incurring the wrath of various Skatalites.

'One Love' was the first song they recorded that day, and it marks the beginning of a new chapter in the group's evolution. The Impressions had recently visited Jamaica where their latest album, 'The Impressions' Greatest Hits' had received rave reviews. Curtis Mayfield's clear falsetto was widely influential, but it was also the strength and depth of his songs that made him such a favourite of the Wailers. More than ten years hence, Bob will fuse 'One Love' with 'People Get Ready' on his 'Exodus' album but the original is a gospel-charged ska track of immense charm, and with a chorus and lyrics worthy of Mayfield himself as Bob exhorts, "Let's join together and feel alright." Bunny steps up to the mic during the second verse, leaving us wondering why he didn't sing lead more often.

'One Love' was issued on 45 with 'Do You Feel The Same Way Too,' which like most "B" sides is quite ordinary. Other songs include 'The Jerk' – another lively dance number – and 'Shame And Scandal,' with Peter on lead vocals. 'Shame And Scandal' was released in the UK on Island during the summer of 1965, credited to Peter Touch and the Wailers, and apparently sold like hot cakes. British comedian Lance Percival had a novelty hit with it around the same time, although the song dated back to the mid-fifties and even earlier. Originally recorded by calypso artists Sir Lancelot and Lord Melody, it tells the story of a young man who falls in love and then asks his father's permission to marry, only to be told the girl's really his sister (and his mother doesn't know!) Further infidelities then unravel throughout the rest of the song, which Peter delivers with wry humour. He's now typecast as the Wailers' calypso singer (and probably for good reason), but that's nothing compared to the assault on their integrity represented by 'What's New Pussycat.'

The song was a hit for Tom Jones that autumn. It stayed on the British charts three months and featured on the soundtrack of a film called 'What's New Pussycat,' starring Peter O' Toole and Peter Sellers. In the wake of Millie Small's breakthrough, Coxsone watched the UK charts closely. He and other Jamaican record producers now had realistic ambitions of getting crossover hits in Britain, provided they chose the right material. London was "swinging," and ska popular as a dance and on record. The Wailers sang 'What's New Pussycat' reluctantly and it shows, despite a typically spirited performance by the band. Bob had asked Cherry along to the session, but her voice made little difference. Jones' version is the better one, and had mainly appealed to older audiences in any case. Instead, it was bands like the Beatles and Rolling Stones who captivated young British pop fans. The Rolling Stones' were seen as rebels with their shoulder length hair and surly attitude – also hard, driving rhythm and blues songs such as '(I Can't Get No) Satisfaction' and 'Get Off Of My Cloud,' which they'd written themselves. Although the Stones were white, their music was influenced by the sound of black America, as was that of other British groups like the Animals, Pretty Things and Manfred Mann. Folk music was also popular, despite having once been described as "an unidentified tool of Communist psychological or cybernetic warfare" by US security forces. That's because at source, it was part of the movement for political, economic and social change, and drew upon a rich history and tradition. It was storytelling music, just like country and western and therefore possessed authenticity – qualities which immediately appealed to youngsters like Bob, Bunny and Peter.

Bob Dylan had initially been cast as folk's Messiah, until committing the cardinal sin of plugging in his electric guitar and revolutionising rock music to the point where it would be viewed as a legitimate art form, rather than mere entertainment. By late 1965, he'd already outstripped the Beatles in terms of lyrical content courtesy of songs like 'Subterranean Homesick Blues,' 'Maggie's Farm,' 'Mr. Tambourine Man,' 'Ballad Of A Thin Man' and 'Like A Rolling Stone,' taken from his last two LPs, 'Bringing It All Back Home' and 'Highway 61 Revisited.' Dylan wasn't making overtly political protest songs anymore, but he'd set exciting new parameters for songwriters wanting to express something of value and meaning. He'd also spawned a host of imitators such as Barry McGuire, whose 'Eve Of Destruction' crackled from transistor radios like some harbinger of impending doom just as riots broke out across America. One of the first places to go up in flames was Watts, a predominantly poor black district of Los Angeles.

"'Burn, burn, burn' was the catchphrase of the riotous sixties," recalled the American author Walter Mosley. "Those words were screaming in my father's mind. He, and millions of other black men and women hated white America for the five days of the Watts' riots. His smouldering wrath was justified by his experience, and he never once questioned his own culpability for the racist institutions and their adherents."

African-Americans in Watts and other deprived areas exchanged gunfire with police and army troops, set fire to buildings and looted stores as the rioting reached its crescendo. Mosley reminds us how African-Americans "had helped build a great nation, yet were denied its sweetest fruits.

"Survival has been our hallmark," he continued. "We were routed and defeated, chained and beaten down. We were murdered and robbed of our language and stories and culture. But still we saved, in our hearts, a ragged flame – something our enslavers thought they had extinguished. We know from bitter experience what it is to be short-changed every day, from cradle to grave. We know the lies propagated by the media, law enforcement and even our own government… It wasn't until we shouted 'No more!' and demanded our share that things began, no matter how slowly, to change."

It wasn't just African-Americans who felt bitterness towards America's predominantly white and wealthy elite, but the country's indigenous peoples too. That same summer, Marlon Brando backed a campaign aimed at sending a Native American delegation to the United Nations, so they could demand international recognition as an occupied people. Brando hadn't got involved for publicity purposes; his views reflected deeply held convictions. Bob would have reason to remember this incident several years hence, during his romance with actress Esther Anderson.

Kingston too, had its share of riots except it was the Chinese who bore the brunt of people's anger and not whites. Hostilities started after a Chinese baker assaulted a black woman for failing to keep up with her hire-purchase payments. News of the incident spread, prompting teenage gangs to go around destroying Chinese-owned shops and houses and attacking Chinese people in the streets, even dragging them off buses. The Gleaner showed little sympathy and even berated Chinese shopkeepers for staying at home, yet six people died and more than ninety others were arrested. There would be a steady increase in shooting incidents from now on as private security firms employed more armed guards.

In such a volatile climate, it was demeaning for the Wailers to sing songs like 'What's New Pussycat.' The group wanted to be taken seriously, and sooner rather than later. In September they recorded 'Rude Boy (Gone A Jail),' which is also known as 'Rude Boy Ska' or 'Rule Them Rudie.' Unusually for a Wailers' song, it begins with pure harmonising. It's as if they're flexing their muscles in readiness for what's to come. The lyrics, "No want you come wheel and turn me, go lick me head 'pon the tambourine" are taken from a mento song by Louise Bennett, whilst "I've got to keep on moving" is borrowed from the Impressions. The Wailers use such devices to get their audiences' attention, but it's lines telling the rude boys to run and scram, and pointing out how "Wantie wantie, can't get it" that are most revealing. The band aren't siding with the rudies, but occupying the moral high ground. "Walking the proud land," as they would have it. (In years to come, Bunny will re-record it as 'Walk The Proud Land.') Released in December, 'Rude Boy' sold over sixty thousand copies, and peaked at No. 4 on the RJR radio chart two months later. It was one of the Wailers' best-selling early hits. The Gleaner even printed a photo of the Governor General doing "the rude boy ska." Although more used to ballroom dancing, he was trying to appear hip, since even the children of middle-class parents seemed captivated by the song. Groups from uptown like Byron Lee & the Dragonaires weren't making music like that and so these kids got into the Wailers by default, even if the group was from Trench Town. They'd show off at school by singing songs like 'Rude Boy,' and this in turn got their parents listening. These middle-class folks might not like what they were hearing, and yet they couldn't ignore it. For a time, the whole of Jamaica was talking about rude boys and the "Rude Boy Ska." People started addressing themselves as "rude boys" and the term

"Wha' 'appen rude boy?" remains a popular greeting to this day. According to Maureen Rowe, a rude boy was defined by a "cool, aloof presence that was quietly menacing. He was macho, defiant and tended to challenge constituted authority at every opportunity." Tony Uter on the other hand, claims the rude boys weren't all that violent.

"People picture it as it is now, but it wasn't," he told Distant Drums. "The rude boys who got a gun, they never really shoot you with it. Shoot it over your head, or shoot you in the hand maybe, but none of the guys kill each other. We all had guns, 'cause it was like a craze to have a .22, just to frighten another set of guys, then when the police come they all have a shoot-out but none of them was killed."

On the back of 'Rude Boy''s popularity Lee Perry used a mix of the same rhythm for 'Pussy Galore' – a tribute to a femme fatale recorded under the name King Perry. The title came from a character in the James Bond film Goldfinger, played by Honor Blackman. It was Perry's biggest hit for Coxsone, and featured harmonies by Bunny and Peter. (It was also an early example of reggae "version.") The original line-up of the Skatalites broke up soon afterwards, although the basic rhythm section would remain intact for some time yet. Personal jealousies and rivalries were to blame, as well as financial considerations. It was said that Tommy McCook and Roland Alphonso often clashed and this was put down to Clement Dodd's nepotism, since he made a personal friend of Roland Alphonso and tended to play him off against the others. Lloyd Brevette had a drinking problem and sometimes wouldn't turn up for gigs or recording sessions, and none of the members earned sufficient money to support themselves and their families in a civilised manner. Their fees for recording sessions barely covered taxi fares, and the band had started to lose prestige in any case. After Tommy McCook left to join the Supersonics, Roland formed the Soul Brothers and Jackie Mittoo took over as Studio One's resident arranger, thereby ensuring some welcome continuity.

It was around this time that Bob Andy, later to enjoy international success with Marcia Griffiths as Bob & Marcia, shared an intimate interlude with the Wailers.

"There was a room at Studio One where we used to listen to records," he wrote on his web site. "Coxsone would give artists music to listen to on this turntable and speakers, but there was another room between Coxsone's inner office and the music room where you could go and lock yourself in and no one else could enter. The Wailers had access to that, and I did too. One particular day, I was the witness to a very special performance. It was like being let into a secret. I was very high from smoking, and they were always high too. It was the first time I had seen each of the Wailers with a guitar, and each time I remember this, it's like remembering a dream. I sat there, and they were just messing around with various songs for a while, but finally it climaxed with a song called 'Ten To One,' which I later found out was a Curtis Mayfield song.

"Bob sang the first line, then Bunny came in on the second, and all three came in on the next line. Peter sang a line, and then all three sang in harmony, then Bob and Bunny sang solo again. When they started that song, I saw a side of the Wailers I felt no one else had seen. It was like my own personal revelation. I've never heard music so beautiful, and I've never seen such love and camaraderie in all my life. I knew then that the Wailers were special people, but they were special by being the Wailers, as a unit. When I reflect on that occasion, it was divine. It was like being on a spaceship, listening to the music of the spheres. I was spellbound, and that memory will stay with me forever."

In October, the Wailers recorded another heartfelt ballad in the style of 'It Hurts To Be Alone' called 'I'm Still Waiting,' which Bob wrote after listening to Billy Stewart's 'Sitting In The Park.' The melodies are certainly similar as is the topic, whilst the lyrics are uncharacteristically soft as Bob sings of how he's sat waiting for his girl in the rain with tears streaming down his face, not knowing whether she feels the same way or not. It's unashamedly aimed at the Wailers' female audience, and taken at tail-dragging pace. Their old friend Delroy Wilson will later revive it for Lloyd Charmers and outperform the Wailers with one of their own songs, which won't happen too often. To be fair 'I'm Still Waiting' is a beautiful song, but let down by rather basic production. It was issued on 45 backed with 'Ska Jerk' (credited to the Wailers & Soul Brothers Orchestra), and reached No. 14 on the RJR chart the following January. 'Ska Jerk' was a direct steal of Junior Walker and the All-Stars' 'Shotgun' and later re-titled 'Ska Jam,' credited to the Skatalites. It can't even begin to match the explosive excitement of the original, but the Jerk was a popular dance craze in America and allaying it with ska was a smart move, despite the throwaway lyrics.

If you're getting the impression the Wailers had ran out of steam, then wait until you hear them tackle Irving Berlin's 'White Christmas.' Bing Crosby's version was the biggest-selling single of all time but the Wailers had been listening to the Drifters' cut, and made slight changes to the lyrics. That's because Peter had complained, saying the words didn't make sense from a Jamaican perspective. Listen carefully, and you'll hear Bob sing, "I'm dreaming of a white Christmas, *not* like the ones I used to know," which alters the meaning considerably. The band has changed as well, to a line-up comprised of Bunny Williams on drums, Bryan Atkinson on bass, Lyn Taitt on guitar and Jackie Mittoo on piano. 'White Christmas' isn't the proudest moment in the Wailers' career and nor 'Let The Lord Be Seen In You.' Beverley and Cherry provide uneven harmonies on that one, whilst Bob's accompanied by a rickety piano – Bunny and Peter are thankfully nowhere within earshot. Bob will cover another Prof. Alex Bradford song, 'Just In Time' with female accompaniment. Both will be credited to Bob Marley & The Spiritual Sisters. His mother Cedella must have wept with joy at hearing them, unlike most of us...

The Wailers were raised on gospel music, as we've already discovered. American groups like the Highway QCs, the Caravans, Swan Silvertones and Sam Cooke's Soul Stirrers were big-name draws on the gospel circuit throughout the fifties and early sixties, until the genre's heightened emotional power became absorbed into soul music, taking many younger listeners with it. Like the Impressions, the Wailers had cut their teeth on gospel and doo-wop material and were busy remodelling themselves in their own image, largely thanks to the writing skills of their lead singer. The Wailers can't be compared to their more illustrious counterparts yet but their cover of 'Just Another Dance' – taken from the Impressions' new album, 'People Get Ready' – has a soulful quality that's equal to the original. Bob sings lead despite Bunny's voice sounding closer to Curtis Mayfield's; the shuffling rhythm is delightful and Bunny and Peter's harmonies dovetail with newfound maturity.

They've settled as a trio now and graduated with distinction, but then so have Toots and the Maytals, whose gospel-drenched songs provide ska with its most direct link to the music from America's deep south. The Wailers weren't so funky, but they were Jamaica's answer to the Impressions. Even their publicity shots echoed those ABC-Paramount issued of the Impressions, like the one used on the cover of their first LP 'The Wailing Wailers.' Peter towers above the other two, looking imperiously cool in shades. More than a decade later this picture would resurface as 2 Tone's Walt Jabsco, after the Specials' Lynval Golding showed it to label boss Jerry Dammers.

'Another Dance' was popular on the sound-systems, but didn't do quite so well on the local charts. Coxsone could have got behind it and featured it more often on his weekly radio show, but chose not to. He had too many other songs to deal with, and by many different artists. He was only interested in sure-fire hits like 'Rude Boy' or 'Love And Affection,' and this left the Wailers feeling disenchanted.

"I've been rebuked. Brothers I've been scorned..." These are the opening lines to 'Somewhere To Lay My Head,' featuring a transitional Skatalites' line-up. It's a spiritual, written to succour the weary and yet just doesn't ring true somehow. It's possible they chose it by way of commentary on their deteriorating relationship with Coxsone – at least judging by the tone of Bob's voice as he delivers the line, "It doesn't matter what the man does, or the heartaches he leaves behind..."

He and the others broke off from writing songs to sing harmonies on Jackie Opel's 'Hairy Mango' and 'My Girl' in October. They also collaborated on Joanne Dennis' 'Don't Cry Over Me' – a song that languished in the Studio One vaults for decades, and probably would have stayed there had it not been for the Wailers' presence. Joanne was best known for 'You're Wondering Now,' which she'd recorded with Reuben Anderson under the name of Andy & Joey. She and her brother Garth (who later joined the Wailing Souls) would often attend the Wailers rehearsals on Second Street.

Peter went missing from the Wailers' next session and so Bob plays acoustic guitar on 'This Train' and 'Where Is My Mother.' Under Peter's tutelage Bob has developed into a competent rhythm guitarist, but it's he and Bunny's near telepathic vocals that impress. Bunny borrows a line or two from Curtis Mayfield's 'Little Boy Blue' on 'Where Is My Mother,' whilst Bob quotes from 'This Train' and 'Who Feels It Knows It'; the band version was overdubbed later. Trini Lopez included a speeded-up cut of 'This Train' on an LP called 'Folk Album' released in 1965, although it's been covered many times – most notably by Sister Rosetta Tharpe, the Kingston Trio and Peter, Paul & Mary. Peter may well have led the Wailers' version had he been at the studio that day, although it's doubtful he would have placed quite so much emphasis on the word "Jesus…"

There's a rehearsal tape with 'Wages Of Love' on it and Bob playing guitar from this same period. Rita stretches for high notes on the first take. Bob then joins in, although his singing's not too serious. Recorded in November, these snippets are of rarity value since none of the other Wailers are present. Peter's still missing because according to Reggae Routes, he'd ordered some records from Studio One and then refused to pay for them. He said the Wailers were owed money and so the records belonged to him. He apparently cursed and intimidated the sales staff but stopped short of fighting with Coxsone, who promptly banned him from the premises. The Wailers were only paid three pounds a week and it was a struggle getting that out of him sometimes.

"We tell Coxsone plain, we don't want a job," states Bunny. "We just sing and he give us royalty. We just Wailers." He says Coxsone would sweet talk them and call them his "sons," but when it came to actually doing something caring or supportive they'd be left "hungry and naked," and "no father treats a son that way..."

They would still go up to Brentford Road every day, singing and writing and recording songs, but then when Friday came and they were supposed to get paid he'd keep them waiting most of the day before dishing out bundles of small notes, so it looked a bigger amount than it really was. He could be intimidating as well. People at Studio One couldn't just go and ask him for something or show displeasure. They'd have to be patient and wait until he took notice of them because whenever artists got angry and impatient, he'd resort to violence. He had a good punch too, but was a dirty fighter since he'd hit people when they least expected it, like when they were turning away or not looking. Joe Higgs said Coxsone once struck him in the eye so hard it partially blinded him. Apparently the producer also threatened to hit Roland Alphonso in the mouth after his right-hand man had mentioned money once too often – knowing that if his lip was damaged, Roland's career was over. Coxsone will later give the impression he'd been running some kind of day care centre, but Bunny says all the artists who went to Studio One were educated already and like the Wailers, just wanted the opportunity of making music.

"It wasn't no little black and hungry pickney up at Coxsone's," he sneers. "Peter's mother had houses in Savannah La Mar, guest houses that she'd rent out. Peter wasn't a man who lived down. My father used to build and sell houses, and at the same time he was Bob's father because my father was taking care of Bob at the time, so where did Coxsone get that from? My father used to drive a Buick Skyline when we used to sing for Coxsone..."

Peter told Sebastian Clarke that Coxsone paid them fifteen or twenty pounds for every side they recorded, plus three pounds a week. He also bought them stage clothes and winkle-picker shoes which were deductible from "royalties," although all three Wailers will deny having seen any statements. Elsewhere, Clarke writes that, "it seemed that Dodd (Coxsone) had a habit of paying particular interest in his artists at a particular period, encouraging them, egging them onto the acceptance of a successful future, but they could never reconcile his words with the way he treated them. Consequently, the artists would unleash their anger, frustration and disappointment against him verbally, either to him personally or to his friends.

Coxsone was reluctant to fight with the Wailers because they were from Trench Town and had a lot of support among the rude boys there. Nobody messed with the Wailers, and Bunny's father had quite a reputation too. Whilst the police didn't care for them too much, they were loved and protected within their community and especially at places like Sang Hu's gambling house, where you could buy food and herb or play dice all night long. People would call round there after they'd been to a show or dance. It's also where characters like Babu Man – a half-Indian man who was always requesting the Wailers sing for him – would hang out.

There was little political violence as yet, although hostility simmered between Jamaica's two parties. In November a JLP march led by Edward Seaga came under a hail of stones and missiles as it passed by Back O' Wall, which was a notorious PNP stronghold at the time. The police didn't interfere until JLP sympathisers defended themselves. They then used tear gas against both sides. Members of the PNP argued the march had been provocative, whilst Seaga's red-shirted supporters lost no time in carrying out reprisals.

The Wailers' next session will give rise to a tune that's the epitome of rude boy readiness, if ostensibly a song of praise. Not for the first time, they draw parallels between righteousness and toughness. To the band's way of thinking it's spiritual authority that bestows power, and not anything physical. Make no mistake; 'I'm Gonna Put It On' heralds a resounding return to form, and the rhythm's fantastic. Fred Crossley does a passable imitation of Motown's James Jamerson on bass and that's Dwight Pinkney, later of the Roots Radics, playing guitar.

"We were working at Studio One," he told Distant Drums. "The Wailers hadn't broken big yet, they were just coming along and hear us working. They like the sound so we did one song, 'I'm Gonna Put It On,' and it went to No. 1 in Jamaica. They wanted the Sharks to be the backing band for the Wailers but we had to leave because we got an engagement in the Bahamas, playing a residency gig at a hotel but to this day Bunny Wailer tells me that if we hadn't left, we would have been the Wailers' band."

'I'm Gonna Put It On' only reached No. 4 on the charts in fact. It'll be the Wailers' last hit before Bob leaves for Delaware and it's a scorcher. The line, "I rule my destiny, Lord I thank you," is an extraordinary thing to say given how disadvantaged these young singers are in certain respects. A statement like that says a great deal about their sense of purpose, with Bob testifying how they're ready to stand up and be counted, "anywhere, anytime..."

Remembering the success of 'Rude Boy,' Coxsone used the same rhythm track for Lee Perry & the Soulettes' 'Rub And Squeeze' – a tune of limited novelty appeal, rife with double entendres and delivered in an impossibly high voice as the Soulettes yowl behind him. It's been suggested this song was played at Bob and Rita's wedding, except that seems unlikely.

According to Bunny, 'Rude Boy' and 'I'm Gonna Put It On' were written by all three Wailers, "but we just say 'Bob' and done. Wailers live good." The group was now writing songs every day, with everyone contributing something. A little part that Peter or Bunny may come up with would be incorporated into one of Bob's songs or vice versa, but they were also singing cover versions whenever the mood took them, or Coxsone found a song he thought may suit them.

'Ten Commandments Of Love' had been a hit for the Moonglows and was later updated by Little Anthony & the Imperials. The Wailers recorded their version in November 1965 and it marks a return to their doo-wop roots with those drawn-out vocals and swooning harmonies. The dirt-slow tempo offsets a tremulous lead vocal from Bob but it's a retrograde move essentially, and especially in the wake of so compelling an original as 'I'm Gonna Put It On.'

As Christmas approached, the Wailers recorded further songs for Coxsone's gospel label, Tabernacle. 'I Left My Sins' was issued on the flipside of 'Just In Time.' Both songs are covers, and may well be Prof. Alex Bradford compositions. The group had a liking for his songs despite him being described as "gospel's Little Richard, letting it all hang out." Reports suggest that he'd be camping it up one minute, and then moving his audience to tears the next. A child star of the vaudeville circuit, he was mentor to the Sweet Inspirations and Dionne Warwick, attracted various Beatles to his concerts and was the finest gospel writer of his generation. Although raised in Alabama, he'd had to leave after running into trouble with the cousin of a local sheriff, who objected to his standard of education and confident manner. He and gospel singer Sallie Martin had a hit once with a song called 'He'll Wash You Whiter Than Snow'... It's early days yet, but let's just pause for a minute or two to reflect upon what Peter thought about *that* one...

On November 29th, all three Wailers contributed harmonies to Delroy Wilson's 'Jerk All Night' which although credited to Bob, is adapted from Lee Dorsey's 'Ya Ya.' Peter's baritone is a key feature of the chorus line, whilst the rhythm must have had dancers reeling courtesy of its insinuous groove and Lloyd Knibb's explosive rim-shots. The sixties were famous for its dance crazes and the Jerk was similar to the Monkey, except the arms swept across the chest, as if conducting an orchestra. It wasn't too dissimilar to how people danced to ska, which meant any synthesis of the two styles was sure to be popular (as already heard on 'The Jerk.') That same session also resulted in the Wailers' 'Lonesome Track' which reprises the train to glory theme and yet never quite achieves lift-off, despite another fiery performance from the Skatalites' drummer.

Rita's group and the Wailers were rehearsing together by this stage, and would soon be sharing studio time as well. The Soulettes' 'Don't Care What The People Say,' with Rita on lead vocals and Peter, Dream and Marlene singing harmonies dates from around this time, and possibly even the same session. Within a matter of days the Wailers would be back with two more songs of their own, and all of Jamaica will sit up and take notice. Bob will later revisit 'Cry To Me' on his 'Rastaman Vibration' album, but we'll miss those mournful, high-pitched harmonies and Roland Alphonso's burbling sax. The lyrics include some of the 23rd Psalm, and continue the Wailers' preoccupation with gospel themes but it's the other song they recorded that day which breaks new ground, and will redefine how audiences view them in future.

The Wailers were automatically classed as rude boys because they came from Trench Town. This wasn't strictly true of course, but that's how Jamaica was at the time. People living in the ghetto were scorned and thought of as criminals. They were discriminated against because of where they lived, and the opportunities afforded middle-class people remained barred to them. After the success of 'Rude Boy,' people would refer to the group as the "Wailing Rude Boys" or "Rude Boy Wailers," even though they'd criticised the rude boys on songs like 'Hooligans.' By late 1965 this perception still hadn't changed and so they decided they'd embrace rude boy culture instead, and teach people just what it was like to be in a rude boy's shoes. Their game plan has altered, and they'll try to win the rude boys more respect in future. 'Good, Good Rudie' was the first song to reflect such a change, and leaves listeners in no doubt of their intentions. Bob even voices it using rude boy slang as he promises "them peego a go lingua" (meaning they'll give the girls from the ghetto something to talk about.) "Can't fight against the youth now because it's wrong. Youth a good, good rudie," he declares, after warning that as baton sticks get shorter, "rudie gets taller." He then dares to voice the unspoken fears in every middle-class heart. "We're gonna rule this land, right now. You can't fight against prediction..." The inference is that rude boys are on the side of prophecy and therefore divine will, hence the closing line, "What has been hidden from the wise and the prudent, will be revealed to the babe and suckling..."

'Good, Good Rudie' is an important song in Jamaican musical history. It marks a turning point for the country as a whole, as well as the Wailers themselves. Coxsone will later rename it 'Jailhouse,' although it's also known as 'Rudie' or 'Rudie Rudie.' It was this track, less than two minutes in length, which cemented the Wailers' reputation as rebels.

"From the start of the Wailers' career they had always strongly identified with the rebelliousness and arrogance of Jamaica's youth," writes Sebastian Clarke. "Poverty was their experience and their environment whilst violence was aggravated by the politicians, and all of these experiences were reflected in their songs. The Wailers commanded a particular response from their audience. Because they identified with and reflected in song the condition of the urban slums, they were greeted with heroic responses."

The Wailers were now celebrated by the people of West Kingston like never before, although other sectors of Jamaican society – their brief flirtation with "rude boy ska" now over – resented them for promoting rude boy culture. The island's two radio stations wouldn't play their rude boy songs, claiming they glorified criminality, but every bar had a juke box in those days, stocked with the latest hits and new record shops continued to open across the city, blasting songs into the streets. The Wailers could now be heard all over Kingston, rendering their lack of airplay almost inconsequential. In early 1966, they would have five songs in the Jamaican Top 10 – 'Simmer Down,' 'It Hurts To Be Alone,' 'Rude Boy,' 'Jailhouse' and 'Put It On.'

The group's live performances, although infrequent, were now wild affairs involving gymnastic style dancing and Bob's dramatic use of play-acting. At crucial moments he'd fall to the floor as if exhausted before being caught by the others. Once recovered, he'd then rush back to the microphone, just like James Brown. Pure excitement! Derrick Morgan was the headliner at one of their shows, which also featured Alton Ellis, the Maytals and Joe White. The Wailers stole the show and got a great response from the crowd. Girls thronged the backstage area and admirers lifted Bob onto their shoulders and carried him out into the street. Such adulation had its dangers however and so the Wailers would always have friends from Trench Town with them, for protection. Lloydie Fowl Foot, who used to play football for the Boys Town team, Jabba and Kinky were all regular members of their crew as was Vincent Ford, whom they called "Tartar Nine Toe." He was one of Bob's best friends, and had already lost a couple of digits to diabetes.

Security was important at the dances since groups of youths would sometimes storm the entrance, hoping to get in without paying. Such events were often held in the open-air, inside fenced-off areas where deejays like King Stitt or Count Machouki would hold sway on the microphone, introducing the songs in rhyming patois. "With a flick of my musical wrist..."

The police often raided these dances without warning. They'd burst through the gate, force the sound-system to stop playing and then scatter the crowds whilst harassing any rude boys or Rastas they found inside. It was as if ghetto people didn't have the right to enjoy themselves unless they bribed the police to stay away, otherwise they were lucky to escape such wanton acts of persecution. Youngsters wouldn't go to a dance in a strange place or some distance away without a posse of friends. That's because anything could happen although there's still nothing so magical as an outdoor, Jamaican dancehall on a moonlit night. Herbie Miller recalls how back in the sixties, little boys would gather outside the venues, chasing among the stalls selling peanuts, oranges, coconuts, sugar cane and even a little herb. Homemade oil lanterns would light up the scene and singers would often stroll up to the record decks, to sing one or two songs by way of greeting.

No one suspected it at the time, but 'Cry To Me' and 'Good, Good Rudie' would be Bob's last-ever recordings for Coxsone. Shortly afterwards his mother invited him to Delaware, where there was a good chance he could find work on a car assembly line and earn some decent money for a change. In the meantime Rita, who already had an infant daughter to take care of, announced that she was pregnant. The news threw Bob somewhat. He needed money to fund his musical career, but now had fatherhood to contend with. The repercussions would alter the dynamics within the Wailers and perhaps irreparably so. Despite having already left the group, Beverley Kelso remained close friends with Bob during this period.

"Bob wasn't talking to Peter or Bunny," she told Roger Steffens. "He wasn't telling them anything so when Rita get pregnant and he didn't know what to do, he came to me. He and Rita don't have any money so I said to go to Mr. Dodd and see if you can get married because that's the only thing they could do. Later he came back and said they were getting married. He said the date was going to be such and such a day, and I was invited although I never make it because I took sick..."

The service took place on February 10th 1966, unbeknown to Bob's friends and members of his family. The first Bunny knew of it was when someone came up to him in Trench Town and asked him why he wasn't at the wedding. Both he and Peter felt angry and disappointed that Beverley knew about it and they didn't. Bunny and Beverley insist that Bob remained in Jamaica for several weeks after the wedding, and didn't leave the following day as reported elsewhere. Getting married had messed up Bob's visa application in any case since he'd been single when first applying, and that meant he'd had to go back and reapply as a married man. The delay prompted the Wailers to perform a farewell show, and try and raise some money towards his trip.

"Bob never want to go to America," Beverley recalled. "Bob said to me that the only reason his mother send for him is because he's singing now and that's probably why she remember him..."

The show raised the princely sum of twelve pounds. It was another "Battle Of The Giants" co-starring the Paragons and ended in chaos after the crowd began attacking the police. No sooner had the Wailers sang the opening bars to 'Good, Good Rudie' than pandemonium broke loose. Rude boys with ratchet knives were in the audience and when a policeman dared make his presence felt, they'd turned on him en masse. These youths refused to act like fugitives anymore. They wore their outlaw status with pride, and felt empowered by the songs they heard blaring out the jukeboxes. Times had changed and as Malcolm X had stated after John F. Kennedy's assassination, "the chickens were now coming home to roost."

Before Bob left for America, Coxsone agreed to pay Rita his weekly stipend in addition to her own allowance as a Soulette. He then expressed his concern that the Wailers were about to lose their main songwriter, as well as lead singer. Bob told him not to worry. He assured Coxsone that Peter and Bunny had the talent to keep the group going in his absence, and yet all was not well between him and the others. Bunny and Peter felt that Bob had broken the rules by marrying Rita, since the three of them had vowed to stay single and commit themselves to the group. Also, they hadn't seen Bob for three days after his wedding and so they suspected he'd been tricked into it, which implied weakness on his part – a development they found deeply troubling. They weren't to know it at the time, but either it was a phantom pregnancy or Rita will sadly lose her baby, since she and Bob's firstborn won't arrive for another eighteen months.

CHAPTER FIVE

Rasta Shook Them Up

Peter and Bunny lost no time in replacing Bob with Dream, whose departure from the Soulettes had left them struggling to keep momentum. He'd now changed his name to "Vision" after a Rastaman from Trench Town informed him that, "old man get dream, young man see vision." Everyone called him Vision from then on. As Rita's cousin he was family to the Wailers, and a decent singer in his own right. He and Peter harmonised well together and whilst Bunny couldn't match Bob for charisma, the new-look Wailers were still a potent force. Before long, they were booked to appear at the State and Ward Theatres in Kingston, which had proved strongholds for them in the past. If they were at all concerned audiences wouldn't take to Bunny singing lead, they really shouldn't have worried. Resplendent in their collarless red tops and cream serge trousers, they got rapturous applause for songs like 'Jailhouse,' 'Rude Boy,' 'Put It On,' 'One Love,' 'Love And Affection' and 'Keep On Moving,' prompting Bunny to declare that Bob wasn't greatly missed. "The sound was there, his presence wasn't. It still had the Wailers' sound and style," he observed.

It was three months before the Wailers' next studio session, in March 1966. Bunny had songs he'd written from even before auditioning for Studio One and Peter certainly didn't lack confidence. Freed of Bob's leadership, they will radically alter the group's dynamic with material aligning them to political and religious causes. First up was a cover of 'Sinner Man,' which Peter will later rewrite as 'Downpressor Man.' Bunny remembers Peter singing 'Sinner Man' at he and Bob's initial meeting with him two years earlier, and he'd waited patiently to record it ever since. It's Bunny who sings lead on the Wailers' version although Peter's baritone shadows him throughout, leaving us to wonder whether he shouldn't have sang it on his own since his is the stronger performance. It's a different sound for the Wailers, and the music's changing too. We're now coming to the end of the ska era, as evidenced by the stripped down band sound. Jackie Mittoo's hammered chords and Bryan Atkinson's cavernous bass underpin the song's warnings of Biblical retribution whilst the slower rhythm is a precursor of roots reggae – a style Bob, Bunny and Peter will come to epitomise in years to come. 'Sinner Man' was credited to Bob Marley and the Wailers when issued on 45 in Jamaica, even though Bob isn't on it. This must have caused a certain amount of disappointment, especially since the others were attempting to create a new identity for the group. Coxsone, who may have considered Bob's name to be the bigger draw, then compounded his "error" by crediting their next recording, 'Guajira Ska,' to the Soul Brothers.

'Guajira Ska' is a charming, light-hearted record, and with a melody similar to that of 'Peanut Vendor.' It's the ideal vehicle for Dizzy Moore, who's been allowed time and space to stretch out on a track that's more of a semi-instrumental than full-blown vocal. The Wailers have never sounded so playful as they fool around, impersonating Spanish girls and singing further praise of the "Ska Jerk," which they've now incorporated with Cuban music. This isn't altogether surprising. Rita, Tommy McCook and

Roland Alphonso all shared Cuban ancestry and so would be familiar with guajira, which had arisen in the period following Emancipation. Derived from the Spanish folk tradition, it had a tendency towards over-romanticism that was quite deliberate. At first glance it was Cuba's equivalent of country music except there was a contrivance about guajira the Wailers couldn't have known about at the time.

"It was in the guajira that the Cuban aristocracy saw their chance to wipe out all traces of the days of slavery, and 'vulgar' black music," writes Ospina. "'Guajirismo' was to drown out all else. At the same time, the playing of drums in public places was banned."

As in Jamaica, freed slaves in Cuba headed for the towns, where they were confronted by mass unemployment and grinding poverty. Unwilling to return home empty-handed, many elected to stay and live in the shantytowns that had sprang up on the outskirts of Havana and elsewhere. Soon ghetto troubadours began to appear, their songs reflecting the joys of liberation as well as tribulations. These bittersweet blues grated with Cuba's elite, who wanted the freed slaves back at work on the plantations. The music they tried to entice them with was guajira, which propagated the myth of a utopian countryside, populated by happy peasants. Needless to say the ruse proved unsuccessful, and guajira eventually fell into decline.

In one sense 'Guajira Ska' couldn't have been timelier since a short time later, Jamaica received a reminder of it's own colonial past when the Queen and Duke of Edinburgh arrived in Jamaica for a four-day stay. It was their first visit to the island in thirteen years, and thousands of people lined the streets to greet them.

Elizabeth II was still titular head of Jamaica by virtue of the island retaining its Commonwealth status after independence, and many preferred it that way. This wasn't true of everyone however. The mood was beginning to change and those who'd grown increasingly disillusioned about church and state weren't slow in expressing their views about the monarchy and organised religion. Take John Lennon for instance, who'd just got into trouble for saying the Beatles were "more popular than Jesus" and predicting that Christianity "will go, it will vanish and shrink." America's militant Bible-bashers reacted like lynch mobs and encouraged people to burn their Beatles' records and merchandise in protest, which thousands did. Figureheads like Lennon held enormous sway over public opinion back then, at least among younger people but the Wailers were more concerned with how such influence could be used, and for what purpose. Curtis Mayfield inspired them more than Lennon, but it's the desire to promote Rastafari "to all four corners of the earth" that'll provide their music with its raison de entre in future.

On April 21st, Emperor Haile Selassie I of Ethiopia arrived in Jamaica to such a clamour of excitement that Bunny likens the event to "the second Coming." It was the first visit to the island by any African head of state and if the Queen's welcome had proved enthusiastic, the one for H.I.M would prove ecstatic. Four years earlier, Edward Seaga had estimated there were ten thousand Rastafarians in Jamaica, "not counting many symphasisers." His figures were either wrong or they're been a massive increase since then as over a hundred thousand people – many of them dreadlocked Rastafarians – poured into the city and flocked to the airport, where joyous scenes ensued. The Emperor's Ethiopian Airways flight had been delayed by two hours due to inclement weather and yet the sun came out just as his plane came into view. This was taken to be a fortuitous omen. Cries of wonderment went up from the crowd, and so many people surged onto the runaway after the plane landed that his appearance was delayed by thirty minutes. When he finally emerged, it was with Mortimo Planno by his side – Planno having met H.I.M in Ethiopia several years previously. Jubilant Rastafarians filled the Emperor's vision, cheering and chanting his praises. Some even lit their chalices under the plane's fuselage, causing the ground staff to flee in terror in case there was an explosion! The sight of so many Rastafarians gathered in one place was extraordinary, even for Jamaicans. That's because dreadlocks were shunned, and often forced to renounce family and friends. The police would beat them on sight, and people round on them in the street. The only places they could live relatively undisturbed were either up in the hills or in ghetto communities like Trench Town and "the Dungle," which is what locals called the garbage dump. The way they commandeered the Emperor's visit was therefore unprecedented, and Rastafarians felt empowered like never before.

During the Emperor's first day in Jamaica, a reception was held on the lawns of King's House. One Rastafarian delegate's welcoming speech proved so passionate, the organisers signalled for it to be drowned out by a military brass band. Later that evening, Count Ossie's group gave a drum recital as the Emperor watched from an upstairs' balcony and Jamaican high society mingled with Rastafarians, dressed in their finest, for the first time. During the remainder of his stay the Emperor will address Parliament and meet with more than sixty Rastafarian elders, whom he described as "blood brothers." This must have caused shock waves in establishment circles except the Emperor was no dissident and apparently dissuaded these Rastas from thoughts of his own deification and also mass repatriation. (Two points that have been the subject of much discussion ever since.) The next day he laid a wreath in King George VI Memorial Park and viewed an exhibition of Jamaican folk art at the Prime Minister's residence before taking the train to Montego Bay.

The Emperor's visit, though brief, caused a seismic shift in how Jamaicans viewed themselves and each other. He'd granted legitimacy to the Rastafarians, who'd been allowed a level of access in Jamaican society many previously thought impossible. Now that they'd witnessed or heard about such scenes, many more people took an interest in Rastafari and especially youngsters living in underprivileged communities, where there was little else on offer that might bring them dignity and self-respect. The day the Emperor had arrived in Jamaica, Bunny, Peter and Vision were broke and hungry, and so they went to ask Coxsone for money. There were celebrations happening all over town, but the Wailers missed out after waiting around at Studio One for several hours. Coxsone came and went twice during that time, telling them he had things to do before finally giving them three pounds. Rita wasn't with them, because she'd gone to catch sight of the Emperor and will later claim to have seen holy stigmata on his palm as he waved to her. The other three walked back into Trench Town where they encountered crowds excitedly waving palm fronds and shouting with joy. Such scenes continued all the way to the quayside, causing them to marvel at how readily people identified with this royal African presence. Rita and all three Wailers will embrace Rastafari soon after the Emperor's visit, although Peter was first to frame it in musical terms. Less than a week after H.I.M's departure, he went into the studio with the Gaylads and recorded 'Rasta Shook Them Up' – a song that's significant in many ways, and not least because he recites a few words in Amharic, the ancient language of Ethiopia, during the introduction. It's the first song he recorded without any of the other Wailers (Bunny and Vision are absent), and it's the first by any of the group – Marley included – to mention Rastafari. As yet, there's no reasoning in the song. It's just a narrative telling the story of what happened, which is how a calypso artist would have approached it.

"A few days ago we had a wonderful time. So good," he begins, by way of setting the scene. "Three days of freedom and not one baton did shake... Everybody was jumping and shaking their body line..." By using the word "we," he's already aligning himself with the Rastafarians and there's also reference to Emperor Selassie's divinity in the line, "Babylon trembles to see our Father's face." Coxsone named the track after the chorus, but Island Records issued it as 'Rasta Put It On' in the UK. Peter does sing that line although the suspicion remains that Chris Blackwell, having noted the popularity of 'I've Gotta Put It On,' tried to pass it off as the follow-up.

The Wailers began visiting Bongo Donald around this time. He was a Rasta elder who lived in Greenwich Park Road, near where Rita's aunt lived. This area was called Ghost Town, due to its proximity to Calvary Cemetery, and is just a short walk from

Studio One. Bongo Donald and other Rasta elders in his circle had a selection of books they'd read or lend to people. Some told of Emperor Selassie I's coronation and African history, which must have been a revelation to youngsters raised on the notion that Africa was "the dark continent," and populated by savages. The Wailers' spiritual awakening grew apace with these visits to Bongo Donald's yard. Rasta had been there amongst them all along but they hadn't really taken a great deal of notice before the Emperor's visit. Now their interest had been kindled, their thirst for knowledge knew no bounds. There was another Rasta elder called Dagoo whom they'd also visit regularly. From now on, the Wailers would drift from one Rastaman's yard to another, reading books, reasoning with Rasta elders and smoking herb – this in-between playing ping-pong or football, and coming up with ideas for songs. Apart from occasional recording sessions and stage shows, they didn't have a great deal to do otherwise. And whilst they'd declared allegiance to the rude boys, they weren't planning to rob anyone or do anything bad, but learn more about their history and their culture.

Larry MacDonald, who grew up in Kingston before playing percussion with Gil Scott Heron says he visited Rasta camps to buy herb as a youth, and that the elders always encouraged him to join in their reasoning sessions.

"There was this elder dread who my instructor and I couldn't leave until I'd sat down with him first," Larry explains. "He wouldn't give me my stuff until I'd done that! He'd say, 'what do you think about the situation in South Africa?' And by this time, your mind is halfway across the island except you'd have to pull yourself together and give this elder dread some coherent discussion. That's how people became informed, because those early Rastas made sure to let people know what was going on man. They knew what was happening and they'd talk about it."

Bunny describes Rasta reasoning as an organic process. He says it's an exchange based on each individual's experience and that Rastas don't learn from one teacher alone, but by sharing testimonies with others. It was the Rastas' mutual quest and experiences that made them equal, but it had been the Emperor's acceptance that had transformed their expectations and elevated them to a social status no one could have possibly imagined prior to his visit. This prompted author and scholar Leonard Barrett, in a discussion with Adrian MacFarlane, to proclaim that, "Rasta has conquered Jamaica. Their presence is like a lion," he said. "If a lion comes into your midst, you know it's there and when a Rasta comes to any meeting or gathering, you know that he is there. His presence alone makes for problems. The natty dread, the long hair, the speech... A Rasta can talk to you about nothing. It may seem like he's talking nonsense but in the long run, he can humble you with his speech. In the beginning of the movement, they were quick to verbally assault anyone who was white, but they've eased these actions. Now the Rastas are free to go anywhere with anybody. They can marry anyone, regardless of their colour. They've made things different in Jamaica. They've actually changed the average Jamaican."

Hot on the heels of 'Rasta Shook Them Up,' Peter went back into the studio with the Soul Vendors and recorded a song that will define his early solo career. According to Peter, he wrote 'The Toughest' after spurning Coxsone's suggestion that he cover James & Bobby Purify's 'I'm Your Puppet.' Jackie Mittoo's arrangement may well have suited a straight cover but it's hard to imagine Peter singing it. That stage of the Wailers' development had now passed, and he and Bunny were eager to show what they could do. 'The Toughest' – issued under the name of "Peter Touch" – will become Peter's first proper hit and put him on the map in Jamaica. It was also the first of the Wailers' material for Studio One to be recorded on four-track, and there's a noticeable difference in terms of production. Yet it's the lyrics that fire the imagination most, and made the song so popular.

"Anything you can do, I can do it better, I'm the toughest," he declares right from the off, and with obvious swagger. Rude boys will rally to the call except Peter is careful to separate himself from their anger and violence. "Stop from doing wrongs, change your foolish plans," he warns them, before asserting his own reality with the line, "You come with your bitterness, but I just use my skill."

By spitting out the words "rough" and "tough," he's mimicking the recently deceased Emmanuel Zachariah "Zackie" Palm, a notorious JLP henchman from Back O' Wall. "Zackie," who was also known as "the High Priest," would belch and then mutter "rough," or "tough" in defiance. His name will appear in several other rude boy-related songs including Derrick Morgan's 'Rudie Don't Fear,' which shares a similar rhythm and chorus. Prince Buster will counteract that song with 'Judge Dread,' thereby initiating a musical feud that'll result in several hits apiece and lots of free publicity for both singers as the rude boy phenomena reached its zenith.

Whilst rude boys came to represent Jamaica's youth culture of the mid-1960s, they didn't stand for anything other than aggressive rejection of the system. Their aims were neither spiritual nor political and the Wailers had recognised this from the beginning, which is why Rastafari – with its religious and cultural framework – quickly drew them into its orbit, together with other reformed rude boys. These newly politicised converts were fired by idealism, and strengthened by events happening in America, Africa and elsewhere in the Caribbean. Momentum was building fast and the music too, will undergo transformation as ska gives way to rocksteady. From now on the bass line will take up the melody instead of the horns, whilst soloing becomes secondary to the vocal arrangements. The principal architect of this new sound was guitarist Lyn Taitt, although it was Keith Scott and Sam Mitchell, who combined running a youth club in Vineyard Town with A & R work for Federal who discovered singer Hopeton Lewis, and his 'Take It Easy' is generally accepted as the debut rocksteady release. Other candidates include Delroy Wilson's 'Dancing Mood' and Alton Ellis' 'Rocksteady,' although Dizzy Moore and Bunny both claim the Wailers' 'Let Him Go' beat them to it, despite Coxsone's reluctance to record without horns.

'Let Him Go' opens with the line, "Rudie come from jail, 'cause rudie get bail. You frame him and say he did things he didn't do..." This suggests it was an answer version to the Clarendonians' 'Rude Boy Gone A Jail,' which Coxsone also produced. The Wailers were trying to make the point that if someone's denied work, even though they're skilled, due to their social background, then who is in the wrong? If they live in Trench Town then no one will trust them and they'll automatically be turned away, so how are they supposed to survive? The Wailers saw how ghetto youths were discriminated against, and the police would intimidate entire neighbourhoods whenever they thought people were harbouring fugitives. Innocent relatives or bystanders faced being searched, arrested, imprisoned and even shot because if the fugitive ran, then the police might fire indiscriminately into the crowd, killing or injuring children and old people. Should that happen the police wouldn't admit liability, but say these people were resisting arrest, or had fired at them first.

'Let Him Go' was coupled with 'Sinner Man' on 45, and the message to the authorities couldn't have been clearer. Bunny, who'd been missing from Peter's last two recordings, was back on lead vocals for the session that yielded 'Let Him Go,' 'Sunday Morning' and 'He Who Feels It Knows It.' Coxsone issued the latter on a "blank" – i.e., a 45 single without a proper label, and that just had "Linger You Linger" scrawled across it. At first hearing it's a dance track, with Bunny inviting the brothers to "get right in the groove," except it conveys a good deal more than that. "Every man thinks his burden is the heaviest," he begins, before reiterating the Wailers' allegiance with Jamaica's poorer class by singing, "Yes I feel it, and I know it..." Just as Peter did on 'The Toughest,' he's imploring them not to be a problem to society, but to make a contribution instead. It's a message that'll resonate throughout the Wailers' oeuvre for many years to come, both collectively and individually. 'Sunday Morning' on the other hand, heralds another return to their doo-wop roots and is delivered in yearning fashion by Bunny, who wrote all three titles. The melody line is beautiful, as befits such a fragile tearjerker. There's even a crack in Bunny's voice as he wrings every ounce of emotion from the song. "We actually recorded

'Sunday Morning' on a Sunday morning," Coxsone told Roger Steffens. "It was one of the first two tracks that I did with Bunny." It was Peter's turn to be absent when Bunny and Vision lent harmonies to Bob Andy's 'I've Got To Go Back Home' and he wasn't there for Rita & Bunny's 'Bless You' either, which was the pair's second duet for Studio One. Being around such a consummate craftsman as Bob Andy could have only strengthened the Wailers' resolve to make music of lasting relevance. The lyrics of 'I've Got To Go Back Home' express the realities of a displaced people like no other. "Can't get no clothes to wear, can't get no food to eat, can't get a job to buy bread. That's why I've got to go back home, even if I've got to run..." And whilst Bunny and Vision's cooing harmonies – framed by horns and a lilting, rocksteady beat – soften the song's impact, there's nothing at all compromising about its repatriation message.

Rocksteady would take over the dances and airwaves that summer. DJs like Charlie Babcock over at RJR ("the cool fool with the live jive"), Rodney Butler, Winston Williams and Jeff Barnes kept the momentum going, whilst label owners such as Coxsone sponsored one-hour programmes, thereby guaranteeing radio play for their latest releases. Despite the best efforts of artists on his roster like Ken Boothe, Delroy Wilson and the Wailers themselves, Coxsone was losing out in the race for supremacy in terms of production, as well as hits. Instead it was his fiercest rival, Duke Reid – an ex-policeman who ran a liquor store downstairs from his Bond Street studio – who dominated the rocksteady era. Alton Ellis, Phyllis Dillon, the Paragons, Techniques and Melodians were among his lead acts and most of them had started their careers with Coxsone. It couldn't have pleased the latter to witness the impact Tommy McCook was having at Treasure Isle because thanks to the former Skatalite's direction, Reid's productions would set the standard for Jamaican music during the mid-sixties. Even Roland Alphonso moonlighted there from time to time but it was losing Alton Ellis to Duke Reid that caused Coxsone most hurt. Alton was now billed as "Mr. Soul Of Jamaica," and deservedly so. He hadn't liked how the Wailers promoted rude boy culture and so went over to Duke Reid and recorded 'Dance Crasher' in retaliation. His successor at Studio One was Ken Boothe, who'd sang in a duo with Stranger Cole, racking up hits like 'World's Fair' before being recast as "Mr. Rocksteady" on records for Coxsone. 'The Train Is Coming' was a big hit for him in the summer of 1966. It's a song that spans ska and rocksteady, and that he'll later revisit for Bunny Lee and with Shaggy. It's the second Jamaican classic members of the Wailers have sung harmonies on inside a matter of weeks, although Bunny was absent from that session and won't return until he and Peter help out on Rita's first-ever solo recordings, 'Friends And Lovers' and 'I'm Sorry For You Baby.' Their harmonies on 'Friends And Lovers' will later resurface in 'Duppy Conqueror' although Rita's vocals are unsteady, and her shortcomings further exposed whenever she ad-libs. You couldn't imagine Duke Reid giving the green light to songs like these or 'That Ain't Right,' which Coxsone held back for exclusive use on his sound-system. It's a song about missing a loved one and Rita may have been singing with Bob in mind, not that she lacks for company on the track itself. Bunny, Peter, Marlene and Vision all join her on backing vocals, whilst the music goes back to the jump era. It's as if the Pointer Sisters had descended on Brentford Road and 'Rock Sweet Rock' is another song to evoke feelings of nostalgia as Bunny leads Peter, Vision and Rita on an irresistible romp, sung in tribute to "the sweetest rocker in town..." It's music with a smile on its face, and that's heavily influenced by doo-wop and New Orleans' rhythm and blues.

The Wailers were also fans of Motown and especially Smokey Robinson, who was writing hits for the Temptations and his own group, the Miracles. Motown had released the album 'The Temptations Sing Smokey' in 1965, and the Wailers weren't the only Jamaican group to sit up and take notice. Their cover of the Temptations' 'Baby, Baby I Need You' (later renamed 'I Need You So' by Heartbeat) shouldn't be confused with another Wailers' song recorded back in 1964, called 'I Need You.' This one's an exquisite slow ballad framed by barbershop harmonies. Bunny's singing with more assurance as the new-look Wailers get into their stride. When Bob was there, he sang lead while the others harmonised around him. Bunny says Bob didn't have the right kind of voice to sing harmonies, "but Vision now, he can twist and turn and go into any kind of lead and come back to harmony."

The Temptations' latest album was 'Temptin' Temptations,' released the previous November. This is the same set that includes 'Everybody Needs Love' and 'Born To Love You,' which Slim Smith will soon cover with distinction. Despite competition from the Miracles, Four Tops, Marvin Gaye and others, the Temptations were Motown's lead act thanks to their two lead singers, a dynamic stage show and fabulous harmonies – attributes that made them the No. 1 choice for Motown's resident songwriters. In the summer of 1966 they were riding high with 'Ain't Too Proud To Beg' and 'Beauty Is Only Skin Deep,' although they'll incorporate a harder, rock feel on 'I'm Losing You,' released at the end of the year.

'Don't Look Back' was one of the songs that Smokey Robinson wrote for the Temptations. Peter sings lead on the Wailers' version and is backed by Bunny, Vision and Rita. In one sense, it's disappointing to hear him sing a cover after the fireworks of 'The Toughest' and 'Rasta Shook Them Up.' He'll revisit the song with Mick Jagger in later years but he's singing with authority, and it's a decent party side from a group now billed as "Peter Touch & the Chorus."

Rita and the Soulettes covered another Smokey Robinson song that summer, and with the Wailers again helping out on harmonies. Originally known as 'Choosey Beggar,' it's given a Jamaican twist and renamed 'A Deh Pon Dem' on the Studio One version. Rita's lead vocals are gawky and naïve, leaving Peter's baritone to penetrate the mix like a welcome shaft of sunlight. This same combination reappears on 'When The Well Runs Dry' although thankfully the other way round, and with Peter singing lead. It isn't one of his finest performances in truth, and his voice weakens towards the end. Also, there's little variation in the rhythm, and the lyrics owe more than a passing nod to the closing track from Otis Redding's 'Otis Blue,' which had been released six months earlier.

At times it feels like the Wailers are treading water, but then they'll suddenly pull out all the stops and deliver an absolute gem. According to Bunny, they also covered the Impressions' 'Little Boy Blue' during this period although the tape has never been found. The Impressions had covered 'Lemon Tree' on their 'Never Ending Impressions' set, released a year or so earlier. Bunny says that Peter suggested the Wailers record it, although Coxsone disagrees.

"It was my idea for the Wailers to sing 'Lemon Tree,'" he told Roger Steffens. "I travelled a fair amount, but Jamaican radio missed a lot and this was one of those songs that I personally loved. I had heard the Peter, Paul & Mary version, and I figured this song could do well."

Peter, Paul & Mary's version dates from 1962. Trini Lopez also had a hit with it but it seems inconceivable that Peter and Bunny wouldn't have taken note of the Impressions' version. The two friends share lead vocals on 'Lemon Tree,' with backing by the Soulettes. The end result sounds more like the Weavers than the Wailers, and is the closest they'll come to recording straight-ahead folk. Perhaps unsurprisingly, it failed to chart in Jamaica and will soon sink without trace. 'Jerking Time' (also known as 'Jerk In Time') would fare much better. It's the last of four Wailers' songs extolling "the Jerk," as then popularised by the Capitols' 'Cool Jerk.' "Jerk in time, after nine," croons Bunny as Peter and Vision do a plausible impression of the Beatles. It was coupled with 'Rock Sweet Rock' on 45 and restored the Wailers' reputation just in time for their performance at Skipper Lawn that July supporting Jackie Opel, who was giving his farewell show in Jamaica before leaving for Barbados. He'd recruited the Wailers to sing harmonies on one of his final Studio One recordings, 'A Time To Cry,' which was a slow tearjerker reminiscent of James Brown's 'Please, Please, Please.' Jackie was so popular that people tore down the fence in a bid to see him. Tragically, he was killed in a car crash shortly after returning to Barbados. There were whispers that Coxsone had hired a girl to drug him and send him crazy in a bid to avoid paying him royalties, but this seems far-fetched. The producer did have a reputation though, and only the brave dared stand up to him.

A month or so later, Peter led the Wailers on three songs brimming with character, despite being radically different from one another. 'Making Love' is rocksteady, and a nursery rhyme romance featuring Rita whilst 'Treat Me Good' won't be released until after the Wailers leave Studio One, and with Bop & the Bell Tones written on the label. The lyrics take the form of a parable. When Peter asks, "where will I wander?" it suggests that he's been thinking of striking out on his own – a notion furthered by 'Can't You See,' which heralds a complete break from the Wailers' usual choice of material (and I do mean *complete.*) British groups like the Rolling Stones had successfully conquered America, but their hybrid rhythm and blues left Caribbean audiences relatively unmoved. Peter clearly thought otherwise. With its "heart of stone" lyrics, slashing rhythm guitar and pounding rhythm, 'Can't You See' is more closely related to songs by the Yardbirds, Kinks or Animals than anything heard in Jamaica but then Peter was nearing his twenty-second birthday and eager to test his mettle.

Bunny will also take the lead on three tracks recorded for Coxsone that autumn. 'What Am I Supposed To Do' has charm, yet is hardly cutting-edge with its rollicking back beat and graceful sax, courtesy of the ever-dependable Roland Alphonso. You can still hear the ska in songs like this and 'Dancing Shoes,' which was a big hit for the Wailers as 1966 drew to a close. We can imagine it blasting out of dances and jukeboxes – also record shops since most of them had speakers placed by the front door, so as to attract more customers. The Wailers were now masters of Impressions' style harmonies, set to ska and rocksteady grooves. Yet we sense they want more, and that Coxsone may not be the one to provide it. 'Dancing Shoes' is a wonderful record, but the piece de resistance among Bunny's three songs is 'I Stand Predominant,' which Coxsone played on sound-system until audiences were weak at the knees. Some heard it as a rude boy classic, of similar stature to 'Let Him Go' and 'Rude Boy'; others as a declaration of intent since the Wailers had not only survived Bob's departure, but also returned with a vengeance. Essentially, 'I Stand Predominant' is a song of praise and written from a Rastafarian perspective – hence the phrase "I and I." Bunny will later revive this and 'Dancing Shoes' for his Bunny Wailer 'Sings The Wailers' album in 1980, and they remain among his best-ever compositions for the group.

Listening to the tracks listed above – some of which differ greatly – it's easy to understand why former Studio One acts refer to the place as a "college" or "university." By having access to the studio on a more or less daily basis, they were able to explore their potential in the company of musicians like Roland Alphonso and Jackie Mittoo, whose arranging skills generally took care of the rest.

"One man who was key in the whole Studio One experience was Jackie Mittoo," states drummer Joe Isaacs. "A lot of people, even those that revere him, don't really know the extent to which he has contributed to the establishment of Studio One and, by extension, Jamaica's music. In our time, we used to make twelve tunes every day and this man, Jackie Mittoo, was the driving force behind it all. He was the man who most times told the bassie what to play, told me what to play and when to roll. He was the man who created all these rhythmical patterns that are now branded as classic reggae, but nobody knows that."

Mittoo was a keen jazz fan, and listened intently to fellow keyboard players John Patton, Richard "Groove" Holmes and Jimmy McGriff. Like them, he'd been amazed by Jimmy Smith's trailblazing exploits on the Hammond, although Richard Ace played organ on the majority of Studio One recordings during this period, leaving Jackie to direct proceedings from the piano stool. Jazz audiences were now split down the middle with free jazz on one side of the divide, and soul-jazz – as typified by Cannonball Adderley's 'Mercy, Mercy, Mercy' – on the other. The genre would become increasingly fragmented, leaving soul as the dominant black music form. All day long, Jamaican radio played hits like the Four Tops' 'Reach Out (I'll Be There),' Wilson Pickett's 'Land Of A Thousand Dances' and James Brown's 'It's A Man, Man, Man's World,' whilst Otis Redding and Percy Sledge did most in popularising the sound of America's deep South. Despite such acts' dynamism, most black music was still rooted in the gospel and harmony tradition, and generally steered clear of social commentary. That would come later. In the meantime, close-knit harmonies were also the mainstay of folk groups like the Byrds, Lovin' Spoonful, Mamas And Papas and Simon & Garfunkel, whose decorative melodies lacked the abrasive potency of Dylan's work, but still generated more hits. The Beach Boys' latest single 'Good Vibrations' will top the US charts in December amidst rumours the track had taken over ninety hours of studio time to complete – an industry record. Together with the group's 'Pet Sounds' album, this song will alter people's perception of pop music, and especially after the Beatles follow it with 'Sgt. Pepper's Lonely Hearts Club Band.' Pop was no longer viewed as ephemera, but something of cultural importance. Following in the slipstream of Dylan and other folk singers, artists began to express sentiments that would have been considered off-limits previously. This shift allowed groups like the Wailers to articulate cultural realities of their own. For the time being however, they're still feeling their way, and using cover versions to explore possible changes of direction. In the words of Roger Steffens, "by singing the most interesting foreign material, from Dylan to Tom Jones, they learned how great songs felt in the mouth, and became matured in their own songwriting."

Their last-ever session for Coxsone yielded two Bob Dylan covers, as well as 'I Need You So' and 'Dreamland.' Dylan will profoundly influence Bob Marley as well. In fact he and Bob Andy, whose real name is Keith Anderson, both called themselves "Bob" after identifying with his music. (Marley had previously been known as "Robbie.") At the time of writing, the Wailers' attempt at 'Blowing In The Wind' hasn't surfaced yet. Bunny says Peter chose to sing it. This could have been after hearing Stevie Wonder's cut, although Dylan's own version had gone Top 5 on both sides of the Atlantic the previous autumn, and received a degree of airplay in Jamaica. As the Wailers entered Studio One on that final day Dylan's latest single, 'Rainy Day Women Nos. 12 & 35,' was blasting out of jukeboxes, promising how "everybody must get stoned," which must have

raised a few smiles.
According to Patti Smith, Dylan "had America in the grip of his fist." He was a singer of conscience, whose songs appealed to black and white audiences alike. After immersing himself in Woody Guthrie's hobo legacy and then revitalising it, Dylan had concentrated on writing songs about what he saw happening around him. 'Blowing In The Wind' subsequently became an anthem of the Civil Rights movement, despite having been written by this young white singer from Hibbing, Minnesota, and who wouldn't have lasted a minute in a Baptist choir. Dylan was always having to wriggle free of constraints. He posed questions in his songs, but was way too smart to hint at possible answers. Instead, he illustrated his truths with mythology and left interpretations to others. His success proved there was a market for lyrics that made people think, whilst that nasal whine demonstrated it wasn't necessary to be a great vocalist – just an honest one. That summer he was involved in a serious motorcycle accident, just a month after releasing 'Blonde On Blonde' and two months after his legendary Free Trade Hall performance in Manchester, where he'd been met with cries of "Judas!" for playing electric guitar and upsetting purists from the folk fraternity.
The Wailers showed no signs of such discrimination, although they do take unexpected liberties with 'Like A Rolling Stone' by giving it a rocksteady make-over and in the words of Greil Marcus, delivering it "in the tone of an elder reading a child to sleep with a fable about the wages of sin." Marcus also credits Bunny, who sings lead vocals, with "putting new blood on the song" by substituting Dylan's lyrics with a single, repeated verse.

"Nobody told you to roam the street," Bunny admonishes. "But that's what happens when you lie and cheat. You have no nights and you have no mornings. Time like a scorpion, stings without warning."

Rita's harmonies are well to the fore, but that fabled "wild mercury sound" which characterises many of Dylan's songs is conspicuous by its absence. Re-titled 'Rolling Stone,' it's one of the most unusual Dylan covers you'll ever hear, and remains strangely compelling. Better still is 'Dreamland,' adapted from the El Tempos' doo-wop hit 'My Dream Island,' issued on Vee-Jay Records two years earlier. It was Coxsone's suggestion the Wailers sing it yet Bunny again makes significant changes, which is probably why he's long claimed authorship. He sings of brotherhood, rather than romance, and the resettlement of an entire nation instead of a lovers' tryst. He also refers to dual utopias Zion and Ethiopia, which makes it a companion piece to Bob Andy's 'I've Got To Go Back Home' - i.e., it's another anthem for fellow Jamaicans struggling to equate a Christian upbringing with their newfound interest in Rastafarianism.

'Dreamland' will remain in the Studio One vaults for over twenty-five years, by which time Bunny will have re-recorded it twice. It's more evocative than confrontational, and an early example of Rasta mysticism. Elsewhere, growing numbers of people were expressing their dissatisfaction with the system, and America's involvement in the Vietnam War. Spreading from its epicentre in San Francisco, the counter culture was fast gaining momentum. New ways of thinking were required and the re-evaluation process would extend to pretty much everything, including race, class, work, health, food, child-rearing, politics, education, sex, clothing and of course the arts, with music serving as a major focal point. 1966 witnessed the emergence of hippies, hallucinogenic drugs, alternative medicine and dalliances with Eastern philosophies – also virtuoso guitarists like Jeff Beck and Eric Clapton, whose experiments with sound effects signalled a break from the blues tradition they'd once sought to emulate. As for the Beatles, they'd quit touring soon after the release of 'Revolver' and bequeathed their pre-teen audiences to the Monkees, whose 'Last Train To Clarksdale' was a No. 1 hit in America.

England beat West Germany in the World Cup final, held at London's Wembley stadium during July. The Wailers' favourite player, Brazilian forward Pele, had succumbed to injury in an earlier round, leaving them disappointed. A lot of Jamaicans supported the victorious England team, whereas West Germany made news for different reasons after donating nearly two hundred tons of tinned meat to Jamaica via the World Food Programme. By the summer, more than ninety tons still hadn't been distributed and so orders were given for it to be loaded onto trucks and taken to a prison farm, for use as animal feed. This decision proved controversial and five hundred looters attacked the convoy before being dispersed by a riot squad firing tear-gas into the crowd. That same day, a child in West Kingston reportedly died of malnutrition.

Earlier in the summer, Back O' Wall had been razed to the ground by government forces – an act of wanton aggression that heightened feelings against the JLP among Kingston's poor, and which the PNP quickly sought to exploit. Trench Town MP Dudley Thompson spoke on behalf of the victims, who included many Rastafarians. Squatters occupied areas of waste ground from Three Miles to Edgewater. This stretch of no man's land included Back O' Wall, where Ras Sam Brown's Rastafarian Movement Recruitment Centre and Prince Emmanuel's Ethiopian African National Congress had their headquarters. Ras Sam Brown's outspoken attempts to join the political process by founding the Black Man's Party had made him a controversial figure, causing him to be thrown in jail and his followers harassed at every opportunity. Less than two months after Emperor Selassie I's visit, the police began clamping down on Rastafarians and attempting to disrupt the island's ganja trade by arresting farmers and burning down fields in country districts, which they knew would antagonise the Rasta communities. Yet the first indication of trouble had flared up the previous October, at an event held to commemorate the 100th anniversary of the Morant Bay Rebellion, when acting Prime Minister Donald Sangster (Bustamante having been confined to his sickbed) had unveiled a monument honouring Paul Bogle and George William Gordon in the National Heroes Park. This ceremony was marred by crowd unrest after Seaga made incendiary remarks to a group of hecklers and threatened to "fight fire with fire, blood for blood." Retaliation wasn't swift, but certainly proved effective. On the morning of July 12th 1966, more than two hundred officers gathered at Denham Town police station armed with batons, pistols, clubs and bayonets before marching to Back O' Wall and attacking the inhabitants without warning, scattering them far and wide and making most of them homeless. Bulldozers then entered the scene, flattening and clearing away the flimsy dwelling places. The wreckage, consisting mainly of poor people's belongings, was then burnt as firemen looked on. Rasta camps in other parts of Kingston suffered a similar fate but it was the destruction of Back O' Wall that smacked of ethnic cleansing, and sent shock waves reverberating around Kingston. This was a new Jamaica – one increasingly torn apart by politics, since the JLP had cleared Back O' Wall in order to reward its supporters with government housing. Blocks of newly built apartments called Tivoli Gardens would soon replace the Rasta camps and shanty-dwellers. The government then built similar structures in Fourth Street, which served to split Trench Town into two rival factions, Rema and Jungle.

Meanwhile, preparations got underway for a showpiece occasion that was intended to promote Jamaica's international stature. In late July, Donald Sangster opened the newly built National Arena, adjoining the National Stadium. Less than two weeks later, HRH Prince Philip, who was making his second visit to Jamaica within just a few months, presided over the Eighth British Empire and Commonwealth Games. More than a thousand athletes from thirty-five Commonwealth countries competed in these festivities, which ended on August 13th. It was the first time the Games had been held outside "white" Commonwealth countries, and Jamaica did them proud. England won most medals but Jamaica managed four silvers and eight bronzes in track and field events, which was a respectable tally.

Events such as this spelt prestige for a former colony looking to assert its independence and excel on its own terms. Back in May, islanders had witnessed the inauguration of Air Jamaica and the airline's first flight to Miami. There were genuine causes for national pride but all was not well under the surface as the authorities struggled to contain political rivalries and an increasingly virulent underclass.

In August, Donald Sangster met with Edward Seaga and Dudley Thompson to discuss the rising violence in West Kingston. Seaga had accused the PNP of subversion in the wake of the Back O' Wall incident, whilst Thompson rebranded his counterpart "the Minister of Devilment and Warfare" (instead of Development And Welfare.) Both leaders were asked not to attend the funerals of supporters killed by rival gangs. Seaga was a known affiliate of the Phoenix gang, led by Frank "Bad Word" Gillespie. He complied whereas Thompson, who had ties with the Vikings, based in Trench Town, did not. Some politicians were now using gangs of youths to safeguard their constituencies and secure votes after supplying them with guns. It's said that this started with Seaga (who was feared for his association with revivalist cults) and Dudley Thompson, who'd studied law in England before standing for office. Others claim such rivalries were inevitable. Thompson had stood against Seaga in West Kingston but lost and so turned his attentions to Trench Town instead. Soon after he and the PNP had seized control there, several opposing gang members were killed by corrupt police officers. Episodes like this, together with the destruction of Back O' Wall resulted in open warfare between rival gangs, who fought running battles along the Spanish Town Road.

When tensions increased and Jamaica's middle classes grew uneasy, the Minister of Home Affairs, the Hon. Roy McNeill, declared a State of Emergency starting at midnight on Sunday, October 2nd. The Jamaica National Reserve was mobilised in case of riots; police and military cordoned off an area of West

Kingston and strict curfews were imposed, thereby silencing the sound-systems. Police also raided both party's headquarters and searched for weapons and evidence of gang-related activities, but without success. The State of Emergency would last just over a month. Three weeks after it was lifted President Kenneth Kaunda of Zambia arrived in Jamaica for a three-day visit, and life in West Kingston settled into more familiar patterns.

Meanwhile, the Wailers' prospects had stalled due to the antagonism between Bunny and Coxsone. Bunny had held back from confronting him whilst Bob was around but as soon as the way was clear, hostilities began in earnest. Bunny was better educated than the others and felt concern that the Wailers still hadn't received any royalties, despite recording so many hits. When they'd first joined Studio One Coxsone told them he needed their help in building an empire, and promised them a share in the label's success. That's why Bunny had grown irate. He felt tricked, and especially after dropping out of high school to pursue a musical career – a decision that had caused arguments with his family. All three Wailers had long abandoned thoughts of doing anything else with their lives, other than music. Peter and Bunny considered they deserved more, and especially after hearing that certain singles had sold over fifty thousand copies apiece. The truth was, the Wailers could barely scrape by. When not on stage they were often forced to wear threadbare clothes and their shoes had holes in them. Coxsone rarely paid them on time, and when royalty time finally came around, those weekly payments would be deducted. Relations between he and the Wailers began to rapidly deteriorate until they reached the point where Bunny couldn't take it any longer.

"This guy don't mean us no good whatsoever!" he exclaimed in disgust. Coxsone didn't take kindly to dissent as Roland Alphonso and Joe Higgs had found out, yet he remained wary of tangling with the Wailers. After Bunny entered his office without knocking one day, Coxsone made some comment about being disturbed, and how he could have been "rudenessing batty" – i.e., having sex with a man. Bunny promptly pulled out a ratchet and held it to the producer's stomach, vowing never to return. It would be he and Coxsone's last encounter. Peter wasn't there when this incident happened but chose not to go back to Studio One either, out of loyalty to Bunny. Fortunately, he still helped out at the dry cleaners and so had a little money coming in, whilst Bunny worked for his father. They'd been through a lot since Bob had left. Musically, both singers had found their own voices, and were writing decent songs. Peter had scored his first major solo hit with 'The Toughest,' whilst 'Rasta Shook Them Up' documented a crucial event in Jamaican history and nailed the group's colours to the wall where Rastafari was concerned – a statement underlined by his use of Amharic. For his part, Bunny had stepped to the plate and written songs like 'Let Him Go,' 'I Stand Predominant' and 'Dancing Shoes,' which had kept the Wailers on the local charts and helped give birth to the rocksteady era. All things considered, the pair had done well in Bob's absence, although Coxsone was glad to be rid of them. Both singers were strong-willed, and with a propensity for truculence. This made them difficult to deal with and such traits will beset each of their careers in future, when the stakes are considerably higher.

PART TWO

Doing The Chicken Scratch

CHAPTER SIX

Freedom Time

The Wailers had gone to Bunny's father and asked him for a loan before Bob's departure, but he'd declined to help. They'd wanted to produce records for themselves, but Thaddeus didn't really understand how the music business worked. That's when Bob first planned to leave for Delaware. He'd originally wanted the group to accompany him, but Bunny wasn't too keen on the idea. He was concerned the Wailers would struggle to retain their Jamaican feel and therefore "lose their essence." He thought they should start their own label instead. After all, they'd learned enough about how things worked by then, and knew what to do once they had the money.

Bob didn't exactly return from Delaware in triumph, despite having saved some cash. He'd written to Bunny whilst he was away, inviting him to come and stay at his mother's house but hadn't communicated with Peter. In fact he'd instructed Bunny to leave Peter behind, even as the pair worked hard to keep the Wailers afloat in his absence. Bunny chose not to answer, which he said caused Bob to greet him with a "lingering screw-face" on his return. Bob even wrote to Tartar, complaining how no one (meaning Bunny) replied to his letters. Yet Bunny couldn't have left without Peter, because that would have spelt the end of the Wailers. This forced Bob to rethink his plans. He'd got homesick in any case and so decided to return home and try and start something from Jamaica.

The first thing he noticed upon his arrival was that Bunny and Rita had turned Rasta. Peter too, although he hadn't started growing dreadlocks yet. He combed his hair, but didn't trim. He just had long hair like the hippies they'd been hearing about in San Francisco, except the cultural revolution in Jamaica went a little deeper and was inextricably bound up with religion. Months after Emperor Selassie I's visit a feeling still hung in the air, like the aroma from a bonfire party. People told Bob the shepherd had been and claimed his flock. They said, "all the sheep now knew the shepherd," and Bob couldn't help but be affected by it. He started growing locks too, whilst looking to see how they could kick-start the Wailers' career.

His first port of call was Studio One, where Coxsone welcomed him with open arms. The wily producer asked if Bob was still in charge of the Wailers. Whilst admitting that Peter and Bunny had improved, he wanted to know if Bob wanted to record solo. Bob refused to break ranks and said he wasn't going to sing for Coxsone anymore either, as the group wanted to make their own records. He also demanded money in lieu of royalties so Coxsone gave him ninety-five pounds, which he said Chris Blackwell had sent from London. Bob took out a little food money for them all, added the balance to what he'd saved in Delaware and then arranged to book Studio One for the Wailers' first-ever session produced by themselves. Apparently, Coxsone only agreed to this so they would see for themselves how little money there was in the record business, which meant he probably had mixed feelings after hearing the two songs they recorded that day.

Bob hadn't even been back in Jamaica a month when the three

Wailers (but no Vision) returned to Brentford Road in November and recorded 'Freedom Time' and 'Bend Down Low' with a stripped-down Skatalites' line-up, augmented by Bob himself on guitar. Led by Jackie Mittoo's rattling piano, 'Freedom Time' – also known as 'Get Ready' – is a gospel song imbued with the spirit of black consciousness, and the harbinger of more militant songs to come. "I'm going to talk that freedom talk, so get ready to walk the freedom walk," he sings, because "this is a time when man must be free." Bob's clearly been influenced by the US Civil Rights movement although unsurprisingly, his voice sounds a little rusty in places.

"Didn't I build the cabin?" he asks towards the end of the song. "Didn't I plant the corn? Didn't my people before me, slave for this country?" He'll revisit these lyrics years later when writing 'Crazy Baldhead' but back in late 1966, 'Freedom Time' served as both a rallying cry for black consciousness, and heralded a new chapter in the Wailers' story.

'Bend Down Low' is a different kind of song altogether. It's delivered off-the-cuff as if written quickly, as B-sides often were back in the sixties. Whilst fans have long believed it's the raunchy calling-card of a man who's been separated from his woman, it's just possible that Bob wrote it about Coxsone after hearing Bunny's tale about him "rudenessing batty." Despite his offer of studio time, the Wailers still viewed Coxsone with suspicion and one or two of the lines could easily apply to him. Their former benefactor's sound-system played at the Success Club on Boxing Day. The show was billed as "This True Nite Of Universal Love," and admission was three shillings. It featured "His Musical Mightiness In Ska, Sir Coxson" but we can rest assured the

Wailers weren't there. Whilst Coxsone still entertained ideas of winning them back, Bob and the others had voiced their last ever session at Studio One.

"We went through about four years of Coxsone's humiliation, exploitation, rip-off and all dem t'ings," Peter told Fikisha Cumbo. "Don't know nothing about my rights and we just go on, not being comfortable and sing and the music sell, and we just never get no money."

With Bob back in the line-up, there was an excitement about the Wailers once more. Now they had their own label, they called themselves "the Wailing Wailers." They'd been carrying this name since they were youths except they'd been through struggles both personal and professional in the meantime, and understood the meaning of the name "Wailers" even more. From now on they would wail for the people as well as themselves, and focus on getting their message across. After meditating on how a Wailer had married a Soulette, they decided to call their new label "Wail And Soul Them." It was Bunny who shortened it to Wail 'N Soul 'M and then designed a logo with three hands intertwined – Vision having melted back into the shadows.

According to Bunny, 'Freedom Time' ended up selling over fifty thousand copies. "In those days, records sold like rice," he recalls. In time, the Wailers would begin to see a little money for their efforts, but they'd have to work hard for it. Under Coxsone, they'd been paid per side, irrespective of sales. By starting their own label they got to keep all the profits, once they'd collected their money from the record stores and small-time retail outlets that were dotted all around Kingston. This could take a while and so the Wailers went hungry at first. They'd suck ice or drink soda

pop to fill up, and then smoke herb until they forgot about being hungry. Such experiences brought the three friends closer together and Bunny even claims it aided their creativity.
"Yes, because you can't sing on a full stomach," he explained. "It's a matter of discipline. It's mind over matter. Singing in those days was a strictly hungry belly business because the singers were made to suffer. I don't know if it's because music takes time to grow. It's a lot of devotion. It's a lot of sincerity. And then when do a song, you don't get paid until the song is actually sold but artists at that time were experiencing what they were singing about, and really feeling the lyrics. They were living inside the song, and literally singing for their supper. You've got to make it work too, because the promoters won't invite you on shows without a hit. If you're a singer, you've got to do it right, because that's where your next meal's coming from. Also, there's always that voice saying there's nothing in it for you and that you're a loser, you're a ten times loser."
None of them had a car as yet, so they'd load up their bicycles with boxes of records, sometimes stacking them so high they couldn't see in front of them. Peter would head out west, through Whitfield Town and towards Waltham Park whilst Bunny headed north and Vision went south. They'd let the bigger stores have test-pressings first of all, which helped generate advance orders. This was the same method Coxsone used, plus they'd give them to sound-systems like King Tubby's and Tippertone, who'd play them at dances all over Kingston. Peter generally took care of the soundmen, whilst Bunny and Bob looked after the jukebox owners. It's said you could sell twenty thousand records to jukebox owners alone in Jamaica during the early-to-mid sixties.

Every rum bar had a jukebox stood in the corner and even the illicit gambling houses had them. Such places were often situated in back alleys, where danger lay in wait for the unwary. Strangers weren't welcome in a lot of these ghetto areas and especially not after dark but the Wailers were determined to make their new label a success, despite such risks. Delivering to more recognised retailers such as G. G's, Clancy Eccles and Randy's was a lot easier, but even that wasn't without its difficulties. One time Bob left the record pressers on Slipe Pen Road and headed for the junction of Brentford Road and Princess Street, steering his bicycle with one hand whilst balancing boxes on the handlebars. In his haste to make deliveries he took the corner too fast, hit the side of a bus and veered out of control before crashing into the kerb and scattering records all over the street. He and Rita were living at her aunt Viola's house in Ghost Town. They'd opened a retail outlet there just before Bob left for Delaware, although to call it a shop is something of a misnomer since it was little more than a lean-to made out of boards, and with "Wail 'N Soul 'M" painted across the front. Rita sold other records from there, as well the Wailers' own and business was brisk at times, despite being confined to people from the immediate neighbourhood.

Coxsone had told them records weren't selling and yet the Wailers were proving him wrong. He hadn't taken kindly to losing them and according to Bunny, was determined to teach them a lesson. The Wailers had pressed 'Bend Down Low' at Specialists, owned by "a nice little white lady" called Miss Benson. Coxsone knew one of the girls who worked there, and she fed him reports about how the Wailers were doing. A short while later thieves broke into the premises; stole the Wailers' records and destroyed the stamper used to press more copies. The Wailers later heard that Coxsone had paid a man called Lascelles from Maxfield Avenue to commit the robbery. Reports also suggest that Coxsone pressed copies of 'Bend Down Low' for himself, and pocketed the money. It's therefore unsurprising Bunny calls him "father of the vampires," and describes him as being "inhuman, with no respect for human feeling."

Dennis Alcapone makes the point that record producers didn't want artists thinking independently, but preferred it "when they hold the handle, and we hold the blade.

"Those producers who were around back then, they didn't want artists to try for themselves," he said. "When the artists find out that the producers were robbing them and then go try a thing on their own, the producers would gang up on them and discourage them because they're not going to be making money out of you anymore and they don't like that. He wants you to come to him and work for him all the time, so he can load his pocket. That's why they go all out to stop you. It's just like in the film 'The Harder They Come.' They had influence with the radio people and would tell them not to play certain records. That means you struggle to get heard, so it's like a big conspiracy against you and we are the creators of the music, and yet not many of us had the means to actually go into the studio and run a session for ourselves. It was difficult in those days. The artist was important yes, but he only get the praise whilst the producer get all the raise."

Bryan Atkinson describes Mr. Dodd as "a good guy, but there was a ruthless side to him as well. There were certain things he didn't know. He was searching, just like the rest of us. He had the opportunity to record all of this great music, and he just went along with it day to day. He was dealing with it as he went along. If he had known, maybe he would have done the right thing by everybody, make sure they had a little pension and proper royalty payments but the business aspect wasn't done properly, and he took it all for himself. That's what drove Don Drummond mad and made Jackie Mittoo so very angry, because there was nothing in writing to say what they and the rest of us did."

The reason why producers like Coxsone were able to exploit so many young artists and musicians isn't difficult to understand. The record industry was booming and the allure of fame, if not fortune, was so inviting.

"That's right because really and truly, no man want to do hard work," explains Alcapone. "No man wants to go down the factory or cut cane, and no man really wants to go out in the sun and mix mortar. That's why as young men, so long as we could buy a beer or get something for a girl, like maybe a pair of shoes, it's nice and we were happy with that at first."

Such opportunities increased with the arrival of a new generation of record producers led by the likes of Bunny Lee, Joe Gibbs and Lloyd Daley, who came to challenge the more established labels. They'll soon be joined by others like Lee "Scratch" Perry, Harry J, Lloyd Charmers, Phil Pratt, Keith Hudson and Prince Tony Robinson as the local industry continued to flourish and the overseas' market – especially in Britain – extended its welcome to Jamaican music. Despite all this competition however, the biggest hits still came out of Studio One and Treasure Isle. Coxsone's latest productions included Ken Boothe's 'Puppet On A String,' the Tennors' 'Pressure & Slide' and Alton Ellis and the Flames'

'Rock Steady.' The latter defined the rocksteady genre but it was Duke Reid's hits with the Paragons, Jamaicans, Melodians and Techniques that raised the bar where standards of musicianship and production values were concerned. This was due to the expertise of Tommy McCook and the Supersonics, who ensured that Jamaican music would become a lot more soulful and melodic from then on. Whereas ska was aimed primarily at dancers, rocksteady lent sophistication to the fledgling Jamaican sound. The arrangements were more polished, whilst the likes of John Holt, Slim Smith and Pat Kelly (who'd just made his debut on the Techniques' 'You Don't Care') had the feel and delivery to rival most big-name American singers.

There were other changes happening throughout Jamaica, and especially in Kingston. In January, even as Parliament was dissolved in readiness for the coming election, acting Prime Minister Donald Sangster announced the formation of the Jamaica Citizens Bank, and commercial activity continued to expand northwards at rapid pace. The old Knutsford racecourse became New Kingston and a number of uptown plazas were built, hastening the decline of shopping centres in King Street and Harbour Street. Plans were also drawn up to redevelop ninety-five acres of real estate along the waterfront, where landscaped boulevards and multi-storey buildings housing the Scotia Bank Centre, the Jamaica Conference Centre and Kingston Mall would soon replace the chaotic sprawl of shantytowns. Despite such modernisation, trouble still simmered on the streets as a result of political violence. In the lead-up to February's election, supporters of the JLP and PNP fought each other with guns and homemade bombs, causing a number of deaths and widespread public concern. After the police were accused of being pro-PNP, they responded by raiding the JLP's Central Kingston headquarters where they found explosives, stolen goods, firearms and rounds of ammunition. Despite this discovery the JLP still won the election, held on February 21st. The PNP were reduced to just twenty seats, one of them held by Michael Manley, who'll join his father in Jamaica's next Parliament.

Two days after the results were announced, Donald Sangster was sworn in as Prime Minister. He would die just three months later in Montreal of a brain haemorrhage. Four hours after the news reached Jamaica, Hugh Shearer took control and preparations got underway for a state funeral. Shortly after Sangster was buried in the George VI Memorial Park, Shearer announced that he did not "expect any policeman, when he tackles a criminal, to recite any Beatitudes to him." Roughly translated, this meant Jamaica's new Prime Minister had granted the police a license to kill, and yet incidents involving firearms continued to rise. Shearer will continue to woo the police despite accusations he'd encouraged them to clamp down on the poor, who he seemed to regard as criminals. This theory ignored the realities of why they might be driven to commit crimes, and the identities of those supplying them with weapons. In a letter published by the Gleaner in July, one concerned reader wrote that, "Violence and hooliganism have been tolerated for too long. The shock troops and the strong-arm gangs, the bully boys and the trouble shooters of the political parties would appear now to be inextricably mixed in with criminal elements and genuine subversives. The question is, can the politicians contain their followers?"

The answer wasn't long in coming. Soon after the election, JLP officials began allocating housing to party supporters in Fourth Street, in an area known as Rema. This was a confrontational move, since Trench Town had many PNP supporters and warfare between the two groups was now inevitable. In the past, gangs armed with machetes and knives had cruised around Trench Town on bicycles, and fought mainly between themselves. Once politicians started recruiting them hostilities increased dramatically, and especially as a result of such deliberate provocation. Dudley Thompson, who'd defended Jomo Kenyatta in the Mau Mau trials, represented the PNP in Trench Town. He and Seaga's deadly rivalry lay at the heart of Jamaica's struggles with political violence during the late sixties, and was clearly exacerbated by Shearer's stance. The situation might have turned out differently had Donald Sangster not died so unexpectedly, and many still believe he was assassinated.

His death was a major talking point as the Wailers began promoting Wail 'N Soul 'M. It coincided with the little-known 'Simpleton,' produced by Prince Buster and credited to the Crackers, but featuring Peter on lead vocals. The Wailers respected Prince Buster for having successfully challenged Coxsone and Duke Reid during the ska era. In addition to making hit records for himself and others, he ran a sound-system called Voice Of The People and had secured distribution for his own productions in the UK, where he headlined tours and enjoyed considerable popularity. He'd recorded 'Simpleton' at West Indies studio with Arkland Parks on drums and Baba Brooks on trumpet, and then released it on his Olive Blossom label. It's an unremarkable song that quickly sank without trace. In fact Peter thought so little of it he didn't even mention it to the others. He and Bunny subsequently sang harmonies on two of Buster's productions, 'Don't Deceive Me' and 'Don't You Know.' The former boxer was a charismatic figure who inspired respect and admiration from those around him. Three years earlier, he'd got to know Malcolm X after performing at the World's Fair in New York. His interest in the Nation of Islam then intensified after he met Muhammad Ali in London during May 1966, prior to Ali's bout with Henry Cooper. After the two became friends, Ali invited Buster to his house in Florida, where he met Sam Cooke. Ali also bought him a brand-new Cadillac, which Buster delighted in driving through downtown Kingston before crashing it the same day. The Wailers were several years younger, and possibly in awe of him. Despite Buster having turned Muslim they knew of his early involvement with Rastafari, and how he'd been the first to record Count Ossie and his nyahbinghi drummers.

"What you must understand is that all of them get the joy from me," Buster explains. "I was the one they look upon, and they all meditated upon what I was doing, because I was the only one who was that successful at the time. Kids like them look at me and say, 'if Buster can do it, then we can do it too, because Buster grew up with we.' They call me Boops, y'know? And so they say, 'if Boops can do it, then we can do it too.' I brought out all of their talent like they were my sons, and they just take it on and deal with it but in those days Jamaica was a tough place, and Rastas weren't well-liked in society. After I went out there, then they knew they could come after."

'Ten Commandments' and 'Al Capone' were big hits in Jamaica throughout 1967 and the latter even went Top 20 in the UK. This was hardly surprising except Buster wasn't smooth like the rocksteady singers, but delivered his lyrics in a rhythmic, semi-talking style that preceded the first deejay recordings by some distance. Infused with larger-than-life personality, his records were a glorious mishmash of ska, gospel and rhythm and blues, and written with keen awareness of popular culture. References to Westerns and TV shows were plentiful, whilst others borrowed from Jamaica's rich treasury of folk and gospel songs. Everyday people loved the Prince because he spoke their language and shared their humour. He had Rasta sympathisers too, who probably turned deaf ears whenever Buster voiced "slackness" – bawdy songs that were well explicit for the times.

He'd got the name "Boops" after Duke Reid and Coxsone had derided his new ska beat as "boop boop music." He took these elders' ignorance as a badge of pride and then watched as they scrambled in his wake. As a former boxer he knew how to take blows as well as deliver them, and it was this fighter's mentality he shared with Muhammad Ali. In April, as Buster rehearsed for his first-ever US tour, his friend caused a furore by refusing the draft. Collective pride in his reigning heavyweight status was shattered and a tidal wave of indignation swept America, much of it fuelled by racism after Ali had declared, "Why should they ask me to put on a uniform and go ten thousand miles from home and drop bombs on brown people in Vietnam while so-called Negro people in Louisville (where he was from) are treated like dogs? If I thought going to war would bring freedom and equality to twenty-two million of my people, they wouldn't have to draft me; I'd join tomorrow but I either have to obey the laws of the land or the laws of Allah. I have nothing to lose by standing up and following my beliefs so I'll go to jail. We've been in jail for four hundred years."

Within an hour of Ali refusing the draft, his boxing license was suspended and he was stripped of his world heavyweight title. Affiliating himself with the Nation of Islam, since branded a "hate organisation," had left him with few influential friends yet the truth of his words and his refusal to bow under pressure inspired far-reaching support among black communities. Ali was a true revolutionary and Peter especially will take it all very much to heart.

Randy Roberts, biographer of another seminal black boxer, Jack Johnson, explains how the main thrust of Ali's message was one of racial pride. It was "the glorification of being black, a refusal to accept that black was anything less than best; a demand for dignity and full entitlements for all black people.

"He came alone at a time when the Civil Rights movement was maturing, and whites were willing to be pushed a bit," he says. "The possibility existed that you could offend white people and still prevail. Ali seized upon that moment and pushed it to the limit."

Some of America's black political activists were beginning to reject Dr. Martin Luther King's pacifism, and felt the need to fight back against the violence and harassment meted out to them by the police. The Black Panther Party for Self-Defence formed in Oakland, California during 1967, demanding equality under the Constitution and declaring that revolution – by any means necessary – was the only way to ensure their rights were respected. By way of illustration, two-dozen heavily armed Black Panthers marched into the Californian State Assembly to protest at plans to tighten gun controls. At the height of their popularity, the Panthers filled the Oakland Auditorium, where Stokely Carmichael gave a rousing speech and H. Rap Brown called for closer links with other disenfranchised ethnic groups in America. The Panthers even hired the Impressions, then enjoying a US Top 10 hit with 'We're A Winner,' to close the show. Undercover FBI agents infiltrated their rally the following night, at the Los Angeles Sports Arena. Thereafter, the FBI instigated a sophisticated programme of destabilisation called COINTELPRO, which caused the Panthers to splinter into rival factions led by Huey Newton and Eldridge Cleaver. Few public figures would dare endorse the Panthers for fear of repercussions as their influence began to wane. Nina Simone and Miriam Makeba did, and their careers immediately suffered as a result.

All three Wailers were fired up by talk of revolution as Black Power made its presence felt in Jamaica. Discussions raged back and forth in the Rasta camps throughout the summer, which was unusually hot that year. The level of rainfall was way down and frustrations began to mount in other areas too, since the Wailers had struggled to raise money for further recording sessions.

This same "Summer Of Love" heralded the emergence of hippies, love-ins, peace signs and a utopian outlook that embraced most things, including the clenched fist of Black Power. It was a time of tie-dyed shirts and dashikis, of campus unrest and civil disturbances, as well as organised resistance to the draft. 1967 was also the year of the Monterey Pop Festival, 'Sergeant Pepper's Lonely Hearts Club Band,' the Human Be-In at San Francisco's Golden Gate Park and a fascination with Eastern mysticism. With the hippies came free love, kaftans, bells, a liking for hallucinogenic drugs and the launch of several influential magazines such as Rolling Stone, Oz and International Times. The generation gap had never been so pronounced, or opposition to the status quo been voiced quite so openly. Nothing would be the same again, or at least that's what it felt like. Speaking on behalf of the counter culture, Hunter S Thompson talked about there being a "fantastic, universal sense of whatever we were doing was *right*, that we were winning" yet victory was still a long way off, and the powers-that-be were quick to register disapproval. That summer, members of the Rolling Stones were busted and then jailed on minor drugs charges as a moral backlash gathered momentum. The Beatles headed a list of signatories calling for them to be released and even the Times considered their treatment heavy-handed. Amidst visions of a brave new world came the inescapable sense that lines were being drawn – an impression reinforced by news of riots in New Jersey and Detroit, where police shot dead one black youth and then callously murdered several others.

It was a turbulent era and the music that came out of it remains a reliable barometer of what actually happened. Rock and soul were the dominant genres and Jamaicans heard plenty of both, especially soul. JBC broadcast a show on Saturday mornings called Top Of The Pops highlighting UK hits by the Yardbirds, Tom Jones and the Beatles etc. That's how youths like Peter and Vision got to hear Jimi Hendrix, whose guitar playing would inspire them both. Acts like the Rolling Stones, Jefferson Airplane, Traffic, Pink Floyd, Janis Ian (with 'Society's Child'), the Doors and Cream didn't sell all that many records in the Caribbean, but it would be a mistake to under-estimate rock's influence during the late sixties. After the pioneering efforts of Dylan and the Beatles rock was viewed an art form, and talked of as if it mattered – a compliment that wasn't so readily extended to black music. That was the kind of impact the Wailers wanted to make. They felt the need to write music that carried a message and stood for something – music that capable of bringing about positive change, first in people's hearts and minds, and then the world at large.

A number of black American artists were intent on doing something similar, only minus the quest for Rasta governance. The Impressions certainly, but 1967 offered a wealth of gospel-trained voices and fatback rhythm sections, of which Sam & Dave's 'Soul Man,' Otis Redding & Carla Thomas' 'Tramp,' the Temptations' 'I Wish It Would Rain' and James Brown 'Cold Sweat' were just a part. It was also the year Aretha Franklin unleashed 'Respect,' 'I Never Loved A Man,' 'Baby I Love You,' 'Chain Of Fools' and '(You Make Me Feel Like) A Natural Woman' – a run of hits that saw her crowned "Queen Of Soul."

Jamaica too, had its share of exceptional singers. The Paragons' songs for Duke Reid all went Top 5, but then Treasure Isle acts had dominated the island's charts all year, relegating the Studio One stable to also-rans. When Delroy Wilson left Coxsone that same year the die was cast, and rocksteady would be forever associated with his arch rival. Duke Reid's biggest hit was the Techniques' 'You Don't Care.' People would request it ten, fifteen times in a row at dances and Reid also signed the Jamaicans, who won the Jamaica Song Festival with 'Baba Boom' after a nationwide tour and the lion's share of radio votes. The group had a young Tommy Cowan in their line-up and their popularity even rivalled that of Byron Lee's travelling show Rock Steady '67 that summer.

The bass line on 'Baba Boom' carried the melody and would inspire numerous other "versions." Jackie Jackson played on the original, causing Johnny "Dizzy" Moore to credit him as the inventor of reggae, along with keyboard player Winston Wright (also known as "Brubeck") and drummer Hugh Malcolm. Dizzy claimed the change happened after Coxsone and the Soul Vendors came back from England during mid-1967. He and Coxsone had disagreed over something during a hastily arranged session in London and the producer let fly at him with a right hook. Dizzy managed to deflect the blow, but wasn't too keen on staying with Coxsone after that. On his return to Jamaica he worked with Kes Chin for a while until Tommy McCook invited him to play at Treasure Isle. That's where the trumpeter says the Supersonics "took the back beat closer to mento."

The Wailers were quick to take notice, and booked a session at West Indies' studio with roughly the same line-up in June. Ranny "Bop" Williams joined Lyn Taitt on rhythm guitar whilst Dizzy Moore and Vin Gordon played trumpet and trombone. Four tracks were laid that day, which Bob had written since returning to Jamaica.

"I remember the first session I played with the Wailers," Jackie Jackson told Mark Gorney. "Bob had just left Coxsone and that was the first time I met him. When Bob came into the studio, he usually had his guitar with him and he had a thing for bass, y' know? Usually when the artists came into the studio, they'd go over to the piano player, sing the song, the piano player would find the key and chord progression, and then all of us fall in. Bob now, he would come and stand in front of me with his guitar and wouldn't say anything. No words, nothing. He wouldn't even say, 'Alright, listen to this.' He'd just pick up his guitar and come right in front of me and stand up and start to play and sing. Close his eyes, with his head up in the air, and sing and play, sing and play and then after a while, he would open his eyes and look at you and that would be the signal for me to start playing a line. And once I start playing, he'd start to sing again, with his eyes closed. I'm following the song and I'll play different lines but then when he hear one he likes, he'd start smiling and the better the line, the broader the smile. When we have the right line now, he would open his eyes and look at me. That's how it was with Bob and all of the recordings I did with him, that's how it was done. No words, nothing. I was the bass player at that moment in time. There were a couple of guys around but he would always ask for me. He never called me Jackie either. He always called me "Bassie." That was his little name for me."

Hugh Malcolm wouldn't take money for playing on Wailers' sessions so they'd just give him a bag of herb instead. Jackson says the drummer had powerful action in his right hand and right foot, second only to Lloyd Knibb. "In some of those old recordings where Malcolm drops his bass drum, it's unbelievable," he recalls. "If any other drummer did that they would soak the song, but Malcolm was a great drummer and his ability to play that instrument was unbelievable."

The music on these early Wail 'N Soul 'M sides isn't anywhere near so polished as Treasure Isle releases, but then the Wailers were still novices at production. That's maybe why these tracks sound a little off-the-cuff. They're rough diamonds, and yet enchanting in their naivety. Even Bob's shaky lead on 'Nice Time' can't detract from the joyous nature of the song. He sings with gusto, whilst the melody is unforgettable. Bob's declaration that, "Long time we don't have no nice time," could only have been inspired by his return to Jamaica and so too 'Mellow Mood' on which he croons, "I'll play your favourite song darling. We'll rock it all night long..." Bob has rarely sounded so romantic, whereas Peter and Bunny's harmonies are sweetly understated.

These songs offer the clearest indication yet that Bob's glad to be back home and in the arms of his young wife. Joyful relief pours from every phrase and whilst it's not a love song (at least not in the secular sense), 'Thank You Lord' expresses similar sentiment. The same month it was recorded, the world's first video link took place as the Beatles' 'All You Need Is Love' was beamed by satellite to more than four hundred million people around the world. Universal love was in the air and yet the Wailers weren't singing of an abstract concept, but personal testimony. The Lord in question is both real and present, and addressed with certainty. "Said I'm in no competition, I make my decision. You can keep your opinion..." The song goes flat after Bunny takes a verse but Dizzy's trumpet soars and the rhythm sparkles. 'Hypocrites' is from the same session but it's a song about man, not God. It's Bob's best vocal performance since returning from America. A roll call of the vain and greedy come under fire in the lyrics and whilst the tone's Biblical, it's never withering – not even when passing comment on "dry land tourists," who claim to have travelled when they haven't. 'Hypocrites' was credited to Bob Marley & The Wailing Wailers upon release, except there's no sign of the other two. Remember, this record was the Wailers' own production. They decided what's printed on the label, and Bob was clearly the bigger draw.

Bob again sings lead on 'Bus' Dem Shut,' but it's a group situation all the way. The three of them wrote it and it sounds like it since everyone gets the chance to sing out; Bunny's higher register being offset by Peter's baritone. The Wailers' vocal magic shines forth whilst the subject matters cuts like a knife. It's a song about being exploited, and you won't be at all surprised to learn that the central character, "brother Pyaka" ("pyaka" meaning greedy and envious) is based on Coxsone; the slave master who works them so hard, their threadbare shirts literally burst at the seams.

'Bus' Dem Shut' will stay in the can for almost a year before being released. It was recorded at the same session as 'Stir It Up,' which Bob wrote after listening to Jackie Opel's 'Push Wood.' Both use the same sexual innuendos - "wood" being a reference to their manhood. Peter and Bunny coo in their best falsettos, as if already imagining the ladies winding their hips in the dancehalls.

The Wailers' next two tracks couldn't have been more different. Both may have roots elsewhere but the Wailers transform them into Rasta pastorals, with funde and repeater drums providing the heartbeat. The songs they put on tape is music you'd normally only hear in some Rasta elder's yard where the brethren chant, play instruments and share a chalice. The Wailers' rude boy phase seems very distant now. The group had managed to reinvent itself, and acquired a more spiritual dimension.

'Lyrical Satyrical' is an instrumental showcasing Peter's guitar playing, which could easily pass for folk or country were it not for the nyahbinghi drums accompanying him. It swings too. The melody's delightful and makes it sound as if Peter's sat on a front porch in the Appalachians. That's his mix of bright chords and blues phrasings heard on 'This Train,' which marks the first time Bunny's been given the spotlight since Bob's return. He seizes the opportunity by taking a song that stretches back to the twenties and beyond, and putting a definitive stamp on it. He'll later revisit it on his classic 'Blackheart Man' album but this early cut exudes a warm sense of belonging. You'd never guess it's the voice of someone who's about to start a lengthy jail sentence.

CHAPTER SEVEN
Thinking Like Wolves

The Wailers initially looked up to Mortimo Planno. He was a man who knew Emperor Haile Selassie I personally: had travelled to several African states and visited His Majesty in Addis Ababa. It was Planno who'd provided reassurance before the Emperor ventured out of the plane that April day at Kingston airport, where tens of thousands of Rastas excitedly awaited a glimpse of their Messiah. As a leading Rasta representative, he'd attended state functions and socialised with Jamaica's elite during the Emperor's visit and was regularly courted by academics. When Planno spoke of ancient African civilisations in a voice thick as tar, it was with grave authority. His persona was that of a man steeped in learning, even as he spoke up about the poverty and injustice that could be seen all around him in Trench Town.

"Planno was a man who was always fighting the system," said Alton Ellis. "He'd say things like 'Let the people have food ta bumbaclaat, and let the blind be led.' The man just cuss and every word 'im speak, it just record in my mind but a lot of what Bob sing about also came from that circle and that teaching, y' know? Because we'd all sit around and read the Bible, eat some food and smoke herb. And somebody might be cooking cornmeal and callaloo or fish as we talk."

Alton lived on the same street as Planno, near the Ambassador Theatre. The Rasta patriarch lived at 35 Fifth Street, at the corner of West Road. His yard was one of the few places where uptown and downtown people could interact and exchange views. This helped both parties gain a better understanding of how the other half lived and more importantly, what they shared in common. In reality, it was Rasta philosophy and not individuals that brought people together, yet it would be a mistake to underestimate the scale of Planno's influence in those heady days, soon after the Emperor's visit. He was a magnet for all sorts, from lecturers such as Walter Rodney to entertainers and local politicians – this in addition to all those penniless seekers who crowded his gate most evenings. Visitors could enjoy a draw of herb and plate of food at Planno's, as well as a welcome sense of fellowship. Primarily though, it was a place of learning. Guest speakers brought news of faraway liberation struggles, and there was a library of books to hand about black history, the Civil Rights movement and religion that Planno and others would read from.

"In those times people would sit down and share with each other," reflects Burning Spear. "We had those who'd go from place to place and explain what they knew. They would share their knowledge and give people the hope that what they were learning could work for them. People don't do that anymore but we'd sit there listening to people talking to us and telling us stuff we didn't know. We learn a lot of good things like that but we had to humble ourselves before receiving that kind of knowledge. For us, learning about things was *hard*."

The Wailers didn't like rehearsing at Planno's yard because it was too crowded. They preferred to be around friends like Tartar, Skipper Layco or Sang Hugh, who allowed them time and space to penetrate the music. According to Bunny, Bob read a lot of "pop" magazines in those days, whilst Bunny himself read

Shakespeare! Peter especially enjoyed books on martial arts, African history and politics. "Anyt'ing wha' say 'Africa,' 'im grab onto that," says Bunny. It was the Bible that took precedence however, and the three friends spent a lot of time reading and reasoning about it together, trying to decipher its' hidden meanings. Planno wasn't a great Bible reader by all accounts but other Rasta elders in Trench Town were, such as Brothers Ging (who was Rasta, but didn't wear dreadlocks) and Daniel. These men weren't ghetto celebrities like Planno; just humble souls who made their living by making and selling crafts. Both encouraged the Wailers to work for themselves rather than be exploited by the likes of Coxsone, and shared the same spiritual beliefs.

The depth of the Wailers' religious convictions – and also their relationship with Planno, who acted as their manager at this time – can be heard in the song 'Selassie Is The Chapel.' According to Planno, he took Bob, Peter, Vision and Rita into JBC for the recording, on June 8th. Clive Chin of Randy's disputes this, and says it was a live session recorded at Planno's yard on Fifth Street. Planno also claims that only twenty-six copies were made although Randy's later repressed at least a hundred or more copies for general sale. The date too, is open to question. Bunny's absence is usually explained by the fact he was jailed in July 1967, and 'Selassie Is The Chapel' therefore must have been recorded in the summer of 1968. Yet Bunny became estranged from Planno before the others, which means he could have still been around when they did it, but refused to get involved. No matter. It's the most devout item in the Wailers' catalogue, and spinechilling in its intensity. Bob sings praises to His Imperial Majesty, his yearning lead framed by high-pitched harmonies, acoustic guitar (played by Peter) and Rasta drumming courtesy of two dreadlocks named Teego and Jeremiah, who play repeater and funde respectively. It was apparently Planno's idea to take the fifties' hit 'Crying In The Chapel,' and turn it into a Rasta hymn. Sonny Till & the Orioles' is the best-known cut but Elvis Presley covered it on his gospel album 'How Great Thou Art,' which made quite a splash in Jamaica on its release in 1967.

'Selassie Is The Chapel' will be Planno's only real contribution to the Wailers' musical oeuvre. Bob and Peter would grow as disillusioned with him as Bunny, and learn to keep their own counsel in future. A woman called Aunty May who lived with Planno would caution them about him, before she left the neighbourhood suddenly and without explanation one day. They hadn't wanted to believe her at first but after they'd witnessed some of his activities firsthand, their trust in him evaporated. Casting his religious principles aside, Planno would head for the whorehouses in Fleet Street, Gold Street and Hanover Street most weekends, where he'd mix with both male and female prostitutes. Sometimes he'd take the Wailers with him but then disappear only to be tracked down in a room with four girls, which he'd proffer them like candy. To the three youngsters, flush with spiritual ardour, this was deeply troubling. Bunny remembered how his father had warned him about Planno, saying that he was "an original rude boy" and shouldn't be trusted. Bunny and the others hadn't heeded him at the time. Living in Trench Town, they'd met their share of characters and learnt how to roll with them. Buzzy Bee could be so intimidating, he even scared the police yet Buzzy treated them with respect, whereas Planno – who they later discovered was involved in scams at the local racecourse – would get Bob to ferry herb around in his battered Volkswagen, thereby putting him at risk.

Bunny was first to rebel, and refused to hang around Planno's yard anymore. Instead, he'd spend time on his own or go and visit Tartar whilst the others ventured up to Planno's on a Friday evening. Tartar's struggle with diabetes was growing worse. He'd already lost several of his toes, and would eventually lose both legs. All three Wailers were supportive towards him. They might buy herb from him or suggest forms of treatment. Bob would even award him songwriting credits in future, thereby guaranteeing him an income but all that seemed a long way off back in the summer of 1967. Bunny found peace in his company, and was friends with the other regulars who dropped by. One Friday evening Bunny was sat with Tartar, smoking and reasoning. The next minute whistles and shouts filled the air and several policemen burst into the yard, brandishing clubs, forcing people to lay face down in the dirt and beating those who resisted. Tartar was arrested for selling ganja but the police rounded up everyone else who was there as well, and charged them with "being in the vicinity."

"In those times, having ganja was like a murder charge," Bunny told Roger Steffens. "You must go to prison, no fines were allowed." For possessing one spliff, a first offender could expect a jail sentence of between six and eighteen months whilst having a seed was classed as cultivation and brought an even longer sentence. Bunny therefore resigned himself to the idea of prison, even though he'd dropped his spliff to the ground as soon as the commotion started.

It would be a while before his trial date so the Wailers decided to leave Kingston and take a break. Bob was having difficulty writing songs, and Peter feeling edgy at the prospect of becoming a father. The mother-to-be was Bunny's sister Shirley, who would give birth to their son Andrew on June 19th.

Earlier that month the Wailers' entourage – including Vision and a heavily pregnant Rita – had left for Nine Miles, where they planned to work the land and sample the joys of rural life. This is the same thing groups such as Traffic were doing back in England, where it was called "getting it together in the country." Bob's grandfather had died some time beforehand and left a plot of land about three and a half miles from the village. It didn't take long for a routine to fall into place. Every day the men toiled in the hot sun planting yams, cocoa, beans, corn, cabbage and pumpkins, and each morning they'd head for a spot about three miles away called Spring, where villagers from Seven Mile, Eight Mile and Nine Mile collected water that gushed from the rocks. People would turn up on foot and donkeys, fill up their oil drums and put them in the panniers, or balance overflowing buckets on their heads before setting off down the winding path to their villages. It was too busy to bathe there during the day so the Wailers would return just before dawn, and greet the morning sun. When they weren't working the land, they'd be rehearsing and trying out new material up at the house – a two-room shelter that had been Bob's first home. A fallen tree lay in the back yard, where Bob would chop wood for the fire. After eating a simple vegetarian meal the group would sit on this tree and rehearse well into the evenings.

They were living healthily except they had little money, despite their records selling reasonably well. Bunny suspected that Bob had been giving money to Planno but decided not to question him about it. To do so would have undermined Bob's authority and caused a split to develop between them. Bob had earned the right to lead the group, and Bunny and Peter didn't have to wait long for another demonstration of why this was the case. One day out in the fields, Bob stepped back on a hoe and cut his heel almost down to the bone. Lesser mortals might have cried out or even fainted yet Bob just packed the yawning wound with earth, bound it with a strip of cloth and carried on working as if nothing had happened.

Bunny had lived in Nine Miles with his father as a young child. It was there where Cedella and Thaddeus had first met and so like Bob, he was used to the country life, as was Peter. There was no electricity in Nine Miles and few distractions unless you count the drunken flights of "peenie wallies," or Jamaican fireflies. After Peter and Bunny had left, Jamaican broadcaster Neville Willoughby visited Nine Miles and filmed Bob singing on the back of his donkey, Nimble, whilst strumming a guitar. This footage was shown on JBC, but is now presumed lost. The Wailers' current hit was 'Nice Time,' which they'd released in July with 'Hypocrites' on the flipside. Two months later and it entered RJR's Top 10. These early pressings were credited to Bob Marley & the Wailing Wailers, and had a red, gold and green label showing three interlinked hands, symbolising unity. The group were making no secret of their allegiance to Rastafari, even as Shearer's government continued to harass cult members.

Bunny was just twenty years old when they found him guilty as charged. He was sent to the General Penitentiary, where his locks were forcibly hacked off and he would spend the next two months before serving a year's hard labour on a prison farm, in Richmond. Bunny told Roger Steffens that jail "is a hell world, made of rails and bars and walls" and populated by "ugly guys with long sticks and handcuffs." The opportunities for exercise were few and far between and since most of the prisoners' time in jail was spent in darkness, they cherished every shaft of sunlight. Each cell held three men, but there was only space enough for one mattress. This meant they'd have to take turns. Two of them would sleep whilst another stood awake in a corner. The standard of hygiene wasn't much to talk about either. A bucket was used as a toilet, with a sheet of cardboard placed over the top to keep the stench at bay. Some of the wardens liked to intimidate the inmates, and put fear into them. Hitting back at them wasn't an option, and any dissent would be swiftly dealt with.

"If you misbehaved you went to the dumb cell, which is a little cell where you cannot stand," said Bunny. "You have to sit or crawl on your knees. That's about the height of it at the entrance, and then it slants down so you can't sit or stand upright. You have to sit or lie down and you're being fed on just water and crackers, sometimes for thirty days or more."

Mortimo Planno came to visit and informed Bunny that it was Thaddeus who'd set him up, to teach him a lesson. Bunny found this hard to believe because whilst his father didn't smoke, he was known to deal a little herb on the quiet. The rest of the prisoners gave Bunny "screw-eye" when Planno turned up, calling him "a batty man.

"These men were West Kingston youths and knew the whole history," explained Bunny, who'll receive one more visit from Planno after being transferred to Richmond. When he asked his father about Planno, Thaddeus had replied that "Rasta business done now. You're supposed to wise up to that now." Bob also visited him once, with a whole bunch of guys from Trench Town. This was useful, as it was good for Bunny to show he'd got plenty of friends on the outside.

"In prison, you have to learn the art of fighting without fighting. That is the greatest martial art ever," he'll recall. He learnt that it's unwise to grant or ask favours, and to talk or act comfortable. "It's nothing for nothing in prison because if you need company, then you're thought of as a coward," he said. "Amongst wolves don't think like a rabbit, not even for an instant."

The other prisoners knew that he was a singer, except Bunny took no notice of them, not even when someone shouted, "Wailers in prison. All rude boys, respect due!" He didn't mingle or talk much, or want to feel too comfortable. Instead, he tried to remain focussed, and maintain a disciplined lifestyle. Once he was moved to Richmond then things eased up a little. A keen batsman, he was even allowed to play cricket for the local parish side sometimes.

Bunny's girlfriend Jean Watt was a dressmaker by trade. Friends have described her as a quiet, reserved person, who took her Rasta vows seriously. She's co-credited with writing some of Bunny's best-known songs from the late sixties and early seventies. Meanwhile the other Wailers' womenfolk had new babies in their lives. Bob and Rita's daughter Cedella was born in August, just a month after Bunny went to jail. The group missed him straightaway. Bob had written several new songs during their sabbatical in St. Ann's but would fling his guitar down in frustration after Bunny was imprisoned, saying the Wailers' sound "get choke up." Peter couldn't recreate the magical blend of harmonies on his own and whilst Vision and Rita were willing to help out, Bob's mood continued to darken. "Wailers a deh in prison," he'd retort although his spirits lifted when 'Bus' Dem Shut' and 'Stir It Up' followed 'Nice Time' onto the local charts. Vision's brother had taken 'Bus Dem Shut' to the US for mixing months earlier, but mislaid the tape. It had taken him this long to find it but no matter; both songs were hits and put the Wailers back in the reckoning, albeit with old material.

December brought with it distractions as the holiday season approached and two prominent entertainers arrived on the island. It had been over two years since South African singer Miriam Makeba's last visit and her shows at the Regal Theatre (where she was supported by the Paragons and Jamaicans) and National Arena were the talk of Jamaica. Dignitaries presented her with the keys to the city at the Ward Theatre and then Prime Minister Hugh Shearer invited her to tea at Devon House, where her Nefertiti style headdress set tongues wagging. Makeba was already the darling of New York's fashion and music sophisticates. Her African dress sense was widely imitated by blacks in America, and her latest album, named after the worldwide hit 'Pata Pata,' had attracted rave reviews.

She and her trumpeter husband Hugh Masekela moved in influential circles. Harry Belafonte, then America's most famous black singer and civil rights activist had sponsored them both, and shared a Grammy winning album with Miriam. A short time after she'd arrived in New York her mother, who was an "isangoma" or spiritual healer, died back in South Africa. When the singer applied to the South African consulate for a visa, they stamped 'INVALID' on her passport, rendering her stateless. Miriam will later address the United Nations and call for a complete boycott of her homeland. The regime promptly banned all her records, although people continued to risk imprisonment by smuggling them into the country and distributing them secretly. "And so I became a spokesperson for my people," she wrote in her autobiography. "The person Miriam Makeba is no longer just an African singer to them. I am a symbol of my repressed people."

Makeba was celebrated for her blackness, as well as musical achievements. Artists like her demonstrated that it was possible to allay music with politics and use it to help raise black consciousness except it was that month's other foreign import who would influence the Wailers' story. Johnny Nash was all over Kingston like a rash throughout December. On Sunday the 7th he appeared at the Hilton Hotel supported by Bob Andy. "For my taste and that of the audience, the surprise offering of 'I Believe' by film star-vocalist Johnny Nash was the highlight of the show," wrote the Gleaner correspondent. "His control and phrasing of this apparently simple but difficult song was really something to hear."

That same month, Nash appeared at Mico College at a "Pre-Christmas Ball" attended by the Governor General. He also starred in 'Nuggets For The Needy,' which was broadcast on Jamaican television just before Christmas. Byron Lee & the Dragonnaires backed him on that occasion. Around the same time he performed as a surprise guest at the Kiwanis Club's "Ladies Night" dinner, held at the Sheraton. On another occasion he handed out medals to the two football teams contesting the

Derek Tomkinson Cup over at Boy's Town. Operation Friendship beat the Red Devils 1 – 0, and skirmishes broke out in the crowd after Operation Friendship missed a penalty.

Nash was from Texas, where he'd been raised on gospel and country music. After signing to ABC Paramount in 1956 he became a regular on the 'Arthur Godfrey Show,' which attracted large television audiences in the US. Acting roles in 'Key Witness' (with Dennis Hopper) and 'Take A Giant Step' followed. 'Take A Giant Step' touched upon black issues in the non-confrontational manner of fifties' productions, and was partially filmed in Jamaica. "America's First Negro Teen Idol" went back there for singing engagements after 'Take A Giant Step' had opened at the Tropicana in early 1961, but would later take legal action against Jamaican promoter Dudley MacMillan, who defaulted on money owed for shows at the State Theatre.

ABC had wanted to establish Johnny Nash as a mainstream act and fed him a diet of lightweight, middle-of-the-road material mixed with a little calypso, country and rhythm and blues. His popularity declined as a result until 'Let's Move And Groove Together' hit in 1965 on a label called JODA (after Johnny and Danny) that Nash shared with Jamaican born entrepreneur Danny Sims. With its light, romantic lead, orchestral strings and choral harmonies, 'Let's Move and Groove Together' was no match for the vocal power of Aretha Franklin or Otis Redding yet Sims insisted that it was "Johnny Nash's biggest hit in the black community ever" due to having been released as race riots broke out in Watts.

"There was a very popular African-American disc jockey in Los Angeles at the time who called himself "The Magnificent

Montague," Sims told Roger Steffens. "He played Johnny's record all the time, and he would yell over the air while it was spinning, 'Burn, baby, burn!' The Feds said that our record was creating the riots... 'Burn baby, burn!' became a slogan all over the black communities in America. I thought I was dead. So many of our people were being killed then so I decided to get the hell out, and we left for the Caribbean. Our favorite country in the world was Jamaica so we headed there to see our friend Ken Khouri the owner of Federal Records, who was JODA's licensee at the time. Ken got us a house near his in the hills above Kingston, in a place called Russell Heights. Ken's son Paul taught Johnny how to play rock steady, which was the music happening in Jamaica at that time, and eventually we started to record Johnny's album 'Hold Me Tight.'"

Nash and Sims had produced tracks with the Cowsills before travelling to Jamaica. The Cowsills were comprised of four brothers who played instruments as well as sang. Nash and Sims produced their debut single 'All I Really Want To Be Is Me,' which flopped. The Cowsills then signed to Mercury and added their mother to the line-up. The group would later inspire the hit television series 'The Partridge Family.' Their wholesome, family image helped to sell millions of records in America and whilst the group's popularity soon faded, Johnny and Danny must have rued having let the Cowsills slide from their grasp. They wouldn't make that mistake again.

Planno claimed that Johnny Nash met Bob on January 7th, and Danny Sims confirms that it was around the time of Ethiopian Christmas.

"Jamaican DJ Neville Willoughby - his father was my lawyer -

told Johnny that he wanted to take him to a Rastafarian religious gathering, something called a "grounation" being held by a man called Mortimo Planno.

"That night, Johnny came home raving about this guy he had met named Bob Marley." He said every song he heard him sing was an absolute smash and that we should sign him immediately to our label. The next day Bob came to our house with his wife, Rita, Bunny Livingston and Peter Tosh, along with Planno. Bob played guitar and sang about thirty songs for me. The following morning I invited him to my house for breakfast but my servants refused to serve him and walked out, saying they wouldn't serve a Rastafarian. The servants I had after that again refused to serve him and they quit too, so Mortimo put a Rasta dreadlock named Jeff in our house to cook and work for us. We were looked on in Jamaica as Americans who came there to cause trouble, working with Rastas and going to Trench Town."

By late January, Bob, Peter and Rita were rehearsing and recording up at Danny Sims' rented house in Kingston. No. 43 Russell Heights is situated in Arcadia Gardens, not far from Plymouth Avenue, where Peter will live during the last few years of his life. The contrast between this leafy, uptown suburb and Trench Town couldn't have been greater. Trench Town had always been a tough neighbourhood, but it was now a virtual war zone thanks to rival gangs of PNP and JLP supporters. Outbreaks of violence were already commonplace because of the poverty and cramped living conditions. Child prostitution and abuse weren't unknown, piles of garbage filled the streets and there wasn't any proper drainage. It must have been a relief for Peter, Bob and Rita to visit Russell Heights, and learn new things at the same time. They were now socialising with industry professionals who knew a great deal about the record business and especially in America. Nash and Sims had know-how, contacts *and* money. They kept abreast of current events and had a reservoir of stories to tell, which made them good company. Yet their main objective was to see if Jamaica's new rocksteady beat could get Johnny Nash back among the hits, and good songs were a crucial part of the equation.

The Wailers, minus Bunny, will record a few demo tracks for Sims and Nash in early 1968, before Bob and Peter return their thoughts to matters closer to home. Peter plays guitar and piano on some of them whilst Rita sings lead on 'Wings Of A Dove,' which the Wailers had earlier recorded for Coxsone. The material on these tapes is unashamedly commercial. Three associates of Sims – Jimmy Norman, Al Pyfron and Joe Venneri – co-wrote 'Fallin' In And Out Of Love,' 'Stranger On The Shore' and 'Splish For My Splash' and whilst these songs may gone down well at the Brill Building, they bore little or no relevance to the Wailers' day-to-day reality. Bob and Peter's readiness to work with such material offers the clearest indication yet that they craved mainstream success, and were willing to compromise in order to get it.

Their first self-productions without Bunny took place at WIRL in January and with the same musicians, plus Tommy McCook, they'd hired last time. 'Pound Get A Blow' came out of that session. Peter had written it after Jamaica switched currencies from sterling to dollars the previous November. His gift for social commentary, driven by concern for the everyday folk all around him, now began to influence his songwriting.

"This devaluation, it cause an eruption. Oh what a destruction, prepare for starvation," he warns, before Bob chimes in with, "All you pyakas, you must get a blow." As in England, Jamaican people feared the cost of living would escalate in the wake of devaluation, and it would be the sufferers who felt the most pressure. Peter will contribute two further songs to this January session. Bunny says he and Peter wrote 'Funeral' as a retort to Coxsone, who was still angry that the Wailers hadn't gone back to him.

"We never stop war with Coxsone, remember that," he growls. Coxsone had been hoping they'd fail without him and wasn't best pleased by their recent run of success. When two more master tapes went missing during a break-in at their shop, he'll be their prime suspect and with good reason after the last incident. "What a big disgrace, the way you rob up the place," they chide. "Robbing everything you can find..." Peter's singing on this track is confident and assured. 'Hammer' is another of his compositions, and will later make its reappearance on 'Never Ending Wailers.' Bunny swears that he heard it on the radio whilst he was inside, although copies have proven hard to come by. Record producers would often sponsor radio programmes in Jamaica, as it guaranteed their records airplay. By the time these latest songs were released – credited, as usual to Bob Marley and the Wailers – the group had a fifteen-minute slot on RJR hosted by Winston Barnes called 'Wail 'N Soul 'M Time,' which went on air every Friday night. Bunny would listen to it in his cell and hear the songs they'd recorded without him, which must have given rise to conflicting emotions. He's claimed that none of them were hits and yet Dave Thompson would later remark that when the new-look Wailers cut 'Pound Get A Blow,' "it marked the true dawn of Tosh's solo career."

Personally I'd award that honour to 'Stepping Razor,' which followed hot on its heels and was credited to Peter Tosh & The Wailers. It will become one of Peter's signature tunes although Joe Higgs wrote it, as he explained to Reggae Routes.

"I wrote Stepping Razor in 1967 for the Festival Song Competition but it was considered a very subversive message so it was disqualified from the top eight because of that," he says, referring to its rude boy aesthetic. "That's when I decided to give it to Tosh. As to who wrote it, well the give away line is, 'don't watch my size I'm dangerous.' I'm five foot four. How can a six foot something guy like Tosh write a line like that?"

Bunny says that the song suited Peter, because he was arrogant. It was certainly a landmark release for the twenty-three year old, whose brashness belied the humour and generosity his friends all talk about. Peter joined Lyn Taitt on guitar that day, whilst Bob and Rita cooed in unison on the harmonies. The group will call other sessions as spring approaches. Rita came into her own on 'Play Play Play,' which Bob wrote for her but the jewel in the crown was 'I'm Hurting Inside' on which Bob – accompanied by Tommy McCook's mournful sax – describes what it feels like when happiness slips imperceptibly out of our reach. "I've done you no wrong, reveal yourself to me," he asks of man, woman or God. He doesn't specify which, but you sense he's referring to something a lot graver than a romance.

"When you get right down to it, what avenues of escape does the average man has to vent his frustrations, his pain and his hurting feelings inside?" asks Ras Cardo in his book Reggae Jamaica.

"Remember when the Wailers sang 'I'm Hurting Inside'? This is the same thing that was affecting us all in Trench Town at those times. Some people have called it songs of protest, but we were not protesting anything. What we were doing was healing ourselves with the hope that others who listened and took heed would also be healed... The average man truly has no other avenue of escape except to call on Jah. We in Trench Town saw this vital link and so created a music that could help us call on Jah when we are sad, hungry, alone, depressed, persecuted, accused, tortured and even put to death. This music is reggae music."

America's black population faced its own brand of injustice. After the riots that had swept through American cities like brush fires just eighteen months earlier, President Johnson had commissioned an inquiry into the causes. The results were outlined in the Kerner Report, published in February. This document informed the US government it was "the frustrations of powerlessness" that had led many black people to express their grievances, and their feelings of alienation and hostility "had led to a new mood of solidarity and racial consciousness, as reflected in the slogan 'Black Power.'" It went on to say that, "self-esteem and racial pride had now replaced apathy and submission to the system, or white power structure," and the police "were increasingly seen as brutal racists, protecting whites but offering little justice to blacks." The Kerner Report couldn't have spelt out the underlying causes any clearer and yet President Johnson rejected its findings out of hand. Black people in England weren't having it easy either. Racism was an on-going problem there, and fuelled by a hostile right-wing press. Harold Wilson's government responded by announcing a tightening of immigration controls, which led to large-scale demonstrations by immigrant communities.

The old order was breaking down, and the genie wouldn't be coaxed back into the bottle all that easily. There was a renewed sense of entitlement in the air, and anger and impatience began to replace the wartime generation's weary reticence. Young people railed against their elders' inability to deliver meaningful change, and went in search of direct action. Students arranged sit-ins at leading universities across Europe and America, demanding a greater say in their administration whilst twenty thousand protesters converged on London's Trafalgar Square in March, denouncing the Vietnam War. News of the My Lai massacre had just surfaced and violent skirmishes broke out between protestors and the police, leading to a substantial number of injuries and arrests. Mick Jagger took part and was moved to write 'Sympathy For The Devil' and 'Street Fighting Man' in the aftermath. Singers like him were no longer content to document what was happening, but wanted to effect change as well. The Beatles had known this for a while, and by the year's end 'Revolution' would sail into the UK pop charts, destroying any semblance of them as "lovable mop-tops."

Jamaica too, had its share of musical revolutionaries. On March 11th demonstrators waving placards descended upon the British High Commission office on Duke Street, demanding that the authorities condemn the recent hanging of Africans in Rhodesia by Ian Smith's white minority regime. Prince Buster joined the demonstration shortly after mid-day, and later posted bail for Peter after he was arrested for obstructing traffic in the Spanish Town Road. Less than two weeks after this incident, Miriam

Makeba sent a message to Jamaican Prime Minister Hugh Shearer, saying "Your understanding and sympathetic gesture concerning black martyrs killed in Rhodesia will be deeply appreciated by freedom loving black people the world over."

The irony in that statement is obvious. No sooner had fears over the Rhodesian prisoners began to subside than another tragedy unfolded, and the repercussions would prove even greater this time. In early April, Dr. Martin Luther King travelled to Memphis to lead a refuse workers' strike. As he sampled the evening air on the balcony of his motel, James Earl Ray shot him and drove away in a white Mustang, leaving Dr. King's body slumped in the arms of his colleagues. Black communities across America reeled at the news. Riots broke out in more than a hundred American cities, but there were surprisingly few deaths. Angry crowds in Harlem pelted the mayor of New York with stones; two policemen were shot in Detroit and a white youth was burned to death in Florida, but people's hurt and rage was directed more at property than their fellow human beings. "We must use the weapon of love," Dr. King had once implored them. "We must have compassion and understanding for those who hate us." It was a message heeded by Nina Simone, who addressed her audience on the night of April 4th with a stirring tribute to "the King Of Love." Artists like her held deep-seated convictions and yet they used their music to heal and unite people, rather than spread dissent. It's a lesson the Wailers will take to heart, even as social unrest continued to dominate the media.

The following month, large numbers of protestors took to the streets of Paris, where students engaged in running battles with the police. Five months later, thousands of students will go on the rampage in Mexico after an estimated three hundred and fifty of them are shot dead by soldiers.

Bunny Wailer, as quoted by Sebastian Clarke: "You've been taught a whole pack of bullshit but then you come to realise a certain amount of truth, and when you start to establish these truths – your teachers, your family, everyone's going to disagree with you because them already drink up the old wine, so now the new wine is being poured out there is no space. You can't put new wine in old bottles. The struggle had to go on. It was just youth consciousness. Every youth had to get conscious of the things around him, knowing what's true and as soon as him find out the things you tell him are false, he *must* rebel against it."

CHAPTER EIGHT

Where It's At

'Fire Fire' rolled off the Jamaican pressing-plants just as America's black neighbourhoods went up in flames. "Will you kindly reduce the temperature on me sir? It's too hot down here," asks Peter, tongue-in-cheek. He and Bob won't co-write another song this good until 'Get Up Stand Up' and the rhythm section – fuelled by Jackie Jackson's driving bass – is hot as the subject matter. "Babylon's burning, they have no water," Peter croons with barely concealed delight.

Hearing this record at the start of 1968 when public dissent was widespread, it felt as if a turning point had been reached. People hoped – sensed even - that victory was just around the corner. The Wailers also recorded 'Them Have Fi Get A Beatin'' that same day, and Peter's revolutionary zeal hadn't cooled any. "Don't you wait until your back is against the wall," he urges. "Just one step to progress, I know God will help you all." He's speaking for the everyday people, and making it clear that those rebelling against the system aren't necessarily hooligans, but defending their rights.

All three Wailers would continue to write songs casting themselves in the role of outlaws and rebels. Reggae is no difference from rock and country music in that respect but full-scale revolution is something quite different and especially when the government of your small island is determined to stamp out any civil disobedience. Peter was prepared to stop at nothing in speaking the truth as he saw it. As his knowledge increased, so did his opposition to the "shit-stem." This headstrong approach will place him in grave danger and ultimately cause his death, but the passion coursing throughout these songs is irresistible.

The Wailers' next batch of recordings couldn't have been more different. The group had rehearsed 'Don't Rock My Boat' before Bunny went to jail, but hadn't managed to record it in time. They'll revisit it in future but this early cut is still beguiling with its sly, romantic lyrics and delicious melodies. 'The Lord Will Make A Way' is straight-ahead gospel whilst 'Chances Are' was written by Mortimo Planno and is more notable for Roland Alphonso's sax playing than anything else.

The Wailers won't produce another session of their own for almost a year, preferring instead to throw in their lot with Johnny Nash and Danny Sims, who were now regular visitors to Jamaica. Nash would record his first reggae hits (including 'Hold Me Tight') at Federal studio on the Foreshore Road, which Ken Khouri ran with his two sons, Richard and Paul. Their father had issued 78s of early calypso artists like Lord Flea, whom he'd record directly to disc on a primitive cutting machine. Whilst he's little heralded these days Ken Khouri is a true pioneer of the Jamaican music industry, and played an important role in expanding its influence overseas. In addition to providing distribution for US labels in the Caribbean, the Khouris maintained a family atmosphere at Federal that turned it into a second home for visiting American musicians.

"Marvin Gaye, Paul Anka, Lloyd Price, Ahmet Ertegun, Tom Dowd and Otis Redding all passed through Federal," Paul Khouri notes proudly. "They loved coming to us because we accepted them as ordinary people. They didn't have to feel like they were big stars. We ran our studio like a family home so when they came there, they felt comfortable and we never had rules and regulations or time limits. If they wanted to work late then it was open twenty-four hours a day. We were just people who loved the music and loved to be involved with whatever was happening. That's how we learnt to take the music forward and to a level. We'd watch these big-name American artists do their thing and then incorporate it into our own music. We did everything we could to develop our musical understanding and learn how to put music together."

The Khouris have been accused of seeking to exploit the island's talent but Paul's comments suggest otherwise. Bob had auditioned for them whilst still at school, and would remain friends with Paul Khouri all his life. Whilst Richard was the entrepreneur of the family, his younger brother played drums, percussion and keyboards, and later produced a catalogue of bestsellers in his own right. He was just twenty-two when Johnny Nash and Danny Sims arrived at Federal. By Sims' own admission, he and Nash had thought of Jamaica as more of a hideaway than a source of musical inspiration, but all that changed once they'd succumbed to Lyn Taitt's irresistible rocksteady beat. Johnny wrote 'Hold Me Tight' at the beginning of his Jamaican adventure and it'll rejuvenate his career, making him a star on both sides of the Atlantic.

"I lost my girlfriend because of that song!" Paul Khouri exclaims. "That's because I was more interested in hanging out with Johnny than enjoying myself with her. That was all I'd wanted to do though. We'd been working on that song since 1967 and Johnny would rehearse it night and day. I remember clearly, we carried picnic stuff to the beach and rehearsed it there first. That was New Year's Day 1967 and we kept singing it over and over, trying to get it right.

"Johnny, he was totally ignorant to what was going on with Jamaican music at the time. As a matter of fact he wasn't even so keen on 'Hold Me Tight' because it was 'Cupid' that he took to the States and got all excited about. He'd wanted to sweeten 'Hold Me Tight' and put horns on it but I'd say, 'No, please don't do that. Leave it alone!' because he'd done that with 'Cupid' and I pleaded with him not to do the same with 'Hold Me Tight.' Remember those ad-libs he's singing halfway through that record? He was actually laying down a guide for the horns but we said to him, 'Are you out of your mind? It's a smash. Just harmonise with what you did' and whilst he did what we suggested, to his mind there no way this song was ever going to work. He and Danny Sims both thought 'Cupid' was going to be the hit but then 'Hold Me Tight' took off and from that happened, they had to revise their opinion because they couldn't believe a song could do so well in that raw state. To their way of thinking it was just a demo, because they never understood or knew what they were hearing at that point.

"It wasn't until after 'Hold Me Tight' that he and Danny realised there was real potential in what we were doing. That's when Johnny started to get these songs from Bob and Peter and realise that it was possible to get hits away from orchestral style productions, because that's where he was originally coming from with ABC and JODA Records. Not having all of that was scary to him though, because I remember him saying, 'my God, I'm being dragged down the tubes here...' But he and I became very close. We virtually lived in each other's houses and Danny Sims left him with me because he knew I'd indoctrinate him to the Jamaican way of thinking. He knew I'd turn this First World singer into an island boy, and I did."

Nash and Sims' label, which they now shared with arranger Arthur Jenkins, was re-titled JAD. Richard Alderson, who'd worked as a live sound engineer for Harry Belafonte, Nina Simone and Bob Dylan – even accompanying Dylan on his first world tour – was invited to Jamaica by Sims to oversee Johnny Nash's sessions at Federal and ended up spending several months there. He says that whilst the Jamaican rhythm players excelled, Nash and Sims couldn't get the sound they wanted and so decided to overdub additional instruments and backing vocals in New York, and hire American musicians to complete the tracks. He also points out that whilst Federal was a decent studio by Jamaican standards, the equipment was quite primitive. There was no substitute for that insidious Caribbean rhythm however. Johnny Nash took to it like a duck to water, and his career would be transformed as a result.

"Johnny had first become popular in the West Indies when he was a singer on the Arthur Godfrey Show and people in the Caribbean carried on liking him from there," says Richard. "In the early days he wasn't a reggae singer at all. At first he was just this cute little black kid with a sweet voice and then he tried to be a rhythm and blues singer, except he didn't have the vocal equipment for it really. All of his artistic expression was then poured into the reggae stuff, which he strongly identified with. His music came alive once he started working in Jamaica but rocksteady really was the best of all Jamaican rhythms. Arthur Jenkins embraced it, and he was a well-practised New York musician who'd worked on sophisticated arrangements for major Latin and r & b bands. He was Johnny's musical guy so it wasn't like a bunch of Americans all at sea in a strange country. Arthur got with it, even though he'd joke about it a little bit. It wasn't like we were disrespecting it or anything, but the initial reaction was, 'What *is* that stuff?'

"We'd go to nightclubs and I can remember the black guys all laughing at me because they had to teach me how to dance to it! In those days there were always a few curious whites hanging out. It was very much a mixed crowd but the rocksteady sound made a tremendous impression on me and the musicians were fabulous. It's remarkable how a tiny country like Jamaica invented a new musical form that took over everything but the music that Bob and Peter were playing back then was a real synthesis. It was a mixture of Jamaican and American influences really."

It had been nearly a year since Neville Willoughby had introduced Nash and Sims to Marley, and they'd been minimal opportunities to record during that time. Fresh impetus arrived after Richard Alderson joined them in Jamaica and happened to see the Wailers perform on JBC's weekly talent show, 'Where It's At.'

"I remember being alone in Danny's house in Jamaica on a Saturday afternoon, turning on the television and watching the Wailers come on," he recalls. "I said to myself, 'Oh my God, this is amazing. This is one of the greatest groups I've ever heard!' They were young and had short hair then, and didn't in any way resemble the reggae icons they'd later become. They were still very amateurish, but when Johnny and Danny came back I brought it up and insisted they get in touch with them. They said they'd already heard about them and were reaching out but then they became friends with Mortimo Planno, who secured the introductions and came to the house a number of times after that."

Planno was still acting as the Wailers' manager and lost no time in demanding a finders' fee for their services. Whilst his intentions were questionable there was no doubting Peter and Bob's commitment, or the extent of their ambition.

"Bob told me right away that he wanted to be a star in the African-American community," Sims told Roger Steffens. "He wasn't that interested in Jamaica; it was America that he wanted to conquer. Bob didn't want to record anymore in what he called 'the Babylonian-type studios, like Federal and Dynamics. So we decided to record him in my house.

"We brought a lot of great musicians down from the States to record with Bob, so we could capture the more r & b oriented sound," he continued. "Many of them were red-hot, cream-of-the-crop studio guys who'd played for Aretha Franklin and people on that level; musicians like Bernard Purdie, Eric Gale, Hugh Masekela, Chuck Rainey and Richard Tee. We wanted them to woodshed with the Jamaican musicians to get that feel. The guys in Jamaica just weren't disciplined enough for us. They weren't dependable. They wouldn't show up on time and they'd play off key. Plus the local technology was way behind the times. We thought that the Americans, once they learned how to play rocksteady, could do just as good as the Jamaicans and I was proved right. The Wailers' vocals were recorded in Jamaica, but not the music. We didn't feel we could get the quality we wanted there so we would go up to New York to lay the music. That's how we always did it. We invariably never kept anything that we did in Jamaica, except the vocals. Our intention was to fit the U.S. and British radio formats. We weren't at all concerned about selling records in the Caribbean. We wouldn't have got paid anyway."

Whilst some have cast doubt on Sims' and Johnny Nash's motives, there's no disputing the hard work and expense that went into nurturing the group's career. JAD will record literally dozens of tracks with the Wailers on a one-track Nagra tape machine at the house in Russell Heights. As Sims has explained, the majority of these recordings – many of them written by Jimmy Norman and Al Pyfrom – were later overdubbed in New York and sound very different from other versions of the same songs. They're brighter and more pop orientated, but unlikely to appeal to all but the most committed Wailers' fans in truth.

Peter, Bob and Rita recorded alternative cuts of 'Bend Down Low,' 'Nice Time,' 'Mellow Mood,' 'Put It On,' 'Chances Are' and 'Hammer' for JAD throughout the summer, together with new songs like 'There She Goes' and 'How Many Times.' If they were at all concerned about their music being watered down, there's no sign of it. Bob and Peter both wanted to succeed, and they had their own label for material that JAD didn't want. It's safe to assume they were excited by the prospect of being signed to a big American star's label and not just as performers, but composers. Sims claims he paid them a weekly retainer and even let Bob stay at Russell Heights when he and Nash weren't there, which implies a level of genuine trust and commitment. Clarke has written that Peter and Bob's relationship with Nash and Sims was an uneasy one and the pair were naïve to believe they were being taken seriously, yet if JAD were only interested in exploiting the Wailers, then why spend so much time and effort voicing them on material that was clearly aimed at the US market, and must have cost a fortune to produce?

As autumn approached, Johnny Nash was putting finishing touches to his latest album, 'Hold Me Tight.' Whilst they're hardly what you'd call grassroots, these early Jamaican recordings did herald a transition of sorts. Johnny had struggled for hits *and* direction after recording 'Let's Move And Groove Together.' He'd also found it difficult to come up with original material, which is why JAD kept songwriters like Jimmy Norman on the payroll. The 'Hold Me Tight' LP, released at the end of 1968, would be his first in four years. His previous set had been a collection of standards called 'Composer's Choice' recorded in the style of another Texan-born singer, Johnny Mathis. The Johnny Nash who'd crooned 'Teardrops In The Rain' had clearly undergone some kind of transformation since then. Nestled among covers of hits by the likes of Sam Cooke, Otis Redding and the Isley Brothers were two of Peter's songs, 'Love' and 'You Got To Change Your Ways,' except you'd never imagine they were written by the same firebrand who'd unleashed 'Them Have Fi Get A Beatin'' and 'Fire Fire' just a few months earlier, let alone 'Stepping Razor.' 'Love' is an attempt at a soul ballad, and was also recorded by the Wailers. It's cloying and repetitive, whilst 'You Got To Change Your Ways' at least has a reggae beat, even if it is over-simplistic. Alas, the lyrics border on the banal, and even a consummate craftsman like Johnny Nash can't lift this song out of the mire. In August, Bob, Rita and Peter were rewarded with a trip to New York where they will be introduced to songwriting professionals, as well as musicians and other studio personnel.

"Danny Sims and Johnny Nash took Peter and Bob to the US because they recognised their potential," says Paul Khouri, when reminded of this visit. "Everybody credits Chris Blackwell with having discovered them, but they were already on the road to success by then."

Bob had already spent several months in the US, but this was Peter's first trip outside of Jamaica and also his first plane ride. When they arrived in New York at the beginning of September, it was to a backdrop of civil unrest and racial tension. President Johnson may have signed the Civil Rights Act earlier that year but people were still talking about the so-called "Glenville shootout," in which several black militants were killed by Cleveland police officers. Watching the news, it was hard to escape the feeling that America was not only at war in Vietnam but also with its own citizens. Senator Robert Kennedy had been assassinated in June and so the Democrats' convention in Chicago – held just a week or so before the Wailers left Jamaica – was always going to be a highly charged affair. When riots had broken out in Chicago after Dr. Martin Luther King's assassination, the city's mayor, Richard Daley, had instructed the police to "shoot to maim or cripple" looters and kill anyone throwing Molotov cocktails. In readiness for the convention he'd called up more than five thousand National Guards, sealed the venue with barbed wire and turned that part of the city into a war zone. For the first three days, his troops restricted themselves to using tear-gas on unruly demonstrators, but then lost all discipline and went on the rampage, arresting more than two hundred people and injuring countless others.

That same month, women bearing placards reading "Women Are Not Meat" marched onto Atlantic City to protest at the Miss America beauty competition. During the protest, many threw so-called "instruments of torture" (mainly high-heeled shoes, girdles and garter belts) into a "Freedom Trash Can," then draped a banner over the balcony of the venue saying, "Women's Liberation." Photos of this slogan appeared in all the newspapers, giving the American people their first glimpse of it. The Wailers' party would be forgiven for thinking they'd entered a madhouse, since there was little evidence of women's liberation in Jamaica. The spoils from centuries of slave trading and colonialism would be nowhere more apparent than in Manhattan, and yet the contrast between such grandeur and the poverty they encountered in Harlem couldn't have been more acute. The rundown streets, lack of adequate schooling and housing and worsening crime rates they found there were sadly all too familiar, although they must have been cheered by the presence of so many black self-help organisations, including the Nation Of Islam.

Danny Sims was well connected in New York circles, and introduced Bob and Peter to a number of influential musicians and political figures. They're rumoured to have included Harry Belafonte who owned Impact Sound on West 65th Street, where most of those JAD productions were readied for release and the Wailers would base themselves during their stay. Belafonte had lived in Jamaica as a teenager, and first discovered calypso there.

His hit versions of 'Island In The Sun,' 'Man Smart Woman Smarter' and 'The Banana Boat Song (Day O)' had put Caribbean music on the map during the late fifties, providing early examples of what's now called "world music." One of his albums, 'Calypso,' had been a million-seller and yet Belafonte was also revered as a matinee idol as well as a tireless advocate of racial equality. He'd been the first black actor to share a screen kiss with a white co-star, and helped to bankroll Dr. Martin Luther King's campaigns in the South. A few months before Bob and Peter's arrival he'd filled in for Johnny Carson on the 'Tonight Show' and used it as a platform to discuss racial issues with a roll call of guests including Sidney Poitier, Bill Cosby, Senator Robert Kennedy and Dr. King, who debated controversial topics such as the government's neglect of blacks in Watts, the high suicide rate among Native Americans and President Johnson's handling of the Vietnam War. Belafonte and Poitier (who'd later star in and co-produce the film 'Buck And The Preacher') even talked about their experiences in Mississippi, where the Klu Klux Klan had forced them to run for their lives. A self-confessed "man about town," Danny Sims was well placed to teach his Jamaican charges a great deal about men such as these, and also the struggle for racial equality as a whole.

"Danny Sims didn't come on like a regular manager," says Richard Alderson, who was resident engineer at Impact and had accompanied Belafonte on many of his campaigns. "He came on like he was your best friend and a great guy but there was a lot of this militant black attitude going on, which was very popular at the time. Danny was acting like he was the protector of the black man and asserting himself into the lives of Peter Tosh and Bob

Marley in much the same way. He gave the impression he was there to stand up for their rights when in fact he was just as much of a predator as any of the white guys. That was his whole shtick because Danny later ripped Johnny Nash off for everything he'd got, causing him to leave the music business for good but they were like buddies when I first knew them."

Danny Sims lived on Fifth Avenue facing Central Park, where Bob and Peter played football most days as Rita, who was seven months pregnant, looked on. Jimmy Norman says the trio didn't go out much in the evenings unless it was to the studio, which was twenty minutes' walk away, straight across the park. That figures. None of the Jamaicans had money of their own or transport, and Manhattan was a whole lot different from Trench Town. The Wailers stood out like sore thumbs with their funny clothes and island accents yet Danny and Johnny were keen to show them the ropes and introducing them to people like Jimmy – a stalwart of New York's r & b scene – was an obvious place to start. Jimmy and his wife lived in the Bronx, and one evening Bob and Rita visited them for an informal jam session with Pyfrom, who lived in the same apartment block. The five of them sang and played long into the night and it'll be this combination, plus Peter, who sing backing vocals on a lot of JAD material from this period.

Whilst the Wailers weren't exactly party people – at least not by New York standards – there was music happening all over the city. Harlem boasted nightspots such as Small's Paradise, Minton's and the famous Apollo Theatre on 125th Street, whilst Greenwich Village was still a Mecca for fans of folk and more experimental styles. Even Indian music had gained in popularity thanks to the influence of Ravi Shankar and the Beatles, whose latest single 'Hey Jude' had just entered the charts. Songs by Sly & the Family Stone, the Doors, Beatles, Rolling Stones, Chamber Brothers, Steppenwolf and Jose Feliciano could be heard blaring from transistor radios the length and breadth of New York that autumn – also the Rascals' No. 1 hit 'People Got To Be Free,' which had tapped into the zeitgeist whilst affording the group's pop sensibilities full rein. Hippies revered Jimi Hendrix, Janis Joplin, Cream and the Grateful Dead, whilst African-American audiences were spoilt for choice thanks to Aretha Franklin, Marvin Gaye & Tammi Terrell, the Isley Brothers and James Brown, whose 'Say It Loud I'm Black And I'm Proud' was the most outright expression of Black Nationalism ever committed to vinyl by a leading r & b artist at that point. This was a dramatic departure from the choreographed sheen of early soul acts like Sam Cooke and the Miracles, and would inspire the Wailers to try their own version of it before long. Even country music was undergoing changes because whilst Jeannie C. Riley's 'Harper Valley PTA' maintained its reputation for homilies (and was a major hit in late 1968), the Byrds had recently shattered stereotypes by becoming the first longhaired rock stars to perform at Nashville's Grand Ole Opry and would deliver a groundbreaking fusion of rock and country on their next album, 'Sweetheart Of The Rodeo.' Popular music was now a kaleidoscope of creative possibilities and with the help of seasoned New Yorkers there was no reason why the Wailers' rocksteady sound couldn't find an international audience.

Jimmy Norman confirms that he and Arthur Jenkins left for Jamaica within days of Peter and Bob's visit. Johnny and Danny would join them there later. 'Hold Me Tight' had raced into the UK charts at No. 4, gifting the singer his first-ever British hit. He had to fly over there for a round of promotional appearances and then two months later, 'Hold Me Tight' went Top 5 in America. That song put Johnny Nash back on the map, and with a brand-new musical bag called rocksteady. It's as well to remember that we're talking about 1968, and the Wailers were still a hard sell. Johnny on the other hand, had movie star looks and PR skills, as well as a marvelous voice. His support team was impressive, and the music itself created from an irresistible fusion of New York and Kingston styles. Like Danny, Jimmy and Arthur were disappointed with the facilities at Federal and also some of the local musicians.

"We couldn't find good horn players and that's why we had to send stuff back to New York," says Jimmy. "We went to the army to see if we could use their horn players and we also approached the local orchestra to use their strings but the people there had never heard the shit we were playing and I think they thought it was very strange! It didn't come out like it should have so we ended up sending it back to Impact and then putting horns and everything else on it up there.

"The rhythm players were very good though, both individually and together. We used Byron Lee's rhythm section a lot and there were a couple of conga players I liked. They hardly ever used to speak to anyone but they were very good, and they played on a lot of stuff we recorded down there. We basically used the same musicians all the time, apart from when someone came down from New York. Danny would sell it to them like it was a vacation so they'd come down for a week or two and then spend all their time in the studio! Eric Gale, he played bass on a couple of things. I can't remember which tracks they were but he and I often worked together – also Cornell Dupree and Richard Tee. Arthur Jenkins and I played piano on a whole bunch of tracks too. It was just the two of us down there doing most of the work. We'd go out and check out various bands, and then work with Bob and Peter on their songs... Between the pair of us we just put it all together and sent it to New York."

Studio sessions aside, Jimmy's main reason for being in Jamaica was to work closely with Peter and Bob, and help them with their compositional skills.

"Danny's neighbours didn't like the idea of Rastafarians so we'd sit out on the lawn all day writing songs, just to annoy them," he says, laughing. "I was down there about seven months altogether but half of the songs we did with the Wailers still haven't been released for some reason."

Richard Alderson recalls Johnny Nash recording several albums' worth of tracks around this time, but says the masters of any remaining material have long since disappeared. The Wailers sang harmonies on some of those songs, with Rita again filling in for Bunny.

"It was interesting the way they did their stuff," Jimmy continues. "It's like they'd stagger their vocals. They'd sing close, but not exact and then sometimes Peter would sing high notes, and Rita would aim a bit lower... They had a fascinating sound I hadn't heard before."

Jimmy was unfamiliar with Jamaican patois, but says he could understand Peter better than Bob. He wrote 'Soon Come' after hearing the phrase bandied about so often. It's a Jamaican saying that means, "don't hold your breath," and in the nicest possible way. Peter was quick to voice that one but Bob, Bunny, Byron Lee and even Neville Willoughby would all record one or two of Jimmy's compositions before he left for New York. The Wailers' versions would surface on albums such as 'Soul Almighty' and 'The Complete Wailers,' issued in the late nineties. Johnny Nash and fellow singer Lloyd Price had previously covered some of them, including 'Fallin' In And Out Of Love,' 'What Goes Around Comes Around,' 'Splish for my Splash' and 'Stranger On The Shore.' This was common industry practise at the time and since the record companies invariably owned the publishing rights, they really couldn't lose no matter whose version proved more successful.

Jimmy had written quite a few of these songs before travelling to Jamaica. As well as playing piano on numerous tracks he also sang bass on 'Chances Are' and 'Soul Rebel' – his deep baritone mirroring Melvin Franklin's role with the Temptations. The Wailers' original cut of 'Soul Rebel' has a radically different style of production from the one they'll voice for Lee Perry. The lyrics are the same and yet the instrumentation and arrangements are aimed to satisfy the demands of record buyers in America, rather than Jamaica. A declaration of personal integrity as well as shared intent, 'Soul Rebel' is among the pick of the Wailers' recordings for JAD, and more representative of the band than anything else they'd done for Sims and Nash up until this point. Whilst not exactly a return to the militant soul power of 'Fire Fire,' it's still a noticeable step in the right direction as Bob casts himself in the role of "soul adventurer." Jimmy was good friends with Sonny Till, of 'Crying In The Chapel' fame, yet hadn't heard the Wailers'

'Selassie Is The Chapel' until Danny Sims reissued it thirty years later. He and Richard Alderson both remember Mortimo Planno though.

"I remember being taken to his house and going round to this little shed in the back and everybody was sat there in a squatting position, listening to him talk," says Jimmy. "He'd talk for hours man, and I'd be struggling to make out what he was saying. I got to know him pretty well in the end. He was the spokesman for Bob, business-wise.

"Another time Peter and Bob took me to this gathering on some wasteland where all these Rastafarians had got together. I was introduced to the head of whoever they were and he prepared a chillum for me. When they'd finished, someone primed it and got it started, then they handed it to me and everything went very quiet. I pulled on this chillum and thank God I was able to hold it down. I didn't choke and when I let the smoke out everybody applauded! They were shouting, 'Rastaman! Rastaman!' I felt so good, y'know? I'll never forget that but the people living round Russell Heights could hear me coughing every night from smoking that stuff..."

"I remember participating in that and getting so stoned I couldn't even stand up because they'd use huge amounts of marijuana each time," adds Richard. "It was marijuana smoking taken to a whole different level. I was a drug journeyman but still couldn't take it. I'd have to go and lie down after smoking that chillum. The degree to which those people smoked was unbelievable."

By Alderson's own admission, drug use was rife in Nash and Sims' circle. The engineers at Impact had to work round the clock to get songs finished, and Richard recalls being at the mixing-desk for three days straight on occasion. Maintaining that kind of schedule just wasn't possible without stimulants, although the scene around Impact quickly deteriorated as the influence of hard drugs made its presence felt.

"We were taking a drug that later got the name "angel dust," but it was really an animal tranquiliser," Richard says, referring to PCP. "Some people would take it and just destroy their minds. The bass player who played on a lot of Aretha's stuff went nuts because of it, and that stuff was definitely part of the Johnny Nash sessions. I got my heroin habit around that time because Danny Sims showed up one day and gave me a big bag of pure, uncut heroin in payment for some of the work I was doing. That's how it was back then. I never saw Peter or Bob take it but the way they smoked marijuana, they might as well have done because it was the equivalent of any hard drug, I can assure you!"

PCP had emerged as a recreational drug just a year or so earlier. It can lead to extreme mood swings, feelings of dislocation and even schizophrenia in some cases. We can assume the Wailers hadn't wished to compromise their religious convictions by trying heroin or hallucinogenics, despite their availability. This mental strength would stand them in good stead later on, when they become more accustomed to moving in rock star circles.

CHAPTER NINE

Black Power

The Wailers' new friends enjoyed Jamaica, but events there were spiralling out of control. Following a dispute over salaries, an island-wide epidemic of "sickness" by members of the Jamaica Constabulary Force had spread fear and uncertainty in its wake. Police officers got three sick days a month but more than three hundred of them took their full quota in September, simultaneously! Soldiers had to man the police stations, whilst the Jamaican Defence Force patrolled the streets. For the sufferers, this meant a brief respite from harassment – a situation even acknowledged in a Gleaner editorial which reported that since Hugh Shearer had made his "no Beatitudes" speech, "truculence, unlawful violence amounting to thuggery by too many police have frightened great segments of the public and made all national leaders anxious."

Shearer's reign as Jamaica's Prime Minister would become increasingly defined by failed, repressive policies and heavy-handed decisions, as well as industrial strikes and go-slows. Government officials had begun seizing the passports of targeted individuals, claiming it was "in the public interest" and issuing exclusion orders with ominous regularity. Shearer then introduced the Immigration Restriction Act, which discriminated against non-Jamaican citizens living and working on the island, such as Dr. Walter Rodney.

Rodney was from Guyana, and taught African History at the

University of West Indies. He was in his late twenties, and said to have been articulate, gentle and unassuming in person. His father had been involved with the labour movement in Guyana, and joined the country's first multi-racial political party. Walter helped distribute their pamphlets before visiting Cuba and then Jamaica, where he graduated from the University of the West Indies in 1963 with first-class honours. After a period of study in Britain with C. L. R James, he lectured in Tanzania for a while before returning to Jamaica in January 1968 and taking up his teaching post. By then, he'd assimilated Lenin and Marx and embraced Black Power, although Rodney was an intellectual rather than insurrectionist. His "crime" had been to give open lectures on the university campus, and address people from all walks of life at informal gatherings in Kingston itself. News of these meetings had spread like wildfire, and prompted Shearer's government to keep a careful eye on him. Dr. Rodney gave talks at the Wembley Sports Ground most Sunday mornings, speaking to crowds of between two and three hundred people, and even visited squatter camps.

"I was prepared to go anywhere that any group of black people were prepared to sit down to talk and listen because that is Black Power; that is one of the elements, a sitting down together to reason, to 'ground' as the brothers say," Rodney explained. "I would speak whenever there was a possibility of our getting together. It might be in a sports club, it might be in a schoolroom, it might be in a church; it might be in a gully. They are dark, dismal places with a black population who've had to seek refuge there. I have spoken in what people call "the Dungle" which is a rubbish dump, for that is where people live in Jamaica. In fact the government doesn't even want them to live in rubbish dumps because they bulldoze them off there and send them God knows where. I have sat on a rusty oil drum and in the midst of garbage when some black brothers and I have grounded together."

These were the same people Shearer had recently described as "criminals and hooligans" in the Jamaican press. It was unthinkable for a university lecturer – someone of learning and status – to associate with such people, yet Rodney praised the Rastafarians for their insight into philosophical matters and their humility.

"It is a miracle how these fellows live," he continued. "They live and they are physically fit, they have a vitality of mind, they have a tremendous sense of humour, they have depth. How do they do that in the midst of the existing conditions? They create too, because some of the best painters and writers are coming out of the Rastafarian environment. The black people in the West Indies have produced all the culture that we have, whether it's steel band or folk music, yet the black bourgeoisie and white people in the West Indies have produced nothing! Black people who have suffered all these years create, and that is amazing."

Soon after his arrival on campus, Rodney had encouraged his students to form a discussion group in reaction to the assassination of Dr Martin Luther King but the main topic was Black Power – a term he described as "a call to black peoples to throw off white domination and resume the handling of their own destinies.

"Black people must now take the offensive," he declared. "If it's anyone who should suffer embarrassment it is the whites. Did black people roast six million Jews? Who exterminated millions of indigenous inhabitants of the Americas and Australia? Who enslaved countless millions of Africans? The white capitalist cannibal has always fed on the world's black peoples. White capitalist, imperialist society is profoundly and unmistakably racist."

In a speech given that spring, he outlined the three main precepts of Black Power, West Indies' style – "(i) the break with imperialism which is historically white racist; (ii) the assumption of power by the black masses in the islands, and (iii) cultural reconstruction of the society in the image of the blacks.

"Black Power is not racially intolerant," he continued, and nor was it incompatible "with a multi-racial society where each individual counts equally." After paying tribute to Cuba for being the only Caribbean country to break free of white power, he asked the audience which side they'd be on in the event of a revolution.

"The choice is simple," he told them. "You either remain part of the white system, or break with it."

Rodney taped a radio programme on Black Power, but the JBC declined to broadcast it. He'd become a controversial figure, and with a growing international reputation. In mid October, he accepted an invitation to address the Congress of Black Writers in Montreal. This conference coincided with the 1968 Olympic Games, which had just opened in Mexico. Forty-four people had died during the build-up after students rioted and police turned their guns on them, firing indiscriminately. Race too, had become a major issue after thirty-two African nations boycotted the Olympics because of South Africa's participation. During the event itself Tommy Smith and John Carlos, who won gold and bronze for the USA in the 200 metres, stepped up to the podium in black socks and no shoes, sporting Civil Rights badges. As the 'Star Spangled Banner' rang out in the stadium, the two athletes bowed their heads and raised their black-gloved fists in a Black Power salute – this during a period when news reports showed heavily armed African-Americans wearing determined expressions, black berets and black leather coats, mobilising in American cities as if they were a revolutionary army. These Games were the first to be broadcast in colour, and the sight of Smith and Carlos stood on that rostrum sent shock waves reverberating around the globe. The two men were promptly suspended from the US team and banned from the Olympic village, but not before fears about Black Power became ever more widespread.

Rodney addressed the Congress with a speech entitled 'Statement On The Jamaican Situation' in which he pointed out how the middle classes of Jamaica "augmented by significant elements of whites and other groups such as Syrians, Jews and Chinese," were the only beneficiaries of Emancipation. He then announced the arrival of a new phase in local politics called "the Black Humanity of Jamaica," whilst deriding the recent decision to enshrine Marcus Garvey and Paul Bogle as national heroes, calling it "a crude manipulation of the symbols of national black pride." By way of explanation, he said the ideals they represented were still far from having been met or implemented and who could argue? He reminded the gathering how Jamaica's political leaders had been forced to take a back seat during Emperor Haile Selassie I's state visit as thousands of Rastafarians – whom he describes as having "completely and inexorably broken with

Jamaican society and its values" – took over the welcoming ceremony. He then noted how Shearer's government had banned Stokely Carmichael, H. Rap Brown and James Forman from entering Jamaica, and also banned the writings of Malcolm X and Elijah Mohammed "at a time when the world is celebrating International Human Rights Year, piously sponsored by the Jamaican government."

Referring to Jamaica's ministers as "local lackeys of imperialism," he criticised the harsh sentences handed down for possession of marijuana, concluding that, "the quality of justice dispensed by the legal system still depends on skin colour." He then claimed the police were being used as "agents of social oppression.

"Their methods have proved increasingly brutal," he said, before reporting how police had shot more than thirty people in the six months leading up to April, killing just over half of them. Summarising, Dr. Rodney declared that, "other incidents of police brutality are too numerous to mention" and said the police force's recent wage demands had been badly handled by the island's politicians, who demonstrated their incompetence "in every direction."

As a postscript, he drew attention to how the majority of Jamaica's resources were controlled by companies based overseas; that nearly a third of the population was unemployed, and over forty percent of them were teenagers. He could well have added that three out of four Jamaican homes had no piped water or sanitation and in Trench Town itself, no electricity either.

The Jamaican government issued an exclusion order against him on October 15th, despite the fact that his job and family were there. Jamaica's Leader of the Opposition, Norman Manley, declared it a breach of human rights and students at the university marched in protest, chanting slogans and holding placards. The police used batons and tear gas to disperse them but as news of the unrest spread, riots broke out in Kingston. Parts of the city started to go up in flames, and more than fifty buses were overturned and set alight. Looters broke into hundreds of shops and well-known public figures were dragged out of their cars and beaten by mobs.

"The lashing squeals of the tyres of the police and military transport were strident and menacing," wrote Andrew Salkey. "The occasional shouts and cries from unseen individuals pierced the stillness... Faint, crackling murmurs of fires hovered over the immediate vicinity. The air began to smell of wood smoke, burnt paint, gasoline fumes and dust."

Peter Tosh was driven by a fierce sense of truth and rights, but he could also be reckless at times. The urgency he'd felt whilst protesting against the Rhodesian hangings was still there, beating ever louder in his chest. As demonstrators' cries filled the air and smoke clouds gathered over the corporate area it finally broke loose. Stirred by the excitement, Peter commandeered a minibus and invited a posse of ghetto youths to join him as he headed for downtown Kingston and drove straight into a storefront, shattering the windows and causing major structural damage. His passengers leapt out and grabbed whatever they could before racing back to their seats. Peter then drove back to Trench Town, where his jubilant passengers flaunted their trophies like returning war heroes.

The riots lasted all day and well into the evening. Bob hadn't joined in because Rita was about to go into labour. In fact she gave birth to their son David, otherwise known as "Ziggy," the very next day. An eerie quiet had settled over the city by then, although army and police vehicles continued to patrol the streets and lanes, which were "littered with overturned garbage, wood and metal scraps from store fronts, ripped-open cardboard packing cases and timber crates, and stacked with tipped-over and burnt-out cars, vans, trucks and buses, some of which had been used as extra barriers to fortify the barricades the night before."

Three people had died, and over a million pound's worth of property was damaged or destroyed. The main targets had been public utilities, but many foreign-owned banks, insurance companies, stores and businesses were also attacked. UWI ordered its gates closed and all lectures were suspended indefinitely. The Jamaica Defence Force sent a helicopter to fly over campus, and barbed wire barriers were erected around the university grounds. Whilst Dr. Rodney's exclusion order had sparked the riots, everybody knew the real cause was a deep, underlying social malaise. Whilst not a Jamaican, Rodney had identified its source with unerring accuracy and then tirelessly exposed it.

He responded to his ban by accusing the Jamaican government of being "white-hearted," and upholding a social structure "which ensures that the black man resides at the bottom of the social ladder." He talked of the myth perpetuated by the ruling class that Jamaica is a harmonious, multi-racial society and praised Rastafarians for being "the leading force of this expression of black consciousness.

"They have rejected this philistine white West Indian society," he said. "They have sought their cultural and spiritual roots in Ethiopia and Africa so that whether there is a big flare up or not, there is always the constant activity of the black people who perceive that the system has nothing in it for them, except suppression and oppression."

After being expelled from Jamaica, Rodney returned to Tanzania where he lectured until 1974. Back home in Guyana, Georgetown University offered him a post as Professor of History, but the government revoked his appointment. After championing the release of a local activist, he joined the Working People's Alliance and later served time in prison for arson. He would suffer persistent government and police harassment until his assassination in June 1980, when a bomb was planted in his car.

Although Dr. Rodney was only in Jamaica for a short while, his influence upon the Wailers and Tosh in particular would be immeasurable.

In the aftermath of the riots, Shearer pressurised the trade unions and warned certain pastors to think twice about what they said in their sermons. Religious leaders associated with the Black Power movement were excluded from Jamaica and their books banned. The government acted as if democracy was under threat and it was, but from those claiming to uphold it.

"What is at stake is present Jamaican society – the repression by the government and the vacillation of the opposition shows that they, at any rate, understand this very well," wrote Richard Small in the introduction to Rodney's 'The Groundings With My Brothers.'

"The racial question is now out in the open, in spite of all the efforts to maintain the taboos surrounding it. Of the greatest significance are the effects at self-expression among black people – pamphlets, newsletters and the like. These independent efforts are essential because of the complete control which imperialism and its local puppets maintain over the various established news media."

Small was referring to independent publications such as 'Black Man Speaks,' 'African Youth Move,' 'Bongo Man,' 'Our Own,' 'The Sufferer' and 'Revolutionary Poems,' which had surfaced in the wake of the Rodney uprising. The most popular was 'Abeng,' whose circulation will reach 20,000 by the following summer. These newssheets had immediate impact. Hidden knowledge came to light in their pages, and inspired everyday Jamaicans to get more conscious.

It was African Youth Move that published 'The Groundings With My Brothers' which reminds us that whilst newly independent Jamaica chose for itself a national flag, motto, anthem, flower, fruit and even a national bird, "what it didn't have was a national consciousness – a sense of where Jamaicans came from, what we have done and to what they should look forward."

An outpouring of music would soon help fill the gap as groups like the Wailers sought a new aesthetic and wrote more message songs. The Dr. Rodney affair had thrown Jamaica's problems into sharp relief and whilst the riots had been quashed, the taste of freedom remained in people's mouths.

Peter wouldn't get to savour it for long, and had to disappear for a few weeks. That's because the store he'd driven into belonged to someone close to Joe Williams – a Kingston police officer Bunny once described as "the baddest man in the world." The

Wailers still had a rude boy following which meant that Williams didn't like them in any case, and especially when they played somewhere within his jurisdiction like the Queens Theatre. Bunny remembers the Wailers playing a show there once and the promoter got so scared, he left a bag of herb for them and split without even staying to watch the concert! The Wailers were the headliners that night and roared into their last song 'Bus' Dem Shut,' not knowing police had surrounded the venue. As the crowd spilled outside, Joe Williams bellowed into a megaphone and ordered "all Clarks booties" to one side – Clarks being the rude boys' favourite shoe. Men would be peeling them off their feet in fear of getting singled out, but then get derided for wearing a suit with no shoes. That's how Joe Williams operated. He exercised totalitarian rule, and yet favoured humiliation over aggression. On that particular occasion he searched everyone in the theatre and kept the Wailers back 'til last, then searched them the most closely, all the while threatening them with jail if he so much as found one ganja seed in their possession. Backing him up were raw recruits wearing white helmets and cradling shiny new rifles they hadn't learnt to fire properly. The majority of them were country boys, and they'd become increasingly jumpy and nervous as ratchet knives, knuckledusters, black jacks, ice picks, iron pipes and the occasional gun clattered to the floor...

CHAPTER TEN

Dream Awhile

Walter Rodney hadn't been the only honorary Jamaican in Montreal during the riots. Johnny Nash had gone there for the "Man And His World" Expo, and performed at the Jamaica Pavilion on the same bill as the Sonny Bradshaw Orchestra. One reviewer described him as "demonstrating the rocksteady dance and promoting rocksteady music" before announcing that, "JAD Records will shortly be relocating from New York to Jamaica after dates in France, West Germany, Italy, Holland, Belgium, Spain, Africa, Australia, Japan, Hawaii and the Philippines." He returned to Jamaica in November, and headlined a show called 'Smashville '68' at the Carib Theatre. King Curtis and the Sweet Inspirations shared the bill but Nash again earned all the plaudits in the Daily Gleaner for "singing in the upper register with thrilling ease.

"Johnny Nash lives each song. His voice is warm and exciting; his stage presence superb and his interpretation of lyrics is enough to make any songwriter deliriously happy. It has been this combined quality of good voice and unique acting ability that has won him audiences from Basin Street East in New York to the Crescendo in Hollywood and virtually everywhere in-between."

He followed this by singing at a number of fundraisers in the lead-up to Christmas. One held at the Regal Theatre called 'Nuggets For The Needy' co-starred the Blues Busters and Gaylettes and raised more than $40,000. Local DJ Jeff Dixon (later known as Free I) was Master Of Ceremonies. Shortly afterwards, Johnny sang at a poolside event organised by the Kingston & St. Andrews Human Rights Committee, which sought to raise money for a library in Trench Town. There's no mention of the Wailers' involvement, but then Peter was still keeping a low profile and Bob taking another break in the country. A couple of weeks later on Saturday December 14th, Nash performed at the National Arena, where Edward Seaga hosted the Grand Christmas Charity Ball. This was a fundraiser held "in aid of the children of Western Kingston and the replacement of the children's home destroyed by fire last Christmas Day." Headliners were the Impressions, who flew in by Air Jamaica and stayed at the Sheraton Hotel – both landmarks of the (relatively) newly independent Jamaica. Desmond Dekker and "Dennis Brown, the 11 Year Old Boy Wonder" completed the line-up. Prime Minster Hugh Shearer, who'd recently announced the launch of Jamaica's first-ever National Lottery was in attendance, together with other leading dignitaries. Byron Lee and the Dragonnaires backed Johnny on that occasion, whilst Arthur Jenkins – described as "Johnny Nash's musical arranger" – was credited with orchestration.

During the build-up to these shows, Nash had appeared on the radio show 'Dream Awhile,' hosted by RJR's Don Black. As well as extolling Jamaica's rocksteady beat he sang extracts from his latest album, 'Prince Of Peace.' Released on Major Minor in the UK, this was a collection of familiar Christmas carols such as 'Away In A Manger,' 'Silent Night,' 'Mary's Little Boy Child' and 'We Wish You A Merry Christmas.' The arrangements were anything but rocksteady but it did contain a cover of the Civil

Rights' anthem 'Go Tell It On The Mountain,' which Peter may have suggested. Rastafarians celebrated Ethiopian Christmas and were less than impressed with the news that the Archbishop of Canterbury was planning to visit Jamaica soon, even though Dr. Michael Ramsay would be the first to do so. Hadn't Dr. Rodney urged black people to repudiate notions of a white Christ and to see themselves with their *own* eyes, instead of the white man's? It wasn't just Rastafarians who reflected on the fact that no matter how poor people were (and how wealthy the pastor was), they were still expected to put money in the collection plate. Many Jamaicans had known people to beg or even steal to get collection money and avoid the embarrassment of going to church empty-handed, and yet it was ironic how most of these churches took little interest in their poorest parishioners.

Once the holidays were over, Bob and Rita opened a shop at No. 100 Orange Street, on Kingston's busiest thoroughfare. Business was brisk, despite plenty of competition, and the music constantly evolving. Leslie Kong – the same man who'd financed Bob's earliest recordings – was top producer with hits by the Pioneers, Desmond Dekker, Jimmy Cliff, the Melodians and Toots and the Maytals, whose 'Do The Reggay' was the first song to mention the word "reggae." Like Bunny, Toots had fallen foul of Shearer's repressive ganja laws. He'd written the classic '54-46 Was My Number' on his release from prison, and transformed his ID number into an uproarious badge of pride. Kong's run of hits would bring him unprecedented success in the overseas' market, but he didn't have it all his own way. Coxsone and Duke Reid were still there, but coming under pressure from newer producers such as Bunny Lee, Harry J and Lee "Scratch" Perry.

Despite Lyn Taitt's departure for Canada, Federal had continued their winning ways with the Gaylettes' 'Silent River Runs Deep,' whilst Keith & Tex followed the Wailers' example and covered the Temptations' 'Don't Look Back.' Other big hits included the Beltones' 'No More Heartaches,' 'Watch This Sound' by the Uniques and the Ethiopians' 'Everything Crash,' which pretty much summed up what a lot of Jamaicans were saying about the local economy.

Even as Johnny Nash continued to affiliate himself with rocksteady, Jamaica itself was jumping to a new beat. Reggae was now the latest rhythm to take the dancehalls by storm thanks to songs like Larry Marshall's 'Nanny Goat' and Stranger Cole's 'Bangarang.' Kingston session guitarists such as Eric "Rickenbacker" Frater, Rannie "Bop" Williams and the Hippy Boys' Alva "Reggie" Lewis had begun to assimilate a little funk into their playing. Jimmy Nolen's "chicken scratch" was coming home to roost in the Caribbean, and Jamaican music will become increasingly rhythm-driven in future. Johnny left for the UK in January, where his latest single 'You Got Soul' went Top 10, peaking at No. 6. It'll stay on the British charts for the rest of the summer, consolidating his star status. He'll be off the island for several weeks, promoting the single and then planning his next album. You'd be forgiven for thinking that his fundraising activities would stand him in good stead back in Jamaica but the authorities were still rattled by the riots, and weren't about to take any risks.

"The Jamaican authorities believed we were a threat to their national security," affirms Richard Alderson. "That's because we were hanging out with Rastafarians who were supposedly terrorists. They were thought to have been plotting to overthrow the government which wasn't even vaguely true, but Black Power terrified the light-skinned Jamaicans who'd replaced the British as the main political force in the country. These people were so scared of the black population in Jamaica. They were convinced the blacks were going to seize power and there was going to be a revolution. They were really afraid of that but what happened was...

"I think it was the second time we went down there. There were eight of us and my girlfriend and I were the only white members of the group. Everyone else was black but we all went through customs together and they looked at me and figured I was some sort of white revolutionary, and then it was Eddie Heath's turn. He was my assistant engineer at Impact. He was a sweet guy but he was very dark-skinned and looked like an African prince. He had an Afro and dressed very black but anyway Eddie had a copy of Mohammed Speaks in his briefcase, which was the Nation Of Islam's newspaper so they saw that and freaked. At first we were worried they were going to find drugs on us but they didn't. In fact they weren't even looking for drugs, they were looking for revolutionaries and then when we got to Johnny's house – this was after we'd been interrogated for hours at the airport – there was a knock at the door and there were these Special Branch people, saying we were wanted back at headquarters. They took us back there and held us in custody for hours and questioned us about what we were doing in Jamaica, which I think was all prompted by them finding that copy of 'Mohammed Speaks.' It's that what had triggered them off and they were convinced we were down there to start something.

They were really wasting their time. I mean there was definitely a growing interest in Black Power, but it was more cultural than political in my opinion. Anyway on top of all that there was this paranoia from people in the Jamaican music industry who were convinced we'd gone down there to take over. That's when I realised that Jamaica is the most corrupt place politically, or at least it was back then."

JAD's retinue weren't the only ones to have their collars felt by Jamaica's immigration authorities. Hugh Masekela received a similar welcome on his arrival in February, and nearly headed straight back to New York.

"African trumpeter Hugh Masekela and one-time husband of Miriam Makeba was in Kingston for a few days rest last week," reported the Gleaner. "He received an unexpected and over-zealous grilling by immigration officials who might have mistaken his trendsetting bell-bottom corduroy pants and other accoutrements as indicative of militant Black Power sympathies. It took some serious persuading by his hosts to stop him getting back on a plane. Let's hope that he'll come again and receive a more appropriate welcome because next time he might be persuaded to play for us."

Nash and Danny Sims first met Masekela at New York's Village Gate sometime in 1965, not long after he'd campaigned alongside Marlon Brando for the release of Robert Sobukwe, leader of the Pan Africanist Congress, who was languishing in a South African jail for speaking out against the Sharpeville Massacre. Back then, Danny and Johnny shared an apartment in Lincoln Towers on West 68th Street that Hugh says was, "always bubbling with beautiful women." He was still married to Miriam Makeba, and the two South Africans were considered the epitome of radical chic in New York due to their revolutionary politics and musical talent. Harry Belafonte figured prominently in both of their lives. Masekela had worked for Belafonte before bringing township jive to America, whilst his former employer had escorted Miriam to Kenya's independence ceremony and then helped launch her singing career in the US. Apart from Belafonte and Brando, the couple's friends included Dihann Carroll, Dizzy Gillespie, Lena Horne, Maya Angelou, Sidney Poitier and Miles Davis, as well as fellow South African music stars Caiphus Semenya and Letta Mbulu. Alas, their vociferous opposition to apartheid came at a price. We've already learnt of Miriam's problems with the South African authorities in an earlier chapter. In the meantime Hugh declared that, "the apartheid administration was painstakingly working with US intelligence agencies to make my life a living hell."

Several years earlier, he'd been invited to return to South Africa as a guest (i.e., "honorary white") so he could "witness all the marvellous changes taking place at home." Masekela had angrily refused, saying he could never accept such an offer whilst the regime continued to "persecute, jail, banish and murder my people in the name of white supremacy."

He and Miriam had separated by the time Danny Sims invited him to Jamaica. He was a marked man by then, and the constant surveillance was getting on his nerves. His phone had been tapped, and the FBI, the Internal Revenue Service and US drug enforcement agencies were all monitoring his activities. A Caribbean holiday would therefore be most welcome, and he gladly accepted the offer.

"One day I flew down to Jamaica with Danny and spent a glorious week at the Blue Mountains' house, which was always full of stunning women and Rasta dudes who kept ganja pipes "full and fired up" during every waking hour," he wrote in his autobiography, 'Still Grazing.' "Working closely with Johnny and Danny's company was a young artist named Bob Marley, whose compositions they were publishing. On several occasions I played the trumpet on Marley's tracks. During the very first Marley session, I was sitting with Johnny Nash's co-producer Reggie, who was from the Bronx, and Danny in the control booth, and I noticed that when Bob was singing, he'd do his fancy, jump up dance steps and often get out of range for the mic to pick up his voice. I finally said, 'Bob, the mic don't pick up the dancing man. Try to stand in one place.' Later, I asked Danny and Reggie why they hadn't told Bob to do that and they told me it had never entered their minds."

There's no mention of Peter, but Hugh played trumpet on the Wailers' cut of 'Love,' which Peter had written and sang, and possibly 'Rocking Steady' as well. 'Love' was still a dirge but brightened by Masekela's trilling, whilst 'Rocking Steady' is a paean to the rocksteady beat, and lightweight by Bob's standards. These tracks, together with 'Rock To The Rock' (with Bob on lead and guitar) had been recorded with the Hugh Malcolm and Jackie Jackson rhythm section before being overdubbed in New York. Coxsone will later release a cut of 'Rocking Steady' after Bob's death, although how he came to get hold of it is still a mystery.

Meeting Hugh Masekela and getting to hang out with him must have been quite an experience for the Wailers. At twenty-nine he was a little older and more sophisticated than them, yet they still had a fair amount in common. The South African township he grew up in wasn't all that dissimilar from Trench Town, and he was more than happy to sit and enjoy a smoke whilst reasoning about current affairs and playing music.

"Back at the house we never stopped smoking ganja, which made me cough deliriously," he admits. "It amazed me to watch Bob and the other Rastas take huge puffs out of the pipe. When they blew the smoke out, they would disappear behind the cloud that formed in the room. I just couldn't get the knack of it. Anyway, we would get so high that we would be speechless and just sit there watching or listening to the rain."

Masekela had studied at the Manhattan School Of Music, and was well schooled in black history. Although classically trained, he could play in any number of different styles, including soul, rock and jazz. The previous year he'd performed at the Monterey Pop Festival, sharing a bill with Jimi Hendrix, Otis Redding, the Who, Janis Joplin and Ravi Shankar. He'd also travelled to Zambia, where his sister gave him tapes of unreleased music from South Africa. That's how he'd found 'Grazin' In The Grass' – an instrumental he'd recorded as an afterthought, but which leapfrogged the Rolling Stones' 'Jumping Jack Flash' to reach No. 1 in America. It'll stay on the US charts for two months during the summer of 1968, building on the success of Miriam's 'Pata Pata,' which had been a hit the previous November. The America market was embracing so-called "world music" like never before, which must have brought hope to the Wailers and stiffened the resolve of JAD Records in finding them a hit.

It was people like Hugh Masekela and Miriam Makeba – black people of achievement who were committed, articulate, gifted and well informed, that helped shape the Wailers' worldview. Like them, they knew what it felt like to be a victim of poverty and discrimination, and yet they could still take pride in celebrating their cultural identity. Above all else they had integrity. Hugh's mother was a leading social worker in the Alexandra township and his family knew Nelson and Winnie Mandela better than most. Hugh had also met Malcolm X, whose call for greater self-determination had echoed the teachings of Marcus Garvey. Hugh described Malcolm as "handsome, hospitable and witty" and "gifted with an ability to gain your intimacy immediately.

"Malcolm X commanded awesome respect even from people who usually felt superior around blacks," he continued. "He became, from that moment forward, a model for me of how a man of African origin should project himself."

Miriam was also a Malcolm X supporter and had got into trouble for reminding African-Americans, "The extent to which you reject and hate Africa is the extent to which you hate yourselves. You cannot hate the root of a tree without hating the tree itself."

Hugh was shocked at how little black people in America knew about Africa. They'd been starved of information and brainwashed into thinking that Africans were primitives.

"Black Americans seemed to have been programmed to avoid and deny any historical or genealogical connection with Africa," he said, after claiming that all the average black (or white) American knew about Africa came from what they'd seen in Tarzan films. "The majority of them were always quick to say, 'No, I ain't got nothing to do with Africa man! I'm pure, full-blooded American. You better believe it!"

Kingston's Rasta communities were far better informed. During Masekela's visit they were busy celebrating Emperor Haile Selassie I's stewardship of the Organisation of African Unity – a coalition formed of independent African nations, and that was intended to promote co-operation between the continent's diverse leaderships. In time, Jamaica would have its own charismatic leader with connections to the Emperor. At the beginning of the year, Norman Manley resigned as Leader of the Opposition and was replaced by his son Michael, who was elected head of the PNP in his stead. In the aftermath of the Rodney riots, Norman Manley had made himself unpopular with Jamaica's middle classes by announcing that, "We have to understand ourselves and dare not ignore Black Power… I salute Black Power."

A few months later he'll define Black Power in terms of black dignity and black pride. Such sentiments were in stark contrast to the Attorney General's description of Dr. Rodney as the "foreign, evil devil who'd introduced Black Power to Jamaica." Within a relatively short space of time, the younger Manley will succeed in seizing the initiative from Shearer's party and establishing the PNP as the voice of the majority black population. He'll achieve this by championing civil liberties and constitutional rights, and protesting at the growing divide between Jamaica's "have and have-nots." Shearer, who people were now calling "Pharaoh," told him to "stop preaching civil disobedience and support the police" when he called for a commission on Jamaica's worsening crime rates. Manley was unrepentant, and also quick to capitalise on Emperor Selassie I's popularity among poor blacks. The Gleaner showed them stood next to one another, with Manley holding "the Rod Of Correction" which he claimed the Emperor had given him. Some people thought it was a fake, and said you could see where the two images had been spliced. Opinion was now divided within the Rasta movement between those who embraced Manley and those who denied him, calling him "a trickster." As political tensions increase many Rastafarians will be considered PNP regardless, even though they hadn't supported "Joshua," as Manley came to be known. And whilst it won't manifest itself just yet, it's this early identification with Emperor Selassie I that'll earn him the respect from reggae artists such as Marley and Tosh in years to come.

Such deliberations coincided with Bunny's release from jail, and Peter's return from exile. He and Bob were still getting a retainer from Sims and Nash, who'd redoubled their efforts in trying to get them a hit. Bunny hadn't been around when the deal was struck and so whilst he was welcomed back into the group with open arms, he still wasn't added to the payroll. Despite getting "a pinch" from Bob and Peter he complained about this to Arthur Jenkins, but it seems people in the JAD camp found him difficult to deal with at first.

Richard Alderson calls him "a paranoid character" but says Bunny was the first of the Wailers to see right through Danny.

"He was the most suspicious of Danny for whatever reason. I don't know why, it was just a feeling I got. He remained a private person and didn't seem to like the foreign musicians all that much."

Jimmy Norman remembers him as "a loner" and calls him "the suspicious type.

"I got the impression he was more of a rude boy or gangster, I don't know which," he says. "Bob and I hung out more and he showed me around more than the others did. I didn't get to know Bunny at all."

'Tread Oh' is said to be the first tune Bunny sang on after his release. It was recorded at JBC, which could be hired relatively cheaply. It's also not very good – Bunny's vocals sound rusty and his lyrics are even worse, since they hinge around the line, "you're like a stick of macaroni in bed." Peter played organ and that's Ras Michael beating on the repeater. Helping out on harmonies is Joe Sarkey – a friend of Peter's from Cockburn Pen, and another stalwart of Kingston's early Rasta community. The presence of these two Rastafarians is significant. They and Peter may have wanted to prepare the ground for Bunny's return with a musical-cum-spiritual cleansing, but the sound is cluttered and the song itself lacks focus. Also, Bob and Rita weren't there, which suggests they were out of town at the time.

A few months earlier, the Wailers had agreed to play a free show at the Ward Theatre. Peter and the Marleys had been getting ready when they heard that Planno was at the venue charging people to get in. Rather than going down there to sort it out they decided not to perform, which meant Planno had to return the money. This incident spelt the end of his temporary management of the group, and also his role as spiritual mentor. Bob left for Nine Miles and considered the matter closed. Planno however, felt angered and humiliated and so he sent some thugs after Bob, seeking revenge. If his idea was to teach Bob a lesson, it soon backfired. When Planno's henchmen arrived in Nine Miles the villagers set upon them, showering them with rocks and almost killing them before Bob intervened and sent them home. Again Planno felt humiliated. He hadn't really wanted to mess with

Peter, but still harboured thoughts of vengeance. Consequently Peter found himself circled by youths on the street one day, brandishing lengths of wood. Using his karate training he seized the leader's stick, broke it into pieces and then gave him a good beating as the others ran off. Peter wasn't troubled again after that but Planno was incensed and threatened to burn down Aunt Viola's place on Greenwich Park Road in Ghost Town, where Bob and Rita still lived. A local gang leader called Frankie Dark warned Bob about this and vowed to protect him, even though Bob wasn't from the neighbourhood.

The Wailers were no strangers to Ghost Town, since they used to walk through there every day on their way to Studio One. They'd often stop and chat with people en route, but none of them had lived there before Bob moved in with Rita. Frankie Dark's gang were called the Vikings, whose members were drawn from all over the corporate area. They were a revolutionary group, unlike say the Sweeties or Zulus, and their fiercest rivals were the JLP supporters based in Rema. It was only recently that gangs such as theirs had divided along political lines. This meant innocent people had started to get caught up in the violence, instead of gang members alone. As soon as politics became an issue, everyone living in a rival area – even dogs and chickens that strayed over the borderline – became the enemy.

The youths Planno sent to burn down Aunt Viola's house were armed with sticks, knives and Molotov cocktails made from crocus bags soaked in petrol and stuffed into glass bottles. Fortunately, Frankie Dark's gang intercepted them halfway to Ghost Town and sent them running back down West Road. From that time onwards, Bob was indebted to the Vikings. This didn't please him but at least the Wailers were now free of Planno and with Bunny now back in the fold, they could concentrate on making music once more. Bunny has been quite scathing about the songs they worked on after his return, calling them "demos for record companies to listen to." He's even said that Danny Sims should never have sanctioned their release. It's easy to see why he should think this, and especially if you compare them to tracks recorded for Lee "Scratch" Perry or Leslie Kong. JAD had crossover hits in their sights however, and were reluctant to stray from accepted formulas.

Jimmy Norman had come to Jamaica with ideas for songs that he and Al Pyfrom had worked on in New York, and he was also writing a lot of new material at this point – most of it penned with Bob and Peter in mind, although Bunny did get to sing lead on 'Treat You Right.' It's wonderful to hear him back on harmonies for songs like 'Touch Me,' 'The World Is Changing,' 'Lonely Girl,' 'Milkshake And Potato Chips,' 'It Hurts To Be Alone' and 'Lonesome Feelings,' which the reunited Wailers recorded around this time. Bob was credited with writing 'Treat You Right' and 'The World Is Changing,' but Jimmy Norman claimed that he and Al Pyfrom were the rightful authors.

Peter sings lead vocals on 'The World Is Changing,' which warns of mankind's capacity for self-destruction over a driving reggae beat. It marked the last time Peter sang lead vocals for JAD, and may well be his finest performance for them. Tosh was always more musically proficient than the other Wailers, and had continued to develop as an instrumentalist. That's him playing melodica on 'Milkshake And Potato Chips' and 'It Hurts To Be Alone.' Augustus Pablo will later elevate the humble "blow organ" to near mythical status but Peter was among the first to use it in Jamaica. Despite his contributions, other JAD productions didn't turn out quite so impressive. 'It Hurts To Be Alone' and 'Lonesome Feeling' were both originally recorded for Coxsone and suffer from over-production, whilst Rita takes the spotlight for 'Lonely Girl' and sounds unconvincing. Peter, versatile as ever, plays harmonica on that one. The Wailers' next recordings will take place at Studio 17, which Vincent Chin had built in an upstairs room above his Randy's record store on North Parade, right in the heart of downtown Kingston.

"We were the ones who put the eight-track desk into Randy's," says Richard Alderson. "Vincent Chin, he only had a two-track machine when we first went there. Bill Garnett was the engineer, and he later came to work at Ralph MacDonald's studio here in New York but we were recording in several different places at that time. We were using Randy's, we were using Federal and I think we even used Coxsone's studio once or twice."

Byron Lee would later buy West Indies studio and rename it Dynamic Sounds after a fire destroyed tapes and equipment there. It'll quickly outstrip every other studio in Kingston and attract international acts such as Paul Simon, Roberta Flack and the Rolling Stones. Yet for the time being it was Randy's that led the field, and which served as a magnet for visiting celebrities. Vincent Chin's oldest son Clive was sixteen and a student at Kingston College when the studio opened.

"There were just a handful of studios in Jamaica at that time, and there was a need for us to offer studio time to some of these independent producers who were coming up like Bunny Lee and Lee "Scratch" Perry," he explains.

"The studio started in late 1968, but it wasn't opened until the spring of 1969 and then the bookings started coming in straightaway. It got so that we could only use it ourselves at weekends, on Sundays. The people from JAD were the first clients to book Randy's, and they had it for weeks at a time – maybe even a couple of months. I remember them being there virtually every day, or certainly every other day. They'd arrive at night, and then work right through until morning before going off to sleep for the day.

"To me, it was exciting whenever those guys came down to the studio because they were completely different. I would see them coming in with beads round their necks and wearing dashikis. They'd wear colourful shirts and tight, bell-bottomed pants with sandals, plus they had Afro hairstyles and wore sunglasses. They were definitely not an everyday set of people. They were these strange and fascinating foreign nationals who'd come down to Jamaica, and the way they worked in the studio was exciting as well. That really caught my attention because they brought in big-time musicians like Quincy Jones and Richard Tee... Hugh Masekela, the trumpet player from South Africa came down and I met Lloyd Price, Harry Belafonte and Cissy Houston... Quite a few people passed through after the studio opened and that's how we got to know Peter Tosh and Bob Marley as well, because they were contracted to Johnny Nash's label. Bill Garnett was the main engineer but JAD were recording several albums at that time, with Byron Lee and Johnny Nash as well as the Wailers. That was around the time they were recording songs like 'You Poured Sugar On Me' and 'Stir It Up.'"

In fact the trio's next recordings would be remakes of 'Nice Time' and 'Bend Down Low' and a new song called 'Soul Almighty' that'll again head for the commercial jugular, but sound a lot more convincing in Lee Perry's hands. All were recorded at Randy's, where the Wailers immediately felt at home – both with the facilities and sometime illustrious company. Jamaican conguero Larry MacDonald was newly returned from Mexico in the spring of 1969, and recalls seeing the Wailers rub shoulders with all manner of star names at that time.

"Yes, they were all there in Jamaica but the success of the records they made were directly correlated as to whether they were doing them for the right reasons," he says cryptically. "We need to ask ourselves whether it was because they were in love with the money, or because they decided it was something current and they could latch onto it, and then get in there ahead of everyone else. But there were a lot of musicians coming to Jamaica at the time, including Lloyd Price and Fats Domino."

Lloyd Price was an old friend of Nash and Sims. A year earlier he'd bought Birdland on 52nd Street in New York and rebuilt it to include a recording studio. He'd named this new club Turntable and would use the same name for its attendant record label. He then hired some of JAD's personnel to take care of production duties, including Jimmy Norman. In an interview with the Gleaner during July, Lloyd was asked if he thought there was a possibility of the Jamaican beat becoming international.

"I have always been impressed by the Jamaican music," he said. "With a little more listening by the overseas public, both the reggae and rocksteady could make it strongly on the US and English markets. The reason for this is simple; it is a true music. It is a history of the people and sound-wise, it is similar to our country and western and rhythm and blues, although I find it stronger.

"The quality of the records has kept Jamaican music from making the big time," he continued, referring to the standard of production. "And then of course there are the lyrics. The DJ has to be in the same groove but the rocksteady has not yet become fully commercialised and Jamaica has the task of educating the music world. It is easier for people like Johnny Nash, Eddie Lovette or myself to carry this music to the world since we are already known."

Lloyd went on to praise Desmond Dekker's 'Israelites,' which he called "a fantastic record." Two months earlier, 'Israelites' had gone to No. 1 in England and become the first authentically Jamaican record to breach the US Billboard charts. Its success triggered a debate as to whether it was necessary to dilute the homegrown Jamaican sound when trying to appeal to overseas' audiences. With its infectious reggae backdrop and opening cry of "Wake up in the morning, slaving for bread sir" 'Israelites' was proof to the contrary, although Desmond himself, talking to Gordon Coxhill in London, seemed more concerned with the lyrical content.

"Jamaica is very limited as far as playing is concerned," he admits, "but with Johnny Nash having hit after hit here, I think there is a definite market in Britain for ska flavoured records. Although ska is thought of as music to dance to, I try to get something across in the lyrics I write as well. I am a firm believer in pacifism and use my songs and singing to try and influence young people to lead a peaceful existence."

Johnny Nash, who was described as "a Jamaica resident" in a July edition of the Gleaner had now scored his second UK Top 10 hit in just a few months with 'Cupid.' This is the same record that he'd wanted to promote ahead of 'Hold Me Tight' and it's another rocksteady classic, taking Sam Cooke's love song into realms the late soul star would have never thought possible.

"Reggae music can fill the British charts only if the dance is given heavy promotion," Johnny told the British press. "It's just as sensuous as any dance. People in Britain have pop, folk, country and western, underground and soul music but now they are looking for something new. Change is inevitable and the reggae could supply that change."

The cover of his next LP, 'Soul Folk,' would depict him sat cradling an acoustic guitar, looking every inch the troubadour. It also sported a hologram, presumably in a bid to get the hippy vote. Apart from 'You Got Soul Parts 1 & 2' every track's a cover version as Johnny tries his hand at ballads, rock and roll ('Love Me Tender'), folk, soul ('Chain Gang') and even calypso thanks to the inclusion of Harry Belafonte's 'Island In The Sun.' Bob Dylan's 'Blowing In The Wind' aside, there's little political content in these songs, which made his new guise seem a bit hollow. That's because a growing number of soul, folk and rock acts were concerned about what was happening around them, and wanted to make their voices heard. They were only too aware that just a few months after being elected US President, Richard Nixon was already threatening to bomb Cambodia. And as criticism of the Vietnam War continued to gain momentum, which of them wouldn't be stirred by the news that the National Guard had used chemical sprays on demonstrators in California, or that nearly fifty students had been injured after attempting to seize control of Harvard? Desmond Dekker was right to be concerned about the lyrical content in Jamaican songs and yet for the time being at least, the Wailers were still some way off from providing it.

CHAPTER ELEVEN

Nuggets For The Needy

It says a lot about Peter Tosh's character that he should walk around Kingston wearing a Black Power pendant at a time when the authorities were so jumpy about would-be insurgents in their midst. Peter had carved a fist out of wood, painted it black and threaded it onto a shoelace as a symbol of solidarity with Walter Rodney and other Black Power leaders.

It was a blatant act of defiance by someone who'd already been jailed, albeit briefly, for his political convictions and then hunted by police after the riots. Bruised by injustices both real and imaginary, the Wailers' rebel-in-chief was no longer content to say and do nothing – not whilst singers like Curtis Mayfield, John Lennon and Bob Dylan were busy writing message songs and making their presence felt. Lennon and Yoko Ono had recently risked ridicule by staging a Bed-In in support of their pacifist beliefs. That same day in a Montreal hotel, they'd recorded 'Give Peace A Chance' – a song released at the height of America's war in Vietnam, and that had put their political agenda on the front page of the world's newspapers. Pop music, more than ever, was a barometer of the times and Jamaica too, would have its share of musical prophets.

"Our music deals with reality, the half that has never been told," Bob Marley was moved to later declare. "The youths tell it through music, and they choose reggae music. Reggae is the news; it's like the people's music. It's news about your own self and your own history."

Inspired by events in America, hip Jamaican men and women now sported Afros, flared trousers and head-wraps, and had adopted a hardened stance towards racial barriers closer to home. Black consciousness was on the rise and the Wailers were keen to lend their voices to the struggle, although they'd yet to convince many of their original fans.

"One time during the Jamaica Song Festival, there was this big show at the State Theatre with lots of artists," recalls singer Dave Barker. "A band called the Vikings backed everyone that night and it was packed. I remember after Glen Brown and I went up and did our song, we came offstage and sat in the audience to watch the rest of the show. Bob and the Wailers came on dressed in their Rastaman outfits and they had these brethrens on stage with them, playing Rasta drums. They were singing some wonderful chanting songs but I couldn't believe what I was hearing because the people booed them! All around me people were passing some nasty remarks and shouting for them to come off the stage. That night, sat there hearing all these people shouting abuse, I felt hurt. I couldn't believe they would do that and it was all because Bob was singing Rasta songs."

In response, the Wailers withdrew from live appearances for a while. This meant money was once again hard to come by. Peter busied himself with session work at Randy's and Treasure Isle, and one of the earliest tracks he played on was Count Machouki's 'Stick Up'. This was during the early days of reggae dee-jaying or toasting. Machouki was a mainstay of Coxsone's sound-system and very popular with Jamaican dancehall crowds. Hip-hop fans please note, because MCs like him and King Stitt were making talking records well over a year before Gil Scott Heron or the Last Poets first ventured into a studio! America's best-known rappers up to that point were Mohammad Ali and Soul Brother Number One, "Mister J-a-m-e-s B-r-o-w-n," who wasn't adverse to letting loose whenever the groove struck home. Grandmaster Flash, himself a leading rap pioneer, told David Ritz "if there's one thing black folks in the ghetto know how to do, it's talk shit. They've been talking shit, singing shit, chanting shit, rhyming shit and mumbling shit since day one. Wasn't hard to see what talking shit over a beat could do to a party…"

Essentially, Jamaican MCs of the day were entertainers who helped pull in the crowds and kept dancers happy whilst they changed the records over. Most modelled their patter on American radio DJs, but it wasn't long before some of them started rapping about things happening around them.

"In Jamaica, things were changing fast," says Hux Brown, who played on innumerable hits for Leslie Kong and Duke Reid. "The dee-jays were one thing but some musicians would go in the studio, make a beat and then all of a sudden everybody else jump on it. It would start with just a little change because the first time I heard reggae, there was this guy called Reggie who played with the Hippy Boys. I went in the studio and heard this "chikka chikka" and I say to him, 'What's this?' He say it's called reggae so I say to him, 'Better you learn a few more chords than that man' but then all of a sudden, the whole music changed over to reggae. It's the truth!

"The Hippy Boys had been around for a little while by then. They were coming like a cheaper recording band. Producers like Lee "Scratch" Perry would use them because those guys never had any money but they were pretty good. They did some nice songs too. They just didn't have any proper training."

"The more established session players in Kingston, they always call us "two chord" musicians," recalls Hippy Boys' bassist Aston "Family Man" Barrett. "We agree and say, 'Yes, but what two chords? And what tempo?" We might not be too versatile at that stage but we had a different concept, which was reggae. Musicians like us used to listen to all types of music. Every time a new album came out we'd study it and try and absorb what was happening. We wanted to learn everything there was about music, whether in the studio or being part of a road band. We didn't shut ourselves off from any of it."

This growing preoccupation with spirituality would take Jamaican music in a different direction from the one mapped out in Duke Reid's rocksteady hits, or the ska tracks unleashed by Coxsone just five years earlier. Studio One was issuing Biblically inspired roots hymns by the Abyssinians and Burning Spear, as Rastafari made its voice heard in the dancehalls. Peter responded by delivering a typically forthright message to the church. "First you came and you sold us Christianity. You taught us of heaven way up in the sky but you can't fool me again..." Recorded at Randy's with unknown musicians, 'You Can't Fool Me Again' is little more than an organ instrumental with vocal interludes. It's not a great tune and the lyrics aren't too special either, but there's no mistaking the sentiments.

"Can you imagine how shocking it is and how angry it makes people to discover they've been brainwashed by the church for so many years?" asks Jamaican actress and filmmaker Esther Anderson. "It's made fools out of your entire family – your granny, your mother, your father and so many other people around you. They do what they do because they've been told it's the right way to behave and then you find out that none of it makes sense, and there must be something else. It's very confusing, and it can make people very angry."

By the time Peter recorded 'Earth's Rightful Ruler,' the Wailers had already recorded 'A Little Prayer', with Bunny on repeater, Peter on shaker and Bob strumming a guitar. They were also attending regular nyahbinghi sessions, where Rasta elders would address their congregation in the language of Ethiopia. Peter had chanted in Amharic on the introduction on 'Earth's Rightful Ruler' – a song that also featured U Roy, the star dee-jay on King Tubby's Home Town Hi-Fi. Tubby's real name was Osbourne Ruddock. He repaired electrical equipment at his mother's house in Firehouse, a little further west of Trench Town. His sound-system was a favourite of those in the Wailers' circle, including Family Man.

"Tubby have a *serious* sound-system," he recalls. "You get the right voice range and top mix. It travel distance and then when you hear that splash of reverb, you know U Roy is getting ready. He'd come on the mic saying, 'Well greetings brothers and sisters. You're listening to the mighty King Tubby's Hi-Fi...' The man talk through just the top alone but then as soon as Tubby make the bass drop, it come like an earthquake pass through there!"

There was no shortage of lawns or outside spaces in Kingston where sound-systems could string up and play, and there were plenty of club venues as well. Dennis Thompson, who'll later work for Randy's as a dub-cutter and engineer, would DJ every Saturday night at a club called The Lotus-A-Go-Go, situated at the back of KG's record store in Half Way Tree. Coxsone used to take him acetates of unreleased material whilst Duke Reid would send down a two-track reel to reel, with vocals on one side and the backing track on the other. Dennis would play the rhythm and get the crowd to sing along, karaoke style. These nights heralded the beginning of dub and "version." Track separation meant that producers could use the same backing tracks for other versions and this led to complaints by musicians who weren't being paid twice, despite their work generating further hits and therefore revenue. Duke Reid will reap spectacular results by reusing old Paragons' hits behind U Roy on songs like 'Wake The Town' and 'Wear You to The Ball', which the deejay delivered just as he would in a dancehall.

'Earth's Rightful Ruler' had none of the swooping, joyous spontaneity heard on those classic Treasure Isle hits but whilst it didn't chart or get any airplay, it's still a good deal better than some of the Wailers' recordings from the same period. During the summer of 1969 an inane contrivance called 'Sugar Sugar', fronted by an imaginary cartoon group called the Archies had dominated pop charts on both sides of the Atlantic. The Wailers' decision to cover this song as opposed to other candidates such as Johnny Nash's 'I Got Soul' and 'Cupid', Marvin Gaye's 'I Heard It Through The Grapevine', the Temptations' 'Cloud Nine', Jerry Butler's 'Only The Strong Survive', Elvis Presley's 'In The Ghetto' or Stevie Wonder's 'My Cherie Amour' is frankly baffling – and especially since other Jamaican acts were busy enjoying crossover success with much better material. Desmond Dekker had followed 'Israelites' with another strong seller called 'It Mek'; Jimmy Cliff charted with 'Wonderful World, Beautiful People' whilst the Hippy Boy's former lead singer Max Romeo weighed in with a smutty little ditty called 'Wet Dream', which he claimed to have written about a leaky roof.

People say it was Wilson Pickett's version of 'Sugar Sugar' the Wailers heard and not the Archies' but that's beside the point. Thankfully there's nothing else like it in their oeuvre except for 'What's New Pussycat,' and that was another mistake. Apparently, Vincent Chin believed 'Sugar Sugar' could be a big hit for the Wailers outside of Jamaica, but he misread the British market by some distance. The Archies' version was light and frothy, and had no pretence to soul whatsoever. It was unpretentious, carefree pop aimed at pre-teens, and there wasn't a chance in hell of the Wailers appealing to that audience. Bob does his best to inject some feeling into it but the song's so trite it simply can't work and whilst Rita's clearly heard on backing vocals, Bunny and Peter's contributions are barely perceptible. Clive Chin calls 'Sugar Sugar' "the bubblegum song.

"It's such an unusual situation because as we know, Bob liked to write his own songs so when he was asked to do that, it must have been intriguing for him to do it," he says. "The Wailers were strong characters too. They weren't easy to work with unless you knew how to deal with them but from you showed them respect, then everything was nice and getting what you wanted from them wouldn't be a problem."

The fact that they agreed to record 'Sugar Sugar' speaks volumes about their relationship with Vincent Chin – a man they liked and respected, and who supported the Wailers by selling and distributing their records. Vincent also liked smoking herb, which Peter would procure for him from time to time. Bunny calls him, 'a good, clean brother that we live amongst. We give him some things (meaning recordings) and he gives us some studio time in return. Him nah really run us down for money at all."

Bunny says that Peter chose to cover 'The Letter', which they renamed 'Give Me A Ticket.' The Box Tops' original was already two years old by the time Peter voiced it and yet it lends itself well to their new arrangement and slightly over-the-top harmonies. It's a bit forced, but nowhere near as bad as 'Sugar Sugar'. Early pressings were credited to the Mad Dogs, but no one knows why. Ultimately, the Wailers' earnest interpretations of pop hits like these are the most unsatisfying recordings of their entire career, and reveal just how far off the pace they were as summer turned to autumn in 1969. By this time the market had split into two. At one end of the spectrum there were acts like the Monkees, who appealed to very young audiences. At the other was rock – music that spoke for a generation now feeling increasingly alienated from mainstream society and that was busy exploring alternatives in every direction it could. The Beatles' 'Sgt Pepper' had provided the dividing line two years earlier. Their latest album contained songs like 'Revolution' and the avant-garde 'Revolution No. 9,' and had left some of their pop following feeling bewildered. The Beatles were coming apart behind the scenes in any case. John and Yoko had bared all on the defiantly unmusical 'Two Virgins' and the Beatles already played their last-ever gig, on the roof of the Apple building in London. There was a sense that rock may be over-reaching itself – a feeling confirmed by the Who's 'Tommy', which had the dubious distinction of being the first-ever rock opera. Recognising the dangers, other leading lights pulled back from the brink and reconnected with their musical roots. The Rolling Stones made 'Beggars Banquet' whilst Bob Dylan headed for Nashville, where he'll record with Johnny Cash. Elvis Presley meanwhile, dressed from head to toe in black leather, made a stunning comeback on NBC TV.

Black music, led by Norman Whitfield's rock-tinged productions at Tamla Motown, would fill the void and redefine the label's sound and reputation. Acts like the Supremes and Marvin Gaye had worked hard to gain mainstream acceptance from whites, but Whitfield's urgency and a series of powerful message songs now put them on the other side of the barricades. The soul and rock genres were moving closer together, as celebrated by Sly & The Family Stone at the Woodstock festival in August, where half a million people had gathered to watch acts like the Who, Joe Cocker, Santana, Crosby, Stills, Nash & Young and Jimi Hendrix, whose electrifying version of the 'Star Spangled Banner' would characterise the rainbow nation's finest hour. Hendrix, like other leading African-American artists, had begun to come under pressure from black activists, who wanted him to endorse their political agenda. Within two weeks of headlining Woodstock he'd play on the back of a flatbed truck at a fundraising event in Harlem, and to an audience that struggled to identify with him. The counter culture was throwing up demons, and thoughts of hippy utopias were unravelling fast, even as Charles Manson and his band of followers butchered Roman Polanski's wife Sharon Tate and her four friends in a Los Angeles mansion. Attitudes were hardening and battle lines being redrawn both in the cultural sense, and on the world stage. Britain sent troops into Northern Ireland, and America was still embroiled in the

Vietnam War whilst witnessing the rise of radical organisations like the Weathermen, who were committed to violent overthrow of the system. This signalled an end to the old "prankster" mentality, as Eldridge Cleaver derided white Yippies like Rubin and Hoffman for practising "infantile disorder."

The previous month, Stokely Carmichael had resigned from the Black Panther party after strongly opposing the party's alliance with white radicals. "History has shown that any premature alliance with white radicals has led to complete subversion of the blacks," he said in a message delivered by his wife Miriam Makeba, whom he'd married the year before. She had recently attracted widespread condemnation after refusing to sing for US troops in Vietnam. Just to make things worse, she and Carmichael had visited Fidel Castro in Havana during April, and were currently exiled in Guinea. The period of optimism that had accompanied African liberation during the early sixties had now given way to something altogether more problematic. The apartheid regime in South Africa was still a stain on the world's conscience and children were starving in Biafra after Nigeria had imposed a blockade, and ordered the Red Cross to leave. 1969 marked the twentieth anniversary of the United Nations. It was the International Year of Human Rights yet several prominent African singers and bandleaders faced retaliatory actions after speaking out against government oppression. Fela Kuti left Nigeria for the US, where he would identify with the Black Panthers and immerse himself in the culture and ideology of Black Power. Eldridge Cleaver meanwhile, journeyed to North Korea as an internal memo, leaked from the White House, warned that, "student disorders will surpass anything we have seen before."

In mid-October, black athletes were expelled from Wyoming University for wearing Black Power armbands. The following month, half a million anti-war demonstrators marched on Washington – scenes that prompted John Lennon to return his MBE in protest against Britain's backing of the Vietnam War. During early December, two Black Panthers were shot dead in their sleep in what appeared to be a covert anti-terrorist operation. The culling of black political activists had begun and it was these unconstitutional actions, even more than the Rolling Stones' disastrous free concert at Altamont, which truly marked the end of the sixties. Back in Jamaica, Dynamic Sound was advertising the Johnny Nash albums 'Prince Of Peace' and 'Love And Peace' in time for the Christmas season. Johnny had arrived from Atlanta too late to perform at Kingston's Hilton Hotel as scheduled, but did put in an appearance at a show in Montego Bay for another round of 'Nuggets For the Needy.' One review claimed that he was nervous, and states this was hardly surprising "considering how callously and insensitively they have treated this fine entertainer in the past."

Just three months earlier, Nash had headlined the Caribbean Music Festival at the Empire Pool in London – an event that attracted more than eight thousand revelers, who flocked to see Desmond Dekker, Max Romeo, Count Prince Miller, Root & Jenny Jackson and the Mohawks. The Wailers could be forgiven for feeling frustrated at this point. Despite trying their hand at "bubblegum," nothing was happening for them. They even auditioned for Lloyd Daley's Matador label during this period. Daley ran an electrical repair shop on Waltham Park Road, and had seen his fortunes as a record producer transformed after recruiting the Hippy Boys on tracks by Errol Scorcher ('The Ugly One') and Little Roy. The latter's 'Bongo Nyah' was a surprise hit in late 1969, since Rasta songs weren't usually played on the radio. This hadn't gone unnoticed by the Wailers, who were desperate to turn their situation around. Unfortunately Daley's wife Deanna, who ran a beauty parlour on the premises, didn't like them and considered the group "too unruly, too ghetto."

Ted Pouder, who worked at Federal, thought otherwise. He convinced the Wailers that he could help but the songs he recorded with them weren't good sellers and left them feeling more adrift than ever. All four tracks are best described as reggae gospel. 'Thank You Lord' is completely different from the Wail 'N Soul 'M version since this one's jaunty, and less ragged. It doesn't have the charm of the original but Pouder was a talented engineer, and invests the Wailers' music with a breezy quality that simply wouldn't have materialised had they been left to their own devices. 'Adam And Eve' has the air of a Biblical fairytale. "Woman is the root of all evil. She was the first one to break the fruit, and now everyone else is living in sin," warns Bob. There's no concession to women's liberation within the Wailers' ranks as yet, that's for sure! Peter sings bass harmonies on that one, and will later re-record 'Wisdom' as 'Fools Die' on his album 'Wanted, Dread & Alive'. Bob's vocals don't quite fit the rhythm although the lyrics are deeply profound. Looking back, it's hardly surprising that Peter saw fit to revive it but then all three Wailers would make a habit of re-recording old songs whenever the mood took them. Bunny first sang a cut of 'This Train' for Coxsone, and will return to it on his 'Blackheart Man' album several years hence. This new version has a barrelhouse feel thanks to Winston Wright's tinkling keyboards, and with Rita's soaring harmonies prominent in the mix. Bob's vocal isn't imbued with so much spirituality as Bunny's was, suggesting that he wasn't always the best choice to sing lead. Did such decisions sow the seeds of future dissent we wonder? Or did the new style arrangement influence the outcome?

'This Train' was a mainstay of Sister Rosetta Tharpe's repertoire, and the Wailers clearly held her in high regard. Old, grainy footage shows a guitar-toting grandmother hollering gospel whilst spraying blues licks like dirt. In the words of Anthony Heilbut, she "could pick blues guitar like a Memphis Minnie. She bent her notes like a horn player and syncopated in swing band manner. Above all, she had showmanship. Grinning, joking... Rosetta was obvious star material."

She'd made her first records in the late thirties, accompanying herself on guitar. One of them was 'This Train', with the lyrics, 'this train don't pull no jokers, no whisky drinkers, no cigar smokers. Because this train's a clean train, this train...' After performing with the big bands of Cab Calloway and even Benny Goodman, she married in an outdoor venue in front of 25,000 paying guests, cementing her status as gospel's reigning Queen. She then committed the cardinal sin of recording blues material and was heavily criticised for it, although her fall from grace did little to diminish her spirits. By the late sixties she'd been recast as a rebel matriarch, hitched her wagon to the burgeoning blues revival and famously took the stage at the 1967 Newport Jazz Festival dressed in a full-length mink coat – this in an era dominated by hippie aesthetics! Three years later, she'll tour

Europe and complain of a sudden, deep chill. After being flown back home she'll suffer a stroke and have a leg amputated but would then recover to complete two more tours – limping on stage in her nightgown, aided by crutches – before dying on the eve of a recording session. Sister Rosetta's tribulations won't generate much media interest, as she was long out of the spotlight by then. In April, Paul McCartney announced the Beatles had split up, just a month before 'Let It Be' became their swansong. Their fans had seen it coming but in any case there were more serious, far-reaching events afoot. America's decision to invade Cambodia had provoked widespread opposition and when students at Ohio's Kent State University mounted an anti-war protest, four of them died and nine were injured at the hands of the National Guard. This happened on May 4th. Five days later, and more than a hundred thousand demonstrators will march on Washington in yet another mass demonstration of public unrest.

News from America spread quickly around the Caribbean. Rastas quoted scripture and talked ominously of these being "the last days" as prophesised in the Book Of Revelations, whilst older folks pined for the world of their youth. The Wailers' career had stalled by this point. Their recent songs seemed out of step with what was going on, leaving fans of 'Freedom Time' and 'Fire Fire' disappointed. Johnny Nash was busy with his own career, and studio time was expensive. Somewhat reluctantly, Bob went to see Leslie Kong at his Beverley's ice cream parlour on the corner of Orange Street and North Parade, just a short distance from the Wailers' record store.

Kong was a tall, skinny man of about thirty who was rarely seen without sunglasses, as his eyes were weak. Bob and Bunny had known him since they were schoolboys and whilst Bob's earliest recordings for him hadn't sold, they'd remained on good terms. The Wailers had sometimes stopped by Beverley's when signed to Studio One – not to record, but to hang out with friends gathered round the piano in the rehearsal room at the back of the shop, where Derrick Morgan and Jimmy Cliff served as Kong's A & R men for a time. Beverley's had the Midas touch and especially in Britain where in the space of the last few months, Kong had tasted Top 40 success with the Pioneers' 'Long Shot Kick The Bucket', the Melodians' 'Sweet Sensation', Desmond Dekker's 'Pickney Gal' and two songs by Jimmy Cliff, including 'Vietnam,' which Paul Simon described as one of the best anti-war songs he'd ever heard. The Wailers had several meetings with him and agreed to record a one-off album project, plus attendant singles. They were paid a decent advance, Kong provided all the facilities they could want and hired the musicians they'd requested. The majority of them had already recorded with the Wailers so it was like a reunion in a way. The rhythm tracks were laid first. Peter would strum the chords and then Gladstone Anderson would work out the actual arrangements on piano. Winston Wright or Hux Brown might contribute a lick or two; Jackie Jackson would start filling in on bass, finding a pattern and then everyone would get excited as the song started to take shape.

"Marley and those guys, they never used to give us any problem," says Hux Brown, who played guitar on most of their Beverley's sessions. "They'd just come in and work like everybody else. They'd sing and we'd play. It was as simple as that and whilst Peter might come out with things from time to time, from a musician's viewpoint, none of them could arrange anything. They'd just write and sing their songs and leave the rest to us but I must say they really had their harmonies together, and you could tell they were well rehearsed. They needed to be, because in those days everything was recorded live – voices, horns, guitar, bass and everything. Nobody could afford to make a mistake and if you did then you were in trouble, and especially if guys like Tommy McCook and Roland Alphonso were there!"

This same team of musicians would often play three or four sessions a day for different producers and then perform hotel gigs at night. Their ratio of hits was extraordinary except Hux pays credit to Leslie Kong for making things happen, and giving them the freedom to create.

"Leslie Kong was a really good producer," he said. "He would come to the studio but leave everything to the musicians, and then if he didn't like it he'd say to try another one. There was never any fuss or anything like that. He didn't interfere with us, and we all accepted the fact he wasn't a musician. He'd just come to the session, and make sure we had everything we needed. We were more or less free to play what we wanted to play and he always got good songs. I never heard him tell the artists what to do either. They'd just say what songs they had or wanted to sing, he'd listen and then if he liked them, he'd book the studio and call us in to find the rhythm and get the thing done. Leslie Kong was a very lucky man, because he never booked a studio session without getting a hit out of it. I'm not saying all of them were big hits, but the majority of his productions always sold. He was a fair man too. The day after a session, we'd go along to his shop and the cheque was always there, written out and all ready for us.

That's why everyone wanted to play for him, because he would never give you any problems. It wasn't like dealing with some of these other producers, who'd tell you to come back next week or make some excuse. Leslie Kong wasn't like that. He paid on time and never owed people money."

Kong ran the Beverley's label with help from his brother Fats and Warwick Lynn, who managed Toots and the Maytals. Most of his productions were recorded at Dynamic under the watchful gaze of studio engineer Carlton Lee, who ensured the band always had time to work properly. The Wailers' recordings for Kong have been described as the first-ever reggae concept album, since it marked a departure from how most Jamaican producers approached the business. At Studio One they'd recorded material with singles in mind. Coxsone would then compile albums from it at a later date, almost as an afterthought. The difference this time round was that the Wailers were encouraged to experiment a little and record a cohesive collection of songs from the start, just like the Beatles and other rocks acts had been doing. At the same time Kong knew they had songs capable of breaking into the British pop market and lost no time licensing 'Soul Shakedown Party' to Trojan, who released it with an instrumental on the flipside. Why it wasn't a major hit in the UK is a mystery. The rhythm's infectious, the chorus immediate and what sweet harmonies! Maybe Bob's lead vocals are just a little unpolished. No matter, because it was a sizable hit in reggae circles and let the Wailers' fans know they were back in business.

'Stop That Train' dates from the same session, which took place on May 5th. Peter sings lead on that one and also played guitar. Again, he expresses solidarity with Jamaica's ghetto people.

"Some living big, but most are living small," he sings. "They can't even find no food at all..." 'Stop That Train' will become the Wailers' second single for Beverley's, and is one of four songs to feature Peter on lead vocals. This is a major departure, since Bunny sang lead on the majority of tracks they recorded during Bob's absence. It implies that Peter was rapidly growing in confidence, and the other two recognised this. He puts in a stirring performance on the American Civil Rights anthem 'Go Tell It On The Mountain', which Johnny Nash had recently covered on his album 'Prince Of Peace'. Peter, Paul & Mary's version was also popular at the time although many still associated it with Fannie Mae Hamer of the Mississippi Freedom Democratic Party, who'd sang it as a protest against Lyndon Johnson's presidential nomination. The sight of this brave woman, surrounded by Southern blacks singing 'Go Tell It On The Mountain' in the streets outside the Democrats' convention hall had left a profound impression on television viewers across America, and it would be nice to think this served to inspire the Wailers' interpretation.

Whilst Jimmy Norman wrote 'Soon Come', Peter makes it his own. Although a love song – or at least written about pursuit of a girl – it's anything but romantic. "I don't like hanging round or to be pushed around," he warns, and without even a hint of pleading. He'll revisit both 'Soon Come' and 'Can't You See' in years to come, after signing for the Rolling Stones' label. The first time he sang 'Can't You See' was at Studio One, with Rita singing backing vocals. This Beverley's version is infinitely better and has a West Coast feel. It's the closest the Wailers have come to sounding like a late sixties' rock band, and it's a shame that no one thought to promote it for that market, rather than leave it stranded on a reggae set. Bunny didn't contribute any songs to the Beverley's sessions, despite having written tracks in jail like 'Battering Down Sentence'. Without him the Wailers had sounded weak, but he'd come back and continued to sing those wonderful harmonies. Whenever Bob and Peter sang together, it made the Wailers sound completely different. Their voices just didn't gell for some reason. It was Bunny's harmonies that provided the Wailers' signature sound, back in the days when they were a vocal trio.

Bob wrote 'Cheer Up' after the frustrations they'd all been through. The intention was to rejuvenate them, and keep the band going. It's a feel good tune – a forerunner of songs like 'Trench Town Rock' and 'Lively Up Yourself', whilst 'Back Out' was inspired by a schoolboy's cheeky remarks. ("Mistress Martin, yah so never sweet like ah yah so…") 'Caution', with Alva Lewis on guitar, boasts some complex harmonies and a rollicking rhythm that stands out from everything else on the album. It could easily pass for a soul track – an impression strengthened by Bob's delivery, and those James Brown-like exhortations of "crazy mother *funker*." (Bunny says the Wailers didn't have to resort to cursing, and that it was only Peter who swore.) The lyrics of 'Caution' tell of a journey, and possibly that of the black race. "Black soul is black as jet. Caution, the road is hot," he warns. "Said you got to do better than that... Don't want to see you on the ground brothers."

Whilst they were wary at first of putting themselves in the hands of another producer and being exploited, the Wailers sound rejuvenated.

"We didn't worry about milk that was spilt," said Bunny. "We just dismissed that. We called that 'paying the dues.' That's how we used to treat it. What happened with Coxsone and Planno, we just put it behind us. We never let it worry us. We were always ready to start again. All that was part of the growing." You can hear the rebirth in their singing, and also the lyrics of another Bob Marley composition, 'Soul Captives,' which blends righteous optimism with inventive use of doo-wop style harmonies. "Now's the time when man must be free, no more burden and pain," they promise. It's as if they're reminding themselves of better days ahead, except their trials and tribulations aren't over yet, not by a long way.

After recording enough material for an album (two further tracks, 'Sophisticated Psychedelication' and 'Baby, Baby Come Home', weren't used), the Wailers left Kong to deal with post-production. They hadn't chosen a title for the album but assumed it would be called 'Cheer Up,' 'Caution,' or at least named after one of the tracks. When they heard he was thinking of calling it 'Best Of The Wailers' – maybe because he sensed it was the only album he was going to get with them – they immediately went to confront him about it, and were assured this wasn't the case. You can imagine how angry they were when it came out, because all three Wailers had been present when Kong denied giving it that title. Bunny warned him that calling it "Best Of" meant it would be the last Wailers' music he'd ever hear, since there was better to come. As it happened, the album wasn't released in Jamaica. It was only released in England and in Bunny's own words, "went back into darkness just as fast."

CHAPTER TWELVE

Living On Our Feet

The Wailers' shop wasn't on the main street but in a little lane where Joe Gibbs would later open a store, right by where the Traffic Court now stands. There was a pressing plant just around the corner and tailors, barbers, a betting shop, cooked food places and other record stores all within fifty yards radius. Wail 'N Soul 'M was small – too cramped for rehearsals certainly – and a convenient meeting place for the band members and their friends. Reggie took Family Man there after Bob heard the Uniques' 'Watch This Sound' and noticed there was something fresh and different about the bass playing. Family Man's style was weighty and melodic. 'Watch That Sound' had been the stocky youth's recording debut, closely followed by Stranger Cole's 'Bangarang'. His younger brother Carlton played drums on that one. They'd played together on several other hits since then, including Slim Smith's 'Everybody Needs Love' and 'Ain't Too Proud To Beg'. As the three Wailers greeted Reggie, Family Man settled himself in a corner from where he watched the singers pass around a chalice and talk among themselves. He saw how the others deferred to Bob, despite Peter and Bunny being strong characters in their own right. Six years earlier, he'd heard 'Simmer Down' blaring out of a jukebox and kept playing it until the other patrons pleaded with him to stop. It was the best thing he'd ever heard and now the Wailers were a few feet away. Within days he'll be in the studio with them at Randy's, and after very little rehearsal – they just ran through the chords a couple of times and took it from there. Family Man noted the Wailers' harmonies were tight and disciplined, and attributed this to Joe Higgs' training. They recorded two tracks that day and both were covers. The Wailers slowed down Junior Walker's 'Hold On To This Feeling' until it resembled a ballad and the new arrangement suited Bob and Rita's tender, soulful vocals to perfection. "We feel like one," croons Rita and she means it.

"'Hold On To That Feeling' was the first release they had after opening their record shop on Orange Street," recalls Bob Andy. "Bunny had come out of jail and the joy and the freedom of doing their own thing and of being resourceful seemed to sweep them along... I saw a fair bit of them around that time and I'd say they were upbeat. Hard times weren't new to them, so that wouldn't have been an obstacle. If anything it would be a driving force."

The other song they recorded that day was 'Black Progress' – an adaptation of James Brown's 'Say It Loud (I'm Black And Proud)' that underlined the Wailers' love of soul music, and showed the whole of Jamaica where the band's sympathies really lay. Lyrically speaking, the gloves were off and jubilantly so. There's a party atmosphere running right through the track and Bob's lead is nothing short of exultant. "Black progress. Got to get it! No matter what the cost. We've been down too long," he chants, defiantly. "We got to stop living on our knees and start living on our feet."

"Bob wasn't even singing on that track, he was rapping!" exclaims Family Man. "He was so advanced, but they were singing real tight in those days and I remember sitting there in Randy's with the engineer, listening to the playback and soaking in those good, good vibes. There was nothing like their vocals at that time. The Wailers had a unique sound and everything was moving in a positive direction because that was the time we start talking about singers and players of instruments coming together to do the works and spread the message. It was the beginning of a new chapter."

James Brown called 'Say It Loud' "one of the most perfect funk performances I ever put out" in his autobiography.

"I don't think it's any coincidence that funk and the civil rights movement found their voices about the same time. The more embedded we became in the movement, the more self-pride our music expressed. Make no mistake, I was warned by everyone I knew – friends, relatives, record people, everyone – not to do it. I was repeatedly told that if I just kept my cool, which I took to mean just continuing to stay in my benign, soul-tinged, polite "black face," I would always be rich and famous and allowed to stay on Whitey's Easy Street for as long as I wanted. 'No way,' I told them. The time had come to paint it *real*, no matter the price. From now on there was going to be more black pride in my music, and a more political element to my show and to my being. Now that I had earned the right to be a cultural influence, I was going to put it to good use and apply it for the good of my people."

Race was the major issue, and African-Americans were not to be denied. A year earlier, riots had had broken out coast to coast. Public disturbances occurred in over a hundred US cities, and police forces across the country reported nearly forty deaths, over three thousand injured and tens of thousands of arrests. Washington was hardest hit, after twelve thousand troops had been ordered into the city and the downtown area became engulfed in flames. As smoke filled the sky and the rioting spread to just ten blocks from the White House, James Brown appeared on television urging restraint. "Don't terrorise, organise," he told the viewers, with obvious sincerity.

Brown was a hero to many, but others found his politics confusing. The Black Panthers would accuse him of being "a capitalist pig" who "worked for the white power structure," yet he'd donated hefty cheques to the Congress of Racial Equality and H. Rap Brown Defence Fund. As he boarded a plane for the Ivory Coast's anniversary celebrations in Abidjan, Life magazine put him on the cover with the headline 'Is This The Most Important Black Man In America?' His next act was to go and entertain the troops. Shortly after his return, he began work on 'Say It Loud' which he described as, "an entirely different kind of song for me, heavily influenced as it was by the murder of Dr. Martin Luther King and my trip to Vietnam. I was eager to record a song with a message of pride aimed directly at my own people, a reminder that standing up with pride was the best way to combat any and all assaults against us, be it murder in Memphis or the defence of liberty in Vietnam. This was the real thing, a wake-up call, a rallying cry, a statement of *pride*."

He described the death of Dr. Martin Luther King as "one of the darkest hours in the history of all mankind." Dr. King had once addressed the crowds at Greenwood, Mississippi and told them, 'you *are* somebody. I want every one of you to say out loud now to yourself, 'I am somebody.' The message took root, and Brown wouldn't forget it. Crucially, the Godfather of Soul made the distinction between Black Power and black *pride* although the US government still feared the extent of his influence and began to lean on him, despite his political alliances. Brown had shared a platform with Democratic Presidential hopeful Hubert Humphrey in Watts. Humphrey, surrounded by bodyguards, was loudly booed at the event. Brown's reputation suffered as a result except he'd only given his support after Humphrey pledged to help black people start up their own businesses. As a self-made man this gesture had meant a great deal to Brown. He then found a bomb outside of his hotel room, just as he was about to record 'Say It Loud.' It turns out the bomb was only a replica, but it was a warning nevertheless.

The SNCC and Black Panthers championed 'Say It Loud' but such endorsements brought him alienation. His records disappeared off the radio, and his friends in high places melted away just as quickly as they'd appeared. The next we heard from Humphrey he was denouncing Black Power as racism, whereas to James Brown it meant black pride and black people owning businesses and having a voice in politics.

Despite all of the controversy, 'Say It Loud' remains a joyous celebration of blackness. It stayed at No. 1 on the US r & b charts for six weeks, and was also a Top 10 hit on the Billboard charts. Released within just three weeks of being recorded, it quickly implanted itself in the African-American consciousness, partly due to a rhyming slogan that people were already familiar with. Brown just crystallised the message is all. "If a man is not proud of who he is and where he comes from, he's not a man," he told an audience in Dallas. His resolve was unshakeable, and the reaction almost overwhelming at times. Black nationalism was on the rise, and many more thousands of African-Americans had registered to vote. Not too long ago Brown been visited by machine gun toting Black Panthers hustling him for money and demanding that he deliver a more confrontational message. 'Say It Loud' would be his response – a song Afrika Bambaata once described as "marking the spot when we transcended from Negro to black. A Negro to us was someone who needed to grow into a knowledge of themselves."

In the absence of Malcolm X and Dr. King, new black heroes had emerged. One of them was George Jackson, who'd been jailed for the murder of a guard at Soledad Prison in January and then gained notoriety after forming a group called the Black Guerrilla Family at San Quentin. Whilst in solitary confinement he'd studied radical politics and written two books, one of which, 'Soledad Brother: The Prison Letters Of George Jackson' became an international bestseller. He'll die in a hail of bullets the following August, during a failed escape attempt. Meanwhile his younger brother burst into a Marin County courtroom brandishing an automatic weapon, freed three black prisoners and took the judge, District Attorney and three jurors hostage whilst demanding the release of "the Soledad brothers." The judge and two of the prisoners were killed in skirmishes outside the courthouse, and political activist Angela Davis was later accused (and acquitted) of providing the weaponry. Already, the waters of black consciousness were becoming muddied. Black people weren't just the victims of white oppression but to some peoples' way of thinking, had allowed themselves to be distracted and led off course. Iceberg Slim's semi-autobiographical novel 'Pimp', published a year earlier, had provided a turning point and from now on black heroes would increasingly be portrayed as criminals, rather than educators or freedom fighters.

Football fans were celebrating yet another kind of black hero as Pele led Brazil to World Cup victory after beating Italy in the final. It would prove the most memorable campaign in the competition's history. All of Jamaica had adopted the flamboyant Brazilian team as their own and whilst players of every shade were represented in their line-up, it was Brazil's black players who the main attraction. Lady Bustamante unveiled a statue of her husband, former Jamaican Prime Minster Sir Alexander Bustamante, in Kingston's Victoria Park during that same month. Things had changed significantly since he was in power. The population of Kingston was now estimated at 625,000, and 150,000 of them were unemployed. These people were excluded from even working-class existence since the majority of them were unskilled, and probably never would find a job. Instead, they were forced to live by their wits and survive as best they could.

During their next session, the Wailers recorded 'Feel Alright'. The sound is much darker than Beverley's and the mood sombre, despite Bob's vocal assertions to the contrary. Peter plays organ, whilst Bunny contributes piano. Family Man would later issue an overdubbed version, except it's hard to escape the feeling that it was an experiment barely worth saving. 'Rhythm' dates from around the same time and was recorded at JBC. Studio time there was cheaper than at Randy's or Dynamic, although the sound quality wasn't as good. 'Rhythm' is an instrumental featuring Bunny on guitar, Peter on piano, Hugh Malcolm on drums, Lloyd Brevette on bass and Ras Michael on percussion. It's a little ramshackle, and originally intended for Bunny's song 'Homeward Bound'.

Bob and the Barrett brothers would be back for two songs recorded at Randy's in the summer of 1970. 'Trouble On The Road Again' will be one of the last releases on Wail 'N Soul 'M, and is chanted over a deep, sinuous rhythm. The urgency in Bob's vocals and his doom-laden lyrics create a mood of dark foreboding, lightened only by Bunny's harmonies and what Family Man describes as a "scrub guitar." Adventurous as ever, Peter's found a fast, rhythmic style of playing derived from country and western and which in due course, will become an integral part of his own musical expression. The other song they recorded at that same session was 'Comma Comma', with Bob again singing lead. Whilst the lyrics are simplistic, the chorus is bright as a new pin and we're left to wonder what this song would have sounded like had Leslie Kong been in charge of production. As it is, Johnny Nash will deliver the more polished version and not for the first time, the Wailers are left counting the cost of going it alone.

Peter's thought to have recorded a number of solo tracks around this same time, including 'Sclassie Serenade', 'Crimson Pirate', 'Moon Dust' and 'Green Duck'. These early reggae organ instrumentals were issued as singles on the Escort, Bullet, Unity and Jackpot labels in the UK. Some are definitely Bunny Lee productions, although Peter will later tell one interviewer they arose spontaneously as a result of him playing along to pre-recorded rhythm tracks. He and the Barrett brothers played on a few sessions together. They'd been laying tracks for Lee "Scratch" Perry, who renamed them the Upsetters. He'd even taken them to

England the previous November, after 'Return Of Django' had reached the dizzy heights of No. 5 in the national charts. The track was essentially a vehicle for Jamaican sax player Val Bennett, who was devastated by not getting the credit for it and then missing out on the tour. Bennett hadn't travelled because Perry chose to take his girlfriend with him instead. Apparently Scratch hadn't liked how Jackie Jackson and Hux Brown had taken "his" sound and given it to rival producers and so after Reggie had introduced him to the Hippy Boys, he decided to let them promote 'Return Of Django' instead, even though they hadn't played on it! Despite him being the headliner, Perry's appearances with the group proved fitful. He'd been busy in other areas though. After licensing the 'Return Of Django' album to Trojan he collected his advance and bought a new Jaguar, which he arranged to have shipped back to Jamaica. He then left the Upsetters stranded in London with no money and no return tickets. They'd been forced to hustle rhythm tracks for their airfares, and wouldn't get back to Jamaica until the beginning of February 1970. A cooling-off period followed and whilst they would continue playing sessions for him, they'll be more wary of him in future.

Scratch's behaviour wasn't exactly unusual by Jamaican standards. The Hippy Boys' other major hit that autumn was 'Liquidator', which they'd recorded for singer Tony Scott. He then sold the rhythm track to insurance salesman-turned record producer Harry "J" Johnson, who got Winston Wright to overdub that distinctive organ melody over the top. Johnson then licensed the track to Trojan and 'Liquidator' duly spent five months on the UK charts, peaking at No. 9 that October. Tony Scott had no further claims on it of course, having sold the rights for a pittance, and the band members hadn't been paid in the first place!

By the summer of 1970, Perry was specialising in instrumentals after having decided that singers were more troublesome than musicians. The exceptions included Junior Byles and Dave Barker, whose 'Prisoner Of Love' was a current Trojan bestseller. Another of Perry's releases, the Untouchables' 'Tighten Up', will lend its name to a compilation series on Trojan whilst the Upsetters' 'Eastwood Rides Again' was a riot of syncopated rhythms, and augmented by Scratch's innovative production techniques. He was the master of gimmicks at this stage of his career, drawing inspiration from spaghetti westerns, TV doctor series, horror films and anything else that happened to seize his vivid imagination. Dressed to kill in fashionable velvet, he cut a dash on the downtown scene and his shop at 36 Charles Street was a popular meeting place for musicians, including the Barrett brothers.

"That was the Upsetter record shop, on the corner of Beeston Street and Luke Lane, and then on the corner opposite was a bar called the Green Door Saloon," says Family Man. "Scratch was driving one of them Jaguar cars from England at the time, and that was green also. Then behind the record shop, we have the rehearsal room. It was once a woodwork shop but they move out and Lee Perry leased or rented the whole scene, so we just set up the equipment in there. After that we were always round there, jamming and feeling good."

Scratch had worked with the Wailers at Studio One, and produced Peter and U Roy's 'Earth's Rightful Ruler' the previous summer. The Wailers started recording with him in August, just as the news surfaced that car rental firm Hertz had applied to the Jamaican Supreme Court in a bid to recover monies owed by Johnny Nash ($1,257. 40 to be precise.) Perry has claimed that Bob was ready to leave the Wailers and pursue a solo career at this point. He's on record as saying that Marley came to audition for him, sang 'My Cup' and then Perry himself suggested he bring back Peter and Bunny. This seems highly unlikely since the Barrett brothers were already playing sessions with him, and Bunny Lee was friends and benefactor to all parties.

"Bob wanted me and them to work, but my stable was full at that time," Bunny recalls. "I had John Holt, Delroy Wilson, Slim Smith and Pat Kelly, you name them. I had the cream of the crop and Lee Perry and myself used to move good so I suggest they work with him and I hear Bob say, 'Boy, me nah want to do nothing with Chicken Scratch.' That was because Scratch used to work with Coxsone, but Scratch is a very good producer. I took £500 from Pama and give it to Scratch so he could start up his own business, because Scratch and myself was at West Indies Records and they fire him, but I make him stay on and give him some studio time. I think it was Roy Shirley make WIRL fire him, because he said, 'Boy, every time I do anything here Scratch carry it to Coxsone so he can do it over.'"

Scratch may have been short of stature but he was no shrinking violet, which is perhaps just one of the reasons why he and Bob clicked. He'd produced several hits for Joe Gibbs, including 'I Am The Upsetter', which they'd written about Coxsone. Their alliance wouldn't last long before Perry again turned rancorous and unleashed 'People Funny Boy,' which was a scathing attack on Gibbs! Scratch was a firebrand, but he'd also acquired knowledge of how the business worked. Distributors (many of them from overseas) would come to Kingston during mid-week, buying up records for export and looking for licensing opportunities. The majority of producers wouldn't know how popular the music was in other territories and so they'd appoint someone like Bunny Lee to represent them. He'd then facilitate deals and see that everyone benefitted in some way. He was Perry's main teacher in this respect, but had more of a conscience. No one played by the rules in those days, but at least Bunny Lee made sure everyone enjoyed a share of the proceeds. That said, the Wailers remembered how Scratch had been Coxsone's right-hand man at Brentford Road, and they respected his abilities. He was a few years older than them, and more experienced. He also had plenty of tricks up his sleeve; knew what it took for a song to hit and was skilled at promotion. That's why the Wailers went into partnership with him, so they could concentrate on music and leave him to take care of the rest. Bunny would subsequently claim that, "people just have him as a comedian within the business," although they may have been referring to Perry's limited abilities as a vocalist! Back then, Scratch lacked the talent to succeed as an artist, and yet he had the drive and determination to make something of himself – hence Bunny's admittance that, "even though he wasn't recording or playing an instrument, his name was being called."

"Man, Scratch was dressing everybody down because he'd wear some green velvet trousers and black high heeled boots, stuff like that... He was living the life, I tell you!" says Dave Barker. "I remember this one night Glen and I were walking past Randy's studio when his Jaguar stopped outside, the doors flew open and

I couldn't believe how many people came from out of that car! They all ran upstairs to the studio and so Glen and I decided to follow them. When the session started I found the darkest spot in the studio and sat on the floor by myself. Busty Brown was there, trying to voice the 'Slip Away' rhythm and Scratch got vexed. He started cussing and carrying on and so Glen said, 'try Dave man.' The Upsetters were in the studio and the booze and the spliffs had been flowing so I walked up to the microphone and Scratch couldn't believe his ears! Scratch got crazy! His sadness suddenly changed to joy and my career start from there. That night we jump in his car and go to a few clubs because that's how he would do it back then. He'd give the DJs in the clubs his records and then watch for when people got up from their seats and danced."

Scratch was up for going to clubs and drinking with the DJs, whereas the Wailers were Rastas and had a very different outlook. They had no wish to get involved personally, but recognised Perry's usefulness in that regard since he loved to be on the scene and wheel and deal. According to Bunny, Scratch hadn't produced anything of real substance by then, and wouldn't do so until the Wailers committed to working with him. "Even until now, those records don't really matter," he sneered. "You couldn't relate to them and they didn't really make any mark. I'm talking about the early ones with the Upsetters, the Hippy Boys... They were mostly instrumentals and didn't really make it but he knew how to get them sold, get them played and all that kind of stuff, so we said, 'Okay, let's have some of that. Let's record and as far as studio time is concerned, everybody understands that because we grant Randy's favour, he grants us favour in return. He won't run us down for money, and so let's go in and start working."

Before starting the sessions, they sat down with Scratch and talked about how things were going to work between them. They didn't need each other, but would fare better by working together and so they decided to split everything right down the middle. None of this was put in writing, yet both parties had come a long way and been exploited by the same person. There was therefore no reason for them to cheat on one another.

"That's how we really started this project with Scratch," says Bunny. "It wasn't a money thing, just a fifty-fifty partnership, and what came off that was to be split between us. Wailers would take fifty percent and share that among themselves; Scratch would take his fifty percent and do whatever he's doing."

Their first session for Scratch took place at Dynamic and yielded 'My Cup', voiced over a bubbling Upsetters' rhythm and with Dave Barker helping out on harmonies. It was the Wailers' second James Brown cover within a matter of months, only this time they dug a little deeper for a tune that's been described as "James Brown's least remembered hit of 1968," namely 'I Guess I'll Have To Cry, Cry, Cry'. Whilst lacking the raucous energy of 'Black Progress,' it's something new. Bob is doing his utmost to reinvent himself as a soul singer, and yet the rhythm is unmistakably Jamaican. "Rannie Bop" Williams filled in for Hux Brown on guitar and Lloyd Parks played bass on the Wailers' second outing for Perry, 'Try Me (AKA I've Got The Action)' but that irrepressible joie de vivre Family Man brings to the Upsetters' sound is absent.

A month or so later they would cut 'Small Axe', with Jackie

Jackson replacing Lloyd Parks on bass. They'll have a couple of attempts in getting it right before finally delivering a track capable of standing alongside the best of their Beverley's output. In a bid to monopolise the local record industry, Coxsone, Duke Reid and Federal had joined together to form "the Big Three." Peter said if they're called "the Big T'ree" (Jamaicans often drop the letter "H"), then the Wailers must be a small axe – hence the lyrics, "If you are a big tree, let me tell you, we are a small axe. Ready to cut you down..." The song opens with a phrase lifted from the Bible, contrasting the acts of those "working iniquity," with the everlasting goodness of Jah. Not for the first time, the Wailers portray themselves as righteous underdogs, battling against greed and injustice. Echoes of Ecclesiastes 10 and Psalm 52 underpin their war cry, which everyone sensed was rather special.

"I'll always remember the night we went into Randy's and they did 'Small Axe'," says Dave Barker. "After they finished, Bob looked up at the ceiling and started talking. He said, 'I know right now nobody want to know of Bob Marley and nobody want to know of the Wailers but mark my words, a time will come when the whole world shall know of Bob Marley and the Wailers' and so said, so done. You know something? He never took his eyes off the ceiling when he was saying that. It was like he was in a trance."

According to the late Clancy Eccles, Scratch wrote the lyrics of 'Small Axe' whilst sat on the WC at the Green Door Salon. Two hours later, he emerged with them written on toilet paper. It's a good story, except Bunny claims Perry played no part in the writing of 'Small Axe'. He says it was Peter's idea, although Bob wrote it. In fact Bunny disputes Perry ever wrote anything for or with Bob Marley, period.

"You see Bob Marley is a selfish writer," he says knowingly. "Only the Wailers can write with Bob Marley and only Peter or I can suggest or say to Bob, 'Put this in your song.' Bob was very funny about that. You can't be around him when him deal with singing or when we're rehearsing, and when him write a song he won't tolerate people around him. He don't want them to hear what him doing, and him don't want any man to peep up them mouth. He was very sensitive like that, so him don't want nobody to tell him nothing. It's only the three of we work together, and then as lyrics come up we can say, 'Try this or try that.'"

There's an alternate cut of 'Small Axe' that's slightly slower. This is presumably the first version. Scratch released it anyway, because Bunny says he cared more for money than the Wailers' reputation. The second, hit version wasn't released until early 1971 in the UK, and wouldn't be included on either of the Wailers' albums for Perry. This is surprising, as Scratch was always searching for a No. 1 record and whilst Bunny may disagree, others have testified that he would often pass on ideas for lyrics or songs to Bob, who was just as keen. It was a creative period for both parties, and a lot of good songs would result from it. Bunny however, insists that Scratch never wrote songs, but would just come up with sketchy ideas and maybe the odd line here and there. He says it was left to the Wailers themselves to construct the songs, work out the arrangements and create the harmonies, before rehearsing them until they knew every note and nuance. Bob apparently wrote in fits and starts. He would jot down phrases as they came to him, and then weave the pieces together at a later stage. He played his guitar a lot too, since he never knew when he might stumble across something of interest. No one had portable tape recorders in those days and Bob couldn't write music, so he devised his own method of storing fragments of melodies and lyrics. He'd rarely finish a song before starting another and often had several in varying stages of completion, which he'd return to as the mood took him. Bunny likens him to "a writing machine" and says the inspiration never stopped.

According to him, Scratch would just walk into a session with nothing prepared – no ideas "or even principles." Bunny says he was incapable of directing the musicians or making suggestions but whenever the musicians hit upon something good, then he'd make lots of noise. In Bunny's estimation Scratch relied on vibes and the inventiveness of his musicians, and wouldn't have had a clue whether an instrument was in tune or not.

Clive Chin disagrees, and claims that Scratch was "very innovative. I saw that man literally lie down on the floor of the studio when he couldn't get the sound he wanted. He *demanded* what he wanted. He didn't have to write scores for the musicians. He wasn't that well schooled musically but he would know what he wanted, and he wouldn't stop until he got it. He would actually make signs to let them know what he wanted them to do. He'd dance in front of them, and make faces and sounds in front of them..."

"Lee Perry was the best producer I ever worked with," adds Junior Dan. "Most of the other producers would just come into the studio, put their tape on the machine, sit down and have a chat with the engineer while we were in the studio working but

Scratch wasn't like that. He'd be in the studio and give you a little time to come up with something then once he got an idea, he'd work with you and get it done. Because of that I'd call him the best producer. As a matter of fact he'd use body language to show you how the beat should go. He'd stand in front of you when showing you a bass line and demonstrate what he wanted by twisting his body up and things like that. He helped the singers a lot too because even Bob Marley, he was singing like Lee Perry at one stage. I know that to be true because there are some songs we recorded with Scratch as demos and then he'd go for Bob and have him pattern what he'd sang on there. Lee Perry would direct him like that. I saw that and I know that happened."

Family Man calls Scratch "creative" and acknowledges that he'd write lyrics, as well as involving himself with the music more than other producers. "He'd come around and start jumping up and down, getting excited, and making everything lively," he says. "He'd encourage us to be bold and say to us, 'I know you can do it, so just give it your touch' and we would, every time! But that vibe we had as Hippy Boys, he never knew it could exist before he heard us, because we played music differently from everybody else. It's just that as soon as he heard it, he knew straightaway we were the right band for what he wanted."

Clive Chin recalls that the Wailers' sessions with Perry took a little time to get going but that when everything eventually clicked, the atmosphere in the studio was electrifying. Bob would be there in his patchwork denim flares, whilst Peter wore brightly patterned trousers and paisley shirts. Their dress sense, like their music, was an amalgamation of African-American black pride and rude boy cool, mixed with a hint of hippy decadence. None of them had dreadlocks yet, Bob having cut his hair some months earlier.

"After Bob trim his locks I was teasing him but he say, 'Striker, I'm a soul rebel now,'" says Bunny Lee. Bob and Bunny played for an amateur football team called Soul Rebels, and had already immortalised the name in song. The tracks that flowed from the band during this period are truly memorable, but then conditions were favourable by comparison to what they'd endured in the past. Their records were selling, they had money to buy decent food and herbs, and Scratch was being industrious on their behalf. All the Wailers needed to concentrate on was making music, since they weren't even doing stage shows at the time.

From September onwards, they'll slip through the unmarked door at Randy's, walk down the narrow corridor and climb the stairs to voice the majority of songs on their next album. The tracks laid that night will prompt one studio visitor to declare them "the greatest group in the world!" Soon the album will be completed with room to spare since other songs were shelved, including 'Shocks Of Mighty'. Bob and Lee Perry indulge in a spot of call and response on that one, as they run through fairly pedestrian dance lyrics. A later cut, re-titled 'Soul Almighty' omits Perry and asks, "don't you know we've got the rhythm?" The answer has to be a resounding 'Yes!' The Upsetters have that soul feel the Wailers wanted to hear in their music. You can hear it in 'It's Alright' and a pulsating 'Rebel's Hop', which is an updated 'Rude Boy', mixed with a cut of the Temptations' 'Cloud Nine'. Scratch always thought they could better their earlier versions of songs – maybe so he could put his own mark on them – but the Wailers were reluctant to revisit past glories. They wanted to do music that was progressive, hence their keen interest in what the Temptations were doing. Under producer Norman Whitfield, the Tempts had radically updated their sound on tracks like 'Ball Of Confusion' and 'Can't Get Next To You'. The impact was immediate, and other soul acts soon followed suit. Edwin Starr's 'War' had as much raw power as any rock track, whilst Marvin Gaye had wrestled free from the constraints of being a ladies' man and was writing perceptive, thought-provoking material such as 'Abraham, Martin And John'. The Jackson Five, with 'I Want You Back' and 'I'll Be There', were soul music's latest sensations although Motown hadn't finished with aching ballads just yet, as demonstrated by Smokey Robinson's bestselling 'Tears Of A Clown'. And of course, Sly & The Family Stone and James Brown weren't just laying the foundations of funk, but redefining the very concept of rhythm-based black music. At the same time all this was happening, two of the Wailers' former colleagues at Studio One – Bob Andy and Marcia Griffiths – were riding high in the UK charts with a reggae cover of Nina Simone's 'Young, Gifted And Black'.

'Rebel's Hop' could well have joined them, except it wasn't issued as a single and the Wailers' thoughts had turned towards exploring their Jamaican roots once more. 'Jah Is Mighty' is another Biblically inspired parable, and with Bob again cast in the role of an outlaw. Peter and Bunny's harmonies are so high-pitched, you can imagine them dissolving into laughter after they'd finished. Some of the same verses reappear in 'Corner Stone' on which they promise, "The stone that the builder refuse will always be the head cornerstone." On that version, the meaning's changed around. That line now refers to a spurned lover, but it could easily refer to the Wailers themselves. 'No Water' finds Bob lying in bed, thirsting for his woman's love, and Peter and Bunny's contributions again take doo-wop harmonising to a different level. As on 'Reaction' and 'Soul Rebel', they're not just repeating Bob's lines, but improvising with rare abandon and if words don't fit, then they'll use other sounds instead. These last two songs are both shantytown anthems. 'Reaction' is a darkly veiled threat to the authorities, with Bob warning that for every action, there are consequences. 'Soul Rebel', along with an alternative cut called 'Run For Cover' are updated versions of a track they recorded for Danny Sims, except it's now transformed into a shuffle and invested with the Wailers' very own brand of Jamaican soul power. The former will lend its name to the Wailers' first album with Scratch – a set that'll also include two songs written and sung by Peter, whose more direct approach can be heard on '400 Years' and 'No Sympathy'.

The latter is an expression of pure melancholy, conceived during a darkening of the spirit when all seems lost and friends are nowhere to be seen. It takes honesty to write songs as revealing as this, whilst '400 Years' is a scathing indictment of post-colonialism on which Peter rejects victimhood, despite lamenting how after "four hundred years of the same philosophy, black people still can't see."

Esther Anderson has likened Peter to John Lennon, who is renowned for being the most political and outspoken member of the Beatles. The militancy of '400 Years' and confessional nature of 'No Sympathy' certainly form parallels with Lennon's own approach since each saw themselves as a message bearer, and both provided the rhythmic driving force to their band's musical output. Scratch knew this, which is why he included an instrumental cut of '400 Years' – featuring Peter's slashing rhythm guitar, and that he'd cheekily re-titled 'My Sympathy' – on the 'Soul Rebel' album. This would be his final act before handing the tapes to Glen Adams, who flew up to London and gave them to Trojan Records for mastering.

CHAPTER THIRTEEN

Shocks Of Mighty

Trojan Records issued 'Soul Rebels' – credited to Bob Marley and the Wailers – in a sleeve depicting a young black woman with bared breasts, dressed in fatigues and cradling an automatic rifle. The Wailers knew this album was coming. They'd helped choose the tracks and given Scratch the go-ahead to release them but the front cover photo was a major surprise and really upset them. Citing how it wasn't relevant to their music or their cause, they regarded it as an affront to their character and Rastafarian beliefs. The only saving grace was a picture of them on the back, stood on a rock by the shoreline and dressed in shirts designed by Jean Watt. Peter, resplendent in bobble hat, African print top and kung fu slippers, is the only Wailer facing the camera and what he made of the line, "all songs written by Bob Marley" doesn't bear thinking about.

Trojan Records were riding the crest of a wave after so many crossover reggae hits but only Desmond Dekker – who'd followed 'Israelites' and '007 (Shanty Town)' with 'You Can Get It If You Really Want It' – invested his songs with any kind of meaningful lyrical content. The Wailers' chances of making it in England were therefore slim. British pop audiences were still in love with Caribbean music and especially once the weather improved, yet they seemed more attuned to the smoother strains of Horace Faith's 'Black Pearl' and Jimmy Cliff's 'Wild World' than anything more radical, and they liked novelty records even more. 1970 had opened with Rolf Harris' 'Two Little Boys' at No. 1 and after embracing Lee Marvin's 'Wand'rin' Star', it'll end with Clive Dunn's 'Grandad' in top slot. To quote Shawn Levy, "1970 was as rotten a year as any England had ever experienced" and whilst he wasn't just referring to the nation's pop music, the description still holds true. The popularity of these novelty records was due to sales at Woolworth's – a chain store that just happened to supply the BBC with most of their chart returns. Woolworth's customers were the reason country songs by Kenny Rogers, Glen Campbell, B. J Thomas and Bobbie Gentry were so popular, and they certainly had a lot to do with the notion that Mungo Jerry's 'In The Summertime' and Bobby Bloom's 'Montego Bay' were somehow reggae songs. Jamaican audiences knew better, as songs by Alton Ellis, Ken Boothe ('Freedom Street'), John Holt, the Melodians and Delano Stewart battled U Roy for chart supremacy. For weeks, U Roy held the top three places with songs grafted onto rocksteady hits from a few years back. Jamaicans loved sentiment too, but only when spiced with something as fresh and exciting as "toasting." U Roy's runaway success will open the doors for fellow dee-jays such as Dennis Alcapone, I Roy and Big Youth, who each had their own distinct style and original catchphrases. Singer Carl Dawkins also managed several hits that year. Scratch took him into the studio during September and came out with a terrific version of Freddie McKay's 'Picture On The Wall' and the Temptations' 'Cloud Nine', featuring the Wailers on harmonies. Working with Scratch revived the Wailers' memories of being at Studio One, and the camaraderie they'd occasionally shared with other artists. All three Wailers backed Glen Adams on 'Never Had A Dream,' and

Peter played guitar and melodica on a couple of Junior Byles' songs for Upsetter, including cuts of 'A Place Called Africa.' Two further collaborations will appear before the year's end and one of them, Dave Barker's 'Don't Let The Sun Catch You Crying', even took the singer himself by surprise.

"What happened was, I went by Scratch's place one evening with this album by Jose Feliciano, which had 'Don't Let The Sun Catch You Crying' on it," he recalls. "I played that song over and over and said to Scratch I'd like to do it so he went in the studio with some musicians to lay the track. A few days later I went to voice it, slipped on the headphones and was amazed to hear the Wailers' voices doing harmonies. Scratch had never said a thing and I was so thrilled! I sang the song and the harmonies almost made me lose concentration at times they were so beautiful and sweet. Man, I was thinking these guys sounded like angels!

"Scratch then wrote 'What A Confusion' for the Wailers but for some reason when they went in the studio to record it, Bob Marley and Peter Tosh refused to do it. I don't know why but they said, 'No man, we nah do it.' Scratch then turned to me and asked if I'd like to try it and I said, 'sure.' This was in Randy's and so Scratch got Errol T to run the track, and gave me the words on a piece of paper. He hummed the melody to me two or three times, then I went around the microphone and started singing, I look round and there's Bunny Wailer coming up next to me and doing the harmony. I was really surprised because when Bunny sings it's just magic and he had a lovely falsetto."

Little Roy, fresh from his success with 'Bongo Nyah', could testify to that. The first copies of he and Ewan Gardiner's 'Don't Cross The Nation' were even credited to Bob Marley and the Wailers before Scratch got the wording right.

"'Don't Cross The Nation' was from 1970," he confirms. "Peter Tosh played guitar and Bunny Wailer played the kette drum. Bob was in the studio too. This was at Randy's the night Bunny Wailer sang 'Dreamland'. Those two songs and Junior Byles' 'A Place Called Africa' were all recorded at the same session. Bunny Wailer was living on Warminster Avenue near Scratch and myself in Washington Gardens at the time. He used to be over by Marcia Griffiths' house a lot. At that time Marcia and Bob Andy were together but Bunny was always there, and he would come and play ball with us sometimes. We wouldn't see too much of Peter Touch in those days, but he and Bob Marley were the stars of the Wailers and I can't really differentiate between them really."

Little Roy's friend Ewan Gardiner will reappear on the flipside of the Wailers' 'Mr. Chatterbox' with a song called 'Goodnight My Love'. Recorded as the rock world reeled over the deaths of Jimi Hendrix and Janis Joplin, 'Mr. Chatterbox' is an update of the Wailers' 'Mr. Talkative,' which Bob voiced for Bunny Lee in a rare fit of pique about Niney The Observer. Legend has it that Niney borrowed the arrangements of a Wailers' tune for his first solo hit 'Blood And Fire' and was rewarded with a good beating but Bunny Wailer disputes this and says Niney wasn't worth the effort. Bob's vocal suggests that he was riled though. "Always carry news all over the place. Mr. Chatterbox, you are a big disgrace," he sings, before threatening to "batter him around" and imitating the blows with his mouth.

Niney, Glen Adams and Reggie all lived in the same Washington Gardens' rooming house. The two Barrett brothers would visit them there, play music and talk long into the night. Family Man and Carly both played on 'Mr. Chatterbox' which is a ska track, and a throwback to an earlier style of production that had definitely run its course by then. It was time for something else, and that better suited the mood of the times.

"Right after rocksteady, there was a period where the music was really chopping," explains Clive Chin. "That was down to the Hippy Boys, and virtually everything that came out was real up-tempo. After a while, some of us younger guys felt there had to be a change and so we started to experiment with something a bit different. Instead of all those fast beats we went for a more down-tempo sound, based around two chords. That was the beginning of the rebel era and it was more of a Jamaican sound, because we began to get away from some of that American soul influence."

Family Man wasn't too literate and so rather than engage in intellectual debate, he searched for the notes and a style of playing that would bring the Wailers' lyrics to life. Musicians like him knew that Rasta songs were unlikely to get much airplay, except they now had other objectives in mind.

"We didn't want to play for high society people anymore," states Junior Dan. "We wanted to play for the people. We started to get into Rasta philosophy more than this 'baby I love you' business. We'd see people on the streets suffering from lack of food and so we started to sing about that instead, but in more of an informative fashion than outright protest. We were different from our parents' generation, who were coming from a colonial perspective so we started to create our own outlook and instead of being romantic, the music started to get more revolutionary. There was a yard just round the corner from Orange Street where musicians like myself would hang out, smoke from a chalice and rehearse. That's where we started to develop music that reflected more of what was happening around us, because we were downtown and could see what was going on. In the early days it was mainly uptown business people who had shops there, but then it started getting rougher and rougher because there would be shootings and all kinds of stuff going on across in the park by North Parade and in the lanes round about. We musicians were protected from a lot of that at first. If we were coming down the street and there was shooting going on, they'd stop because street people respected us. We'd just put our hands up and pass through but Clancy Eccles, Phil Pratt, Winston Riley and Prince Buster, they all had places on Orange Street..."

One of the yards where Junior and other musicians would hang out was Busy's. This was behind Lee Perry's Green Door Salon, on the corner of Charles Street and Matches Lane. There were at least two other such places in the downtown area, including a yard on Matches Lane called Gong's where they could buy herb and smoke a chalice in-between sessions. The police and soldiers would come there, but not to arrest people. They knew the musicians weren't criminals, but were waiting for producers on their way to play sessions at Randy's, which was the focal point of Jamaica's music scene at that point.

That's where Scratch took the Soul Syndicate to record the original rhythm used for 'Duppy Conqueror' – a song that he's supposed to have co-written with Bob one day after suggesting he use the phrase, "yes me friend. Me deh pon street again." He'd talked Bob into giving these young musicians a chance after falling out with the Upsetters, who'd grown restless at how little money was coming their way. As Christmas approached, they decided to cut a track for themselves and came up with 'Clint Eastwood' – a semi-instrumental designed to counteract King Stitt's 'Lee Van Cleef', and that Family Man Barrett claims is the "first drum and bass."

Scratch released it after settling up with his star players, but not until after trying to replace them by recruiting some other (more inexperienced) musicians. Unfortunately Bob didn't like the rhythm that Soul Syndicate had come up with for 'Duppy Conqueror' and insisted that Scratch bring back the Upsetters, who'd been rehearsing the song with them in any case. Family Man says "a lot of grievance" went into that second cut of 'Duppy Conqueror.' The Upsetters were out to prove a point, and with Family Man laying down one of his characteristically mesmeric bass lines, they did.

"I witnessed he and his brother Carlton working in the studio and they were brilliant musicians," says Dave Barker. "They'd play a few notes and then they'd stop to discuss certain things, like how the drum should be played and all that and then when the tape started to roll again, you couldn't believe the sound you were hearing! What we all gave back then, we gave from the heart. We were living for the moment really."

'Duppy Conqueror' was an immediate hit went released on 45 in Jamaica. It was hailed as a triumph for both Lee Perry and the Wailers, who'd risen above adversity and definitely weren't for turning. Bob's use of Biblical imagery, even as he cloaks himself in the guise of acquitted outlaw is magnificent but it's the line, 'I'm a duppy conqueror" that resonates most. Challenging the supernatural in a place so riddled with superstition as Jamaica required real courage. Duppy is the name given to an implacable spirit, and practitioners of "obeah" or black magic were greatly feared on the island. Banishing these dark forces with such swagger was just as revolutionary as promoting Rastafari, and furthered the Wailers' reputation for daring. Yet the song is joyful too and the mood lightened by cooing harmonies, some of which sound like the bird calls Peter would make back in Westmoreland, when out hunting in the woods.

The cut of 'Duppy Conqueror' that would appear on the Wailers' second album for Perry was mixed differently from the single. Bob's vocals have lost their lustre, and the track sound's more muted than when it first appeared. Just to confuse matters further, the Soul Syndicate's original rhythm will resurface behind 'Mr. Brown' – a song written and produced by Glen Adams, who got Peter to add backing vocals and then sat him down at Randy's trusty Wurlitzer for some additional organ phrases. It was Scratch who'd suggested Glen give the song to Bob, as a follow-up to 'Duppy Conqueror'. Whilst not in the same league as 'Conqueror', it still caused a stir on account of the lyrics. Back in the autumn rumours had spread like wildfire about crows perched on a wheeled coffin that had been seen careering through the countryside, 'from Mandeville to Sligoville, coffin running around..." Bunny dismisses these tales as a publicity stunt, staged by a local funeral parlour. If that's true it was a smart piece of marketing and the Wailers at least got another hit out of it.

'Duppy Conqueror' had hardly left the pressing plant before Vincent Chin began pressurising Scratch to pay his studio bills. He got Errol Thompson to ask Scratch for the money before releasing the tape, but hadn't realised just how desperate they were. Bunny reacted by reaching for a length of timber and aimed it at the hapless engineer, who ducked in the nick of time. The wood smashed against the door and splintered, so Bunny took the jagged edge and pushed it under Thompson's throat whilst warning him how this "wasn't any of Randy's business." Errol gave them the tape. The Wailers clearly weren't going to be intimidated by anyone although the group then turned their attention to Scratch and made sure he paid Randy's what they owed. Although quick to exploit others, Scratch shied away from violence, and couldn't defend himself in the same way they did. He'd learn from this incident though, and be more cautious of them in future.

As Christmas approached, he arranged a few shows to promote 'Soul Rebels.' Over three hundred people turned up at the Sombrero Club on Molynes Road, and there would be further dates in Negril before the holidays were over. The band hadn't performed in a while, and yet the shows went down a treat.

"The Wailers were very confident on stage," says Junior Dan. "They were well rehearsed and never made mistakes but if something went differently from how they'd planned it they'd quickly adjust to it, and it just became a part of their show. They were very professional and that came from being serious about what they were doing. It's like they were prepared for anything."

The Wailers would become the first Jamaican group to project a militant look on stage. They even strolled on wearing vests and no shirts, as if they'd just stepped from a ghetto sidewalk. Apart from the Sombrero, they would also play at Skateland, the Glass Bucket, Silver Slipper and VIP Club in the coming months. The latter was in the centre of Half Way Tree, near the Clocktower Plaza, where the Upsetters had also played on occasion. Family Man recalls performing at the Blinking Beacon and Green Miss on Mountain View Avenue, as well as places like the Rainbow, Flamingo Hotel and the Jonkanoo Lounge, as the Sheraton's ballroom was known.

The clientele at such places went there to drink and socialise, and weren't necessarily all that familiar with the Wailers' cultural and political aims. Most of them wouldn't have registered that Emperor Haile Selassie I had declared a state of emergency in Eritrea, where the Eritrean Liberation Front were making their presence felt, but news of this had certainly spread around the Rasta camps, together with reports of Portugal's attack on Guinea and a recent assassination attempt on the Pope. Soon, and for the first time in the island's history, a native son will head Jamaica's Roman Catholic Church but this wasn't of great concern to Rastafarians, who were far more interested in what the Ethiopian Orthodox Church represented. Emperor Haile Selassie I had reacted to Rastafarians' claims that he was the Messiah by telling Jamaica's Minister of Education, "I am a man, and man cannot worship man." In the wake of his state visit, he'd sent an Ethiopian delegation to Jamaica to teach people Amharic and introduce them to his own faith, which wouldn't be officially established on the island until 1969. The head of the Church in Jamaica was Abba Mandefro, who petitioned the Jamaican government "to stop the demoralisation of Rastafarians," and demonstrated his willingness to intercede on behalf of cult members who'd been arrested or beaten by the police. Such kindnesses wouldn't go unnoticed, and may have played a role in

Bob and Peter's decision to join the Ethiopian Orthodox Church towards the end of their lives.

Once the holidays were over, the Wailers' thoughts turned back towards recording. On 'Fussing And Fighting' – a song inspired by disagreements between Scratch and Glen Adams over money – Bunny and Peter switch harmonies as Bob calls for an end to "the cheating and fighting." There's more than a hint of exasperation in his delivery, which suggests the Wailers were already tiring of Scratch's dubious business practices. 'Long, Long Winter' was originally recorded by the Impressions and possibly in tribute to the group, since lead singer Curtis Mayfield had left them, and was busily establishing himself as a solo act with songs like '(We People Who Are) Darker Than Blue,' 'Move On Up,' and 'Miss Black America.' It was the end of an era – a feeling reinforced by news that Tom Cringle's cotton tree on the Spanish Town Road, reputed to be more than two hundred years old, had suddenly collapsed without warning. It was as if a hand had reached from the skies and crushed the life out of it but then Jamaica is a land of spirits after all, and alive with Bible stories.

When Peter revisits 'Sinner Man', he conjures up visions straight out of the Old Testament. They'll be no mercy on Judgment Day as the oppressors flee for their lives, only to be met by boiling seas and melting rocks. Peter's love of wordplay is never just about humour. He's calling these people "downpressors" because that's what they do – they keep their fellow man down so they alone can reap the benefits. It was his second attempt at Nina Simone's 'Sinner Man', and his best by some distance thanks to the mocking in his voice and Family Man's loping bass line. Lee Perry would often suggest the Wailers re-record some of their

Studio One material. All three Wailers had songs they felt could be improved upon, and everyone took delight in trying to better Coxsone. The group had recorded 'Put It On' twice before but the version from early 1971 is a real gem, revolving around Peter and Bunny's tightly meshed harmonies and with Bob only interjecting here and there. They'd recently befriended Usiah "Sticky" Thompson, whose hand drums add to the sense that this song is an evocation, and contains echoes of the band members' early religious upbringings. The Wailers have now found their metier, and a sound that goes to the very heart of their own culture thanks to the Barrett brothers. Those chants of "I rule my destiny. I'm not boasting" shouldn't be taken lightly. Suitably empowered, the trio cast aside one last taboo and recorded their first-ever herb tune. Shearer's repressive drug laws were still in effect and Bunny had only been out of prison a year, yet there's no sign of apprehension. Not unless they were playing it safe by calling the song "Kaya" – a slang name for marijuana and the term given to coconut husks, which poorer Jamaicans used as mattress filling. Bob apparently wrote 'Kaya' on a trip to Hanover with Lee Perry, where they visited the producer's family. It's written in the style of a love song as Bob croons, "I'm so high, I even touch the sky, above the falling rain..." 'Kaya' was the follow-up single to 'Mr. Brown,' and their first release of 1971. It immediately registered with the downtown crowd who no doubt smiled in recognition as the music caressed their senses, and the rhythm slowly uncoiled like smoke from a high-grade ganja spliff.

On the dub, they went one step further by sucking on a chalice. An alternate cut – mainly instrumental – begins with Peter intoning, "A who that sah?' before opening the door to their dealer. Bob then scats over Peter and Bunny's harmonies, singing "ease this pain of mine, and then turn me loose..." Not every Rastafarian smokes herb (or wears their hair in dreadlocks), but those that do justify marijuana's healing properties by quoting from Genesis 1:29: "God said, I have given you every herb bearing seed which is upon the face of the earth... to you it shall be meat," it reads. According to Ennis B. Edmonds, Rastafarians value ganja "for its physical, psychological and social therapeutic powers" and regard it as a source of physical healing.

"They contend that their use of ganja, particularly in its ritual smoking, ensures perpetual health," he wrote in 'The Structure And Ethos Of Rastafari.' "Psychologically, ganja smoking is a source of illumination that gives access to inner and worldly knowledge. It's also a means of creating and celebrating communality. In this respect, the Rastafarian perspective on ganja smoking is opposite to the generally held view (in Jamaican society), which is that ganja smoking predisposes the smoker to violence."

He goes on to report that Rastafarians believe "ganja dispels gloom and fear, induces visions and heightens the feelings, creating a sensation of fellow love and peace. It also aids in dissolving the barriers and hastening the return home to the reality of Jah. In the visionary state induced by ganja smoking, Rastas come to the "I and I consciousness;" the merging of the individual with all life forces and the realisation that all life flows from the same source, and the collapse of the distance between internal and external, subject and object."

That Bob wrote the Wailers' first herb tune and not Peter is surprising. Maybe he was preoccupied. He certainly had women trouble by the sounds of it. On 'Brand New Second-hand' he's accusing some girl of being used goods. "Don't exalt your painted face girl," he warns, "because underneath that face, you're just a disgrace. You're just a brand-new second-hand..." That's Bob singing harmonies, and Peter's baritone adlibbing between verses. "You better go back round there so," he tells her at one point, and you can almost see the sneer playing around his lips as he voiced it. It's cut from similar cloth to 'Can't You See' but more vitriolic. Bunny, who's nowhere within earshot, disputes that Peter was hurt romantically and says he liked to just fool around with girls, but never got too serious.

"Peter was a hit and run guy," he assures us. "It was just a tease, and he enjoyed it. He's just commenting that you get some girls out there who seem nice and proper, but they aren't really – they're well experienced!"

Peter played guitar on that track. Keyboard duties went to a teenager from Cockburn Pen called Tyrone Downie, who'd moonlighted from King's College to play in Family Man's Youth Professionals – a bar band also featuring bass player Robbie Shakespeare. The Upsetters may have been spearheading a new chapter in Jamaican music, and yet there still wasn't enough money coming in without them playing extra sessions and club dates. In March, they backed Dave Barker at Skateland, just after 'Shocks Of Mighty' had raced up the local charts. Barker is a soulful lead singer, but his biggest hits were those where he yelps and screams, James Brown style, over funky reggae beats. 'Shocks Of Mighty' proved so popular, Scratch used the name in place of Green Door Salon but only he really profited from its success.

"I remember after doing 'Shocks Of Mighty' I'd have to walk home because I didn't have any bus fare," Dave recalls. " I lived in Franklin Town so it was quite far. I'd be walking home after say two in the morning and on a Friday or Saturday night, when you have dances all over the place. Every sound-system is playing and then all of a sudden I'd hear, 'This is upsetting...' These sound-system guys, they'd put horns up in the trees and that made the sound travel even more. It's like the songs were coming out of the sky and I'd be walking home, hearing my music being played so loud and sweet... The feeling it gave me, it was like my feet weren't touching the ground. I'd be floating. You can't believe it's you!

"Artists weren't treated fair by those early producers, but we were happy to get the chance to record. We were filled with so much music and so much warmth that was a thrill to go in the studio and be in your own world. You lived for that moment so even though we were robbed, we'd shrug it off and then when you heard your music played on the radio or in a dance like that, it lifted you up and made you feel good. It was only later the troubles start."

The Wailers' sessions for Lee Perry would continue until around Easter and their winning streak continue unabated, even allowing for 'All In One' – a medley of their hits culminating in 'Duppy Conqueror', and with an introduction by Scratch. Medleys were useful reminders of past success, but prone to sounding naff – a fate 'All In One' managed to avoid because the vocals and harmonies are so damn good. There was more backtracking on 'Dreamland', which would have made the perfect coda to their stay with Perry. Coxsone still hadn't issued the cut Bunny sang for him, but this one's definitive. Bunny's enunciation is immaculate and his adaptation of the El Tempos hit more of a complete reconstruction, rather than cover version.

Bunny again sings lead on 'Brainwashing', and his vocals are full of character. This isn't an occasion for that soaring falsetto, but it's still a command performance. His delivery's soulful and theatrical – taut in places, expansive in others as he tells a tale that's part nursery rhyme, part parable. Peter sings bass harmony and played piano on another of Bunny's songs called 'Riding High,' written about a woman who's been giving him the run-around. The rhythm sounds lop-sided and it's Bob who's noticeable by his absence this time. The three Wailers write about women in markedly different ways. Peter can be abrasive and Bunny a little detached, whereas Bob is more poetic. 'Stand Alone' is country and western in all but genre. "They you are, crying again but your loveliness won't cover your shame," he warbles, after being left with only memories.

Family Man and Peter were massive country fans, and they loved funk too. You can hear the strands intertwine on tracks like 'Memphis' – an instrumental featuring Peter's melodica. He's become more proficient since last year but Peter's best melodica performance is on 'Sun Is Shining', where it dances in and out of Bob's quasi-mystical lyrics. Members of Soul Syndicate claim to have played the languorous rhythm, although Bunny disputes this. Bob would later rename this song 'To The Rescue' and it's a work of considerable maturity, despite its simplicity. This early version would be the first single issued on the Wailers' new Tuff Gong label, which Pama Records distributed in the UK.

Bob's other classic song from spring 1971 is 'Keep On Moving', which again casts him in the role of fugitive. The authorities want to hang him for a murder he didn't commit, except there's no hint of fear in his voice – only slight weariness. Bunny and Peter each get lines for themselves, separate from their harmonies. Peter's line, "I've got two boys and woman. They're going to suffer now" lends the song immediate poignancy, whilst Bunny's adds a spiritual dimension. The vocals are mesmerising but then so too, is the Barrett brothers' groove.

"When we were with Wailers, it was strictly singing and playing instruments together, with each of us bouncing off each other," says Family Man. "Looking back, it seems like we co-produce a lot of those tracks because we'd always be discussing how each particular track should go, and what they needed to make them sound better. I was more involved than many people realise but working with the Wailers come like a thrill to me because I was always wondering what was going to come next."

'African Herbsman' was one of the last songs they recorded for Scratch. It's an adaptation of 'Indian Rope Man' by Richie Havens, who'd appeared in the Woodstock film facing a crowd half a million strong, armed with just an acoustic guitar and a handful of songs. They'd come across the song after Jubbie, who ran Scratch's record shop, discovered the 'Richard P. Havens 1983' album and played it full blast most days. The original's a fast shuffle, and Havens' lyrics a rich mix of poetry and philosophy. "Indian rope man while looking on. Tells common clay he's heavenly born. Retired layman looks on in scorn with a transplanted heart."

The Wailers slow the rhythm right down, replace "layman" with "slave man" and write new parts for Peter and Bunny. Family

Man says they changed the chorus around in honour of a soldier they called "the African herbs man" who would regularly pull up outside the Green Door Salon and sit in his jeep, smoking herb and taking in the music. Peter was very fond of him apparently. He and Bunny were growing disenchanted by this time, and may well have stopped working with Lee Perry before Bob. Neither of them feature on 'Don't Rock My Boat' (also known as 'I Like It Like That'), which has the kind of sensual rhythm that graced the best of Treasure Isle's rocksteady recordings. Bob responds with a song that reeks of sex without once resorting to cliché, and then recruits the Soulettes for a raggedy gospel number called 'Love Light'.

An important chapter in the Wailers' career has now come to a close. Perry again licensed the majority of their tracks with him to Trojan, in readiness for a UK release. The Wailers' second album for Scratch would be called 'Soul Revolution', and it's a more coherent, balanced effort than their first. The songs, all credited to Bob alone, are stronger, and even the sleeve is better. Glen Adams photographed them posing as armed revolutionaries in Lee Perry's garden, pretending to fire toy guns. They look like Caribbean desperados, styled from a mix of spaghetti westerns, Trench Town rudies and Black Power. Perry Henzell's film 'The Harder They Come' was already in production at this juncture, and captures the essence of that time. The Black Panthers' influence was also felt in the Caribbean, as Walter Rodney had discovered. David Brun Lambert thinks they embodied "a certain black American revolutionary romanticism.

"A lot of black kids from the ghetto identified with those rebels who claimed the right of their people to carry a weapon. They felt like heroes, ready to challenge the government, to fight or even die for their ideas if need be."

Black Panthers had established canteens, schools, nurseries and free clinics in American black neighbourhoods, and provided these communities with legal aid and healthcare – initiatives that were largely ignored by the press, and would later inspire many Rastafarians to attempt something similar. Leadership was crucial and yet in the wake of Dr. Martin Luther King's assassination the majority of black leaders had been rounded up, silenced, driven into exile or killed. Fear of a black uprising hung in the air amidst simmering resentment and only a few brave souls dared speak up. One of them was Nina Simone, who came out in support of a black separatist state and said black people wouldn't get their rights any other way. Such pronouncements were now rare; new freedoms seemed further away than ever and yet fear had been replaced with a newfound sense of entitlement – hence the Wailers' readiness to portray themselves as revolutionaries.

Neither of their albums for Lee Perry would sell that well. In fact they'll barely register with audiences outside of the group's small following in the UK, despite later being described as "the two most important albums to have come out of Jamaica" by film director Theo Bafaloukus. Perry mastered 'Soul Revolution' during a trip to London but decided to issue it on his own Maroon label in Jamaica, then strip off the vocals and release the instrumental tracks as 'Soul Revolution Part II.' The Wailers had no idea he'd planned to do this until Bob saw it on sale somewhere and by then it was all too late.

They were still recording for him in March, when Dave Barker left for the UK to promote he and Ansel Collins' 'Double Barrel'.

The Upsetters backed him on his farewell show at Skateland as the Wailers looked on, wondering why they hadn't been so lucky. They'd left Scratch in charge of the money whilst recording for him. Bunny says they didn't go to him for "even a penny until it mattered, so session was nice. We had everything we needed to make the music sound the way it did." That Bunny disliked Scratch isn't open to question. He claims the producer robbed them, sold the rights to their songs and left them frustrated.

"Me don't deal with them kind of people," he told Roger Steffens. "Any time me buck him up is pure kick him get, and two times me kick him down already."

He says Perry never liked how Bob always had a crowd of youths around him, and that Coxsone and the Wailers both gave him beatings on occasions – Coxsone when Scratch was running his sound-system, and the Wailers after they'd stopped recording for him. The first time they fell out with him was at the Sombrero, where bands would play every Friday night. Friday night was also when you'd hear the local hit parade on radio, and 'Duppy Conqueror' had just entered the Top 10. The Wailers were getting airplay at last, and playing stage shows again. Things were looking up and so when they saw Scratch that night, Bob merrily suggested they should have a money talk. Scratch mumbled something about how he could only pay them a royalty of ten cents per record, instead of the fifty percent they'd agreed. Bob and Peter were nonplussed but Bunny just went and sat in a corner, rolled a spliff and meditated on how the Wailers always seemed to be facing some problem or the other. In this instance, there was no point crying. They didn't have anything on paper, and would be defenceless from jibes of how they'd learnt nothing since getting ripped off by Coxsone. All these things went through Bunny's mind as he sat there. After a while, he rejoined the others and started yelling at Scratch, who told him not to interfere. That was it. Bunny punched him to the floor, spilling their drinks and sending tables and chairs flying. Bob, who was a little drunk, looked shocked, as if he couldn't understand what was happening, and the Wailers' party left soon after that.

This incident brought shame on the Wailers. A day or two later, they called in at Scratch's shop on Charles Street. They were at serious odds with him now, and everyone felt badly towards him. Bunny went up to him and demanded money, demanding that Scratch either play them what's due, or show them where the money went. Motioning towards his new bodyguard, Scratch smiled and asked Bunny if he thought he could do the same as he did at the Sombrero. This was all Bunny needed. He immediately let fly with a right hook and decked Perry, then whipped out his ratchet knife and held it against the bodyguard who stood stock still, as if frozen in fear. Other people arrived at this point, and further trouble was diverted but it would be open warfare from now on. Scratch promised to come up with the sales figures, and a meeting was arranged for later that same week.

When they returned, they walked into the office at the back of his shop and noticed the table was piled high with papers. Scratch whispered something to his girlfriend and she fetched a bottle of yellow liquid from his car, which he placed on the table next to him. Peter wasn't called "Touch" for no good reason and feeling curious about the bottle, picked it up almost absent-mindedly. Scratch immediately became uptight and yelled at him to put it down. Peter had the cap off by now and began smelling the contents, which Scratch said was acid used to cut metal stampers. Bunny realised it was meant for him, since Scratch had no reason to try and disfigure the others. He quickly grabbed Scratch and made to pour the acid over him. He was just bluffing, but wanted to know if there really was acid in the bottle. Scratch wriggled free and tumbled over four times in a frantic bid to get out the door he was so panicked. Peter let him go, then smashed the bottle on the table, which gave off lots of smoke and burnt a hole clean through the wood. A few days later, after tempers had calmed a little, they got to sit down with Perry and go through the figures. That's when Scratch showed them the invoices for records that Rita had taken. According to him Rita had taken thousands of them, which she'd then sold without any of the Wailers knowing.

This latest blow hit them hard. They'd wanted to let their funds accumulate with a view to buying a house or at least a piece of land since all three Wailers remained dependant upon relatives. Peter was still living at his auntie's house, Bob was at Aunt Viola's in Ghost Town and Bunny lived with his father in Washington Gardens. They wanted a place to live or at least congregate, and therefore hadn't asked Scratch for a penny. They'd understood that he had no money when they started out, and so hadn't asked him for an advance yet Vincent Chin had let him have studio time on credit, which meant his overheads were minimal. Ever since recruiting the Hippy Boys, Scratch had been making good money in fact – certainly more than he'd earned in the past. Bunny claims it was spent on "whoredom and foolishness" and that Scratch hadn't struck good deals in England, but settled for amounts that were too small.

Peter and Bunny felt disgraced after this incident and didn't want anyone to know about it, least of all people from Trench Town. To have Bob's wife steal from them was bad enough, but their relationship with Scratch was over. As far as Bob was concerned Scratch had been exonerated, which is why the two of them remained friends. Peter and Bunny thought otherwise, knowing that Rita could never have betrayed them without Perry's involvement. Their minds went back to another incident that had happened a few weeks earlier, after John Holt had openly mocked them for staying with Perry. Bunny Lee had bought Holt a brand-new white Ford Cortina after 'Stick By Me' topped the charts, and yet Scratch hadn't given them a penny for 'Duppy Conqueror.' Fired with a mix of anger and shame, they'd manhandled Scratch that day, whilst warning him about the consequences of betraying them. Danny Sims and Johnny Nash were back on the island, and Bob sought diversion in their company for a while. He and Peter were still signed to JAD's publishing company, and had continued to visit Russell Heights whenever they were around. Glen Adams recalled them rehearsing 'Concrete Jungle' up there before he and Bob left for the US. The reality of life back in Ghost Town after harbouring dreams of having his own place had hit Bob hard. It was at that point Johnny and Danny invited him to join them in New York and then Sweden, to help Johnny write new material. Bob will be holed up in a Stockholm suburb for two months, writing songs for the soundtrack to a film that won't stay in the cinemas a month.

CHAPTER FOURTEEN

King Street Shuffle

"No Wailer made any money out of our career together until we split," Peter would lament. "No one made a dime. Ten years of just work, and nothing. And yet we never quarrel or blame one another, never!"

Rita had been undercutting Scratch, and selling records on the cheap. Bob was mortally embarrassed by this and had walked out of that final meeting feeling dazed. Bunny went to talk with him but Bob shrugged him off, muttering something about how Rita was at least feeding his children. Bunny wasn't a father yet but Peter was and he just walked away without saying anything, nursing his frustration. The Wailers had left Scratch with all those songs and Peter guessed – correctly, as it happened – they wouldn't see any money from them, despite having given so much in return. The injustice of it all left him feeling empty inside, and wondering if he was living in a dream.

"Frustration just mad you, you start talk to yourself and walk and look up in the sky," comments Bunny, who saw that Peter now harboured resentment towards Bob. For his part, Bob swore he'd repay the money that Rita had swindled from them. Bunny said he didn't want his share, but to keep it in the business account. "Let it stay there and grow," he said, but Peter could ill afford such luxury. He was left with little alternative but to play sessions, and spent the rest of that summer recording tracks for Duke Reid, Joe Gibbs and Randy's, contributing keyboards mostly. Clive Chin says the majority of Peter's sides for Gibbs were recorded at Randy's, and the first session yielded a No. 1 reworking of 'Maga Dog' that sold 75,000 copies in just two weeks. Joe Gibbs would claim that Rita and her friend Judy Mowatt from the Gaylettes sang harmonies on 'Maga Dog', although it may have been Hortense and Cecile from the Soulettes, given Rita's recent exploits. Peter himself plays guitar, piano and organ, and transforms the ska-meets-calypso version the Wailers recorded for Coxsone into something altogether different. This new one is much slower, and set to a sinuous reggae groove. His vocals are a lot more distinct, and the raucous energy of the original now replaced by a wonderfully relaxed use of space. Several other songs will result from Peter's sessions with Gibbs including 'Black Dignity,' which urged black people to wake up from their "slumbering mentality, and come closer to reality." It's said to have been inspired by the recent Ali versus Joe Frazier fight – the so-called "Fight Of The Century" that boasted a cool $US 2.5 million in prize money. There was more at stake than money alone though. Ali had got his boxing license back a year earlier and both men were previously undefeated. One was the very symbol of black pride and the other criticised for having white management, yet Frazier won by a unanimous decision after knocking Ali down in the fifteenth round. It was Ali's first loss and he took it badly saying that, "All black people know I won," despite evidence to the contrary.

'Arise Blackman,' with Bunny on harmonies) was recorded at Randy's during a Wailers' session. It shares much in common with 'Awake Rasta' – a song that Scratch had introduced to Peter. Just as they had during Bob's previous absences, Peter and Bunny had gone into the studio in a bid to keep the Wailers' name alive. Peter did this despite having further solo success with 'Rudie's Medley' and 'Here Comes The Judge,' which speaks volumes about his allegiance to the Wailers' cause.

'Them Ha Fi Get A Beaten' dates from around the same time, and is one of his best protest songs. "Don't you wait 'til your back is against the wall," he tells the people. "Just one step to progress and I know Jah will help you all." He's addressing the common man again, and at a time when elections loomed on the horizon. This song made Peter a folk hero in Jamaica. Two months after it had followed 'Maga Dog' into the charts, Gibbs offered him $500 to record a solo album but Peter rudely declined, and would later complain that he only ever got money out of Gibbs by threatening him with violence. He and Bunny were busy with a new Wailers' venture in any case. The shop on Orange Street was too small and so they moved to a new place on King Street, close to Beeston Street and Chancery Lane. 127 King Street was L-shaped and had two entrances – one on King Street itself, and the other on Orange Street, which increased their chances of attracting passing trade.

Bob had helped make the arrangements before he left, and got a friend called Jack Wise to help out. It was Jack who painted the walls in psychedelic colours and then nailed egg boxes to the ceiling, as soundproofing. Peter and Bunny took care of the stock, pinned up a selection of posters and flyers and made sure the hi-fi system was in good working order. The Wailers called this shop (and also their new label) "Tuff Gong," although reports vary as to how they arrived at the name. Lee "Scratch" Perry and Bob's friend Alan "Skill" Cole have both claimed authorship, whilst another version of the story has them naming it "Tuff

Gang," before the Wailers disassociated themselves from any rude boy connotations.

"People say it was Scratch who name Bob Marley "Tuff Gong" but it wasn't like that," says Bunny Lee. "It came from the films, and the guy who used to hit that big cymbal before the movie start (meaning the Rank Organisation's opening credits.) Bob saw it and said, 'It tuff eh?' Someone say it called a gong, and that's how it originated right there. The gong part represented how far sound can travel, because the echo lasted so long."

The Wailers launched their new label with 'Sun Is Shining', and were delighted when it quickly sold out. Rita was now back in the picture, and would help out in the shop as Ziggy and Cedella played behind the counter. It's said the others were upset when she fired an assistant called Dudley without their consent, but there was no shortage of other willing helpers like Django, Selwyn and Johnny Lover, who was a part-time MC and toasted over cuts of 'Rock My Boat' and 'Sun Is Shining' as Tuff Gong got up and running.

The Wailers regarded these songs as their own, despite them having been recorded whilst they were with Scratch. They'd also booked the odd session for themselves before Bob had left for New York, although these tracks didn't sell very well or receive as much exposure as their hits with Scratch. Bunny reckons that's because they'd been singing more serious songs on their label. He says whilst they could always "rough up a gimmick tune" for Scratch if called upon, the Wailers' own productions were "eternal." (He also concedes they should have saved certain songs for Tuff Gong, instead of letting Scratch have them.)

They'd recorded 'Send Me That Love' at West Indies studio as their sessions for Perry drew to a close, and there's nothing else like it in their entire oeuvre. The Wailers' gospel roots always were a touchstone and they're evident again here as Bob implores the Lord to "send me that love I've been created for," and the band plays a waltz. (Yes, that's right – a *waltz.*) Bunny's on bass and that's Peter playing xylophone. Hugh Malcolm is recalled on drums, whilst Rita and Hortense sing harmonies. It's a style of accompaniment that's far removed from anything people normally associate with the Wailers, but then they always did pride themselves on their versatility.

When Bob returned in late June, he was delighted with how the shop looked and wasn't at all surprised to learn that Peter had severed his relationship with Joe Gibbs. After Peter had spurned his offer to record an album, Joe Gibbs took the rhythm of 'Maga Dog' and issued several versions of it. This infuriated Peter, who felt that he hadn't been properly compensated for 'Maga Dog' in the first place. With vengeance in mind he and Bob headed for Randy's and recorded 'Once Bitten' on which Peter warns, "I don't want to hear a word you say – step back with your lies." He then used the same rhythm for 'Dog Teeth,' with spoken lyrics promising that "no dog who bite me will ever bite me again.'

Peter issued it on his own label Intel Diplo – a derivation of "Intelligent Diplomat." He and Bunny would both own their own labels whilst still members of the Wailers. They enjoyed hanging out at their new shop entertaining friends like the Barretts, who were currently Jamaica's most in-demand rhythm section. Family Man had been born in Beeston Street, right near where Tuff Gong now stood. He'd call by there and reason with Bob, sharing ideas about music whilst drinking a juice out in the street and sampling the atmosphere of Kingston's busy downtown district. Other times they'd buy a breadfruit and eat it round the back of the shop or sit and spar with Keith Hudson, who rented the office upstairs and would soon produce classic songs with Dennis Alcapone, Big Youth and others.

Bob and the other Wailers also spent time with Danny Sims and Johnny Nash whenever they were on the island, and Family Man recalls going up to Russell Heights and rehearsing 'Let The Sun Shine On Me' with them, which JAD later re-titled 'Pour Down The Sunshine.' Johnny Nash wasn't around too often but he and Danny Sims openly admired Bob's talent for composition and wanted their relationship to continue. In the meantime, work got underway on a number of recordings for Tuff Gong, beginning with "Screw Face.' It's a song with attitude because whilst "screw face knows who fi frighten," Jah Jah children have divine protection. Bob hoped that 'Screwface' would emulate 'Duppy Conqueror' in launching a new chapter for the Wailers although they quickly shelved it once 'Trench Town Rock' happened.

The mood on that track is defiant, and even jubilant at times. Family Man was laid up in bed with a cold the day they went into Randy's. In his absence, Bunny started fooling around on bass, playing the riff from a song he'd written called 'Scheme Of Things.' Bob began scatting and fitting words to it and that's how 'Trench Town Rock' was born. According to Bunny, 'Trench Town Rock' was the song, "that really made us start to search." After their frustrations with Perry they'd wanted to reassert themselves, just as Peter had done with 'Maga Dog' and 'Them Ha Fi Get A Beaten.' 'Trench Town Rock' fitted the bill perfectly, and on several different levels. It would offer further proof of their resilience, and demonstrate that they weren't reliant on outside producers for success. More importantly, it was an act of defiance relating to where they'd come from, and where Peter and Bob still lived. Many Jamaicans looked down on people from Trench Town ("cold I up") and so there was always this challenge to prove them wrong. Trench Town residents had their work cut out persuading outsiders they were just as good as everyone else and so it's natural they'd want to exult their community in some way, whether in music, sport or even badness. The Wailers had learnt to thrive despite this handicap, although they still took such criticisms personally. Like most Trench Town residents they had principles. Anyone transgressing the unspoken code would end up hounded, beaten or dead. Either that or people would set a trap for them and carry their name to the police, forcing them to flee the community. "It's not what you do in Trench Town, but how you do it," says Bunny, sternly. Ultimately, Trench Town people policed themselves. Trust was very important, and those who lived there were quick to search out neighbours they could call on for help and support if necessary.

'Trench Town Rock' spoke to them like no other tune before or since. It became an anthem and not just for the residents of one embattled community in Kingston but for ghetto people worldwide. "One good thing about music, when it hits you, you feel no pain," sings Bob who revels in the sensation, even calling for it to "hit me harder, brutalise me." If that's a reference to James Brown, then it's a subliminal one because the Wailers have now fully assimilated the Godfather's influence, and won't be covering any more of his songs in future. 'Trench Town Rock' was a No. 1 hit in Jamaica and would soon inspire a bestselling deejay cut by U Roy called 'Kingston 12 Shuffle.' After 'Trench Town Rock' sold three thousand copies, Red Stripe presented Bob with an award that he accepted wearing the kind of gaudily patterned trousers you'd find in a Haight-Ashbury thrift shop. The Wailers' lead singer wasn't renowned for his dress sense but during August he was back in the limelight again after being invited to crown Miss Musical Chariot at the Sombrero, as part of that year's Miss World celebrations. 'Trench Town Rock' had put Bob and the Wailers back on the map, and yet it failed to chart anywhere else – even after Scratch surreptitiously licensed it to Trojan as part of the 'African Herbsman' album.

"The Wailers, they hit me with the 'Trench Town Rock' right on my head and behind my back," says Lee Perry, ruefully. "I was in London trying to get my music released by Trojan Records and them think me get thousands of dollars from it, but I didn't even have control of my records and so had to set up the Upsetter label to survive. And without any payment, 'cause I only got two thousand for it, I never get ten thousand like they say but nobody else realised this. That's why they plan to hit me with 'Trench Town Rock' and fill Kingston town with devils. That was my part."

Scratch wasn't doing too badly without them. Junior Byles' 'Beat Down Babylon' was Record Of The Year, and accompanied by a number of other hard-hitting songs commenting on Jamaica's political situation, such as 'Joshua's Desire' and 'Pharaoh Hiding.' Byles would later suffer from mental illness brought on by poverty and neglect, despite having provided Perry with some of his biggest-selling hits, including 'Curly Locks.' Bunny says Bob wrote 'Craven Choke Puppy' about Scratch, which tells the story of a dog gorging itself, only to splutter and choke. "Want all, lose all..." Other reports suggest it may have referred to Leslie Kong who'd just died aged thirty-eight, the victim of heart failure. This seems unlikely however, since Kong was regarded as being a generous man. Bunny's reputation as a mystic was greatly enhanced by his passing, as he'd predicted the Wailers' recordings for Beverley's – which Kong had named 'The Best Of' – would be the last he ever heard and so it proved.

Kong passed away around the same time the Wailers were in Randy's recording songs Bob had written in Sweden like 'Guava Jelly.' Others were inspired by conditions closer to home. Peter chants in Amharic on the intro of 'Concrete Jungle,' which is a dark prototype of the song that would later appear on 'Catch A Fire.' It must have been hard for Bob to reacclimatise to life back in Trench Town after the relative luxuries he'd enjoyed in Sweden and London. Since his return, he'd been faced with the responsibilities of feeding a young family and reviving the Wailers' fortunes, and such tasks were made even more difficult by the circumstances he found himself in. Whereas 'Trench Town Rock' promoted and even exulted in ghetto life, 'Concrete Jungle' laid bare the realities of living amidst degradation and despair. The two songs are sides of the same coin, and 'Concrete Jungle' harrowing in its use of bleak imagery.

"Darkness has covered my life, and turned my day into night," Bob sings mournfully. "No chains around my feet, but I'm not free. I am bound here in captivity." It's not the kind of song anyone would write with hits or radio play in mind, but a lament from the heart, delivered with real feeling. The concrete jungle he's singing about is the network of government housing schemes built in outlying areas of Kingston and that offer shelter, but little else for the city's poor. Such neighbourhoods are invariably hotbeds of violence and poverty, and from where there's little hope of escape unless it's to the cemetery, jail or madhouse. Judging by the title, 'Redder Than Red' should be a ganja tune although it's more a declaration of love, whereas 'Lick Samba' is the admission of a man who's been hurt, yet is still willing to take another turn on the roundabout of romance.

The other big hit they recorded in the run-up to Christmas was 'Lively Up Yourself', which had all of Jamaica leaping to its feet after monopolising jukeboxes for months on end. The word "infectious" doesn't even begin to do it justice. The Wailers had exhorted audiences to dance before but never in such irresistible fashion. 'Lively Up Yourself' will remain among their key recordings, and is still guaranteed to keep a party rocking even more than forty years later. The success of songs like this, 'Trench Town Rock' and 'Screwface' will ensure Tuff Gong's ongoing viability, and allow the Wailers to dream of turning their label into what Family Man has described as "a little Motown." Right from the start, they'd hoped Tuff Gong would become a vehicle for other acts as well as themselves, and there was no shortage of worthy candidates. Members of the Wailing Souls still lived in Trench Town where they too, had learnt harmonies under Joe Higgs' tutelage. Lloyd "Bread" McDonald confirms that he and Winston "Pipe" Matthews sang backing vocals on 'Trench Town Rock' – also 'Redder Than Red' and 'Lick Samba' – and says the Wailing Souls' 'Back Biter' was recorded at the same session. George "Buddy" Hayes and Norman "Fats" Davis, who'd also sang harmonies on 'Here Comes The Judge,' were members of this same Wailing Souls' line-up, and 'Harbour Shark' and 'Back Biter' were both released on Tuff Gong as the year's end approached.

Keyboard player Glen Adams had left Jamaica by now, and three different musicians will take his place over the coming months – Bernard "Touter" Harvey, Earl "Wya" Lindo and the teenage Tyrone Downie, who's said to have made his debut on 'Lick Samba.' The Wailers had entered yet another new phase, and the music they were making was not only straining at the boundaries of their own creativity, but also that of Jamaican music as a whole. In the minds of fans overseas, reggae was defined by songs like Dave & Ansel Collins' 'Double Barrel,' the Pioneers' 'Let Your Yeah Be Yeah,' Greyhound's 'Black And White' or Bob & Marcia's 'Pied Piper.' Catchy tunes and happy beats were the order of the day, and whilst mainstream radio DJs often derided reggae for being too simplistic, no one could deny its popularity. Back in Kingston however, the Wailers had embarked down a path that allowed them more freedom of expression than they'd ever thought possible.

'Satisfy My Soul Jah Jah' and 'Satisfy My Soul Babe' were both voiced over the same rhythm, and aimed at two different kinds of listeners – those favouring love songs, and those preferring more spiritual fare. The gap between songs of praise and romantic ballads has always been slight, as the likes of Ray Charles and Sam Cooke had discovered, but not even they had come up with such a radical departure as heard on these two tracks. The overdubs vary quite a lot, but it's the deep roots sound of the rhythm that stands out and provides the epitome of "word, sound and power" – the mystical science of sound vibration that can alter a person's consciousness just by the notes they're hearing. Family Man ventured into this domain with the same, methodical approach he used when mending bikes or musical equipment – i.e., in the manner of a consummate craftsman. He took upon himself the task of translating the Wailers' spiritual quest into music, and searched for the notes and chords that would best complement their lyrics. His mission coincided with the birth of what's now known as "roots music," as defined by acts such as the Wailers, Abyssinians and Burning Spear.

National Heroes Day fell on October 18th that year, the day before Peter's twenty-seventh birthday. Shearer's administration marked it with a military parade and then awarded Sir Alexander Bustamante the Order of National Hero, which the Governor-General, Sir Clifford Campbell, presented to him. Meanwhile Kingston's growing army of soul rebels – and even many Rastafarians – had their eyes on Michael Manley, who was contesting the forthcoming election with great charisma. Although light-skinned, Manley was attracting widespread support among Jamaica's poor, who liked how he sympathised with Rastafari and his promise of social reforms. Manley wasn't called "Joshua" for nothing, and nor could they fail to notice his black celebrity lover, local television presenter Beverley Anderson. His campaign trail took him to all fourteen parishes, and in the company of singers like Dennis Brown, Ken Boothe, Alton Ellis, Max Romeo and the Wailers, who performed as part of his "Caravan Of Stars." This tour would later be called the "PNP Musical Bandwagon." Bunny has subsequently claimed the Wailers were "teenagers and never understood politics" when taking part, yet the facts dispute this. All three Wailers were already in their mid-to-late twenties, and are known to have endorsed Manley.

"Hear me now. The Wailers were PNP and big Michael Manley supporters – especially Peter Touch, that's the truth," says Roger Lewis, whose band Inner Circle toured with Manley. "Peter Touch, Bunny Wailer and Bob Marley, they were on ninety percent of the shows we did on the PNP Bandwagon as little youths. Those times we were fifteen, sixteen years old, jumping around the stage and travelling around the island. We were still at high school and didn't get even one dollar from the government. The most I can say we get from the PNP Bandwagon was a drink and maybe some food and yet we back up everybody, because Bob, Bunny and Peter didn't even have a band back then."

The Wailers played about thirty shows in total, spread over ten parishes. Bunny swears they didn't do these dates in order to promote Manley, but Rastafari. He also claims it was Bob and Peter who were drawn to the socialist cause, not him. That said, they were treated well, food was provided and they got $150 a show, which was the most they'd ever been paid by anyone. On the minus side, Bob fell over on stage and hurt his head at least twice, and they'd occasionally have to dodge stones thrown by opposition supporters. Even the PNP crowds would get restless during Manley's speeches sometimes, as they waited for the acts to perform. Bunny says people came to see the Wailers and not the politicians, and with a set list that included 'Duppy Conqueror' and 'Trench Town Rock,' that's not surprising. The Wailers were back in demand except they'd nailed their colours to the mast by backing Manley, and would later regret it.

"Michael was really quite radical," says Bob Andy by way of explanation. "He was very much pro Black Power and Rastafari, and he walked through the grassroots to get to power. His theme for that election campaign was "The Word Is Love" and he had a staff rumoured to have come from His Majesty, which got a lot of people's attention. He was head of the National Workers Union, which was formed by his father, and he received much love and admiration for having married a black Jamaican. Apart from being quite Hollywood with his looks and charm, I must say he was also erudite and articulate. The first time myself and many other Jamaicans learnt about multinational corporations was because of his teachings so I'd say that Michael Manley played a key role in opening up the political consciousness of Jamaican people, including Rastafarians."

Hundreds of cars drove around Kingston sporting 'Better Must Come' and 'Time For A Change' stickers, and fresh graffiti appeared daily on walls in the city, proclaiming allegiance to the PNP. Posters sprang up showing Manley dressed in a Kariba, the sleeveless beige suit favoured by African leaders, while sound-systems played pro-Manley songs such as Max Romeo's 'Let The Power Fall On I' and Delroy Wilson's 'Better Must Come.' Despite leaning towards the PNP the Wailers were generally cautious around politicians, and made sure they didn't sign anything. For the most part they just stayed close to people they could trust and in Bunny's words, "found it easier being around thieves than politicians."

He and the others had seen how singers like Joe Higgs and Alton Ellis had been hounded after making politically sensitive statements, and knew that if you shed light on people's activities

– and especially those of politicians – they could soon turn against you. Bunny wouldn't have anything to do with politicians, which explains his feelings about the PNP Bandwagon. He'd seen how showing support for either party could damage an artist's career, and wouldn't sit down and eat with them, or let them do him any favours. The politicians saw that singers were unprotected and didn't know how to defend themselves. All they knew to do was write and sing songs. They just wanted to get their names on a record and get it played on the radio. Also, as Bunny pointed out, if the politicians cared so much for artists, then why were there still no copyright laws in Jamaica?

The election was scheduled for February. Bob wouldn't be around for it as he'll be in London with Danny Sims and Johnny Nash. In fact he won't return to Jamaica until the following May. His last recording with the group before leaving was 'Why Should I', and it reads like a diary extract. "The hard work has ended, and a new world has begun," he proclaimed. No sooner said than done because in December – and despite Bunny's reservations – the Wailers' participation on Manley's campaign trail finally paid off after PNP man Anthony Spaulding arranged a handful of dates for them in New York. These shows would be their first outside of Jamaica, and mark Bunny's first trip overseas. As they headed for the airport, 'Screwface' was already blaring out the rum bars along the Palisades Road, near where they'd posed for the 'Soul Rebels' photo session just eighteen months earlier.

They would play three shows in the US over the holiday period, backed by a pick-up band led by Jamaican guitarist Eric Frater, who everyone called "Rickenbacker." The first show took place on New Year's Eve at the Concord Manor on East 161st Street in the Bronx, and was an unqualified success. Bob had injured his shoulder whilst playing football before leaving Jamaica, but a woman grabbed his arm as he leaned into the sell out crowd and inadvertently yanked it back into position. What a cure! The second was held at the Manhattan Centre and the third at a Brooklyn club called the President's Chateau, where Glen Adams sat in with them on keyboards. During this last show the atmosphere became tense as a local rude boy started shouting out requests for 'Screwface' and then fired his gun in the air, which sent people racing for cover. Within minutes the police had arrived, shut off the power and escorted the Wailers backstage. This brought to an end Bunny's only performances with the band's original line-up in America. Some sources report that the Wailers also played dates in Pennsylvania, Queens, and Delaware throughout January 1972, although there's no evidence to support this. What we do know is that by the end of that month Bob was in London, and Bunny and Peter were safely back in Jamaica.

PART THREE

High Tides, Low Tides

CHAPTER FIFTEEN

Midnight Ravers

The election took place on February 29th 1972, a leap year. The PNP won and Michael Manley replaced Hugh Shearer as Prime Minister. Jamaica's charismatic new leader had achieved the near impossible by politicising factions of the Rastafari movement, and would soon repay their support by commissioning a government report into the decriminalisation of marijuana. The mood was optimistic, and especially after the report recommended an overhaul of existing ganja laws. Family Man issued an instrumental called 'Herb Tree' by way of celebration, even as many older Jamaicans shuddered at the thought of Rastafarians being heeded so seriously.

Count Ossie and the Mystic Revelation of Rastafari were now playing at the Harambe Room in Kingston most Sundays. Jamaican popular music and Rastafari were becoming increasingly intertwined, but there was concern about those who'd embraced Rasta without accepting the responsibilities that went with it. Peter called a session at Randy's attended by Bunny and the Barrett brothers. Family Man had brought Tyrone Downie along, then watched as Peter voiced 'Lion' and a cover of George Harrison's 'Here Comes The Sun,' with Bunny singing harmonies. "Lion" was street slang; a greeting Rastas would use instead of "Hail" or "Greetings," as one Rastafarian to another. In the past, no one but Rastafarians wore dreadlocks. Madmen and wanted criminals were the only exceptions, but that situation had changed. Some youths now grew them because they thought it was cool, and gave them something to identify with. They weren't necessarily interested in observing the precepts, but just liked the music and hanging around singers – the Wailers included. "I only hear your words, yet I don't see works," Peter sneered on 'Lion.' "Locks on your head, talking about you're dread. And you believe that is all."

Bunny also worked on a few solo productions whilst Bob was away, starting with a session at Dynamic that resulted in 'Life Line' and Heat, Air & Water's 'Searching For Love.' Both tracks were released on his own Solomonic label, designed by Bunny himself. The artwork's divided into halves of bright red and yellow, overlaid with drawings of geometric patterns and reptilian eyes that hinted at hidden mysteries. Bunny is most intriguing of the three Wailers, and renowned for being elusive. His critics have portrayed him as a shadowy figure with a propensity for violence – at least in the far distant past, whilst others cast him in the role of Rasta mystic. He sings of a love like fire, burning in his soul on 'Life Line' and the language is sheer poetry. Secular and spiritual love are fused, whilst the rhythm's another undulating groove from the Barretts, and decorated by Bunny and Peter's harmonies.

Bunny's next session was at Aquarius studios in Half Way Tree. It was there he recorded 'Bide Up,' which is the kind of narrative Curtis Mayfield once delivered with such certainty. Essentially, Bunny is saying that the only way to advance in life is within a religious framework, just as he did on 'This Train.' He's encouraging us to "bide up with reasoning" – to humble ourselves so we can receive divine protection and ultimately salvation. Rasta is presented as a route out of the hardships and frustrations, to a place where's "no more worries, worrying and pains. No more crying, shedding tears like rain..."

American troops had finally withdrawn from Vietnam, after failing to secure victory. Back home in the US, important battles had been won and lost. The Black Panthers were now a spent force and when Angela Davis was freed in June, it felt like the closing of a chapter. It was only two or three years earlier that Black Power and the hippy movement had caused the system to shake a little, before being quashed by a determined and at times, brutal response from government forces. By the summer of 1971 most musicians, black and white, had already excused themselves from politics and the naïveté of those who remained, such as John and Yoko, would soon be exposed. For all of Lennon's bluster on 'Power To The People' it had been George Harrison, aided by Bob Dylan, Eric Clapton and others, who'd succeeded in making his political ideals count when hosting the Concert For Bangladesh. Many took this as a demonstration of how musicians could still make a difference given the right platform because whilst expectations weren't so high anymore, the struggle was far from over. In late May 50,000 people flocked to a Liberation Day assembly in Washington and called for a repeal of the Byrd amendment – a piece of legislation which had lifted United Nations sanctions against the minority white regime in Rhodesia. Peter had been arrested whilst demonstrating against this racist, illegal state several years ago. Rastafarians like he and Bunny called the white power structure "Babylon," and longed to see it fall. At its core resided the Pope and English royal family – rulers of an empire that had subjugated millions in the name of God and

King, and continued to exploit them at every turn. Yet thousands of poor, black Jamaicans loved the Queen and called their sons Winston, after Winston Churchill, or regularly put more than they could afford in the church collection plate, so as not to attract criticism.

Bob was still off the island when robbers broke into Tuff Gong and stole an amplifier, turntable and a couple of stampers. It was the Wailers' friend Jack Wise or "One Eyed Jack" as he was known, who discovered that Coxsone was behind the heist. The animosity he felt towards them was probably due to jealousy. Coxsone's store was just a few blocks away, at the corner of Beeston Street and Love Lane, but Tuff Gong had been attracting a younger crowd, drawn by the Wailers' music and reputation. Business was good and so Peter and Bunny were able to replace the hi-fi equipment relatively quickly, but the stampers were a different proposition. These were the metal discs used to press records, and their loss meant that new ones had to be created from the original master tapes, which wasn't cheap. Also, whoever had stolen the stampers could press as many copies of the songs as they liked, without paying royalties. This was a serious situation and could have affected the group's relationship with Trojan and Pama, who issued their records in the UK. Pama had issued 'Screw Face' on 7" whilst Trojan snapped up 'Lick Samba', 'Guava Jelly', 'Grooving Kingston 12', 'Trench Town Rock', 'Redder Than Red' and 'Lively Up Yourself' for their various subsidiary labels, including Green Door. Whilst none of these singles troubled the UK national charts, they were popular with Caribbean audiences living in England, thanks to the reggae sound-systems.

Bob arrived in London from Sweden in late January 1972 and moved into a house on Queensborough Terrace, which he shared with other members of the JAD entourage - Nash and Sims included. Five minutes down the street and then across the Bayswater Road was Kensington Gardens, where he could play football when not holed up in his room writing songs, or meeting with friends from Jamaica who'd since moved to England. Bob liked London and would spend a lot of time there in future, but the skies were often dark and a chill worked its way into every part of him, no matter how well he wrapped up. Danny Sims still had hopes of promoting him as a solo artist and persuaded CBS to grant them some studio time, in anticipation of Bob getting his own record deal. Some of the musicians from Johnny Nash's backing band The Sons Of Jungle were used on this session, but the results were lacklustre compared to the Wailers' recent output. Bob had met Nash's bandleader, Texan born John "Rabbit" Bundrick in Stockholm the previous summer, when they'd worked together on a film score. The two had become good friends, but just couldn't find the right sound or chemistry to make these recordings work, despite Bob having written some decent songs. Johnny Nash's next album would include three of Marley's compositions – 'Stir It Up,' 'Guava Jelly' and 'Comma Comma' – as well as 'You Poured Sugar On Me,' which the pair had written together.

'Stir It Up' was a hit for Nash in April, and gave Bob his first taste of what it felt like to connect with an overseas' audience, albeit by proxy. Repeat performances, only with himself as the singer, would take a bit longer. CBS released one of his tracks, 'Reggae On Broadway' as a single but it was poorly received, despite reggae music continuing popularity. Paul Simon had recorded his current hit 'Mother And Child Reunion' in Jamaica, whilst Greyhound had a Top 10 hit with 'Moon River,' confirming their role as Mick Jagger's reggae band of choice.

By this time, Bob had already written songs like 'Slave Driver,' 'Concrete Jungle' and 'Midnight Ravers,' which signified a change of direction from more commercial material such as 'Reggae On Broadway.' It was if he'd given up trying to sound like an American soul singer, and brought his own uniquely Jamaican expression to the forefront instead. He'd win full marks for artistry, whilst appearing to have turned his back on chart success. Danny Sims must have had reservations but was preoccupied with Johnny Nash, whose latest single 'I Can See Clearly Now' was tipped for chart success. Marley's benefactors had urgent work to do, and sent him back to Jamaica with expectations of the Wailers touring behind Nash later in the year.

Bob returned home with renewed enthusiasm, but there was something not quite right within the Wailers' camp. According to Peter, Rita told him that Bob had planned to rob the group and take their money back to England with him. This had left him in a difficult position. He couldn't confront Bob with it directly so he told him that he'd had a vision, and outlined what Rita had said. Astute as ever, Bob said it didn't sound like a vision but something that had really taken place. He suggested they look for Bunny, whereupon Peter repeated the story about the vision and Bunny got annoyed. He'd heard about it already and told Peter to forget it, since that kind of thing could only harm the group. It was a lie, and intended to stir up trouble. Bunny told him that Bob would never do such a thing and "Satan a trick him," which shamed Peter. He'd carried a woman's gossip to her husband and in doing so, created mistrust between him and Bob.

Shortly before Bob had left for Sweden, he stopped Rita from seeing a bunch of uptown guys including Derrick Harriott, Tony Laing and the Conservative Connoisseurs, who ran club nights at the VIP and Sombrero. Rita had got excited when they invited the Soulettes to sing with them. The group had all but folded but Bob ordered her to stay at home with the children and made no secret of his dislike for them. They were party people, and their views differed greatly from those of Rastafarians. The Wailers held fast to certain principles, and Bob didn't want them to be associated with such lightweights. Rita was furious and went around saying how she was going to break up the Wailers, just like Bob had broken up the Soulettes, since they disbanded soon afterwards. Hortense left for America and then Cecile stopped going to sessions after becoming romantically involved with Alva "Reggie" Lewis, whose drink problem was getting the better of him. Whether the Soulettes would have rallied after taking up the Connoisseurs' invitation is debatable but Bob was adamant they weren't going to have the opportunity, even threatening Rita with violence if she disobeyed him.

"Bob was very stern," Junior Dan recalls. "He never told jokes or anything like that. Peter was more the joker in that respect but all three were stern characters. They were serious guys. They weren't pussycats but Bunny was especially rigid. He never messed around. He would drive fear into people if they weren't strong. Having said that, Bob would be the first one to put a man out if he didn't like you. The three of them were quite something I tell you! People say that Bob was the leader but Bunny was the front person because he'd be the first one to question you and find out what you're up to. Bob was more quiet and reserved. He'd be sat in the background, summing everything up and getting ready for his next move, which may well include showing someone the door. None of them were pushovers. They weren't easy at all."

Bunny admits that Bob was driven, and never let up. Nothing was going to stop him in his mission and even Peter acknowledged his leadership. Bob was all about working hard and achieving what had to be done. He wouldn't force anyone to help out, but leave them to do whatever they believed was necessary until he disapproved of something they did. Peter and Bunny accepted this, and clearly felt the same way. Neither of them complained and yet they would get dispirited at times, just like everyone else. Coxsone, Lee Perry and Rita had resorted to stealing; Leslie Kong had died on them and they hadn't even begun to uncover Danny Sims' machinations yet. Shit happens, and it's how you respond that matters. The Wailers held firm, and forged a hard-bitten mentality that helped them combat frustrations and bad treatment. They knew that no one was going to hand them success on a plate, and that it would take a lot of hard work and self-discipline to achieve their goals. That's why they made an effort to refrain from quarrelling among themselves or apportioning blame. Musically, they had everything going for them. All three Wailers were impressive in their own right and as songwriters, as well as singers. The Barrett brothers had an intuitive genius for finding the right groove and those latest Tuff Gong releases were big hits on the reggae underground. The Wailers were stars on the island, but a bigger stage continued to elude them. Bob felt they needed a bit more business acumen to help them along their way and with this in mind, he invited his friend Alan "Skill" Cole to join Tuff Gong's cause.

Cole was Jamaica's most famous footballer, and therefore someone Bob respected right from the start. Both excelled in their own fields, and were aware of just how useful fame could be in furthering their political and spiritual aims. Cole was also a Rasta, although he'd attended Kingston College and met with criticism for having crossed the social divide. This intrigued Bob, and it had made Skill a hero to Jamaica's poor who celebrated the fact that he'd recently played in Brazil, home of the current world champions – even attracting favourable comment from Pele. His return to the island had been widely publicised, and attendances soared whenever he turned out for Kingston teams such as Boys Town and Universe 11.

When the Wailers got to know him he was dividing his time between playing football and dabbling in the local record business. A mutual friend who worked at Dynamic had brought him to the Wailers' shop. Some claim this person had been releasing the Wailers' material in the US without their knowledge but Bob trusted Skill, and that was enough to quell any rumours. Due to Bob's endorsement, Skill rapidly began to exert influence over the Wailers' affairs. His speciality was persuading radio DJs to play their records, and by any means necessary. Prior to this, the Wailers had received precious little airplay in Jamaica. As one-time rudies turned Rastafarians they had no friends in high places, and some DJs made no secret of the fact they thought the Wailers should have stayed with Scratch. Skill's methods may not have been strictly legal at times, but they were certainly effective.

"It was a difficult time," he'll later admit. "We had to put out a lot of strength, what you call muscle, to get played by the various disc jockeys so it was my duty to see that these things happened... Sometimes we had to go there and beat disc jockeys and deal with programme directors... We had to send guys to smash their cars or things like that. Threaten them... if you don't play the records you better leave the station... Quite a few people left the station during that year. Disc jockeys and programme directors... some even left the country. That was the period he got most of his No. 1 songs in Jamaica."

Bunny Lee concurs that DJs regularly played their records after being paid a visit by the band's "business manager."

"They certainly never enjoyed a level playing field before Skill was involved with them," agrees Bob Andy. "I remember them having to kidnap Halford Plummer to get their records played on the radio but you could buy air time if you had the money. Coxsone, Randy's, Treasure Isle and G. G's all bought fifteen minute slots on the radio but the Wailers had more of a cult following, which was unusual back then. 'Bend Down Low' had been a big hit, with or without radio play yet Bob Marley just couldn't get a No. 1 hit in Jamaica for some reason. In those days, you'd sell your first couple of hundred to the jukebox people for cash, and then go and get more pressed with that. The Wailers had been through some rough times but I would say no more so than when we were with Coxsone, because at the same time they were enjoying their independence and freedom. There was nothing insurmountable for them as far as I remember."

Everything the Wailers released on Tuff Gong now charted and sold well. For the first time since leaving Coxsone they had a run of good sellers, and which brought them some decent money at last. Previously, the Barrett brothers had earned more than the Wailers just from playing sessions. Family Man's latest triumph was teaming the Youth Professionals with Errol Dunkley, whose 'Black Cinderella' was a major hit that summer. Roots and culture music was now taking over from what English audiences called "skinhead reggae" and Coxsone, whose recent tracks with Burning Spear, Horace Andy and the Gladiators all expressed Rastafarian values, was again at the forefront.

It was still rare to see Rastafarians outside of the Jamaican countryside or Kingston's downtown areas, despite their mounting influence. Film director Perry Henzell's 'The Harder They Come' would soon help change this on a scale few could have previously imagined.

Henzell's film starred reggae singer Jimmy Cliff in the lead role of Ivanhoe Martin, based on the life of a notorious Jamaican outlaw. It had taken two years to finish, mainly due to lack of funds, but will be hailed as a cult classic for decades to come. Kingston's Carib Theatre was jammed to the rafters on June 5th for the premiere, attended by most of the cast and crew. The entrance was so crowded Jimmy Cliff couldn't get in and Perry Henzell's wife Sally had to be passed over the heads of people waiting outside. Inside, tumultuous reaction greeted every scene. 'The Harder They Come' marked the first time many poorer class Jamaicans had seen themselves on screen and they cheered Ivanhoe's every move from their one-dollar seats in the stalls. Reports in the Gleaner claimed the opening was "a fiasco" due to rowdiness but the film itself was an unprecedented success, grossing $37,000 on the first day, and $2,000 a day thereafter once it was shown in local cinemas such as the Tropicana, which is where the Wailers and Barrett brothers first saw it. Those riveting performances by Jimmy Cliff and Toots & the Maytals were filmed at Dynamic studios, where the Wailers had recorded for Leslie Kong just two years earlier. The cutthroat nature of the local recording industry was thrown into sharp relief after Ivanhoe finished singing 'The Harder They Come,' but then refused to sign away his rights for a pittance. His rebellious attitude ensured the song got shelved until after he'd turned killer and his face appeared on wanted posters all over the island. Cliff's character then attained Nirvana, Jamaican style, by becoming a celebrated outlaw *and* topping the charts, all at the same time. ("I told you I'd be famous one day," he said admiringly.)

Some of the more memorable scenes portrayed Rastafarians and the ganja trade in a sympathetic light, which was virtually unheard of at the time. There's so much reality in the film that every character's believable, whether it's the preacher whipping his congregation into a near frenzy, or the middle class housewife who struggles to conceal her fear whilst acting superior. The settings too, were entirely authentic. It was 'The Harder They Come' that gave overseas' audiences their first glimpse of a Jamaican shantytown, with its tumbledown zinc fences and unforgiving aura of poverty. Those scenes were filmed in West Kingston, where Bob and Peter still lived. Jamaica's reputation as a tropical paradise – a world of white sand beaches and palm trees inhabited by American playboys and characters from Ian Fleming novels – had been shattered. We now understood a little more about why people migrated from the Caribbean. Over 17,000 Jamaicans arrived in England during 1972, searching for a better way of life. The majority would take refuge in West Indian communities dotted around the country and face racism on a regular basis, whether it involved housing, work or education. As ever, music offered release from hardship and Caribbean house parties, also known as "blues dances" or "shubeens" could now be found in every major English city, providing the police didn't close them down first. Reggae had exploded onto the mainstream less than a decade earlier, but those recent chart entries were hardly representative of what was happening at grassroots level. Just a few months earlier novelty record producer Jonathan King had recast a couple of session singers as the Piglets and made a song called 'Johnny Reggae' that went to No. 3 on the UK charts, and characterised the music as belonging to skinheads. The follow-up was 'This Is Reggae,' released the same year as sound-system favourites by Burning Spear, the Abyssinians, Horace Andy, Prince Jazzbo and many others, including the Wailers. A rebel strain had emerged, fuelled by righteous zeal and intent upon radical social change. Its music celebrated blackness whilst preaching love and unity, and drew from the same rich source of inspiration as the ancients. These artists weren't interested in making hits, even if their producers were. They wore their dreadlocks in defiance of Babylon's rules and gave a voice to poor ghetto people who otherwise didn't have one. This was a long way removed from what British audiences were hearing on their transistor radios, or watching on 'Top Of The Pops.' Perry Henzell's film 'The Harder They Come' would start to close that gap but not in terms of the soundtrack, which was made up of older material, dating from at least two years earlier. There were many brilliant tracks on that album – not least those by Jimmy

Cliff – but nothing of the real dread variety, to make "all weak-heart drop." That style of music hadn't surfaced from the reggae underground yet, and the Wailers were acutely aware of this fact – Bob especially, after those months he spent in England.

In July, Danny Sims invited the Wailers to support Johnny Nash on a series of UK tour dates, beginning in a month's time. The news was met with real optimism. Peter and Bunny had heard a great deal about England from Bob and friends like Bunny Lee, who remembers an air of excitement surrounding their trip. First however, they had to take care of business closer to home. The Wailers had a joint Tuff Gong account that required two of their signatures on any cheques they wanted to cash. Skill Cole was now their business manager, so he was given a twenty-five percent share in Tuff Gong and granted power of attorney in their absence. Once assured that everything was in order, the Wailers' party boarded a plane to London. It was mid-August, and yet Peter and Bunny immediately felt the cold. They were the only two making their first trip to England. Family Man and Carly had been with the Upsetters, and steeled themselves for another rollercoaster adventure.

"Johnny Nash and Danny Cash" as Bob called them, were still at the same house where he'd stayed a few months earlier. John "Rabbit" Bundrick and his girlfriend were also living there, and space would be at a premium now the Jamaicans had arrived. 3 Cromarty Villas was on Queensborough Terrace, just off the Bayswater Road. Bob liked the location but found the company hard going at times, as did Peter and Bunny. Johnny Nash was now a major pop star. 'I Can See Clearly Now' had been a Top 5 hit in England just a few weeks earlier, and the album was selling fast. The kind of reggae he specialised in was lightweight, but very melodic. His vocals were impeccable and the production exquisite but it was nothing like the hardcore Jamaican sound that reverberated with spiritual power and flew the flag for Rastafari, which all three Wailers carried within their breasts.

There was mounting tension over Northern Ireland when they arrived. Fourteen people had recently died there after British troops had opened fire on a civil rights march. This incident became known as "Bloody Sunday" and led to inevitable reprisals by the IRA. A majority of English people were all for a united Ireland, but Paul McCartney's 'Give Ireland Back To The Irish' was promptly banned, just weeks before Britain imposed direct rule. Bomb threats intensified after a plane crashed whilst taking off from Heathrow, killing over a hundred passengers. A national dock strike then brought trade shuddering to a halt. Britain was ill at ease with itself, but otherwise characterised by rundown seaside resorts, Saturday night variety shows on television, bingo halls and working men's clubs, where every weekend couples sat shrouded in cigarette smoke, downing beer and eating scampi from baskets whilst singing along to cabaret singers imitating Tom Jones and Engelbert Humperdinck. Either that or they'd laugh as comedians told scurrilous jokes about Jamaicans, Pakistanis and the Irish. Prejudices went largely unchallenged, even on TV. White actors blacked their faces and indulged in racist typecasting on 'The Black And White Minstrel Show,' which still attracted millions of viewers each week. Budget airlines hadn't materialised yet and the majority of working class people still didn't have passports. Many of those young, white, working-class males who piled on the make-up or wore skin-tight, silver lame jump suits with platform boots back in 1972, at the height of the glam rock craze, remain eternally grateful that camera phones hadn't been invented yet. David Bowie's 'The Rise And Fall Of Ziggy Stardust' was album of the year, whilst Marc Bolan ruled the pop charts. There were also plenty of skinheads around. This was Britain's most unsavoury youth cult, and with a well-earned reputation for violent, racist behaviour. Three shivering soul rebels, wearing military style clothing and matching scowls therefore had to tread carefully.

Cromarty Villas became overcrowded with all three Wailers staying there. Nash and Sims liked groupies, and visitors have described women of all different nationalities wandering around in various stages of undress, eager to experiment with drugs and group sex. It was scenes like this that inspired Bob to write 'Kinky Reggae' – not that he or the others were especially prudish. In a bid to make the Wailers feel welcome, Danny Sims had invited some girls to entertain them one night. One was the daughter of Michael X, who stole all their money after she'd spent the night with Bob. He and the others quickly locked the door, then rounded on the rest of the girls and beat them mercilessly. Danny protested, bought the girls' silence and then gave the Wailers some money by way of compensation. Bunny looked after their stash from there on, although they'll add precious little to it during the rest of their trip.

Peter, Bunny and the Barrett brothers moved to the nearby Queensborough Hotel after this incident. They were still close to the shops and underground station, and continued to spend most days and evenings at Nash's apartment in any case. Delroy Washington, who'd befriended Bob on his first visit to London, rejoined the Wailers' circle at this juncture. He knew Peter already, and has fond memories of Peter giving him a ride to school on the handlebars of his bicycle some mornings, back in Westmoreland. That was more than ten years ago. Delroy's family had left for London shortly afterwards and so he'd grown up in England, although whilst sticking close to his Caribbean roots. A talented singer in his own right, he was an invaluable ally to the Wailers during this visit. It was Delroy who'd helped recruit the musicians who played on Bob's tracks for CBS. He'd known members of the Cimarons and Greyhound since they were at school together, whilst Rannie Bop had been an obvious choice after backing the Wailers in Jamaica. Delroy had also convinced Bob that he should return to London with Peter and Bunny in tow, as the group had a strong following among young Caribbean music fans. The addition of the Upsetters' rhythm section was a real bonus, and heightened anticipation ahead of the forthcoming tour dates.

Danny Sims had hired two soundproofed rooms in a basement below Condor Music in Kingston-upon-Thames where the bands could rehearse. The facilities were good, but they were several miles out of London and the Wailers had no car, which meant they had to use public transport to get there every day. Their journey entailed changing trains at least twice each way, and waiting around on station platforms whilst trying not to look too conspicuous. Needless to say Johnny Nash and his band The Songs Of The Jungle didn't have to suffer such indignities. They rehearsed in the big room, whilst the Wailers crammed into a smaller space across the hall. This wasn't ideal but they enjoyed having the space to play music and all the musicians got on well with one another, or at least for the time being.

"When I first knew him Bob had a massive Afro," recalls Cimarons' guitarist Locksley Gichie. "His manager Danny Sims talked to us about doing a couple of gigs in London, so we started to rehearse with him and Johnny Nash. Bob was quite big in Jamaica by then, but not in England yet. He was a nice brother, and we used to move with him a lot at that time. Him and Johnny Nash, they were sharing this big flat in Bayswater. I remember we did a gig at the Bouncing Ball in Peckham and also one in Bristol. (The promoter there was Tony Bullimore, now better known as a round-the-world yachtsman.) We also did a couple of shows at the Apollo in Willesden High Road, which was Jeffrey Palmer's club. This was before Bob met Chris Blackwell, when he was here in London on his own.

"After a while Bob went home to Jamaica and when he came back, he brought the other two Wailers up with him to do some recordings, and that's when we began rehearsing at this place in Surrey. All of the Cimarons were with them at first but then Franklyn our bass player went to play with Johnny Nash instead. Maurice stayed though and so we ended up with two drummers, which I think was the first time this had happened in reggae. It was definitely something new..."

James Brown was already experimenting with two drummers, except the Wailers would barely get to perform with this new line-up before it splintered apart. Only Bob performed at the shows that Gichie mentions. He would open for Johnny Nash singing 'Reggae On Broadway' and 'Oh Lord I'm Gonna Get You' with the other two Wailers sat in the audience. Rumour has it that Nash was scared of their talent and didn't want his audiences to hear them, especially as he was billed "King Of Reggae." Family Man says that Nash never looked in on their rehearsals, despite being just across the hall. One of his musicians did though. "This must be reggae!" the mystery man had exclaimed, before asking the Wailers why they'd let Johnny Nash take their sound and their music. Hearing this must have gone down like a lead balloon with Peter and Bunny, who weren't exactly enamoured with their English escapade so far.

In his book 'Jah Music,' Sebastian Clarke claims that Sims and Nash had intended to tour with the Wailers, but used them for recording purposes instead.

"The backing tracks for Nash's 'I Can See Clearly Now' were laid down by the Wailers," he writes. "The band members were annoyed at the manner in which they were handled and disgusted with the treatment they received. In that same year Marley released a solo single through CBS Records called 'Reggae On Broadway.' CBS showed no interest in the record and it was through the efforts of Nash's promotion manager (and Sebastian's brother) Brent Clarke that it eventually sold 3,000 copies. The Wailers were staying at a hotel in Bayswater where they had no proper facilities to cook or conduct themselves in the manner they preferred.

"Brent Clarke, a young Trinidadian promoter who had previously been involved with the music business through promoting dances and putting on bands, first met Nash, Sims and Marley at Mr. Bee's Club (later known as the Bouncing Ball) in Peckham, South London. Sims introduced himself and they struck up a conversation. According to Clarke, Marley was quite happy to meet a Caribbean person he could talk to, since he hadn't met up with his Jamaican friends who were living in London by then. Clarke accepted Sims' invitation to be Nash's promotion manager. After Nash had his biggest hit with 'I Can See Clearly Now,' he got a great deal of abuse from the Wailers through the mouth-piece of Bunny Wailer, and so Sims suggested that Clarke devote all his time and energy to the Wailers. The first thing Clarke did was to move the Wailers out of their hotel and into a small, three bed-roomed house in Neasden. This was a morale booster for the Wailers for they began to attract young black musicians in London, and also met up with a number of their friends."

Neasden was an urban backwater in NW London, surrounded by industrial sites and railway sidings. Its best-known landmark is the North Circular – a busy ring road designed to take traffic away from Central London. Brinsley Forde, singer with Aswad, lived nearby and became a regular visitor to the house Brent Clarke had found for the Wailers, in The Circle.

"I went up there with Delroy Washington the first time," he says, "and I was round by them quite a bit after that because I took my instruments over and we'd all be jamming and stuff... We'd play football over at the Welsh Harp sometimes as well, but none of them went out a lot. I remember being at work and seeing them walk up and down the street a few times but they went completely unnoticed, and no one was any the wiser as to who they were. At that time Bob wasn't dread yet. He wore his hair in plaits and they were slightly twisted at the end. Only Bunny had dreadlocks. He and Peter kept their own company more than Bob. Peter was a solitary figure and really didn't socialise that much. To be honest I had more of a relationship with Family Man because he and I really locked. He wanted me to play bass, but I wanted to sing and I could never do both at the same time."

The house was quite roomy, and had a back room where they could store their instruments, including Brinsley's guitar and amp and a keyboard borrowed from Courtney Hemmings, who would later join him in Aswad. Peter and Bunny shared one room and the Barrett brothers another. Bob had his own room where he entertained Franklyn's girlfriend Janet – a development that had undoubtedly hastened the Cimarons' bass player's departure. Early in the mornings Bob, Family Man and Delroy Washington, who often slept over at the house, would jam and work on songs together. They would then tape whatever they came up with on two small cassette recorders, sometimes adding rudimentary percussion by drumming on items of furniture or even an aerosol can. Whilst Bob and the others worked on new material Peter would be practising his martial arts or reading. He was still heavily into Black Power, and had pinned a picture of Che Guevera on the wall. According to Delroy, "none of the Wailers were dunces." Bunny spoke proper English and had a way with words, whilst Bob listened carefully as Delroy advised him not to use too much patois in his lyrics, otherwise he'd limit his chances of connecting with a mainstream audience. Bob took such counsel seriously, and was grateful for the tip.

"One minute you speak Jamaican, the next you're an Englishman!" he told him, laughing. Delroy's home life wasn't too satisfactory, and lack of parental guidance could have sent him down the wrong path had he not met up with Bob and the Wailers, who treated him like family and provided him with a sense of direction – one based on a moral and spiritual code emanating from Rastafari. Anyone coming into the Wailers' orbit was expected to observe the same principles and woe betide those who dared take liberties.

"Everybody was petrified about meeting the Wailers," recalls Delroy. "They'd heard they were some strict people, and the environment at the house could be very tense. There was an intense kind of atmosphere around them. You didn't want to be messing up so people would come in and sit down in a corner and not move an inch. A lot of people assume Peter was the troublemaker but it wasn't like that, and it wasn't just Bunny either. The thing Bunny really didn't like was people going into the kitchen but everybody was very rigid and kind of militant whenever visitors came there."

Not everyone was greeted suspiciously. Ethnic Fight producer Larry Lawrence would stop by regularly and also friends like Chicory and Jah Rennie, whose tam concealed a massive set of dreadlocks. Rennie would soon leave for Ethiopia after taking the rap for a ganja bust involving the Wailers, or at least that's what some people say. Delroy disputes this story and says it was Chicory who arranged for herb to be posted from Jamaica and delivered to the Wailers' address. The band hadn't sanctioned this, and had no idea Chicory had already put his plan into action. Bob especially was very cautious when it came to procuring herb, but none of the Wailers would have taken that kind of risk. Bob and Delroy were out shopping in Brixton market with Family Man and Carly when police called at the house, disguised as postmen. Chicory signed for the parcel and everyone in the house was promptly arrested. When Bob and company got back around late afternoon, the neighbours told them the police had come and taken everyone away. Peter and Bunny will later be released without being charged, cursing the fact they'd been dragged into Chicory's scheme and the loss of so much good herb, which was expensive by Jamaican standards.

As Rastafarians, all three Wailers adhered to a strict dietary code and prepared their own meals wherever possible. They avoided eating at restaurants – even those selling West Indian food like Caribbean Sunset in Harlesden or Mr Patties, although at least they didn't get the cold shoulder in such places. When they walked into other cafes or restaurants looking for something to eat, sometimes the customers would get up and leave. This wasn't just because they were black. The Wailers didn't look like typical West Indians either and especially Peter, who could have passed for a Black Panther in his black beret, and with that ever-present black fist dangling from his neck. Caution was the bye-word although they did enjoy exploring their surroundings from time to time.

"Brent Clarke had this little car and used to drive everybody round sometimes but the Wailers were pretty down to earth, and would take a train or a bus to get where they wanted to go," says Delroy. "It was only if there some kind of emergency that they'd take a taxi but otherwise they'd want to see and get to know London. That's what set the Wailers apart from everybody else because groups like the Pioneers, they'd wear flash suits and drive flash cars. They'd be changing clothes like three times a day but the Wailers really couldn't have been more different and that's one of the things that attracted me to them."

Delroy had seen how elder Caribbean people had formed associations devoted to their respective countries. In NW London there were associations for Trinidadians, Grenadians and several other nationalities. Whilst still at school he'd founded a more open-ended group, drawn from all different parts of the West Indies. By the time the Wailers pitched up in Neasden this association had several hundred members, most of them youngsters, who'd flock to a nearby hall where he and Mikey Campbell ran a Monday night talent show, backed by the Cimarons. Jamaican singer Pat Kelly, riding high with 'How Long,' did a PA there once but even Delroy was amazed when the Wailers accepted his invitation to drop by one night.

"The Wailers actually turned up around six o'clock that night. I told them to come early because we had to get everything ready and it was weird man but there they were, just hanging out and enjoying themselves. A lot of people saw them as cult figures at that time, even among reggae artists because they were different from everyone else. Not too many other artists were doing music that talked about Rasta but they weren't on a star trip or anything like that. I remember people disappearing to tell their friends the Wailers were there and to come down to see them. They got so excited. I guess for them it was like meeting God from heaven or something so the whole place was rammed out by the time the music started."

"We had some nice times," adds Brinsley. "I had this old Cortina that I'd rubbed down, ready to be sprayed... I remember we broke down by the Four Aces in Dalston once and Lloydie Coxsone and his crew came out front and helped us push it down the road. Coxsone's sound-system also played when we went to see U Roy perform in London somewhere..."

This was the Grand Rastafarian Ball, held at Woodland Hall in

Acton during September. It was the first public Rasta function in England and a milestone in Anglo-Caribbean affairs. The Wailers were beginning to sense their time had come and yet their management team were largely conspicuous by their absence. Brinsley visited the house many times and never saw Johnny Nash or Danny Sims there once. In fact he doesn't even recall their names being mentioned. According to Sebastian Clarke, "Johnny Nash had a tour of the UK and the Wailers were supposed to be the support act but it seemed that whether it was done purposely or whatever, their visas ended up at the Jamaican Embassy and they only managed to do two shows in the time they were there. They sat and they waited and waited to go on this tour but it never materialised."

"That's true. We had a couple of gigs planned," says Gichie. "The first one was by the seaside. I think it was in Portsmouth or somewhere like that and it was a flop. It wasn't promoted well enough and it was very cold. We went there and although the venue wasn't all that big, it was still really empty."

The Wailers played the Telegraph Club in Brixton on August 27th, and they're also known to have performed at the Commonwealth Social Club in Croydon, South London. "When we perform, the whole place tear down," Peter would later brag to Fikisha Cumbo, referring to one of these shows. "After we done sing and tear the place down for an hour and a half we have to walk to get food and when we get it, the food stink so much we have to dash it away. The next day we get paid three pounds."

Bunny also recalls them supporting Nash "in a place where no black people were." This was unfortunate since the Wailers were proud of their cultural stance, and had recently taken to wearing red, green and gold on stage. The first time they opened their set with 'Rastaman Chant' was at one of these UK dates, and it had happened by accident after some instruments went missing and they reverted to chanting nyahbinghi, accompanied by just Carly and Bunny on congas.

"We didn't have enough instruments with us and Johnny Nash's band didn't want to lend us theirs," says Family Man. "One of them finally lent me his bass but it wasn't tuned, because some musicians used to wind down the strings when they weren't playing, so they'd last longer. It was lucky that I'd trained myself to play on just one string from my early days because for our first song, that was all I had. Then after the first number I had to tune it fast, right there on stage! By the second tune I was ready, and from there we just tear up the whole show…'"

Bunny remembered them performing 'Small Axe', 'Duppy Conqueror', 'Put It On', 'Rude Boy', 'Nice Time', 'Bend Down Low', 'Stir It Up' and a cover of War's 'Slipping Into Darkness,' which they'd rehearsed until it was note-perfect. He says there was a nice atmosphere to the gig, despite the majority of fans being "skinheads with tattoos and wearing Dr. Martens." Even the security guys seemed happy. Things then really got lively during 'Keep On Moving,' as people began snake dancing around the auditorium. They'd rehearsed 'Reggae On Broadway' but decided to save it for the encore along with 'Love And Affection' or 'One Love,' Bunny couldn't remember which. Not that it mattered; the crowd were already won over, and Johnny Nash struggled to keep the momentum going. Someone in his band played a Mellotron rather badly, and his musicians seemed confused as to how to play reggae in any case. By the third number people started to leave or made their way to the back of the venue, where the Wailers were enjoying an after-show spliff and basking in some well-earned compliments. Danny Sims was nowhere in sight which was just as well, since Johnny Nash came off stage looking to kill him! He was still wearing his silver-studded denim suit and patchwork boots when the Wailers caught sight of him ten minutes later, beating his fists on the wall and swearing he was never going to play with them again.

A night like that wouldn't have gone down too well, no matter how much he and Sims valued Marley's songs. The prospect of further tour dates had now faded but in the absence of anything more significant, the Wailers were determined to make use of the rehearsal facilities. Those trips to Kingston-upon-Thames now took on a different feel. The band had renewed purpose, and that basement room became the launch pad for a new Wailers' album that would make their previous recordings obsolete.

"Right from the start, when I first began working with him, Bob would say to me, 'There's a sound that I want, I can hear it in my head. I want to create a sound that's new and that everyone will follow.'" says Gichie, whose fluent guitar runs also inspired Bob to conjure 'No More Trouble' out of thin air one day. "We used to rehearse songs over and over and then after we start 'Concrete Jungle,' I played some blues licks behind it and Bob went crazy man. I stopped playing and Bob said, 'Gichie. That's the sound I can hear in my head all the time. That's the one I've been looking for – the blues guitar on top of the reggae rhythm.' It was more of a crossover sound than what you normally heard coming out of Jamaica but it's funny because once we'd gone in the studio to record it, Bob swore that I was playing it differently to how I'd done before. I told him it was the same thing but he wouldn't have it so I got mad and walked out. That's why he had to bring in that other guitarist, Wayne Perkins, to play on tracks from 'Catch A Fire'."

Despite this misunderstanding, Gichie proved an influential figure around the Wailers and got to know them well, with the possible exception of Bunny.

"Bunny was the philosopher, and he was the force behind Bob where Rastafari doctrine was concerned," he says. "He was more radical than Bob or Peter, and he'd always be asking these loaded questions like, 'A where yuh come from?' and 'What's your name?' I'd say, 'Gichie,' and he'd say, 'Your name's not Gichie!' Bunny really didn't like England and as a matter of fact, most days he was depressed. He didn't like the cold at all and found staying in England really grim."

Bunny's mother had spent nine years in England, working in a toy factory making dolls. She'd only returned to Jamaica once, at Christmas time. Perhaps Bunny blamed England for having taken her away from him, or maybe his disposition wasn't all that sweet to begin with. Lest we forget, Bunny was the only Wailer to wear dreadlocks. He was fiercely committed to the Rasta cause, and self-disciplined with it. Whereas Peter and Bob both enjoyed female company and sought it, Bunny was withdrawn and meditative. According to Clarke, Bunny "was more conscious of food and hygiene and the right way of living. He read the Bible and thought about his woman in Jamaica."

The Wailers went into the studio and recorded five tracks – 'Concrete Jungle', 'Stir It Up' and 'Midnight Ravers,' plus new versions of 'Keep On Moving' and maybe '400 Years' – during their stay in Neasden. They were playing as a proper band by this time. Peter and Bob were creating unique rhythm patterns on guitar as Gichie played lead, whilst the Barrett brothers provided their usual rock solid anchor. It wasn't aimed at the pop charts like Dandy Livingstone's 'Suzanne Beware Of The Devil' or Johnny Nash's latest hit, 'More Questions Than Answers.' The Wailers' music now catered more to rock audiences than the fickle demands of pop fans. They'd become focussed on making albums rather than crossover hits, but still didn't know how to market themselves properly. It turns out the band didn't have work permits, and that's why they didn't get to play more shows. They couldn't even return to Jamaica when they wanted since Danny Sims had lodged their passports at the Home Office and then forgotten about them once 'I Can See Clearly Now' had begun its ascent of the US Billboard charts. It would hit the No. 1 slot in November, by which time Johnny's remaining UK dates had all been cancelled and the pair were long gone.

"Nash and Sims left the country for the United States to pursue their own business and abandoned the Wailers to themselves," writes Clarke. "On their departure, Brent Clarke sought a job as promotion manager with Island and was assigned to work on Greyhound's 'Dream Lover' and Lorna Bennett's 'Breakfast In Bed'. He later approached Chris Blackwell and showed him the songs that Marley had written for Nash. Blackwell was impressed and divulged that he had wanted to sign the Wailers for several years, but hadn't approached them because of their reputation as rebels and non-signatories. At the same time Island's biggest reggae act – Jimmy Cliff, star of 'The Harder They Come' – didn't want to remain with Blackwell because he felt he wasn't being paid enough money. Also Island had suppressed certain songs he'd wanted to record – songs such as 'Let Your Yeah Be Yeah', which became a chart hit for the Pioneers and 'You Can Get It If You Really Want It' which became a hit for Desmond Dekker. Cliff was reputed to have received £14,000 for his original contract with Island and asked them for £20,000 to re-sign, but they didn't want to pay that kind of advance."

Island Records' offices and studio were in a converted church on Basing Street, in Notting Hill. Bob and Brent Clarke had gone there one day, walked into the lobby and handed over a tape box marked "CBS." What was on the reel, we ask ourselves? Was it material Bob had recorded on his last trip to London, after he'd tossed aside the artifice of 'Reggae On Broadway' and bared his soul on songs like 'Concrete Jungle' and 'Midnight Ravers'? Or was it the more advanced cuts he'd recorded with Peter and Bunny just recently, and featuring Gichie on guitar?

I suspect the latter. In any event Blackwell was intrigued enough to call a meeting. He'd known of the group from their Studio One days and whilst their previous albums hadn't sold too well, he recognised how they were spearheading something different. The Wailers joined him on the roof of Basing Street one day. He said that he'd wanted to meet them for years, but people had told him they were dangerous people to deal with. He'd been warned off them in other words. Blackwell said that he'd given Coxsone "thousands of pounds" and was surprised to hear they'd only received a one-off payment more than four years earlier. All three Wailers bristled with indignation at this and only Bunny stopped to consider whether it was a psychological ploy, designed to ensnare them.

Brent Clarke hammered out a two-album deal with Chris Blackwell on the Wailers' behalf. It was agreed they'd be paid £8,000 per album, and retain the rights to release them in the Caribbean.

"The reason for this was that the band was based in Jamaica," continues Clarke. "There was no certainty about how well their records would sell internationally, and they would therefore not have to depend on overseas royalties for sustenance. The terms were agreed to and contracts signed. A cheque for £1,000 was paid over to Clarke by way of commission and the remaining £7,000 was paid into Byron Lee's bank account in Jamaica, which the Wailers would receive on their return. Clarke loaned the Wailers £750 towards their return tickets to Jamaica. When the contracts were signed the Wailers seemed to become suspicious of Clarke's good intentions and refused to sign a management contract. It is true to say that Bunny Wailer was the most obsessively mistrustful of all the members of the group."

Family Man disagrees with certain aspects of this account, and claims that Brent Clarke came to him with news of Blackwell's interest. He and Carly were then upset when Bob, Bunny and Peter signed without them. Yet at this stage the Wailers were still a vocal trio and the Barretts hired sidemen, despite their importance to the group's overall sound. Danny Sims paid them a retainer of twenty pounds a week but the Wailers' rhythm section had been earning more than that playing sessions back home, and resented the idea of being paid "pocket money, like schoolchildren."

"We start to lick out after that and Bob took it personal, saying how he'd invited us to England but Danny Sims wasn't acting fair," says Family Man. "Bob say to him, 'is it war yuh want fi deal with? Well, let us go out into the street then' but them nah want fi war, and things just cool off for a little while. Bunny Wailer, he don't like how there's trouble between we and them, but me tell him we've been up in London already and have an idea of what goes on. I tell him you have to be like a soldier on guard but he don't say too much to me, so me and him don't stay so chatty after that."

Bob's friend Rabbit had been touring Japan with Free, supporting Emerson, Lake & Palmer, but would continue to play the occasional session with Sons Of The Jungle after his return to England that autumn. Shortly before Nash and Sims left for the US he overheard Bob arguing with Danny, saying he wanted to sign with Island Records. This indicates that a deal had been agreed, but it was dependent upon Danny Sims releasing the Wailers from any legal obligations to him. Chris Blackwell wouldn't have sole control of the group until that happened but he could see their potential and was particularly impressed by Bob's manner.

"When we sold Bob's contract to Chris Blackwell and Island Records in October 1972, Bob was ready," Sims would later tell Roger Steffens. "He was an established, polished artist who was able to co-produce with Blackwell or any other producer. He was able to use what he had learned from Johnny Nash, Arthur Jenkins and all the other great people we put him with from 1967 to 1972. That was enough for anyone to get his Ph.D. and be able to go out on the stage of the world."

CHAPTER SIXTEEN

Island Hopping

Soon after the Wailers' got back home, they discovered that most of their money was missing. They'd set off for England with $15,000 in a shared Tuff Gong account, but now there was only $4,000 of it left. The balance had gone to pay gambling debts resulting from late night poker games and visits to the racetrack. The thing was, Skill was Bob's closest friend, which put Peter and Bunny in a difficult position. Once the dismay had eased a little, Bunny declared he didn't want anymore of it. He told the others to deal with the problem between themselves. He also reminded Bob how they'd worked hard and paid serious dues to get this far, and they were supposed to know how to safeguard their earnings by now. Not for the first time, he and Peter had to suffer the consequences of Bob's poor decision-making. The two of them were growing tired of pouring their heart and soul into Wailers' projects, only to see their hopes dashed by the actions of people close to them. It was Skill who influenced Rita to go and see Tony Spaulding, who was Housing Minister for the PNP. Rita asked for Spaulding's help in getting new accommodation, and he duly delivered. Soon, she and Bob would own a plot of land out in Bull Bay, just a few miles east of Kingston. Bob was allegedly incensed at having a politician grant him favours, but it's unlikely that Skill would have broken ranks in that way. Bob may well have engineered the situation, whilst being seen to oppose it and it's typical of his machismo that Rita will be left to build her house and make it into a home for their children virtually single-handedly, whilst he concentrated on music. Bunny and Jean Watt lived nearby, and in a house on the beach whose design reflected the same creative, spiritual energy that went into their songs. Peter meanwhile, had moved to Bridgeport – a government housing project in Greater Portmore, just a short drive from Kingston. He'd recently met a green-eyed beauty called Yvonne Whittingham who shared his passion for knowledge, and from whom he'd soon become inseparable. He and Bunny still had their doubts about Chris Blackwell, despite his success in promoting Jamaican music overseas. Their instinct was to mistrust any wealthy, white Jamaican looking to get rich from exploiting black talent, but Bob welcomed Island Records' involvement, and viewed it as an opportunity not to be missed.

The band had already rehearsed most of the songs for their new album, plus there were a few others they'd recorded before but felt could be improved. Some of the tracks were laid at Randy's, although the engineers there were having difficulties recapturing the same sound, after Vincent Chin had dismantled the desk and used it for some outside recording. Randy's misfortune would motivate Lee Perry to build the Black Ark studio and gift Channel One a head start in the race for hits, whether produced by the Hookims, who owned it, or former Randy's clients such as Bunny Lee and Niney The Observer. The Wailers turned instead to Dynamic, where they'd recorded 'The Best Of' album two years earlier. Dynamic would soon be rocking to the sound of the Rolling Stones, looking to follow 'Exile On Main Street' with an album steeped in tropical haze. Keith Richards joked how Jamaica was the only country that would let him in but ironically, it's also one of the few places where the Stones weren't treated as celebrities.

It was October by the time the Wailers strolled into Dynamic and recorded 'Catch A Fire.' They recorded it onto eight-track, and doubled up the guitar and piano to give their music that extra rhythmic thrust they liked so much. According to Bunny, they recorded five rhythms on that first day, and five more the next. The Wailers weren't used to recording at a leisurely pace and so approached 'Catch A Fire' just like always – by making sure they were well rehearsed, and then nailing the tracks in as little time as possible. They put the voices on last, within a week of laying the rhythms, and the entire album was ready to mix inside a month.

"As soon as we get back to Jamaica, we couldn't wait to start work on the new album," says Family Man. "That was when everyone's soul was together. We just book some studio time and get right in there man. Boom, boom, boom, and it done! And not just 'Catch A Fire,' because we do most of the 'Burnin'' album at the same sessions too. We didn't have to rehearse those songs too much either, because they were there in our heads already. We'd been rehearsing a programme, like an album and showcase, when we were in London with Johnny Nash. We'd be running through all of those 'Catch A Fire' tracks in that basement studio so we were definitely well rehearsed, and that's how we were able to record them so quickly."

Despite the speed and fluency of those initial sessions, the Wailers were only too aware that they needed to raise the bar on this new record. Everyone agreed they hadn't managed to capture the right sound on their previous recordings, and they were determined to get it right this time after listening to albums like Curtis Mayfield's 'Roots' and Marvin Gaye's 'What's Going On,' which weaved their spell on the Wailers as those Dynamic sessions began. Freed from its three-minute straightjacket, contemporary black music was no longer restricted to shaking tail feathers, walking the dog or doing the popcorn. Artists like those mentioned above – and also Stevie Wonder, whose 'Talking Book' would be released before the year's out – had embarked on a search for the music's humanistic core, and raised topics that few producers would have countenanced just five years earlier.

Bunny had played bass (with his thumb, no less) on that first version of 'Concrete Jungle' from 1970. The re-recording of it may just be the sweetest lament you ever heard. "Where is this love to be found?" asks Bob, who's answered by high-pitched harmonies from Bunny and Peter telling him, "sweet life must be somewhere." The latter strums guitar on the intro and to a rhythm so understated, it creeps like a thief in the night. Lyrically it's full of hurt, although in place of the Wailers' usual ire we hear loss and uncertainty. For once, Bob has come up with an outlaw character struggling with doubt and a dimming of the light. He and Peter had lost all appetite for ghetto life by the time 'Concrete Jungle' was written, and it shows. 'Concrete Jungle' was among the tracks they finished first, together with 'Midnight Ravers,' 'Stir It Up' and 'Slave Driver.' They'd all been around a while, just like Peter's two songs, 'Stop That Train' and '400 Years.' They may well have re-recorded 'Small Axe,' 'No Sympathy' and 'Duppy Conqueror' at these sessions too although it's more likely these were completed later, once the Wailers had returned to London. Bunny even had another attempt at 'Walk The Proud Land,' plus he'd written several new songs including

'Reincarnated Soul,' 'Hallelujah Time' and 'Oppressed Song' – offerings so delicate and individual, they really couldn't have been penned by any other member of the group. The Barrett brothers hadn't become official Wailers by this stage, and yet they were fast proving indispensable. Bunny has underlined their importance by describing how they'd tune their instruments to perfection, which made the mixing process so much easier. He says Carly was the first drummer in Jamaica to pad out his bass drum and that Family Man was so good at running repairs, he'd make the Wailers' well-worn instruments sound just like new. The Upsetters had disbanded by now. Glen Adams and Rannie Bop were still in exile, whilst Reggie played a little on 'Catch A Fire' but would soon drift from the Wailers' circle. Since Bob and Peter could both play guitar, his input wouldn't be missed. Reggie had lost faith in the music, and lacked the professional attitude needed to take the Wailers forward – qualities the Barrett brothers had in abundance. They respected the Wailers; they were young and they took telling because that's how the band operated. Musicians did what they were supposed to and wouldn't even think about fooling around, because Bob could get very angry if they played something he didn't like.

"When the Wailers recorded with Lee Perry, he said he wanted the rhythms to sound like you were stepping in glue, which is a very good description," reflects 'Rockers' director Theo Bafaloukos. "The way that Family Man and his brother played, they would always leave a tiny bit of space between the bass and drums. They wouldn't play together at exactly the same time, and that's the glue Scratch was talking about. Chris Blackwell was quick to pick up on it and embellish it, because that was something new..."

This interplay between the Barrett brothers would lend 'Catch A Fire' such cohesion, Island Records were able to market it to rock and soul audiences weaned on great rhythm sections and instrumental prowess. They were augmented on 'Catch A Fire' by an assortment of guests, including organist Winston Wright and members of Inner Circle. Family Man also brought in Robbie Shakespeare, who played bass with the Youth Professionals. In their ranks was schoolboy Bernard "Touter" Harvey, who might have toured with the Wailers had he been a little older.

"During those 'Catch A Fire' sessions I'd probably end up playing piano and Winston would play organ," Family Man explains. "If the lead instrument was going to be piano, then he'd play that but Winston was definitely the better organ player. I'd always get to learn something from guys like him. They were there before you, so you'd pick up what you could from them."

Musicians like him and Seeco, who played percussion, wouldn't receive any credit for their contributions to 'Catch A Fire' and 'Burnin'' because Island wanted the Wailers to be viewed as a self-contained unit. Touter would later join Inner Circle, who played on 'Stir It Up' and 'All Day All Night' – also 'Walk The Proud Land,' which remains unreleased nearly forty years later. Inner Circle had recently played on Eric Donaldson's No. 1 hit 'Cherry Oh Baby' and often worked at Dynamic on sessions. 'Stir It Up' is pretty sparse, yet still swings thanks to its dancing bass line. This version's much improved from the one the Wailers cut for Danny Sims and there's an ethereal cast to Bob's lead, despite the steamy lyrics. This song and 'Rock It Babe' – later renamed 'Baby, Baby We've Got A Date' – seduce with their lithe rhythms and doo-wop harmonies whereas 'Hide Tide Or Low Tide' is a ballad, and could easily pass for a soul track. 'Hide Tide Or Low Tide' and the achingly beautiful 'All Day All Night' will be left off the album, possibly because Island wanted to keep love songs to a minimum and promote the Wailers as rebels instead. Chris Blackwell would later admit this may have been the wrong decision, except it's not hard to see why he might have been distracted by tracks like 'Slave Driver,' 'No More Trouble' and a brace of songs from Peter.

'400 Years' has a swagger that's missing from previous attempts – most notably the earlier incarnation on 'Soul Rebels.' Every instrument is clearly heard in the mix and Peter sings with greater authority as he attempts to rouse the youths into following him, Pied Piper style, towards "a land of liberty where we can live a good, good life and be free." Rarely had the invitation to stage an uprising been delivered with such a well-informed sense of history. 'Stop That Train' is much improved too. The lurching rhythm and shifts in tempo inspire a more relaxed vocal performance this time round, and allows his guitar playing to sparkle.

In late November, Bob set off to London with the 'Catch A Fire' master tapes. If he was expecting to hand them over to Island and leave just as quickly then he would be disappointed. Chris Blackwell sat behind the console in Basing Street with engineers Stu Barrett and Tony Platt, listened to the new album and decided they wanted to give it more of a rock feel. If the Wailers were going to connect with hippies and students, they needed to provide them with familiar reference points. The roots of rock lay in the blues, and so it was decided they'd add some lead guitar solos. The problem was, Bob had fallen out with Gichie from the Cimarons and rock style lead wasn't Rannie Bop's forte. Enter Wayne Perkins – an American session guitarist who'd backed the likes of Joe Cocker and Stevie Winwood after replacing Duane Allman at Muscle Shoals. His latest group, Smith, Perkins, and Smith had signed with Island earlier in the year and were about to tour Europe with Free and Fairport Convention. They'd stopped off at Basing Street to do some recording but were interrupted when Blackwell asked Wayne if he'd like to play some reggae. "What the hell is that?" he'd replied before reaching for his Les Paul and following Chris downstairs, where he was introduced to Bob and got his first taste of real "island" music. The Alabama born Perkins couldn't understand a word Bob said to him but Blackwell advised him to be guided by the bass, rather than the melodies, and to play what he felt. Wayne wasn't expected to embellish every track – just those needing a lift, and that could accommodate a style fusing blues, rock and country. The Wailers' temporary guitarist took the opportunity to try out a sustain pedal he'd recently bought in New York. This device could hold a note for up to three minutes, and then feedback a whole octave higher towards the end of its cycle. Tony Platt doused Wayne's solo on 'Concrete Jungle' in additional echo and Bob was delighted with it. This was the sound that he'd been carrying around in his mind's eye for months, and the Wailers' ticket to a wider audience. With the arrival of 'Catch A Fire,' there would no longer be any reason for white rock critics to dismiss reggae as badly produced novelty music, devoid of meaningful content. The songs on this album were different, both lyrically and musically, to those masquerading as reggae on the UK charts, and popular misconceptions of Jamaican music would have to change.

A handful of other musicians lent flourishes to 'Catch A Fire' before it was transferred to sixteen tracks and mastered. Chris Karen overdubbed some percussion, and John "Rabbit" Bundrick added synthesiser, clavinet and organ. He'd just played on sessions with John Martyn and Free and will earn the princely sum of thirty pounds for trying to decipher Bob's instructions, and helping 'Catch A Fire' to attract the attention of listeners more accustomed to the likes of The Band, Neil Young and Little Feat. We can be sure that Bob and Rabbit exchanged a few words about Johnny Nash and Danny Sims before the sessions were over. Johnny was enjoying the biggest hit of his career with 'I Can See Clearly Now,' which some believe is a Bob Marley composition, despite being credited otherwise. JAD engineer Richard Alderson disagrees, saying it bears all the hallmarks of Nash's own writing style. Also, if Bob did write 'I Can See Clearly Now,' then why did he never record it himself?

It was at this point that CBS sent their lawyer Bob White over to Island to inform them Marley was signed to CBS through Danny Sims. The contract he showed Chris Blackwell was only half a page long but it was binding enough to prompt fears of legal claims. Blackwell wanted to avoid a costly and lengthy court case so he suggested Bob fly to New York, explain the situation to Danny Sims and ask his terms for a speedy release. It was New Year before a determined Bob boarded the flight to New York with the cassette of 'Catch A Fire' nestled in his pocket. He met up with Sims backstage at a Johnny Nash concert in Manhattan. Johnny was promoting a new album called 'My Merry Go Round' which contained a version of 'Nice Time.' He and Danny Sims agreed to let Bob sign with Island providing they received £5,000 by way of compensation and Marley renewed his publishing contract with Cayman Music, which they owned. In addition, JAD wanted a two percent over-ride on the Wailers' first six albums. After quickly weighing up the options, Chris Blackwell agreed to the terms and a deal was struck. The Wailers were now solely contracted to Island and their tenure with Sims was officially over. The only outright loser was former PR man Brent Clarke, who never did get his £750 back.

Chris Blackwell's long-time associate Dickie Jobson was in New York and took Bob to a Traffic concert in Manhattan. It was there he met Jamaican actress Esther Anderson, who'd recently starred in 'A Warm December' with Sidney Poitier. She'd rekindled her friendship with Blackwell after relocating to London during the early sixties, and had witnessed his entrepreneurial skills firsthand. Jobson also introduced Bob to Lee Jaffe after taking him to an after-show party in Traffic drummer Jim Capaldi's room at the Windsor Hotel on West 56th Street and 6th Avenue. Jaffe had studied sculpture at Penn State and was part of the art establishment in New York's SoHo district. A born adventurer, he'd already travelled to Brazil and filmed local musicians in the shantytowns. After exhibiting in a landmark show of conceptual art at MOMA, he'd become the youngest artist to exhibit in the Paris Biennial. This was in 1970, when he was barely out of his teens. He was working on a project in the French capital with the son of Marguerite Duras when he met Esther and her friend Maria Schneider, who'd been filming 'Last Tango In Paris' with Marlon Brando. Jaffe and Esther Anderson then flew to London, where they attended the premiere of 'The Harder They Come.' Sat there in the darkness of Brixton's Classic Cinema, watching images of Jamaica on the flickering screen proved a Road To Damascus type moment for the twenty-two year old. It was a few months later, once back in New York that he met Bob Marley, who looked and spoke as if he'd just stepped from a scene in that film. The pair immediately became good friends. Lee showed Bob around New York and entertained him at his loft on Greene Street, which was situated above a gallery popular with New York's art intelligentsia. This must have been quite an experience for Marley – one eased by copious amounts of herb thanks to Jaffe's underworld connections. Lee would tell biographer Roger Steffens that for the week he and Bob were together in New York, "the 'Catch A Fire' album became the soundtrack for what was at that time the centre of the art world," and that Marley had walked into an environment "where being a poet and musician was regarded without suspicion."

Jaffe and Esther Anderson will occupy key roles in the Wailers' story over the next two years. She and Maria Schneider had been on their way to New York for the US premiere of 'Last Tango In Paris' when agreeing to appear in Jaffe's next movie, based on the life of sculptor Gordon Matta-Clarke. Filming was due to take place in Chile, where the political situation had worsened because of opposition to President Salvador Allende's social reforms. Prompted by seeing 'The Harder They Come' and what he'd heard from Bob and Esther, Lee suggested they film in Jamaica instead. Chris Blackwell was planning to return there soon for a spot of Caribbean island hopping, and he invited both Lee and Esther to join him.

"I'd been offered an eight-picture contract with Sidney Poitier," recalls Esther. "We'd recently finished 'A Warm December' but I just put everything on hold and went with Chris to go and meet the Wailers in Jamaica and take pictures of them. I'd met Bob in New York during the last Traffic tour. Bob was dancing backstage but I didn't see him again until arriving in Jamaica..."

Like Bob, Esther was mixed race and born in a country parish (St. Mary's in her case, as opposed to St. Ann's.) Her father was a Scottish architect, whilst her mother was of East Indian descent. Esther may have been a movie star, but she'd grown up in modest circumstances and so had more in common with Bob than might be imagined. She also had strong affinities with the local music thanks to Chris Blackwell, who'd launched Island Records in England with her help. Esther ended up virtually managing Millie Small and Jimmy Cliff, whom she'd coached for his role in 'The Harder They Come' at her Chelsea apartment. In-between modeling assignments and her work with Island Records, she appeared in several films and also television series, including 'The Avengers.' Shortly after meeting Bob, she would be nominated for an Oscar and win a NAACP Image Award for Best Actress for her performance in 'A Warm December' – a film that's often been described as a "soul western," which must have pleased the Wailers greatly.

"I'd met Sidney Poitier when I was nineteen, when he was acting in 'The Bedford Incident' with Richard Widmark," she explains. "He definitely had a big impact on me because Sidney wanted to uplift the black race, and he was always focused on that. That film helped to expose sickle cell anemia and some of the dialogue transferred itself to my real life and how I felt about my own country. The character I played was an African princess who worked as a diplomat and knew she was going to die, and yet she was still trying to build her nation. I always remember that, but then I put my own career on hold to work with Bob. I never saw what might happen in future. It's just that once I'd gone home to Jamaica in the early seventies, I knew I was going to have to try and help build our nation in my own way."

In April 1972, just six months before Esther met Bob in New York, Poitier had donated receipts from the film's premiere to the New Jersey branch of National Black Political Convention. His political aspirations rubbed off on Esther, as did those of her former boyfriend, film star Marlon Brando. Bob and the other two Wailers were about to receive quite an education from their newfound friend, who combined beauty and intelligence with rare insight into the social issues they held most dear.

Back in Jamaica, everyone was talking about the world heavyweight title fight between Joe Frazier and George Foreman, held in Kingston on January 22nd. Frazier was undefeated in twenty-nine fights but Foreman dominated from the outset, knocking down his opponent three times in the first round and then again in the second. After Frazier was knocked down a sixth time, the referee wouldn't allow him to continue and awarded the victory to Foreman by technical knockout. True to form, Jamaica's musical fraternity rose to the occasion and immortalised it in song. Dennis Alcapone and Big Youth ("George Foreman got you now...") recorded the most memorable tributes. Meanwhile, at Chris Blackwell's Blue Mountain retreat, various Wailers and Island Records' personnel gathered for a preview of 'Catch A Fire' which the label planned to release in a couple of months' time, just as soon as UK tour dates could be arranged.

Peter and Bunny were both eager to hear the finished mix and approved of what they heard. They were already convinced the album was going to wake up Jamaica and send reggae in a different direction. They'd watched how soul music had evolved into a social and political mouthpiece for African-Americans and wanted the same for Jamaica – not because they'd tired of ska and rocksteady, but due to the fact that a fresh outlook was needed. Neither had been present when the overdubbing took place but whilst they trusted Bob, Chris Blackwell was a different proposition. At the playback meeting, he produced contracts and told them Dickie Jobson was going to be their manager. This made them suspicious, since they could easily be jumping from the frying pan into the fire. Jobson would be reporting back to Island and whilst now a liability, Skill Cole was still around, acting as if he was the Wailers' manager.

"Skill Cole was a very uncompromising individual," recalls Al Anderson. "He and Bob wanted to switch with one another. Skill wanted to be a singer and Bob wanted to be a footballer; their little thing clicked and they were very amusing for a time but then it just got out of hand. Skill wanted to take over and manage the band but he didn't have what it took beyond a certain level..."

Both he and Chris Blackwell were gamblers, yet whilst Skill hung around the local racetrack, Blackwell played baccarat for high stakes in places like Monte Carlo. There could only be one winner, and Cole's influence waned considerably thereafter. This incident marked the start of a steep learning curve for the Wailers. They discovered that despite his laidback charm,

Blackwell insisted on pulling the strings and the group would be expected to trade a good deal of their independence in exchange for Island's favours. Despite concerns over their management, the Wailers were generally pleased with what they heard that day, and everyone left in high spirits. Their album now had the rock feel they wanted, and everyone was impressed with Wayne Perkins' guitar playing. Bob had re-voiced certain tracks in London, and 'Concrete Jungle' had benefitted especially – hence his exclamation of "We've got it!" right near the end. 'Kinky Reggae' again sounded more exuberant compared to the original mix whilst '400 Years' had additional guitar and piano, and almost baroque keyboard lines courtesy of Rabbit. The latter plays like he's just joined the Doors instead of Jamaica's most celebrated soul rebels. Maybe he felt more at home on Peter's songs, which partially draw from the American tradition in any case. 'Stop That Train' is noticeably different from the other tracks on 'Catch A Fire.' It's a storytelling song with strong moral content, as found in the best of folk and country music. Peter's cast in the role of a seeker after truth; an itinerant teacher who's grown tired of trying to enlighten those around him, yet retains a desire for social justice. Listening to '400 Years' and 'Stop That Train' it's amazing that Peter struggled to get his songs featured on previous Wailers' albums. To therefore have two included on their flagship Island release wasn't bad going, all things considered.

Family Man was also pleased with what he heard; although he considered Rabbit's keyboards a little too dominant in places and thought Peter and Bunny's backing vocals weren't prominent enough. Lowering their harmonies in the mix had switched the emphasis from the Wailers as a vocal harmony group to Bob as a solo performer, which is not how he or the rest of the group had envisaged it.

"The harmonies aren't supposed to be in the background like that," says Family Man. "They must be out there, close to what Bob was doing, and the only things that are supposed to be in the background are the fills, like if you use horns. The Wailers use a different concept of harmony. It's music using harmony, melody and expression, created by three voices in unison. The Wailers' harmonies, they were unique."

"Basically what Chris did, he speeded up the rhythms so it had more of a rock feel and I think it worked," counters Esther. "Christopher wasn't the greatest producer; he couldn't dance and he wasn't an academic person either. He left Harrow and was sent straight to Charterhouse because he's an accountant really but he put himself in the music and met all of these rhythm and blues people like Fats Domino… Every time one of these musicians came to Jamaica, Chris had some hand in it. He used to buy records and supply jukeboxes in Jamaica before moving to England and plotting how to put the competition out of business. The Blackwells weren't one of Jamaica's ruling families and they weren't involved in the drive to build a new, independent nation either but when you've been schooled in England and then return to Jamaica, you do have some kind of leg up over the rest. You become mixed up with the uptown, middle-class Jamaicans and that's why Chris Blackwell only signed poorer, working-class artists from England or Jamaica. Anyone from a wealthy family could take him to court, so he would always sign people who came from the lower echelons of life, and who didn't have too much else going on for them."

Carnival was held in early March that year and the Wailers wouldn't be touring until April, which meant they had a more than a month to rehearse and prepare for their return to England. Since Peter had declined the offer and Bunny wasn't even invited, Bob was the only band member to board the plane Blackwell had chartered for their Caribbean hi-jinks. The other passengers included Traffic's Jim Capaldi, Dickie Jobson, a US attorney called Abe Somers and his wife Phyllis, Esther, Lee Jaffe and his Brazilian girlfriend Liani Do Rosario. On the way to Trinidad they visited Martinique and Tobago, then stopped off in Haiti on the journey home, where they were met by security guards touting machine guns. Blackwell's party was held overnight in police cells before being escorted back to the plane and allowed to leave. Somehow Bob became separated from the others, and he wasn't best pleased by their indifference. Chances are he felt more exposed as a black man, and also someone who had little money at his disposal. Esther says Bob avoided hanging out with Blackwell after this incident, and never really trusted him. In her photos of their trip Bob looks like a fish out of water and is standing some distance away from Blackwell and his friends.

"Bob and I had been left behind by Christopher and his team," she explains. "They'd forgotten us but then after we'd got back in the plane, they did apologise. It's just that Bob decided he couldn't trust Chris after that and didn't want to do business with him. He was already signed to Island by then, but he was really angry. That's when we wrote 'Get Up Stand Up' together, as we were flying back home but then once we arrived at Island House, Bob disappeared and we couldn't find him. We wanted to take pictures and for them to start rehearsing, but nothing happened. I hadn't even met Family Man and Carly yet, although I'd heard plenty about them. Anyway there we were waiting around and then Peter came by Hope Road one day. I asked him where Bob was and he said, 'So wha'? You like him?' He was so charming and handsome. I said, 'Yes, but that doesn't matter, because you guys are supposed to be rehearsing.' He said, 'You want me to go get him?' I said yes so Peter went and got him and brought him back to Hope Road and that's how the Wailers came back together, except we went through hell getting Bunny to come to the rehearsals. It was like hellfire and damnation and cursing and I nearly starved to death out there in Bull Bay because it was evening by the time they'd smoked ten pounds of ganja and persuaded him to come and rehearse, but then once I heard them all sing together it was beautiful."

CHAPTER SEVENTEEN

Isms And Schisms

Whilst Bob was away, Peter recorded two songs for his own label. 'No Mercy' featured Bunny on conga drums, and is a searing indictment of police brutality. The other track was 'Can't Blame The Youth,' which turns the blame around on the authorities, and lays bare the anger and frustration felt by Jamaica's army of poor, disaffected youth. His lyrics expose the lies perpetuated by church and state education – institutions largely determined by white self-interest. Peter is letting his audience know that young people can see through such deliberate attempts to deceive them. It's one of his best songs to date; voiced with genuine passion and with a chorus that stays in the brain long after the track's finished.

Bunny Wailer has suggested that 'Mark Of The Beast' was recorded within just a few weeks of this session and it sounds like it, although Peter won't release it until a good while later. Also Bob's not on it, which means he's probably still in London or New York. "I see the mark of the beast on their ugly faces. I see them congregating in evil places," begins Peter, who then accuses the police of framing him for ganja. By his own admission, 'Mark Of The Beast' is purely autobiographical. No sooner had he sat down to write the song – and with a spliff dangling from his lips no doubt – than the police burst in his apartment and gave him a pistol-whipping, smashing his ribs and clubbing him over the head with a rifle butt. His head injury will later require seven stitches and cause persistent headaches. Neighbours had apparently been keeping a dance in the yard where he was living. The police came to raid it, but had to pass by Peter's place to get where the action was. They'd smelt herb from outside his window and stopped to investigate. The situation then turned violent after Peter resisted arrest and began to curse them.

It was easy living at Island House by comparison. Esther Anderson and Lee Jaffe had moved in after returning from Carnival. Chris Blackwell had bought the property from an elderly English lady called Miss Goff, who sold it to him for a knockdown price of £3,000 on condition that she could stay there for the rest of her life. For the next few years she would live in modest quarters round the back of the house, next to the rehearsal room. Dickie Jobson and his sister Diane were also based at Island House and Bob too, will spend an increasing amount of time there in future.

He and Esther were now an item and they were writing together too, which was a new experience for Bob. Esther resisted his urgings to fall pregnant and this is what inspired 'I Shot The Sheriff' with its refrain of "Every time I plant a seed, he say kill it before it grows." Her role as Bob's muse will be a collaborative, rather than passive one. Esther was Jamaican too, and well capable of holding her own in their relationship. Bob respected her, and learnt a lot during their time together. Esther had lived in "swinging" London throughout most of the sixties and befriended many of its principal characters, including well-known filmmakers, artists and musicians. She was accustomed to a cultural milieu that was far removed from anything found in Trench Town, but it was her love affair with Marlon Brando (and then working association with Sidney Poitier) that had sharpened her political awareness and lent purpose to her artistic endeavours. She'd met Brando, twenty years her senior, in London during the spring of 1966 on the set of 'A Countess From Hong Kong,' directed by Charlie Chaplin. Brando was already a legend, and certainly no stranger to controversy. His 1953 film 'The Wild One' had dramatised tensions between the older and younger generations to the point where he'd become a worldwide symbol of rebellion – both on and off the screen. It was soon apparent he held the Hollywood film industry in contempt and by 1955 he was expressing a desire to make films that "had social value and would improve the world." He'd later become involved in fundraising ventures on behalf of the Congress of Racial Equality and meet with Bobby Seale and Eldridge Cleaver after expressing concern over Huey Newton's jail sentence. Brando helped fund the Panthers for a while; attended Bobby Hutton's funeral and paid for several members of the party to attend Dr. Martin Luther King's memorial service, although he remained opposed all forms of violence. After disengaging himself from the Panthers he made donations to the SCLC and visited Alabama, where he spoke to black people in their homes and learnt of their day-to-day realities firsthand. He even contemplated giving up acting altogether, so he could pursue his civil rights activities. As the sixties drew to a close, he participated in 'King: A Filmed Record: Montgomery to Memphis,' a three-hour documentary about Dr. King that featured a host of other leading actors, including Harry Belafonte, Charlton Heston and Paul Newman. This little-heralded film was screened in the US during early 1970 and billed as a "one-time event," with the larger than usual admission fee being donated to a fund set up in Dr. King's memory.

Brando had turned down parts in 'Butch Cassidy & The Sundance Kid' and 'Ryan's Daughter' in order to make such films. Despite being a major celebrity, his acting career had been on the wane before making 'The Godfather' in 1972. He and Esther had ended their relationship by then, but would still see each other occasionally. Brando's next film was 'Last Tango In Paris,' which has been called "the most powerfully erotic film ever made" and was screened in New York shortly before Esther left for Jamaica. Newsweek described it "a piece of talented debauchery" with the reviewer claiming it made him "want to vomit." It even sparked obscenity charges in Italy. Fortunately the judges ruled in favour of director Bernardo Bertolucci, whose film had arrived in the midst of blossoming feminism, gay rights and sexual promiscuity. In March 1973, just as the furore over 'Last Tango In Paris' was at its height, Brando won an Oscar for 'The Godfather' but refused to attend the ceremony and sent Princess Sacheen Little Feather in his place. Upon taking the podium, she read out his declamation of how the US – and also its film industry – had treated Native Americans. "For two hundred years we have lied to them, cheated them out of their lands and turned them into beggars," she intoned, to a chorus of boos. Brando sensed that might happen but had wanted to inform the Oscars' two billion television viewers of some home truths concerning America's indigenous peoples. With Little Feather's help he succeeded, only to sharply divided opinion.

Several years earlier, he'd accompanied Esther and Millie Small on a tour of West Africa, where he'd delighted in the local music scene. Brando had played drums as a youngster and also attended Afro-Caribbean dance classes, where he'd come into contact with blacks, Haitians and Latinos for the first time. To quote Patricia Bosworth, "sometimes he pounded on the congas for hours, until the skin on his hands split. His drum teacher was Henri "Papa" Augustine, the company's hungan or voodoo priest, who taught him that every rhythm has a purpose, such as healing or warding off evil spirits."

Esther would be reminiscing about Brando's love of drumming soon after she and Peter set off in search of Bunny, who was at home in Bull Bay.

"It was Peter and I who went to get Bunny, because that's how I discovered Bongo Mattie," she recalls. "That's how the whole Rasta thing got tied in with what the Wailers were doing because I saw all of that in Bongo Mattie's yard – the red, gold and green and the Rasta drumming, that whole expression... When we got to where Bunny lived, he was cursing and carrying on and said I couldn't come inside. Peter told me to stay outside and said that once Bunny had calmed down, then he'd call me. I said okay and then I heard all this drumming coming from nearby. It sounded like some Pocomania ritual I remember seeing as a child so I marched up to the gate and there was Bongo Mattie, who welcomed me inside. We sat around talking for hours whilst they were singing and playing drums and that's the first time I heard 'Rastaman Chant.' Before that, I'd been to Hellshire beach and met Countryman and all these other Rastas but what I experienced out in Bull Bay made a deep impression on me, because I'd never seen anything like that before. I'd left St. Mary as a young girl of fourteen and lived in Kingston for two years so

I'd witnessed these colourful fellows who'd shout at people in the street about Babylon and all that, but I'd never really understood what they were talking about. They were thought of as bogeymen and I was a bit scared of them, but this was something altogether different."

Esther had developed a keen interest in photography and lost no time in capturing what she'd seen in Bongo Mattie's yard on film. Some of those images will later be used on the inner sleeve of the Wailers' next album. She also took the bold step of getting the gardener at 56 Hope Road to paint the woodwork of the main house and outbuildings in Rasta colours. Such an act would have been unthinkable just a short time previously, and especially since Island House was situated just a few hundred yards from the Prime Minister's official residence. Esther had been absent from Jamaica for over a decade and in her excitement, had given little heed to possible repercussions after stumbling across a cultural and spiritual tradition that had remained all but hidden to outsiders until surfacing in 'The Harder They Come.' Viewing Rastafari through a prism of art and politics, Esther had immediately seized upon its potency as a revolutionary force. It was she – unwittingly perhaps – who persuaded Chris Blackwell of its promotional value, despite Bunny Wailer's reminder that "eighty-five percent of the musicians who created ska were Rastafarians.

"The way they played music, it had to be coming from some divine source for it to have survived until now, and for it to still be making a great difference in people's lives,' he opined. "The drums and the horns used to herald the comings and goings of His Imperial Majesty, which is how the Order of the Nyahbinghi originated. That's why the nyahbinghi also plays in reggae songs. It's a relationship, but no one taught us to do these things. They were instilled in us from we were in our mothers' wombs. I used to play drums, as well as make guitars and play them as a child. That was in me naturally, from birth and it was something I brought out from within. It came from rapture, and was phobic."

Author Leonardo Acosta seems to echo this view by asserting that, "If we wish to find a symbol that embraces the cultural identity of Africans brought to the Caribbean by the slave trade, and which has been able to represent that identity throughout four centuries of resistance despite the most inhuman and alienating conditions known in history, that symbol would be the drum."

Beginning with 'Selassie Is The Chapel,' the Wailers had already embarked down the road of incorporating the sounds and symbols associated with Rastafari into their music. What they lacked was marketing, and the ability to maximise its impact in the visual sense. Chris Blackwell and Esther Anderson both helped in this regard but the other, more essential ingredients were already there, as Lee Jaffe can attest.

"The Wailers were really, really tight, spiritually and politically. I felt it in their music. They were amazing together. They were articulate, powerful, focussed on where they wanted to go and the message that they had and how to get it out there, and they were so incredibly uncompromising that I was left defenceless. I couldn't think that any other mission could be more important. I knew that they were not going to compromise to get a hit record. It was the most fierce, pure attitude I had ever been confronted with, and it left me very humble. I had always considered my work radical, and to meet the Wailers and sense the enormity of what they were doing – well, I just wanted to be part of that. I knew absolutely it was where I wanted to be."

Lee spent the early part of 1973 with the Wailers and saw them every day. All thoughts of filming in Chile evaporated as he fell under the group's spell and assisted them however he could, whether by contributing ideas for lyrics, running errands or just hanging out and keeping them company. He was especially close to Bob, which meant the others readily accepted him in turn. Bob was now dividing his time between Island House and Bull Bay when he wasn't back in Trench Town playing football with old friends like Seeco. Either that or he and Skill Cole would be out running somewhere, accompanied by whoever could match them for pace and stamina. Personal fitness and an ital diet were crucial components of the Rastafarian lifestyle, and all three Wailers took such things very seriously. Most days they'd run along the beach near where Bunny lived then go for a dip at Cane River Falls, where Esther filmed them relaxing with Ras Daniel Hartman – a talented artist who'd starred as one of the main Rasta characters in 'The Harder They Come.' Chris Blackwell had given Esther a Sony video recorder and the black and white footage she and Lee Jaffe took of them during those early months of 1973 provides a most intimate glimpse of the Wailers at rest and play. (Her documentary 'Bob Marley: The Making Of The Legend' was finally premiered in 2011.)

Rita was safely out of the way in Bull Bay, raising Bob's children during this period. Bob still visited her, but loyalty to his creative muse came first. Esther's involvement led him to write some of his best songs to date including 'Burnin' And Lootin',' with lines inspired by their incarceration in Haiti. "Oh God I was a prisoner too," he laments. "Could not recognise the faces standing over me. They were all dressed in uniforms of brutality." 'Burnin' And Lootin' was re-titled 'Curfew' when the Wailers issued it on Tuff Gong, possibly to avoid censure although the radio stations hardly played it in any case, despite its anti-drugs message. 'I Shot The Sheriff' we've mentioned already, except Lee Jaffe also claims to have contributed towards that one after suggesting Bob add "the deputy" to his list of characters. Where Esther's presence is really felt is on 'Get Up Stand Up,' which she and Bob wrote soon after their first meeting.

"Bob and I wrote the original song in about twenty minutes," she told me. "I wasn't there when Peter wrote his part but Bob said, 'boy, me want the Wailers to be famous and so I give it to Peter because him say that too many of my songs deh pon the album.' When I heard the verse Peter sings, I know that is Peter's voice and so to me it's his contribution no matter what anyone else may say. Bob said he gave half to Peter because they'd had a row and Peter wanted to leave the group but then I remember asking him about 'I Shot The Sheriff,' and why just his name appeared on that. He did the same thing with 'Burnin' An' Lootin,' which he and I also wrote together, and said it was to make the band bigger. I was a successful actress and so I was doing it just to help them. I didn't think for a minute about money and stuff like that, but I did want my credit – as an artist, I wanted to be recognised for my contribution and I think that's only natural. Joe Higgs, he used to throw in some lines too, but none of us were thinking these songs were going to become so famous."

Esther likens Peter and Bob to Lennon and McCartney and says there was definitely less friction between those two than there was between Bob and Bunny. If there was a falling out between Bob and Peter it was over the wording of 'Get Up Stand Up,' which was even more explosive in the first instance.

"I was writing this tune 'Get Up Stand Up' with Bob," he'll later tell Fikishka Cumbo "and my verse said, 'We're sick and tired of this bullshit game, dying and going to heaven in Jesus' name. We know and we understand that Jah is a living man.' The guy tell me I can't say "bullshit" and that I must say something else but him can't tell me what to say so I just say "ism schism." It's bullshit, but in this society only certain people can say certain words."

In years to come, Amnesty International will adopt 'Get Up Stand Up' as an anthem for the dispossessed. Poor people have long been brainwashed into believing their happiness depends on crumbs from the rich man's table, and the two Wailers were having none of it.

"Preacher man, don't tell me Heaven is under the earth," Bob sings in the first verse. "I know you don't know what life is really worth." A little later this same point is made even clearer with the lines, " Most people think great God will come from the sky. Take away everything and make everybody feel high. But if you know what life is worth. You would look for yours on earth."

Have the Wailers ever recorded a more incendiary lyric? And doesn't this song sound a lot more like Peter's than Bob's? Because Bob's rebel songs are usually a lot less direct and cast him in the role of an outlaw – witness 'Duppy Conqueror' or 'Iron Lion Zion,' which they recorded back in 1973 but won't surface until many years later, as part of Tuff Gong's 'Songs Of

Freedom' box set.

Bunny meanwhile, was penning the kind of pastoral hymns that'll completely transform perceptions of Rastafarians as madmen or drug addicts, and portray them as Jamaican holy men instead. Lee Jaffe describes Bunny and Jean Watt's simple bamboo dwelling overlooking Bull Bay as "exquisite." That's where Bunny wrote 'Hallelujah Time,' 'The Oppressed Song' and 'Reincarnated Souls.' Island chose the latter as the flipside of 'Catch A Fire,' and thought about giving the Wailers' next album that title. Chris Blackwell had impressed upon them the need for additional material as there would be little opportunity to write and record once they'd began touring, and they'd responded magnificently. Some of these songs were recorded at the same time as 'Catch A Fire' or started whilst Bob was away, with the remainder being recorded at Harry J's during the spring of 1973. Apart from 'Get Up Stand Up,' Peter's only contributions will be 'One Foundation' and a re-recording of 'No Sympathy' that will remain unreleased for quite some time. The initial recordings didn't work out but the second, recorded soon after Bob's return, are well in keeping with Peter's legacy. 'One Foundation' is an appeal for unity, and with lyrics far removed from the polemics of 'Get Up Stand Up' or 'Can't Blame The Youth.' It's the kind of all-inclusive message you'd expect to hear from a rock or folk act, rather than an embattled Rastafarian from Trench Town.

"All of the Wailers were quite political but I think Peter had a greater worldview than any of the others, including Bob," says Esther. "He and Bob would talk all this superstitious nonsense, but Peter had the capacity to see things on a broader scale unlike Bunny, who was a very violent person in my opinion. When I tried to photograph him later on, he took this big stick of wood and knocked me down to the ground with it. He almost killed me, but what could I do? Bunny caused a lot of problems for Bob and I when we were together. He used to tell people Bob had left Rita for some middle-class woman but that wasn't true. We never had too much money when I was growing up and my mother was descended from Arawaks and Tamils so there was no name for me or my brother Winston, who had long hair and was calling himself an Israelite by then. What Bunny failed to realise was that my family had a long history of being humanitarians, because my great-grandfather William Anderson was sent to Jamaica by the British authorities to look out for the newly freed slaves. He'd gone there to protect poor blacks from his own white people."

It's possible that Bunny felt jealous of Bob, who had this knack of falling on his feet and getting the kind of breaks denied his band mates. Friends of theirs have hinted there were sometimes racial overtones to Peter and Bunny's criticisms of Marley, and that they considered his lighter complexion to be an unfair advantage – especially when it came to dealing with record companies like Island. Fortunately for them, Island had struck a deal with Harry J, whose studio in Roosevelt Avenue was well-equipped by Jamaican standards. Some of the tracks they recorded there were newer versions of songs they'd originally recorded for Coxsone or Lee Perry. 'Put It On,' 'Small Axe' and 'Duppy Conqueror' all fall in this category. There were several reasons for doing this, apart from the fact they had access to better recording facilities. For one thing, the band had grown tighter than ever. The Barrett brothers' rhythm section was now an integral part of the Wailers' sound and their playing so intuitive, it brought magic to everything they touched. They and Bob had grown especially close, and Family Man in particular was constantly searching for ways to improve their material, whether by learning new instruments such as the clavinet or subtly altering the arrangements of songs like 'Small Axe.' He's referred to some of the tracks recorded during these sessions as "demos" – most notably 'Pass It On' and 'Get Up Stand Up.' These will be finished properly at Island's studio in London. The last track they recorded before leaving for England was 'Rastaman Chant,' which manages to combine the earthy spirituality of a Rasta grounation with decent production values. It's the Wailers' best attempt yet at capturing the authentic sound of nyahbinghi in a studio environment. Led by Bob, 'Rastaman Chant' is exactly what it suggests – a righteous invocation, and a near perfect demonstration of the Wailers' close harmony skills. Carly Barrett had become a father for the first time in December and played a central role on 'Rastaman Chant,' as you might expect from a master drummer. The lyrics are rooted in the hymnal tradition, and yearn for a final resting place. This will be the last track Bob, Peter and Bunny ever sing on together, although no one – not even those closest to them – had any inkling of this at the time.

To all outward purposes, the Wailers' camp was a relatively happy one. Bob and Esther made a fine couple and would often set off for the countryside in his battered old station wagon. Nine Miles and Negril, which was a day's drive to the west, were favourite destinations. Peter and Bunny were also more settled than in the past and unlike Bob, didn't have to lie about their current relationships (since Bob had told Rita that Esther was Lee Jaffe's girlfriend.) It was around this same time that music publisher Don Williams, who shared office space with Shelter Records' Denny Cordell in Los Angeles, entered the Wailers' orbit. Williams had first visited Jamaica with his girlfriend, who was the stills photographer on 'Papillion' – a film starring Steve McQueen and Dustin Hoffman and partially filmed in the area around Seaford Town in Westmoreland, close to where Peter was from. Filming went on for three weeks and so Don had lost no time in journeying to Kingston, where he'd sought out music and business opportunities. He'll visit Jamaica regularly from then on, and befriend many of the people within the Wailers' circle. His love of reggae music was ignited after Denny Cordell – already a close friend of Chris Blackwell's – had returned from a trip to London, where he'd struck a deal to distribute Coxsone's material in the US.

"Denny had come back with a stack of Jamaican records and when I heard them I went berserk!" says Don, excitedly. "Shelter was based in a house. My office was at the front and Denny's was in the back. There was a hallway some fifty or sixty feet long between us and as soon as I heard this track by Toots & The Maytals called 'Never Grow Old' I raced into his office saying, 'What is that?' I started grabbing up all these records and he said, 'I was wondering when someone around here was going to get it.' It's still one of my favourite Jamaican recordings but that's what started me off. Shortly after that, I went to Kingston and stayed in this apartment right next to 56 Hope Road; all that separated the two buildings was this hedgerow, they were that close together. That's when I first met Bob and Lee Jaffe, who were sat in the living room at Hope Road together. Bob was having some concerns with his publishing deal with Danny Sims at the time. Johnny Nash's 'I Can See Clearly Now' album had already charted, it was a big success and Danny was sending Bob contracts for these individual songs he wanted Bob to sign. I was a music publisher and I was connected to Chris Blackwell through Denny but I was also white so maybe I was a little suspect in Bob's mind, but he really didn't want to sign all of these individual contracts. Danny had exclusive writer agreements with Bob and Peter but those agreements expired just at the point where I happened to appear on the scene. I said, 'hey, there's some money I can give you.' We were all pretty young at the time and I didn't have too much experience with the Jamaican side of things but Peter wanted to get his songs recorded, just like how Bob was getting some of his songs recorded so I signed him, Bunny and Joe Higgs to song-writing deals, and I also signed Bob Andy as well..."

Shelter would release just three songs licensed from Jamaican labels, including the Wailers' 'Duppy Conqueror' and U Roy's 'Flashing My Whip.' None achieved a breakthrough, despite the growing cult status of 'The Harder They Come' in the US. There wasn't the same network of Caribbean communities in America as there was in the UK, or a similar number of reggae sound-systems to help promote new releases.

"Capitol Records was our distributor at the time and the radio stations just didn't know what to do with them," says Don. "Those records were just so different. There was nothing even remotely close to them at that time..."

Recognition in the US would have to wait. In the meantime, the Wailers' thoughts had turned towards England, where the 'Catch A Fire' tour was due to commence in late April. The band had used several different keyboard players on the album, and yet they couldn't tour with any of them. Glen Adams had left for the USA; Winston Wright was already committed to touring with Jimmy Cliff, whilst Tyrone Downie and Bernard "Touter" Harvey were still at school. Their replacement would be Earl Lindo, whom everyone called "Wya." He'd learnt to play whilst a student at Excelsior High School and then in local bands such as the Astronauts, the Meters and Generation Gap. Peter and Family Man had already played sessions with him at Treasure Isle, where he'd been tutored by Aubrey Adams and cut the odd instrumental, including a hit version of U Roy's 'Wear You To The Ball.' Wya was playing with Now Generation, who used to feature Wailers' songs such as 'Trench Town Rock,' 'Screwface' and 'Man To Man' in their set list, when Bob had gone to see them play at the Sombrero one night. Soon after that, Now Generation backed the Wailers during a show at the VIP Club, where everyone got a little more acquainted. Family Man especially was taken by Wya's wide-ranging tastes in music, which encompassed soul, jazz, funk and progressive rock, as well as reggae. Although only twenty years old, the youngster from Trelawny had already mastered piano, Hammond organ, clavinet and even the mellotron – an instrument that had baffled most Kingston session players after Federal and then Dynamic had invested in one. Rabbit's quasi-symphonic flourishes on 'Catch A Fire' held no fears for him and yet he also had a great sense of rhythm, because he'd slotted right in with Family Man and Carly's rebel grooves from the very first time they'd invited him up to Island House for rehearsals.

Wya had been a fan of the Wailers ever since hearing their earliest

Studio One releases. He remembers poking his head around the door of Randy's studio one night, and witnessing them cutting sides for Scratch in a near impenetrable cloud of ganja smoke. The Wailers weren't like any other Jamaican group. They were unafraid to take risks, and had a strong sense of identity that spilled over into everything they did. Touring with them was a dream come true and yet would entail a level of discipline no amount of musical schooling could have prepared him for.

According to Bunny, the Wailers were "pure ghetto rock stones" and posed a serious challenge for Wya, who'd joined them just as the group had embarked on something different for Jamaica, and for reggae music as a whole.

"You had to adjust yourself to meet the Wailers," he growls, "because the Wailers don't bow or fool around. You knew that you couldn't mingle with the Wailers. Your heart would have to be geared for it, and your whole mind would have to be ready for it."

CHAPTER EIGHTEEN

Rockin' At Mr. B's

'Catch A Fire' was released on April 13th. Island advertised it in England's leading rock publications – the NME, Sounds and Melody Maker – and the sleeve design immediately gained attention, even if the name "Wailers" didn't. Zippo windproof lighters were must-have accessories for cannabis smokers and the vinyl LP was housed in a cardboard replica that opened on a hinge, just like the real thing. It was touches like this that made Island everyone's favourite independent record label. They knew what was happening at grassroots level, and were clever in how they used it. Esther disagreed, thought the sleeve was a gimmick and said it didn't represent what the Wailers were about. Her portrait of Bob smoking a spliff – which he'd felt uneasy about posing for – was used on the cover of subsequent pressings. Esther was taking a strong personal interest in the Wailers, and felt justifiably proud of the photos she'd taken of them. She also knew what she was talking about after being mentored by Robert Freeman, who'd designed album covers for the Beatles. The artwork on the Wailers' next album will reflect more accurately what she had in mind for them yet there's no mistaking the impact that original 'Catch A Fire' design had, even before people heard the actual music.

Prior to 'Catch A Fire,' most reggae albums were singles' compilations housed in tacky sleeves decorated by cartoons or scantily clad black girls. The music was presented as if it was of little worth and with no thoughts of visual sophistication. Rock fans on the other hand, had grown accustomed to seeing cover art by the likes of Hipgnosis and even Andy Warhol. Unfortunately reggae wasn't held in the same regard and its best lyricists went largely ignored. This situation will change as the markets converge and hippies disillusioned with the artificialities of glam-rock begin to find similarities between their vision of an alternative Woodstock nation and the Rastafarians' rejection of Babylon. Much has been said and written about reggae's affinities with punk, but it was the student crowd who first embraced Rasta music outside of Jamaica.

'Catch A Fire' surpassed everything the Wailers had recorded to date. The quality of production and marketing was so much better, and they'd achieved this without compromise. There was no 'Reggae On Broadway' or 'Sugar Sugar' on 'Catch A Fire,' which marked a watershed in the music's evolution and rang the changes loud and clear, yet during its first year of release 'Catch A Fire' will sell just 14,000 copies. That's a poor return for an advertising budget reputed to be twice that amount, and Island knew they could only improve on it if the Wailers managed to build a substantial live following. The forthcoming UK and American tour dates would be crucial, since there was little likelihood of them having chart hits. (The low-key response to recent Tuff Gong 7" pressings of 'Baby, Baby We Got A Date,' 'Midnight Ravers' and 'Concrete Jungle' had proven that.) Instead, Island would emphasise the Wailers' musical strengths and remind everyone that here was a group powered by Jamaica's No. 1 rhythm section, and spearheading a revolutionary new genre rooted in dread heavy drum and bass.

Bunny nearly didn't make the trip. He'd wanted to take his handmade conga drums with him but insisted on waiting until the skins were stretched properly. The group left for the airport without him, but then decided to turn back. As their car entered the driveway of Island House he was sat on the front steps, chastened but unbowed, his drums stacked neatly by his side.

The same day they arrived in London Chris Blackwell's grandmother died, which meant he wasn't there to meet them. That's perhaps just as well since the band members were housed in a flat recently vacated by one of Island Records' rock acts, and immediately felt affronted by the state of the place. Bob meanwhile, stayed with Esther in an apartment just off the King's Road. Taking advantage of a week's break for rehearsals, she took them down to the Thames embankment for a photo session. Peter's in the foreground wearing khaki, sunglasses and a rather fetching bobble hat. He looks the friendliest of the bunch, because no one else is smiling. Bob's looking stern and has his hands pushed deep in the pocket of his raincoat whilst Bunny appears sullen and is tightly wrapped up in scarf, hat and at least two jackets. After their previous stay in London they knew what to expect from the British weather and clearly weren't about to be caught unawares.

It wasn't just the climate making them feel apprehensive. Travelling around the country in a Ford Transit wouldn't exactly be a picnic and the lack of a designated sound engineer left them at the mercy of people with no experience of mixing reggae. Nor did their problems end there because in the absence of a proper road crew, the Wailers had to hump their own equipment in and out of venues. Benjamin Foote was their tour manager, but had little experience. His father was Jamaican Governor General Sir Hugh Foote, who'd once employed Chris Blackwell as his aide de camp. We can therefore assume his appointment was due to nepotism, rather than any practical reason. There were no proper motorways in those days, which meant using 'B' roads and eating at a succession of transport cafes that served up greasy, fried food and virtually nothing else. They'll survive on a diet of fish and chips and the occasional curry after venturing beyond London's city limits, but at least Nottingham's sizable West Indian population had ensured them a decent turnout once they'd rolled up at the Coleman Club. This was the first gig of their tour, on April 27th. The following night they played at Lancaster University and performed to a mostly indifferent crowd of white students. It would take time to win over the college circuit, despite the Island press department's best efforts. In the meantime they headed back to London, where a warm reception awaited them at Mr. B's in Peckham. This was the same venue where Bob had met Brent Clarke, and the mainly Caribbean audience welcomed the Wailers with open arms.

A few days later (on May 1st), they recorded two sessions for the BBC at the company's newly refurbished studios in Portland Place, just opposite Broadcasting House near Regent Street. The former Langham Hotel was a training centre, as well as recording facility. It had an air of faded grandeur compounded by a wizened, but stately doorman in full uniform, complete with epaulettes. The first session was for John Peel's radio show 'Top Gear.' The Wailers performed three songs – 'Concrete Jungle,' 'Rastaman Chant' and 'Slave Driver' – for a programme due to be broadcast in two weeks' time. When John Peel had joined Radio 1 in 1967, the station was limited by the amount of needle time each show was allotted. This meant DJs would have to talk more, as they could only play a certain number of records. Peel had got round this by broadcasting live sessions and not just by major acts, but also new or unsigned ones. To quote Mick Wall, "nobody was obliged to perform their singles or even any of the tracks from their current albums; bands could play anything they fancied on the night. John later said he saw it as 'an opportunity to actually advance the music a little bit, which is what he did.'" Wall describes how Peel remained, "at heart, an irredeemable fan," and "the same shamelessly myopic music worshipper he had been since schooldays."

"The one thing all the different artists that appeared on Peel shows had in common, and the theme that would become the backbone to all future Peel shows was that they had begun from an unpromising starting point so far removed from whatever currently passed for the mainstream that without Peel they would have had little or no hope of receiving airplay on what was still the UK's only national pop station," he continued. Peel was an unashamed supporter of minority genres such as reggae, but later recalled senior members of the BBC management team being dismayed that he'd continued to play "music of the black criminal classes."

Later that same day, still ensconced in the labyrinth of studios at the Langham, the Wailers recorded further songs for the BBC 2 television programme 'The Old Grey Whistle Test.' Bunny has claimed the Wailers recorded the entire 'Catch A Fire' album at this session, and not just 'Stir It Up' and 'Concrete Jungle.' This seems unlikely, as featured acts rarely performed for longer than five or six minutes. As with 'Top Gear,' bands didn't need a hit single to get on 'The Old Grey Whistle Test,' which served its viewers a diet of mainly rock, folk and country music. The Wailers were the first reggae act to appear on the programme and they were mesmerising. From the opening shot of Bob strumming the intro to 'Stir It Up,' viewers knew that something special was about to happen. Johnny Nash had recently charted with his own version, but it was nothing like this one. The tension in their music was almost unbearable, yet soothing at the same time. Peter, imperious as ever in shades and red, gold and green bobble hat, barely moved whilst picking out lead runs on his guitar. Bunny, a fez perched on top of his dreadlocks, hovered over his drums like a praying mantis whilst Wya played keyboards borrowed from Pink Floyd's Rick Wright. The way that he and Family Man grooved to the music was a reminder that we can dance to it, as well as become transfixed by it, because the anguish on Bob's face as he sings 'Concrete Jungle' left us in no doubt as to the reality of his lyrics. It was Jamaican style soul at its best, and the Wailers' performance that day is still the most exquisite expression of sufferers' music ever seen on British television.

"Bob had this charisma, this spiritual thing that's in his voice - it's there in every song I heard him sing," says New York engineer Joe Venneri, who worked on most of their JAD material. "It's not musically perfect. It just seems to be an association with the earth. He's got this honest thing that just comes across. Whether he's sharp or flat or sideways, there's something to everything he sings."

Whilst all the vocals were sang "live," both rhythm tracks had been recorded earlier in the day. The group had originally felt insulted having to mime playing their instruments, but this was soon offset by the satisfaction of making their television debut. Island Records were delighted as the tour still had three weeks left to run. They more than anyone, understood the value of what had just taken place since very few people owned video recorders, there was no YouTube, and it was still decades before the advent of social networking sites.

As the Wailers trooped out of the Langham that evening the doorman, who'd worked at the BBC for over fifty years, leant over to Family Man and murmured, "I like your noise." He'd heard a vast number of bands during that time, and so this was praise indeed. Family Man says the Wailers' party would remember him with affection, and Peter make them laugh afterwards by mimicking the old man's upper-class accent.

Soon, they'll climb aboard their Ford Transit and journey up north once more. Previous apprehensions about skinheads were confirmed when a gang of them smashed the van's windscreen, which left the band feeling distinctly uncomfortable but attendances will noticeably improve after their appearance on 'The Old Grey Whistle Test,' and especially at college gigs. They played at Hatfield Polytechnic, York University, Manchester University, Wolverhampton's 67 Club, Essex University in Colchester, Boobs in Bristol and North Staffordshire Polytechnic in Stoke before driving across to Teeside and then returning to London for a second show at Mr B's on May 13th. Four nights at the Speakeasy would follow in-between recording sessions at the Island studios on Basing Street, where Bob had supervised the final mixes of 'Catch A Fire' just six months earlier.

They'd brought tapes of material recorded in Jamaica with them, since these tracks were going to be mixed and mastered in England once they were finished. Apart from completing 'I Shot The Sheriff,' the Wailers redid the backing vocals on 'Reincarnated Souls,' which they assumed would be the title track of their next album. 'Reincarnated Souls' also benefitted from some quick-witted improvisation by Family Man, who simulated the sound of rainfall by pouring water onto a sheet of newspaper that he'd spread out on the floor of the studio. Although the band were pleased with Wya's contributions on stage, he was a spectator during these sessions and it was Family Man who played piano and clavinet on 'Get Up Stand Up' – a song that had taken on fresh meaning after the May Day demonstrations. On the same day the Wailers had visited the BBC, England had come to a virtual standstill after the TUC had called for a one-day strike and national rail services had been halted or disrupted. Protest rallies had taken place in Birmingham, Manchester, Liverpool and Glasgow prompting Jack Jones, leader of the Transport & General Workers' Union to warn the British government it would be foolish to ignore the millions of people "who are fed up with the way prices are continuing to rise."

Chris Blackwell had been impressed with the Wailers' first night at the Speakeasy, and noted how Family Man had taken good care to get the sound levels and balance just right. The band's 'Top Gear' session, recorded two weeks earlier, was broadcast that same day, on May 15th. Awareness of the Wailers was growing and since several influential rock writers had caught their shows at the Speakeasy, Island were expecting further press coverage in the coming weeks. The small, dimly lit club was a renowned media hangout on account of its central location in Margaret Street, just north of Oxford Circus, and the fact that it had been an important launch pad for artists like Jimi Hendrix, David Bowie and King Crimson. The Wailers were paid £250 per night for their four shows. Manager Laurie O' Leary told Marco Virgona that Chris Blackwell had approached him with a view to promoting the Wailers, but he'd turned them down at first. "'Not our scene Chris, we're a progressive music club,' was my initial reaction but how wrong was I?" he asks. "Fortunately Chris persevered and the rest is history." O' Leary describes the shows as "sensational" and notes "the crowd of an eclectic mix were spellbound with the rhythms of sound never before experienced.

"Chris wanted a week in the club and I gave him an unheard of four consecutive dates. Marley's the only artiste to have ever had that option in the Speak'."

He remembers seeing Eric Clapton, Jeff Beck and members of the Who there, taking in the hypnotic sight and sounds of Jamaica's soul rebels. Family Man talks of them having cast a spell on the Speakeasy audiences, and makes reference to the Wailers' spiritual mission when describing how they delivered "lyrics of roots, culture and reality, for the young people worldwide.

"It was just like the gospel crusaders, singing these songs of freedom," he tells us. "These redemption songs that bring wisdom, knowledge and overstanding, and that give you true inspiration, coming directly from the Father of course. The most we do is just smoke our herbs to give us a little inspiration, and that's it you know? Then we let the good times roll..."

The analogy with gospel is a good one, since the parallels between what happens in church and what the Wailers were doing on stage wasn't all that different essentially. They too, wanted to raise consciousness and save souls, but with music instead of religious dogma.

"The thing was to get the roots and reality message across," says Family Man, "so our opening track would always be 'Rastaman Chant.' Bob, Bunny, Peter and my brother played the nyahbinghi drums; I played bass and Wya played organ. It was the six of us who start it and 'Rastaman Chant' that create the spell because even in the rehearsals, we knew we'd got a magic different from everything else we'd heard on Island Records at that time."

Prior to Dylan and the Beatles becoming cultural spokesmen music was simply entertainment – a commodity to ease the dull ache of everyday life and shake off inhibitions. During the days of ska and rocksteady, people liked to dance and hadn't worried too much about what the lyrics were saying, but this wasn't the case with roots reggae. Rasta artists like the Wailers had developed their own unique worldview, their own ethics, values and language, as well as their own brand of music. They'd adopted a lifestyle based upon the principles of love, peace and harmony, and yet which sought to overthrow the inequalities that continued to oppress poor people. They were revolutionaries, and determined to sweep all before them in a bid to get their message heard.

Trojan Records brought them crashing to earth after issuing a "new" Wailers' album called 'African Herbsman.' This was a compilation of leftover tracks from their Lee Perry sessions, grouped around 'Soul Revolution.' The same label will reissue 'Soul Rebels' as 'Rasta Revolution,' even as Scratch reused the rhythm tracks from 'Dreamland,' 'Kaya' and 'Keep On Moving' as part of his landmark dub album, 'Blackboard Jungle.' Needless to say, the Wailers had no prior knowledge of these releases and worried they might detract attention from 'Catch A Fire.'

Their next gig was at the Greyhound pub in Fulham Palace Road on May 20th. That's where radio DJ David Rodigan saw them and then watched in amazement as they huddled in a nearby doorway after the show and lit up enormous spliffs, sending clouds of smoke into the cool night air. Dates at Fantasia in Northampton and Leicester Polytechnic followed before the band returned to London on May 24th and played at the Paris Theatre on Regent Street. This show was recorded by the BBC and broadcast as part of Radio 1's 'In Concert' series. The producer was Jeff Griffin, who'd started the series three years previously, whilst radio and TV presenter Pete Drummond was MC. The Paris Theatre was a converted cinema that the BBC had been using for light entertainment programmes since the end of the war. Griffin recalled that when Drummond introduced the Wailers, he told the crowd their music was "very danceable," and that the band would be more than happy if some of them got up and danced.

"Eventually two or three couples started dancing, and towards the end there were quite a few more," he told a reporter from Distant Drums. "I think the band were almost oblivious of it. Whether that was because they were in a certain frame of mind or because of certain substances they had partaken of during the previous hour, I don't know. I remember going into their dressing room to check everyone was okay and to give them the five-minute warning and I could hardly see anyone for the smoke! The mood was great though, very relaxed. At the time they were beginning to get a bit of a reputation. They weren't big yet but they were growing, so I was keen to get off on the right foot."

He says the Wailers played for nearly an hour, although only thirty-five minutes were used for the actual broadcast. As on previous shows, they'd opened with 'Rastaman Chant' before virtually playing 'Catch A Fire' in its entirety. The Wailers had now enjoyed more radio exposure during the past month than they'd ever received in Jamaica, and left for shows in Exmouth and Bristol in good spirits. The mainly black crowd at Tony Bullimore's Bamboo Club in Bristol greeted them warmly, which buoyed their mood yet further. Their next stop was in Hitchin, Hertfordshire and then Birmingham's Top Rank Suite, where they were given another rousing reception. The tour would end a day later at the Coach House in Southampton – a show that proved anti-climatic compared to the highs experienced in Bristol and Birmingham. As the adrenalin waned, tempers had begun to fray and Bunny's especially. Family Man notes how relations between the three main Wailers had deteriorated ever since they'd played the Speakeasy and says that Bunny, whose face "wore a permanent screw," rarely stopped complaining.

When the band had first arrived at the Speakeasy they'd headed downstairs and been greeted by the sight of someone dressed as a vampire, lying in a coffin. It was a publicity stunt for 'The Rocky Horror Show' but Bunny and Peter weren't amused. Both got stroppy and Bunny even turned round and headed back up the steps, threatening never to return. The atmosphere got tense, and Bob had to go out on the street and remonstrate with him. The pair of them only just avoided coming to blows, since nothing was going to deflect Bob off course and if the rest of them had to go on stage without Bunny then so be it. Bunny finally went back inside but remained sullen and withdrawn for the rest of the evening, scorning the opportunity to shine in front of celebrities like Mick and Bianca Jagger. It's little wonder Chris Blackwell would become exasperated by Peter and Bunny. From his viewpoint they were churlish malcontents who sought to find fault with everything. Both envied Bob despite lacking his star quality, and let this sour their relationship. From this point onwards Blackwell gravitated towards Bob who unlike Bunny, wanted success at almost any price.

"We were going to show what could happen when singers and players of instruments come together and Bunny, he was one of those who'd been talking a lot more than the rest of us," Family Man explains. "In fact, he was reciting that kind of talk a lot more than even Bob himself, because Bob was a man who'd take note of something and then meditate on it before reaching a decision but then once he'd decided on something he'd say, 'this must be done by all means!' That's because you've got theory, and then you've got practise. Both of them are nice yes, but they have to work together in harmony, and Bunny wasn't practising that."

The US leg of the 'Catch A Fire' tour was due to start in mid-July. The Wailers had a meeting with Chris before leaving England, and someone asked him what kind of venues they would be playing over there. "Freak clubs," he'd replied, meaning hippy places. Bunny was aghast and said he wasn't going. "If you don't do these clubs, then you're nobody," Blackwell retorted. Bunny got even more irate at hearing this since Rastafarians believe that only dead people have "no body." He effectively left the group at this juncture; Bob became upset and the meeting ended in disarray. The others decided to continue with the US tour dates with or without Bunny, but his departure cast a shadow over the group as they prepared to head back to Jamaica.

Bob would inform Jamaican broadcaster Dermot Hussey that Bunny left because he didn't like touring. "If you don't want to work that's your business and I don't care," he said. He made the point that if someone sang on the Wailers' records but then refused to promote them, they were wasting his time and "them nah defend nutten."

"Bunny didn't want to travel with us, it's true" adds Family Man, in response to reports that Bunny had left the group because he didn't like flying. "Yet he knew the Wailers had to tour because with music, we get to understand you have to go out there and promote your product. If you're a musician, you're going to have to perform live for people too but it seems like Bob, Bunny, and Peter have a little friction developing between the three of them at that time and I don't know the details behind it, but it was plain enough for me to see. And whilst I wasn't privy to what was being said between them, actions speak louder than words, and I could see the cracks begin to develop in their relationship, for sure."

CHAPTER NINETEEN
Turn Me Loose

"Bunny was scared of flying, that was his main problem," recalls Esther. "He didn't want to go and tour with the Wailers because he was afraid the planes were going to fall out of the sky or something. He was Bunny Livingston in those days, because he didn't take up the name Bunny Wailer until after the others had gone through hell in putting the name out there, and worked so hard to promote it. I'd like to ask him, 'what did you do to promote the music and the message of the Wailers? What was your input?' Because he was always bad-mouthing Bob, whilst pretending they were best friends. He was constantly going on about Bob's father and how people loved Bob because he was half-white and not black like them."

On May 30th, a Rasta assembly was held at Success Hall on Wildman Street, where the Wailers had once performed with Coxsone. Members of the Ethiopian World Federation (EWF) and Ethiopian Orthodox Church flocked to hear the services, including an address by His Holiness Abuna Theophilos, Patriarch of the Ethiopian Orthodox church. A week or so later, His Holiness put in an appearance at the Federation headquarters on Maxfield Avenue and the celebrations – led by Rastafarian chanting and drumming – stretched far into the night. Such occasions offered an opportunity to meet with friends and learn something new, as well as rejoice. Rastafari was now the most potent spiritual force on the island and with Manley in power, anything felt possible. Manley however, had no taste for theocratic government. Like Jose Marti in Cuba, he believed that his country's problems needed a social, rather than political or religious solution. Not so the Wailers, who sought change through spiritual awakening. They saw themselves as crusaders and that's how they'll approach their forthcoming US tour dates – as musical messengers. Joe Higgs, who'd subsequently moved into Island House, was recruited to fill Bunny's place on conga drums. Peter told Reggae Routes that Higgs had been "a brother among the Wailers for years," and credited him with providing encouragement and inspiration, as well as keeping the group together. His appointment found favour with everyone. Higgs' harmonies were faultless, and he would be a steady presence on the road.

The tour began in July and would last throughout August. Peter took Yvonne along with him which was unprecedented, and therefore must have taken some negotiating. Family Man remembers her as fitting in with the other band members well enough, but having a temper and standing up to Peter on occasion. She wasn't the type to be intimidated and nor was she in thrall to Bob, who steered clear. Their first stop was Boston, where the band played a five-day residency at Paul's Mall, beginning on July 11th. There were two venues on the site – one in the Mall itself and the other in an adjoining basement called the Jazz Workshop, which the Wailers' party would often visit during their breaks. A local man named Alan James found them some strong Columbian herb and loaned them his record player, which meant they could listen to music whilst relaxing during the day and working on new songs like 'So Jah Seh,' 'Talking Blues' and 'Natty Dread.'

Ray Charles, who was a long-time favourite of the Wailers, had recently played Carnegie Hall but rock was still the biggest draw in popular music. Led Zeppelin were in town preparing for sold-out shows at Madison Square Garden and everyone was talking about Watkins Glen rock festival in late July – an event that would attract even bigger crowds than Woodstock. Whilst it still couldn't compete in terms of sales or exposure, black music had evolved along parallel lines as rock, and was enjoying a rich vein of form. The advent of "black exploitation" films had afforded opportunities for artists such as Curtis Mayfield, Bobby Womack, Marvin Gaye and James Brown to expand their horizons and compose soundtracks. They too spoke for a generation as well as their race, and their influence on the Wailers was undeniable. Just to recap, 1973 was the year that Mayfield released 'Superfly' and James Brown wrote the soundtrack to 'Black Caesar.' Brown had supported Richard Nixon in the lead-in to the 1972 election and would pay a high price for such misguided political alliances. When he played the Apollo in May protestors had gathered outside with banners demanding, 'Get The Clown Out Of Town.' Interestingly, Brown had recently met Marlon Brando and described the actor as "one of the greatest cultural touchstones in America. He had been part of a growing community of white performers who stood solidly and proudly on the side of black equality, not just in show business but every aspect of life in America. He was as important an inspiration to me as any musician I'd ever heard."

Lee Jaffe, who'd missed out on the Wailers' UK tour, had returned to New York ahead of the band. Chris Blackwell installed him in a room at the Windsor Hotel and put him to work securing gigs for them. It was Jaffe who booked them to appear at Max's Kansas City and then served as their tour manager for the rest of the dates. Clutching a copy of 'Catch A Fire' he'd gone to see Sam Hood, the manager of Max's, who said the Wailers sounded "like the Drifters with raised consciousness." Suitably intrigued, Hood offered them a slot supporting Bruce Springsteen, who was due to open on July 18th. The Wailers supported him from July 19th to the 22nd inclusive. Springsteen would then play a further two nights without them.

Max's was a two-storey bar/restaurant on Park Avenue South, off Union Square. Apart from the black and white awning there was little else to distinguish it, at least from the outside. Owner Mickey Ruskin had opened the place in late 1965. Previous to that he'd ran a Village bar called the Ninth Circle but it was the poetry events (and also free, cocktail hour buffets) he'd sponsored at Les Deux Magots on East 7th Street that had first endeared him to New York's bohemians. At Max's, the art intelligentsia had gathered round the bar whilst a younger, fashionable crowd occupied the backroom. He would make structural improvements later on, as Max's reputation grew. This would be largely thanks to the patronage of Andy Warhol, whose studio was just a block and a half away. Five years earlier, Warhol had been shot and almost killed by a crazed hanger-on and the days of Edie Sedgwick, Viva and Lou Reed's Velvet Underground were long gone. There was a different crowd there now, although Max's still attracted creative types.

"You'd walk in and the bar was on the left," recalls Lee Jaffe. "Immediately behind the bar was a Warhol "Most Wanted Man" painting in black and white. All the way in the back, on the ceiling and using the corner walls as part of the sculpture was The Cross Of Fire, which consisted of red fluorescent lights in the shape of a cross. It gave the whole back room, which was a dining area, this incredible red glow. It was the intellectual centre of the Western world, where the avant-garde went to eat hamburgers, but then it changed because they added another room upstairs where they started having groups play in the early seventies.

"It could hold a few hundred people I guess. It was long and narrow, like a loft type of thing. It was tight, but when they started to have groups there, the whole atmosphere at Max's began to change. It was no longer a place for just artists. It became the place where glam rock started. The New York Dolls started at Max's. You'd have David Bowie when he was in New York, you'd have all the people from the Warhol movies – Holly Woodlawn, Jackie Curtis… You also had people like Todd Rundgren, Patti Smith and Lou Reed. All kinds of brilliant people were hanging out there. It started to become a rock star place."

The Wailers played at least three half hour sets every night during their stay at Max's, and often played older songs like 'I'm Gonna Put It On,' 'Bend Down Low' and 'Rude Boy.' One night Bob's mother, her husband Edward, their children Anthony and Richard, Bunny's sister Pearl and also Rita's father Roy Anderson turned up, lending a festive air to the occasion. The band was camped at the Chelsea Hotel on West 23rd Street, where the management had grown accustomed to larger-than-life characters. Janis Joplin, William Burroughs and Leonard Cohen had all stayed there over the years, and no one was likely to be fazed by seeing a cavalcade of Rastafarians troop through the lobby. Everyone liked the Chelsea. It was just a short cab ride from Max's and had rooms with a kitchen, which suited them perfectly.

Springsteen would soon be described as "the future of rock and roll" and evoke comparisons with Dylan. In order to stoke up media attention, Columbia had bought up a lot of tickets for journalists, many of whom got their first taste of reggae whilst watching Bob lead the band through songs like 'Concrete Jungle,' 'Slave Driver' and 'Get Up Stand Up.' Glen Adams was there one night, and invited Peter and the Barrett brothers to play on a session in Brooklyn the next day for producer Brad Osbourne. Bob reacted angrily when he found out and was only pacified when Chris Blackwell slipped him $500, "to take his mind off it." Later that same evening, Glen tried to film the Wailers at Max's but Chris Blackwell stopped him. In late July, the Wailers headed for A & R Recording studios on Horatio Street, where they put finishing touches to 'Get Up Stand Up.' A & R was where the likes of Burt Bacharach and Paul Simon recorded. The facilities were first-rate and work on 'Get Up Stand Up' went smoothly from the minute they decided to quicken the tempo, and Peter and Bob found another gear. Their vocals were now charged with newfound exuberance, and resulted in a rallying cry of tremendous power. Family Man says that everyone agreed it was the best song they'd ever done, and gives Peter most credit for the transformation – especially where the lyrics are concerned.

After this session, the Wailers prepared to tour with Sly & The Family Stone. Gary Kurfirst, manager of the rock band Mountain, knew Sly's agent and when he learnt they were looking for a black support act, he'd immediately recommended the Wailers. This is how they came to join soul music's most controversial superstar on a jaunt around America that would end with them stranded in Las Vegas with little more than they had on. Five years earlier, Sly had revolutionised black music by combining rock and psychedelic influences, together with soul, funk and political commentary. Rickey Vincent has written that James Brown "was identified with black ghetto folks who would never be leaving the ghetto, whereas Sly represented everyone in the new melting pot. The Godfather opened the door, but Sly let everyone in."

Despite his groundbreaking antics, Sly already had a bad reputation. He'd been on the bill at the Newport Jazz Festival four years earlier, after rock and soul acts were admitted for the first time. The crowd had rioted during Sly's performance, broken down fences, set off firecrackers, set wooden chairs on fire and thrown bottles and rocks at the police. A month or so later he played at Woodstock and gave a sensational performance but his appearances would grow increasing erratic from thereon. Over a hundred and fifty people were arrested and nearly the same number injured after three hours' of rioting at a free concert he'd headlined in Chicago during 1970, and the crowd had pelted him with bottles during his performance at the Isle Of Wight Festival. By the end of 1971, he'd missed almost a third of the shows booked for him in the previous twelve months because of lateness, illness or simply not showing up. He was now all but unreachable thanks to worsening drug problems and the constant demands of dealers, hardcore hustlers and hangers on. His band members were reportedly unhappy and so too his record label, who were beginning to despair of ever seeing any new product. Despite being a champion of inter-racialism, Sly had also come under pressure from black militant groups demanding his support for initiatives that were often ill thought out and impractical. Several black radio stations in the US had even dropped his records from their playlists after he'd made derogatory remarks about them. Just to make matters worse Sly had given his support to the Black Panthers, and suffered relentless police harassment as a result. This was during a time when black leaders were being illicitly targeted, and Sly was arrested no less than five times in 1972 alone. There were rumours of Mafia involvement amidst reports of payola and drug trafficking and back in March, Sly had been arrested at his Bel Air mansion along with five other people and charged with possession of cocaine. The police report later stated a variety of drugs and weapons had been found at the house, "including twenty pistols, three rifles and a shotgun."

The arrest had disrupted Sly's plans to tour earlier in the year, but his reputation had already suffered irreparable damage in any case. By the time his rearranged dates with the Wailers got underway, he'd lost a lot of his support in the media and was playing to smaller, mainly African American audiences, rather than large-scale rock venues. He'd also lost drummer Greg Errico and bassist Larry Graham, who'd once formed the core of his celebrated rhythm section but had since tired of Sly's erratic behaviour.

The Wailers were scheduled to play seventeen dates with him but were dumped from the bill after just four. This is unsurprising, despite claims that the Wailers blew Sly off stage every night. The truth of the matter was revealed in a Washington Post review of their show in Annapolis, which mentions how the audience had remained "unmoved," and "applauded loudest for the end of the Wailers' set."

"In that era, Sly was a total influence, the in thing of the time," Joe Higgs later admitted. "People came to see Sly because of what he had to say, what he looked like and his latest design. How was Bob a threat to Sly Stone? People said they couldn't hear us; that they couldn't understand our accents and our rhythms were too slow. We weren't happening, our outfits were inappropriate and we were rebels.

"All I can remember is that we were opening for Sly & the Family Stone and when we get to Las Vegas, we were fired. Next thing I knew, we were out on the street, rejected from the hotel. We were on the street with our luggage, then someone took us to Sausalito, and we made a broadcast there..."

Sly had cut his first record aged nine and been singing in front of audiences since he was around five years old. All of Jamaica had thrilled to early hits such as 'Dance To The Music' and 'Everyday People,' which blazed with such irresistible energy and excitement. In their own way, the Wailers were also intent on breaking down musical barriers, just as Sly had done. Maybe they'd hoped there'd be some mutual regard yet Sly was too self-absorbed to care and made no attempt to interact with anyone from outside his immediate circle.

Las Vegas was no place for a group of penniless Jamaican musicians, but help was at hand. Chris Blackwell put them in touch with a Jamaican attorney called Gus Brown and their next stop would be San Francisco, where a local promoter was willing to put on a couple of shows at short notice. This is how they came to play at the Matrix on October 19th and 20th. In the meantime,

Blackwell also contacted Bay area photographer Chuck Krall, who'd previously met Bob, Joe Higgs and Peter in Jamaica, whilst serving in the US Peace Corps.

After leaving the Peace Corps, Chuck had returned to his native New York and hung out with Jimi Hendrix for a while before heading west and working in rodeos as a bull rider. His next stop was Aspen, Colorado, where he studied photography with Robert Capa. He and school friend Lenny Kaye – now better known for his guitar playing with Patti Smith – then took off for San Francisco, just as the counter-culture approached its zenith. Kaye introduced him to rock journalist Ed Ward and by the time the Wailers bowled into town Chuck was a familiar face on the 'Frisco scene, with close ties to Bill Graham and regular commissions from magazines like Creem and Rolling Stone.

"Back then I was shooting a hundred rolls of film a week easily," he says. "I'd get home from a concert at two o' clock in the morning, go into the darkroom and develop the prints before going to sleep. Then in the morning I'd wake up, have coffee and doughnuts and take them over to the record company. It was a lot of work..."

Shortly before the Wailers' arrival he'd documented Crosby, Stills, Nash & Young's appearance at Winterland, on Post Street. The Faces and Rory Gallagher had headlined Cow Palace that same week yet Chuck wasn't just a rock photographer, and his portraits of country, soul, blues and reggae acts are unrivalled for that period. He took some unusually relaxed shots of the Wailers at their motel in San Francisco during that trip. News bulletins were announcing US Vice President Spiro Agnew's resignation at the time – an event that brought fresh resonance to the line,

"Babylon, your throne come down" from 'Rastaman Chant,' which the Wailers still played nearly every set.

Those first two shows at the Matrix weren't sell-outs, as has been widely reported elsewhere. In fact attendances were quite low, possibly because two people had been hacked to death just a week or so earlier. They were the first in a string of unsolved killings that would later attain notoriety as the "Zebra murders," and discourage people from venturing out in San Francisco at night. Also, the Matrix had recently moved from Fillmore Street to new premises on Broadway. It was no longer the same place where the Jefferson Airplane had been discovered, or where patrons would be greeted by a mural of the Four Horsemen Of The Apocalypse, dressed like hippies and clutching musical instruments. The Matrix of old, where Hunter S. Thompson and Ralph J. Gleason once held court, belonged in the past and at a location several blocks away. Many concertgoers hadn't got used to the switch yet, but those who did go to see the Wailers weren't disappointed. Rather than feel dejected about recent events, the band had determined to prove their worth and were firing on all cylinders by opening night, which coincided with Peter's birthday. Word of these concerts soon spread like wildfire, prompting the same promoter to book them for a further two dates on October 29th and 30th. Both nights would be filled to overflowing thanks to support from local station KSAN-FM.

After their debut at the Matrix, station manager Tom "Big Daddy" Donahue had invited the band to record a session for KSAN-FM at the Record Plant in Sausalito. Donahue was known as "the Orson Welles of rock" on account of his deep voice and commanding presence. In the Bay area he was renowned for turning records into hits. Jim Marshall described him as "San Francisco's reigning Top 40 disc jockey" – a man who "owned racehorses, a nightclub and record company, ran a radio tip sheet and promoted concerts, including the final public appearance by the Beatles at Candlestick Park in 1966."

Forsaking "pimple cream ads and Herman's Hermits' records" Donahue had discovered the joys of FM radio circa 1967, just as progressive rock got underway. He and B. Mitchell Reed (AKA "the Beemer") joined KMPX-FM and played what they liked, including plenty of album tracks. Other DJs would soon follow suit but for a short time at least, KMPX-FM was the hippest station in San Francisco and there was nothing else like it on the airwaves. Two years later the staff staged a walkout and switched over en masse to KSAN-FM. Donahue was installed as general manager and would remain so until his death in 1975. He'd championed the Wailers from early and like John Peel in England, knew how valuable a "live" radio broadcast could be to up-and-coming acts.

Seven of the ten tracks he recorded that day would finally see release on the album 'Talkin' Blues.' The title was well chosen. Michael Lydon, author of 'Rock Folk,' calls the blues "the music of a people profoundly alienated, a people making their way in a foreign land to which they were brought as captives. On one hand attempting to deal with the cruel or absurd reality facing them as best as they can, they are also searching for a surer, more essential reality – their past, their historical, racial and primal selves, and the web from which they were ripped."

He could have easily been talking about reggae – the blues music of the Caribbean that's steeped in slave rebellions and sufferers' cries. The Wailers would seize the opportunity to get their message across with both hands, and the exposure on KSAN-FM served them well. As a band they had unbelievable authenticity and whilst Bob was the main attraction, the musicians were razor-sharp. No one played rock solid bass like Family Man, whilst Wya sounds truly inspired. His keyboard riffs and Peter's wah wah guitar formed an essential plank of the Wailers' rhythm section. They brought a distinct edge to the Wailers' music, and every track bears their stamp. 'Burnin' And Lootin' is a tour-de-force whilst 'Slave Driver' rips away all vestiges of romance from black people's history. 'Kinky Reggae' fair leaps from the speakers and 'Get Up Stand Up' starts off lazily enough, but then builds to a crescendo after Peter takes control and prompts Bob into a flurry of adlibbing. Apart from 'Bend Down Low' they didn't play any other love songs during their set, which meant no 'Stir It Up' or 'Baby We've Got A Date.' It's a rebel selection but with the odd surprise thrown in for good measure like 'Walk The Proud Land,' which they'd re-recorded during the 'Catch A Fire' sessions but then shelved.

In addition to the Record Plant session, KSAN-FM continued to play extracts from 'Catch A Fire' and the Wailers' latest album 'Burnin,' which had just been released in the UK. Queues soon snaked down Broadway as the Matrix filled with an assortment of pot smoking hippies, curious African Americans and a handful of Jamaican expatriates. The band's set list still included 'Duppy Conqueror,' 'Lively Up Yourself' and 'Small Axe,' but the focus was now on more recent material. Peter raised a few cheers when stepping up to the mic for 'Can't Blame The Youth,' but there was no room for solo hits like '400 Years,' 'The Toughest,' 'Maga Dog,'

'Stepping Razor' or 'Mark Of The Beast.' Much to Peter's dismay, the Wailers had become a vehicle for Bob's talents alone – a development Chris Blackwell may well have initiated, but that Bob hadn't exactly resisted. Peter was reduced to being Marley's backing singer, giving rise to feelings of indignation, disappointment and betrayal. He knew that Bob wasn't going to change and he'd soon be forced to leave, although he didn't allow this to spill over into rows or arguments – at least not yet. Instead he tried to bide his time, and kept a close eye on everything happening around him.

In-between their triumphs at the Matrix, the Wailers had headed down the coast to Los Angeles, and amidst a spate of UFO sightings. Reports had flooded into the sheriffs' office of "strange lights in the sky" and there was much talk of alien landings, or even imminent invasion. According to the Bible, these were "the last days" and so anything was possible. The Wailers' party muttered prayers and stayed vigilant, whilst taking stock of their new surroundings. The usual Hollywood temptations held little interest for them, apart from the Troubadour and Tower Records. Food and music were their primary concerns, and radio had been a lot more interesting in San Francisco. Most LA stations specialised in rock, which meant listeners were served a steady diet of Cher, Joe Walsh, the Allman Brothers and Rolling Stones, whose latest hit 'Angie' had been recorded in Jamaica, and could be heard everywhere. Peter wasn't alone in preferring songs by Marvin Gaye, Gladys Knight ('Midnight Train To Georgia'), Stevie Wonder ('Higher Ground') and Billy Preston, whose 'Space Race' was the theme tune to American Bandstand and featured an early Moog synthesiser. Few realised it at the time but black music was headed in the direction of disco, and its quotient of soul power will diminish dramatically. The revolutionary, cutting-edge of black music would soon belong to reggae, and Bob and Peter in particular.

The Wailers already knew people at Shelter Records, and so went to visit their offices on Sunset Boulevard. Denny Cordell and Chris Blackwell were old friends, whilst Don Williams had met the band in Jamaica. Denny and his partner Leon Russell had recently formed a film production company called Shelter Vision and were keen to put their state-of-the-art equipment to good use. Music videos were still a long way off, but the success of rockumentary films such as 'Woodstock' and 'Mad Dogs And Englishmen' had opened new possibilities for promoting music in cinemas, rather than just being reliant upon print and radio. The industry was changing and Shelter – like Island – intended to stay ahead of the curve. It was agreed they'd film the Wailers playing a closed-door session at the Capitol Record Tower in Hollywood on October 24th, using three cameras and high definition colour film. Shelter and Island could then decide what to do with the footage later. Rumour has it that Cordell may have already been harbouring ambitions to sign Marley to Shelter but he and Blackwell were still on good terms and Don says the project came together easily, without any fuss or bother.

The band members were well rehearsed, and knew the material inside out. Only a dozen or so people were in the audience that day and yet the lack of atmosphere clearly didn't affect the performance. As the film opens, we're shown a close-up of Peter sat on the floor, beating a big bass drum as the Wailers sing 'Rastaman Chant.' His ever-present shades and the flannel jutting out of his back pocket denote a rude boy stance, but it's the floppy, yellow hat with toggles hanging from it that really gives the game away. Wearing this hat was more an act of defiance than fashion statement. Peter wasn't trying to look cool or impress. On the contrary, he was letting people know that he was unashamedly ghetto, and totally unconcerned with vanity. Not that he had a monopoly on unusual headgear. Family Man had contemplated wearing the bowler he'd bought in London, but wore his US Army helmet instead.

'Rastaman Chant,' as always, was an invocation. Once the spirits had been appeased, Peter strapped on his axe ready for 'Duppy Conqueror' and the band launched into another round of songs, some of which they rehearsed several times. 'Midnight Ravers,' 'Kinky Reggae' and 'Get Up Stand Up' were among the highlights. Bob grandstands on the latter, but Peter sings his verse with barely a flicker. It's close to being an Elvis moment, when everything's won on a curl of the lips. Am I imagining it, or does Bob try and steal Peter's thunder by adlibbing so much? And is Peter's lack of reaction a sign that he's already disengaged from the band, and so can't be bothered with Bob's antics? He gets to sing 'Stop That Train' and 'Can't Blame The Youth' before the film ends, except they're not among his best performances. The stagecraft Peter will be renowned for isn't fully developed yet and he makes no attempt to steal the show, even when singing lead. His role is a supporting one, and any frustrations hidden behind those wrap-around shades. Interestingly, the band members scarcely look at each other and there's no banter between them, although Joe manages a smile now and then.

After filming the Shelter session, they'll return to the Matrix for those last two shows and then head back to Jamaica. Not for the first time, their foreign travels will have yielded trials and tribulations, as well as triumphs. Don Williams had already begun to detect a change in Bob, and says he looked "hustled." The responsibilities of keeping the band together, being the lead singer and appeasing Peter whilst meeting record company demands was beginning to weigh heavy on his shoulders, even at this relatively early stage of the Wailers' international breakthrough.

"I probably spent more time with Joe Higgs than I did with any of the Wailers except Bob and they were all really nice guys," recalls Don. "Joe and I spent a lot of time together. He was a very thoughtful fellow. He was a senior to the rest of the Wailers. Joe liked to reason. Joe would come around every once in a while and just talk and chat, whereas Peter was a more difficult character. He was the only one who had this really mean streak."

Joe had already decided to leave the group when the tour finished. He didn't relish the prospect of further hardships on the road and although Island had scheduled another round of UK tour dates beginning in just two weeks' time, he wasn't having any of it. He came back from America feeling badly run down and with sores on his head, as well as the inevitable empty pockets.

"Joe couldn't take the strain of being on the road," says Esther Anderson. "It was too hard for him. I remember Bob saying he was too old and couldn't manage it or something like that, but Joe Higgs was wonderful. He was the teacher for them all."

Peter's spirits visibly lifted once he was back in Jamaica. Soon, he'll make his way over to Bull Bay and visit Bunny, Jean Watt and their newborn daughter Iyata. It's possible that Bunny hadn't wanted to be away from home for the birth and wasn't prepared to lose face by admitting it, but only he would know that. The couple greeted Peter warmly and then heard how the Wailers had "mashed down Sly Stone," although Peter admitted that it hadn't been a happy tour. After listening intently, Bunny decided that he hadn't missed anything, and wouldn't be persuaded to rejoin. The present Wailers' set-up wasn't to his liking, and he knew Peter didn't care for it either.

The latter played a few sessions before turning his thoughts to the Wailers' forthcoming dates in England. He played guitar on Larry Marshall's 'She Is My Woman' and melodica on a cut of John Holt's 'It May Sound Silly' for Spanish Town producer Harry Mudie. These sessions just happened, and weren't part of any revised career plan although he did press up three further singles on Intel Diplo. 'Foundation' is taken from 'Burnin',' and a subtle reminder of his contributions to the Wailers' new album. The other two were recorded at Treasure Isle, with Bunny on backing vocals and percussion. A re-worked 'Funeral' – now called 'Burial' – reasserts Peter's Rasta credentials, and may just refer to the break-up of the Wailers. With hindsight, it's easy to assume that lines like "Make your friend come claim you are the general," now apply to Bob's relationship with Chris Blackwell, but that's by no means certain. Bunny's presence lends weight to this argument, but then he'd probably be there in any case.

'What You Gonna Do' is another of Peter's calypso-inspired songs, just like 'Maga Dog.' The melodies have a traditional air whilst his lyrics strike a fine balance between humour and social commentary. The narrator is describing a police raid, which he escapes by jumping a fence. Alas, his friend's not so lucky and is taken to jail, leaving his family to struggle without him – all because of a little ganja the man had in his possession. It's a situation Peter saw happen many times in Trench Town, and that he'll continue to rail against for the rest of his career. The production on that track's clean as a whistle. Robbie Shakespeare played bass and that's Lee Jaffe on harmonica. Peter was now feeling increasingly confident about leaving the Wailers behind. As far as Bob's concerned, Peter would be coming on tour but that's far from clear at this point. Peter was enjoying being back in Jamaica, and had little desire to go out on the road again so soon. Not only that, but his suspicions about Island came roaring to the surface once he finally saw a copy of 'Burnin'.' Esther Anderson had supplied Island's art department with photographs she'd taken in Jamaica, and the label had responded by issuing the new album in a gatefold sleeve containing at least a dozen of her images. Some were of street scenes in and around Kingston, whereas others were taken on Hellshire beach or at Bongo Mackie's Rasta camp in Bull Bay.

"All them bloodclaat pictures of Lucifer! All the same guy," Peter exclaimed, pointing at a photo of Bongo Mackie. "I don't know nothing about this, I was in America when all things happened. When I come to Jamaica and I see that, I was grieved. You see any of my pictures there man? Not one picture is there for I, and yet still I sing on the album so there was something within those fuckers trying to keep me out."

At least he couldn't complain about the front cover since they're all on it, including Bunny, the Barrett brothers and Wya Lindo. The sleeve looks as if it's made of wood, and the photo's been burnt into it with a branding iron. Bob's head admittedly takes up more space but at least the album's credited to the Wailers and not Bob Marley and the Wailers, even if a close-up photo of him smoking a spliff does dominate the back cover. It's a memorable image, audacious in its disregard for Jamaica's drug laws, and would later appear on t-shirts and posters as part of Island's promotional campaign. Presumably, Peter already knew that only one of his songs would feature on 'Burnin'.' Bunny, who still believed Chris Blackwell had dropped the original title of 'Reincarnated Souls' to spite him after the "freak clubs" incident went one better, and 'Hallelujah Time' and 'Pass It On' are both exquisite. Unfortunately 'Reincarnated Souls' and 'The Oppressed Song' were dropped and won't become available until many years later, by which time Bunny will have re-recorded them on 'Blackheart Man.' On the inner sleeve of 'Burnin',' he's shown standing in front of a poster advertising a sound-system clash between King Tubby, Tippertone and Emperor Faith. Esther had to sneak the shot, as she says he became violent and abusive whenever she tried to photograph him. It's little wonder that Bob was singled out as the Wailer most likely, and Blackwell felt he could deal with him more easily than the other two.

Such thoughts would occupy the Island supremo as the Wailers' tour dates loomed closer. Bob was still spending a lot of time with Esther, who was glad that Lee Jaffe had abandoned his film after hearing about Chilean leader Salvador Allende's alleged suicide. This happened during a coup organised by General Pinochet. There was much talk of CIA involvement but then Egypt and Syria attacked Israel, which prompted the US to intervene and orchestrate the biggest airlift in history. Arab nations responded by imposing a trade embargo on the US and NATO countries that would last until spring 1974. Jamaica, in common with many other places, would suffer chronic oil shortages as a result. Bunny wrote 'Arab's Oil Weapon' about the crisis and recorded it at Randy's, with Peter again helping out on guitar and harmonies. The lyrics are suffused with Biblical prophecy. "By the sign of the times I know the end is showing," he sings. "With all your scientific research, you'll never reach completion. No more trains, no boats, no planes..." He's warning how the system – i.e., western civilisation – will crash, taking all of the money and technology with it.

Esther discussed such issues at length with Bob and Peter, and agreed with those who declared US foreign policy "manipulative, divisive and a major cause of bloodshed." The other news story that caught their attention was the famine in Ethiopia. The region had long suffered from drought but by late 1973 an estimated 300,000 Ethiopians had died from hunger, and many more were refugees. Helping them was a priority and so when the Wailers were asked to play at a benefit show for Ethiopian Famine Relief as a curtain raiser for their UK tour, they readily agreed. The concert would take place at the Sundown Theatre in Edmonton, North London during early November. The Wailers' performance was filmed but only ten-minutes' worth has survived. Friends of the band lined the stage as the Wailers played using equipment borrowed from Eddy Grant's latest discoveries, 90 Degrees Inclusive. MC Dennis Bovell introduced them as "Bob Marley and the Wailers" and later admitted to feeling sheepish after his group Matumbi stole the headlines. "They were our heroes," he says, referring to the Wailers. Instead of opening with 'Rastaman

Chant' – possibly because they hadn't found anyone to replace Bunny or Joe Higgs on percussion – they launched into 'Slave Driver.' Peter remained inscrutable as ever in his dark shades and bobble hat, his wah wah guitar lines scything through the mix like tracer bullets. Bob was effusive by comparison, and strutted around like a Caribbean rock star in his satin, patchwork jacket – his hair teased into a large, shapeless Afro that to paraphrase Bob Dylan, sat on his head "like a mattress balances on a bottle of wine." Whilst the Barretts were coolness personified, Wya got a little over-excited and his jarring chords made Bob wince once or twice, especially on 'Slave Driver.'

The second leg of their UK tour was due to start a week or so later, in mid-November but the first five dates had to be cancelled after Peter contracted bronchitis, or at least that's what Island Records claimed. Nottingham, Bradford, Birmingham and Stafford all missed out. The tour eventually opened at the Locarno in Blackpool on November 22nd, and in far from ideal weather conditions. Winter had set in, and a blanket of snow covered the ground. The following night they crossed the Pennines and played a blistering set at Leeds Polytechnic after being introduced as "one of the greatest bands in the world." This late 1973 edition of the Wailers differed from that premiered just seven months earlier, as heard on the lengthy intro to 'Duppy Conqueror.' Inspired by their American adventures, they'd added a Jamaican twist to the fusion of rock and r & b that bands like War and Sly & The Family Stone helped pioneer. Bob's singing was free and easy; the rhythm section tighter than ever and Wya's excesses kept firmly in check. That night in Leeds they played near definitive live versions of 'Midnight Ravers,' 'No More

Trouble, 'Put It On,' 'Kinky Reggae' and even 'Lively Up Yourself.' The latter turned into a thirteen-minute magnum opus, with Bob singing as if he's in a trance and proving the adage that "when music hits, you feel no pain."

The following night they played in Liverpool and then Doncaster before returning to London for another radio broadcast hosted by John Peel. This session took place on the 26th, at Kensington House in Shepherd's Bush under the watchful eyes of John Walters and Pete Dauncey. The band played just three songs, including 'Kinky Reggae' and 'Can't Blame The Youth,' and they're evenly split between Bob and Peter. Was Bob trying to appease him we wonder? The show wouldn't be broadcast until Christmas Day and so it's ironic they ended with 'Get Up Stand Up,' which explodes the myth of Christianity. If the producers had noticed this, they certainly didn't let on.

Britain was still in the grip of glam rock, and the charts filled with a succession of acts sporting feathered mullets and eyeliner. The androgynous antics of Bowie, Lou Reed and Marc Bolan had a lot to answer for, and even the Rolling Stones camped it up for a time. We can only imagine what Peter thought of this. It was hard to decide what was worse – the sight of all those "midnight ravers" or the middle-of-the–road fare dished out by the Osmonds, Carpenters and then current pre-pubescent heart throb, David Cassidy. Elton John was at No. 1 in the album charts with 'Goodbye Yellow Brick Road' and even Max Bygraves, a crooner who appealed mainly to old age pensioners, couldn't be denied as 1973 stumbled to a close.

Once back in London, the Wailers met up with old friends such as Pepe Judah, who'd started to hold regular meetings at 28 St.

Agnes Place in Kennington, South London. This same address will become the headquarters of the Twelve Tribes organisation in London and was partially funded by artists like Bob, who contributed what he could. Manchester was next. The Wailers then played their last gig in Northampton on the 30th. The tour had been scheduled to last longer but the remaining eleven concerts were cancelled, including the all-important London shows. Reports in the media claimed the tour had been terminated because of the weather. If this were true, it would have been a first in rock history. Peter's mood had certainly plummeted with the temperature and rumours soon began to circulate, claiming the Wailers had split. Island denied them, stating that Peter was suffering from bronchitis and "had been advised by a doctor to return to Jamaica immediately." He and the Barrett brothers shared a flight home, whilst Bob stayed behind for a few days to discuss business with Chris Blackwell. Bunny would later announce that "the only reason why Peter drop out the group is because he didn't have me harmonising with him and he couldn't harmonise with anyone else," but that's not what Peter told Malika Lee Whitney.

"When I left the Wailers it was not directly any conflict between me and Bob," he explained. "Bob was manifesting what was in him. I was at that time decorating what was inside of Bob to make it beautiful and the time had come for me to decorate what was inside of me, so I did."

CHAPTER TWENTY

Pass It On

Island Records could tell the English and American press what they liked but in Jamaica, there were persistent rumours that the Wailers had finally unravelled. Neville Willoughby interviewed Bob for his radio show just before Christmas. Bob was guarded when answering questions about the break-up but insinuated that Peter and Bunny had betrayed him by refusing to tour. This was deceptive and unfair. Peter and Bunny's problems hadn't concerned touring as such but Chris Blackwell, who they thought was exploiting them. If Blackwell is to be believed, 'Catch A Fire' and 'Burnin'' wouldn't recoup what Island spent on them for another few years at least. I guess those full-page advertisements in the music press hadn't been cheap and nor the sleeve designs but it's heartbreaking to think the Wailers were finally closing in on success and yet couldn't stay the course. Despite Peter and Bunny's suspicions, they were signed to the best label for reggae music at that time – one with strong links to Jamaica, and that was renowned for fostering original talent. Also, there was still no other vocal group to touch them, despite a surfeit of young hopefuls pouring out the shantytowns, singing about ghetto life and promoting Rastafari far and wide. Esther Anderson knew Chris Blackwell better than most and years after the event, still thinks it unfair that he got blamed for the Wailers' break-up.

"Bunny Wailer broke up the Wailers!" she insists. "When he took off that caused Bob to be in a real quandary because by the time they left for England with Peter, Bunny had already mixed it up by saying how much songs Bob have on the album and all that. The man never stopped! He was always spreading bad feeling until in the end, Bob and Peter came apart as well and yet those two were so close before all of that happened..."

"Bob was mixed race, and that's something else which throws further light on that whole situation," reflects Delroy Washington. "I'd often hear people saying that if Bob hadn't have been mixed race then he wouldn't have reached so far and that's major grounds for insecurity in my opinion. Certain people felt resentment towards the fact that he was half white and I do believe that was a problem. Sometimes people would talk to him disrespectfully, and I'm talking about his brethren who were in the group with him as well.

"It was inevitable they'd have to break up because Bob could have just gone and got anyone from Jamaica and that's literally what happened in the end. He was destined to make it; it was on the cards. There was something about Bob that set him apart from everyone else. He understood things in a way the others didn't, because Bunny and Peter would get things mixed up. It was as if they expected to just do whatever they wanted and still make money but Bob knew he had to make concessions and that was the difference. He was prepared to compromise, whereas the others weren't and that couldn't work."

Esther recalls that Peter and Bunny used "to bad up" Chris Blackwell whenever they saw him. They'd treat the Island boss with thinly veiled contempt and demand money from him, like bullies in a school playground. Bob didn't care for this and was embarrassed by their actions. He'd point out that Blackwell had given them money when they needed it and demonstrated faith in them. As far as he was concerned, Island's backing had enabled the Wailers to get their music across to different audiences and alienating Blackwell made no sense.

"Bob had the better attitude towards the business and decided he was going to do it properly and that is what Chris Blackwell wanted from him too," says Hux Brown. "Chris wanted to make some serious money but then after he'd picked the group up, he realised Bob was the only one thinking along the right lines, and the three of them couldn't work together. Peter turned that around and said Blackwell was trying to mash up the group and so he got crazy and start to run him down with a machete and all that. After that now, Bob decided he was going to stick with Chris. He had his own band by then and could pay them weekly so they wouldn't have to go anywhere else, plus he carried on writing all those good songs except no one sang harmonies like Peter and Bunny..."

There would be one last, shared recording session before the three principal Wailers parted company and went their separate ways. In early January, dreadlocks from all over Jamaica assembled in Clarendon, where they staged a nyahbinghi in the Bull Head Mountains to celebrate Ethiopian Christmas. Four sets of drums would send the sound of a thousand Rasta heartbeats echoing across the hills, plus there were singers, priests and dancers aplenty – all of them adding to the carnival atmosphere. Patriarch Bongo Burru was among those giving speeches on Rastafarian doctrine. A key theme of this meeting, which lasted seven days, was meditation on the phrase "death to all black and white oppressors." The drumming, chanting, dancing and herb smoking went on all week, sending some adherents into a religious trance or heightened state of consciousness Rastafarians term "the Irix."

It was this nyabinghi that inspired 'Distant Drums,' which shares the same rhythm as Yabby You's 'Love Thy Neighbour.' The producer was Family Man, who'd begun recording tracks like 'Eastern Memphis' for his own Cobra and Fams labels.

"This particular track here, 'Distant Drums,' features Robbie Shakespeare on bass, Carlton Barrett on drums, myself on rhythm guitar, and Bob Marley, Peter Touch and Bunny Livingston on percussion," he says proudly. "Peter and Bob play repeaters and Bunny the funde, then you have Vin Gordon on trombone and the late, great Herman Marquis and Dirty Harry on clarinets. It was recorded at Randy's on North Parade in downtown Kingston, where we used to make all those hits for Lee Perry. Bob, Peter and Bunny often played drums together in the early days, including on that first 'Catch A Fire' tour, so I wanted to go back to that same groove..."

Those mournful clarinets lent 'Distant Drums' a melancholy air. The overall impression is one of longing, whether for spiritual redemption or maybe an ancestral homeland that's now lost in the mists of time. The three Wailers' drumming isn't passive by any means. They beat on the skins with great force and energy, although without ever disrupting the feeling of impending, religious dread.

"It was a frustrating time for the Wailers," explains Lee Jaffe. "It was very hard because no one had any money. Bob had a little money from the songs that Johnny Nash had recorded, but Peter and Bunny didn't have anything coming in and they were big stars in Jamaica. They'd had a hit with 'Trench Town Rock' earlier on, but the radio stations in Jamaica had boycotted it. When I was among them the first song of theirs to get any airplay was 'Three O' Clock Roadblock,' and I'd already been with them a good two years by then. Every so often I'd drive Bob and Skill Cole around in this rental car. Skill was a big guy. He was like six foot three, and would go training every day in the mountains. He had this baseball bat that he'd bring to the radio stations. He and these two rude boys, Tek Life and Frowser, would leave me in the car with the radio on and no air conditioning while they were inside making the DJs play 'Three O' Clock Roadblock.' They'd leave me in the car so they could make sure the station was really playing it. That went on for weeks and weeks, and the song went right to No. 1 as a result of that. They weren't authorised by Bob to do it, but the Wailers started getting a lot more airplay after that."

No sooner was he back on the airwaves than Bob was approached by local promoter Stephen Hill and asked if he would open two shows for Marvin Gaye, due to be held in Kingston during late May. He agreed immediately, and invited Peter and Bunny to join him. None of the Wailers had performed solo yet and despite rumours that the band had split, many Jamaicans still thought of them as a trio.

The first show was a fundraiser for a new Sports Complex in Trench Town, held at the Carib Theatre on May 28th. By the morning of the show the Wailers still hadn't heard from the organisers and so Bob send word to Anthony Spaulding, Jamaica's Housing Minster and MP for Trench Town, to let him know they wouldn't be appearing. Several hours later Spaulding turned up at Island House where they'd been rehearsing and began threatening them. Bob and Peter were only too aware of his influence and chose to stay quiet, but Bunny wasn't having any of it. When he challenged Spaulding, the man turned around and said he didn't know him. He said that he knew Bob and Peter, but didn't know Bunny. This wasn't true and Spaulding knew it, since he and Bunny had both lived on the same street some years back. In fact Bunny was the only Wailer to have been born in Kingston! As the atmosphere continued to darken Bob stepped up and said the Wailers would perform but Bunny refused to change his clothes and ended up walking out on stage at the Carib Theatre in bare feet and without a shirt, his frayed trouser legs rolled up in defiance, exposing his scrawny legs.

It was the Wailers' first show in Jamaica for some time, and they brought the house down. Tyrone Downie made his stage debut with the band that night, joining the even younger Bernard "Touter" Harvey on keyboards. The latter had played on 'Catch A Fire' but missed out on the tours due to his age and the fact that his parents wouldn't have approved. He assures us there were no signs of nerves, despite all 1,700 seats being sold out. Marcia Griffiths was the support act that night, and she invited Rita and also Judy Mowatt – then in a relationship with Alan "Skill" Cole – to join her. The trio got an ecstatic welcome, and especially after launching into the Sweet Inspirations' 'That's How Strong My Love Is.'

After their set had finished, the three women lined up behind the Wailers, who opened with 'Burnin' And Lootin'.' The crowd roared with approval at seeing Bob, Peter and Bunny stroll on stage together but despite appearances, it wasn't strictly speaking a Wailers' reunion. Bob planned to use the women as his backing singers and in his mind Peter and Bunny weren't part of the group anymore, but special guests. Peter sang 'Can't Blame The Youth,' then Bunny wheeled into 'Arab Oil Weapon' – a song lent additional relevance by the petrol shortages in Jamaica. 'Get Up Stand Up' was next and Bob and Peter shared it every inch of the way, although without trying to outdo each other. The biggest response was reserved for 'Three O' Clock Roadblock,' with Lee Jaffe wailing on harmonica and Bob crying out, "Why can't we be what we want to be? We want to be free..."

Three days later and the Wailers would repeat their triumph in the National Arena. "Yes and with Peter acting like him was the boss, but that was cool," chuckles Family Man, who noticed how Marvin Gaye later "put away his tuxedo, put on his tam, and start showing himself all natural" after watching the Wailers from backstage. Gaye was accompanied by a seventy-piece orchestra and came out swinging, a full band roaring behind him. American soul music was no longer the preserve of the chitlin circuit but strove for a level of sophistication that no Jamaican act could match at that time. Most of his repertoire was taken from 'What's Going On' and had the girls screaming with delight – especially after he'd launched into songs like 'Distant Lover' and 'Let's Get It On.' Those two shows would remain a highlight of Jamaica's musical calendar that year, whilst serving to whet local fans' appetites for any future Wailers' appearances.

In August, Bob and the Barrett brothers headed for London, with reels containing tracks from Bob's forthcoming solo album. Family Man had turned the rehearsal space behind Island House into a demo studio and there was now a creative buzz about the place. Bob had moved the Wailers' record shop into the compound, where it'll lure visitors with all the latest reggae and dub releases, and the yard was always full of visitors. He and the Barretts had grown close since Peter and Bunny had left. At night, they'd climb onto the roof and lay on their backs under the stars, talking music and discussing future plans before slipping away to their beds at dawn.

During lulls in his schedule Bob still toured the island with Esther, having fun and searching for a place where they could build a love nest, away from the pressures of Island House. Eventually they found the perfect spot in Little Bay, just up the coast from where Peter was born and raised in Westmoreland. Esther bought the land with money she'd earned acting in a US television series. She and Bob then built the house themselves using thatch and local timber. Peter and Yvonne occasionally visited them there, as did Family Man and Carly. Lee Jaffe was another frequent guest, and his musical tastes would impact on both Bob and Peter as he played them Chicago blues by the likes of Muddy Waters and Howling Wolf. It was the latter's cut of Roy Brown's 'Hard Luck Blues' that had inspired Marley's 'Talking Blues,' with the lines "cold ground was my bed last night, and rock stone was my pillow too."

Bob recruited additional musicians when cutting the 'Natty Dread' album, whilst Family Man served as co-producer. His input was now proving invaluable and Marley's first solo album would be widely acclaimed later that autumn.

"The blessings were flowing, and people around us could see clearly what we were trying to do," says Family Man. "We had this feeling that nothing could stop us at that time because Jah will must be done, even though we were being watched by many different eyes, whether it was Island or people who'd already dropped out. It was then that we realised that there is really no end to this music, and that nothing really could stop us as we worked to get the music established, and to find it's rightful place."

Peter played on sessions with Eric Clapton at Dynamic during late August, although neither of them seemed to have enjoyed the experience all that much. Eric – who'd recently come off heroin, albeit at the expense of a serious drinking problem – was recording the follow-up album to '461 Ocean Boulevard,' which had included his cover of Marley's 'I Shot The Sheriff.' Clapton tried out a couple of Peter's songs but none would feature on 'There's One In Every Crowd' when it was eventually released in April 1975.

Meanwhile Bob had been in San Francisco collaborating with blues artist Taj Mahal, who'd covered 'Slave Driver.' He and the Barrett brothers then flew to London, where they finished 'Natty Dread' and met American guitarist Al Anderson, who played an unforgettable solo on 'No Woman No Cry.'

'Natty Dread' was released on October 25th 1974, after a three-month delay. Island credited it to "Bob Marley And The Wailers," which angered Peter and Bunny no end, since Bob had no right to the name "Wailers" in their opinion. They had a point too. When Curtis Mayfield left the Impressions, he didn't call himself "Curtis Mayfield & The Impressions." He'd closed that chapter of his career, and opened a fresh one using a different name (his own.) In response – or rather defiance – Bunny assumed the title of "Bunny Wailer" and no one dared challenge him except Marley's seizure of the "Wailers" brand would have massive implications in future, after Family Man and the other musicians continue using it for themselves. This simple act – instigated or at least agreed to by Chris Blackwell – will plant confusion in people's minds and serve to cloud the original group's legacy, which is what Peter and Bunny had suspected all along. They weren't happy about that or the lyrics of 'Talkin' Blues,' which Bob wrote specially for them. "Your feet is too big for your shoes," he sings before asking, "so who's going to stay at home, when the freedom fighters are fighting?" There's no evidence that Peter and Bunny took this personally, but they were now in danger of becoming spectators, and both would redouble their efforts in getting solo projects underway.

By late November, Eric Clapton's version of 'I Shot The Sheriff' would be sat at No. 1 in the US Billboard charts. Such unprecedented success did wonders for Bob's profile (and his bank balance), although reggae music wasn't doing all that badly on its own terms. Ken Boothe had a No. 1 hit in the UK with 'Everything I Own,' and John Holt was threatening to do the same with 'Help Me Make It Through The Night.' Trojan meanwhile, rehashed the Wailers' 'Soul Rebels' album for Lee Perry, added a few extra tracks and called it 'Rasta Revolution.' Although a cash-in it was admittedly well named since musically at least, there really *was* a revolution happening. Rasta was taking over and a new generation of dreadlocked warriors had arrived to challenge the Wailers' supremacy. "When the right time comes, them haffe charge fi murder," warned the Mighty Diamonds over a new style rhythm called "rockers." If further proof of reggae's acceleration towards mainstream acceptance was needed, Stevie Wonder's 'Boogie On Reggae Woman' went Top 3 in the US during January 1975. Two months later and the Jackson Five would arrive in Jamaica for a show on Saturday March 8th at the National Stadium attended by every schoolgirl on the island, or at least that's what it seemed like.

These girls had been pouring over pictures of the Jackson Five in American teen magazines for months. Their favourite was Michael who was not only cute as a button, but also supremely talented. When he sang 'Ben,' many fantasised that he was singing about them. They would talk about Michael and his brothers incessantly, comparing their looks, smiles and dress, and then practise the dance routines they'd seen the Jacksons perform on television. Scores of them gathered outside the Sheraton Hotel on the day of the show, eager for a glimpse of their heartthrobs. When the brothers finally emerged, dressed for a basketball game against a team of high school students in the National Arena, the girls all screamed and charged forward, causing the Jacksons to rush back inside and stay there until show time.

Bob was again booked as support and invited Peter and Bunny along, despite recent upsets. Unfortunately the concert – which lasted a mammoth six hours –had to be stopped twice because of problems with the seating arrangements. By the time the three Wailers ambled on stage the atmosphere was tense, although an opening 'Trench Town Rock' soon dispelled any misgivings. Bunny then toasted the Rasta contingent with 'Blackheart Man' before Peter launched into 'Mark Of The Beast' and a full complement of Wailers' hits got underway. The band was on top form that day. Tyrone Downie and Wya Lindo shared keyboard duties, whilst Bob's old friend Alvin "Seeco" Patterson helped out Bunny on percussion. Even the Jacksons were impressed, and said as much whilst visiting Island House the following day.

A few weeks later, Peter, Tyrone and the Barretts would collaborate with rock singer Joe Cocker who was still a master of gospel-drenched blues, despite suffering from alcohol problems. The Wailers' contingent took him to Randy's Studio 17 and played on his cover of Bob Dylan's 'The Man In Me,' taken from his 'Stingray' album. Peter would later play on sessions with American guitarist Eric Gale after returning from Oklahoma, where he recorded tracks with Eric Clapton's bass player, Carl Radle. Lee Jaffe was helping Peter with plans for a forthcoming solo album named after his latest single 'Legalise It,' which called for the legalisation of ganja. The White Panthers' John Sinclair once termed marijuana "a revolutionary force," and claimed that smoking it becomes a political act once it's made illegal. He said it promotes "outlaw consciousness," and "drives people to become enemies of the state." He must have been thinking about Peter, who reacted to the Jamaica Broadcasting Authority's decision to ban 'Legalise It' by taking out a advertisement in the Daily Gleaner quoting the song's controversial lyrics in full, including the line "even judges and the lawyers smoke it." Peter had previewed 'Legalise It' on the Jackson Five show and wasn't in the mood to take such censure lightly.

"Those who say, 'don't smoke herb,' sell it and make millions of dollars every day," he thundered to the press. "Why banana not illegal? Herb was created for the use of man, so who gave anyone authority to pick out one specific herb to say this one is dangerous?

"Herb was created for medicinal, scientific and spiritual purposes, so no man is coming to tell me that I must not smoke herb... No force or power can force me not to smoke herb. If you're going to hang a man for smoking it, hang me 'cause I'm not going to stop!"

When Bob and the new-look Wailers toured behind 'Natty Dread,' few people asked about the switch in personnel. Yet Al Anderson had replaced Peter on guitar and the I-Threes now sang harmonies, which changed the sound of the group out of all recognition. Peter and Bunny were in danger of being forgotten, and Bob's manager Don Taylor was opposed to further reunions. Among the highlights of this 'Natty Dread' tour was a gig in New York's Central Park, where the new line-up played to 15,000 people as part of that summer's Schaeffer Music Festival. They would wind up in Los Angeles at the Roxy Theatre on Sunset Strip, where rock luminaries such as Mick Jagger, George Harrison, Ringo Starr, Billy Preston and members of the Band and Grateful Dead all caught the band during their five-day residence. Sell out shows in the UK had followed, including two nights at the Lyceum Theatre in London which Island Records had recorded and will later release as 'Bob Marley & The Wailers Live!'

Peter and Bunny had some catching up to do, and weren't found wanting. Bunny had been hard at work on his first solo album 'Blackheart Man' ever since Chris Blackwell had paid him a record advance, separate from any involvement with the Wailers. Peter, the Barrett brothers and even Bob contributed towards the sessions, which yielded one of those landmark releases that redefine their genre, and deserved to take its place alongside other seventies' classics by the likes of Stevie Wonder, Marvin Gaye and Curtis Mayfield.

"It's coming from the Wailers, and the knowledge that I'd acquired having been with the Wailers all that time," he explains. "Before I embarked on my solo career I was being trained and prepared to deliver an album like 'Blackheart Man.' I had to be making sure I stayed within the concept of the Wailers, and to make sure people wouldn't stray from the messages given to the Wailers. We were solo by then but the messages that came from us individually were all pointing to the same practices and customs. We were looking at it like a one big family type of situation because the Wailers never sang any songs with racism in them or that suggested any kind of superiority or inferiority complex. We never tried to put down or put up people. The Wailers just served the dinner, and we had to make sure we all ate from the same pot."

On August 27th it was announced that Emperor Haile Selassie I had died of respiratory failure after a prostate operation. It was widely believed he'd been assassinated, since doctors had already testified that he'd recovered well from surgery. The news sent shock waves among Rastafarians. Bob went into Harry J's studio to record 'Jah Live,' which went a long way towards allaying doubts about the Emperor's divinity. He then voiced 'War,' which he'd adapted from a speech Haile Selassie I had given at the United Nations twelve years earlier. He would write further songs like 'Rat Race,' 'Crazy Baldhead,' 'Heathen' and 'One Love/People Get Ready' before the year's out whilst having to fend off criticism in Jamaica about his new BMW, which he said stood for "Bob Marley and the Wailers." His latest single, a live cut of 'No Woman No Cry' recorded at the Lyceum, went Top 30 in England in late September. It was his first crossover hit. One of the Wailers was finally "bubbling on the Top 100," just as he'd prophesised.

Marley's success prompted Virgin Records to try and sign Peter, despite his reputation for being difficult and having once threatened Chris Blackwell with a machete. True to form, he treated Richard Branson with disdain. Peter twice invited him to his home in Ensom City, but then made sure he was out on each occasion. Virgin would eventually release his first solo album 'Legalise It' in Europe, after Columbia won the race for his signature in the US.

Reggae's cult following in America would grow by leaps and bounds over the next few years as the rockers style underpinned a flood of righteous reggae songs, informed by black history and the Bible, and voiced on irresistible rhythms. Back in Jamaica, Big Youth's chant of "lightning flash, weak heart drop" sent the Rastafarians' dread message ricocheting around the dancehalls, where Johnny Clarke, Cornel Campbell, U Roy, the Mighty Diamonds and Dennis Brown held sway. Jacob Miller was also very popular at this time, thanks to songs like 'Tenement Yard,' 'Baby I Love You So' and 'Tired Fi Lick Weed In A Bush.'

As October approached, talk in Kingston centred on two things – Mohammad Ali's rematch with Joe Frazier ("the Thriller In Manila") and Stevie Wonder's forthcoming "Dream Concert" at the National Stadium, due to be held on October 4th. Ali's bout was shown on giant screens, and had the whole island talking. Shortly afterwards, Stevie Wonder flew in for the one most keenly anticipated shows of the year. Alas, there'd been a stampede at the same venue the week before and several people had died, which may explain why only 15,000 showed up. The organisers had hoped for twice that number after adding Harold Melvin and the Blue Notes to the bill, but then lead singer Teddy Prendergast quit and they didn't make the trip. No wonder the organisers quickly renamed the Dream Concert "the Nightmare Concert."

The Wailers, or rather Bob Marley & The Wailers, were again invited to be support act. This time Peter and Bunny's participation came as even less of a surprise. The two of them joined the rehearsals at Island House, which Bob had now arranged to buy from Chris Blackwell. Fikisha Cumbo has written of dreads milling around in the yard, their forms melting into the darkness. Clouds of ganja smoke filled the rehearsal room where Family Man and Carly held down the rhythm, bathed in the murky glow of red and green light bulbs. Bob and Peter were stood in the centre of the room, strumming guitars as Bunny crouched over his conga drums. There was a unity between the Wailers that belied their recent difficulties. It was music that brought them together, even as external influences continued to push them apart.

To get to the stage, they had to walk through the crowd. Bob and Peter led the way, cradling their guitars and flanked by entourage of Rastafarians who ignoring the police barricades, pushed into the VIP section by the front of the stage. In an evocation of times past, the Wailers opened with 'Rastaman Chant' before running through a selection of old favourites, including 'Nice Time,' 'Simmer Down (still a crowd-pleaser, more than a decade later) and 'One Love.' Bunny then sang lead on 'Dreamland' and 'Battering Down Sentence' before Peter, dressed in a white judo outfit and with an unlit spliff in his hand, took centre stage for

'Mark Of The Beast,' 'Can't Blame The Youths' and 'Legalise It.' The latter got one of biggest cheers of the night, after Peter had defiantly brandished his spliff for all to see. The strength of these individual performances demonstrated only too well why Peter and Bunny had chosen to go their separate ways. Bob then took over for 'So Jah Seh,' 'No Woman No Cry' and a rousing 'Jah Live.' The Wailers' journey had finally come to an end but if any of them sensed this in their hearts, there was no sign of it on the stage that night.

Stevie Wonder went on late yet still received a tumultuous welcome. A trio of groundbreaking albums – 'Talking Book,' 'Innervisions' and 'Fulfillingness' First Finale' had seen him outgrow the confines of Motown's hit factory and become one of the world's leading black superstars. Although no stranger to Jamaica, his arrival in late 1975 meant a lot given the island's perilous economic state and recent political upheavals. Midway through his set, he handed over a cheque for US $23,000 to representatives of Jamaica's Salvation Army School for the Blind – a sum that was larger than his appearance fee. His band was still playing the last few bars of 'You Are The Sunshine Of My Life' when the Wailers filed back on stage, hugging the shadows. The crowd began to stir as they realised what was about to happen. Stevie then beckoned them up front for a grand finale of 'I Shot The Sheriff' and 'Superstition' that sent everyone home wreathed in smiles, performers included. It was three in the morning and Trench Town's finest had just taken their final bow, singing in tandem with an American soul legend at the National Stadium. What a way to go... Also, Stevie had sung his heart out on 'I Shot The Sheriff.' He'd recently visited Africa for the first time, and was captivated by the music from Jamaica. He would perform with Bob again in future and produce tracks for Third World, who also played at the "Dream Concert." The Wailers were no more however, and their thirteen-year association would leave only recriminations in its wake, at least as far as the band members were concerned.

In the aftermath of the "Dream Concert," Peter told the Gleaner that according to Island Records, the Wailers still owed $41,000 in touring and recording expenses. He said it was this that had caused disagreements within the band, and not personal differences.

"The Wailers will always stay together because as it was in the beginning, so shall it be in the end," he said. "What really cause the rumour is the fact that Bunny and I refuse to sing for Island because of its poor treatment of us, after singing so many hits..."

Typically forthright, he called Island Records "pirates" and warned that, "Bob will find out someday they are only using him..."

Relationships between Peter and Bob would deteriorate even further after the Dream Concert. At one stage there was talk that Bob's manager, Don Taylor, was going to try and negotiate a joint deal for solo albums by all three Wailers. The proceeds would have then gone towards buying Island House and building a studio but Taylor had chosen to concentrate on representing Bob's interests instead, and even the Barrett brothers would lose out eventually. Insiders claim that just like Chris Blackwell, Don Taylor never understood the chemistry between the Wailers and preferred to deal with Marley alone. Bunny and Peter are said to have viewed this as a betrayal, whilst Bob had grown tired of such squabbles and wanted freedom to pursue his own musical destiny.

He and Peter would perform together just one more time, in Burbank during the 1978 "Kaya' tour. Bob and the Wailers had worked their way down the West coast before arriving at the Starlite Amphitheatre on July 22nd. Mick Jagger and Diana Ross were backstage that night but it was Peter alone who strode out to join Bob for a rousing duet on 'Get Up, Stand Up.' "The Pope felt that one!" Bob exclaimed, as the pair slapped hands backstage. Two weeks later, Pope Paul VI died and his replacement followed suit just a few weeks later. Rastafarians view the Pope as the anti-Christ and so the two deaths were regarded as highly significant. No wonder Peter had called his band Word, Sound & Power. He was signed to the Rolling Stones' record label by then and as their support act on the 'Some Girls' tour, was performing to mammoth crowds across America. It had taken him a while, but Peter had become a major star of the reggae firmament and especially after the release of his 1977 album 'Equal Rights,' which featured songs imbued with fiery Black Nationalism.

Try as they may, but no other reggae act could compete with Bob Marley. Everything had turned in his favour during the 'Rastaman Vibration' tour of 1976, when he'd reaped comparisons with Dylan and Jagger, and Playboy magazine called him "a prophet." The Gleaner told of UK audiences succumbing to "Marleymania" but then in December, just weeks after his girlfriend Cindy Breakspeare was crowned Miss World, he was injured in an assassination attempt at 56 Hope Road. The wounded superstar performed heroically at the Smile Jamaica concert just days later, surrounded by people willing to take a bullet for him if necessary. Forced into exile, he recorded the bestselling 'Exodus' and 'Kaya' albums in London, enjoyed several chart hits and completed a critically acclaimed tour of Europe despite suffering from a toe injury, which doctors later declared cancerous. The following April – just weeks before the Burbank performance – he'd returned to Jamaica and headlined the One Love Peace Concert – an event that brought the country's warring political parties together in a rare, public display of unity. Near the end of his performance Marley had invited Prime Minister Michael Manley and Edward Seaga – then Leader Of The Opposition – on stage with him, and joined their hands above his head whilst chanting "Jah, Rastafari." This iconic moment would become a defining landmark of popular culture and dwarf Peter Tosh's incendiary appearance at the same concert, despite his courageous speech deriding the police and local dignitaries.

During the next two and a half years, Marley would be awarded a Third World Peace Medal on behalf of "five hundred million Africans" and play at Zimbabwe's independence celebrations after writing the rebel forces' theme tune, 'Zimbabwe.' The album it was from, 'Survival,' went a long way towards reaffirming his credentials as a revolutionary. His last tour would be of the US, promoting 1980's 'Uprising' – a set containing 'Could You Be Loved' and the unforgettable 'Redemption Song.'

The melanoma cancer he'd been diagnosed with in early 1978 had spread throughout his body by then, causing him to collapse whilst jogging in New York's Central Park. He would perform for the last time three days later, at the Stanley Theatre in Pittsburgh on September 23rd 1980. Several months later, after treatment at a specialist clinic in Bavaria, he would head for Jamaica but die en route at a Miami hospital on May 11th 1981, aged just thirty-six.

The whole of Jamaica and half the world's media turned out for his funeral but not Peter nor Bunny, who declined to attend because of their religious beliefs. Later that same year Bunny released 'Tribute,' on which he covered some of Bob's best-known roots and culture songs. It was swiftly followed by another album entitled 'Sings The Wailers,' aimed at keeping memories of the original line-up alive. Whether that message ever reached beyond grassroots' audiences is debatable. Indeed, there would have been no need for this book if it had succeeded. No one's disputing the depth of his talent, but with the aid of skilful and persistent marketing, Bob's memory would turn into a juggernaut and relegate such considerations to a mere footnote. In the years ahead, he'll be recast as a cultural icon and come to symbolise reggae and Rastafari to millions of people around the world. The BBC will name 'One Love / People Get Ready' "Song Of The Millennium" whilst 1984 compilation 'Legend' will become the second longest charting album in the history of Billboard magazine and sell nearly three million copies in Britain. By 2006, he'd made Forbes' Top 5 list of biggest earning dead rock stars and was outperforming John Lennon. Such achievements went way beyond the title of "first Third World superstar," and led to his life story becoming blurred with mythology.

As this process began to manifest, Peter made the occasional bitter comment about his dead friend, whilst fending off attempts to crown him "the new King Of Reggae." In December 1982, he and Bunny co-hosted a benefit concert held at Kingston's National Stadium called "Youth Consciousness." This show marked Bunny's return to the stage after a lengthy absence, and was intended to raise funds for youth projects in Jamaica. Although dogged by inclement weather it was a resounding success musically, and offered solid affirmation of he and Peter's legitimacy as reggae figureheads. Several years later, they would embark on a joint project with Junior Braithwaite and Vision Walker under the heading of 'Never Ending Wailers,' which found the surviving members voicing over archive recordings. The resulting album was intended as a reminder of the Wailers' enduring potency, even without their charismatic leader (although Bob's ghostly vocals can be heard on certain tracks.) It was finally released in 1993 on Tuff Gong, and greeted by tepid reviews for the most part.

The other Wailers had already been relegated to supporting roles in the Bob Marley story by then – even Peter, who was shot and killed just weeks after Carlton Barrett was murdered by a hit man hired by his wife and her lover.

Peter was killed after an incident at his detached home in uptown Kingston on September 11th 1987, not far from Johnny Nash's old house in Russell Heights. He'd been relaxing with girlfriend Marlene Brown and three friends (including drummer Carlton "Santa" Davis) when Dennis "Leppo" Lobban, who'd recently been freed from prison, forced his way into the house accompanied by two other men, both armed. Peter and company were already face down on the floor when local radio DJ Free I and his wife Joy called at the house. They too, were ordered to prostrate themselves on the floor, shortly before Leppo and the other gunmen opened fire. Peter, herbalist Wilton "Doc" Brown and Free I all died as a result of injuries sustained that night. Some claim that Leppo, who still languishes in a Kingston high security prison, had taken the rap after Peter was caught with a gun a couple of years beforehand, and that Leppo's family hadn't been cared for as promised. Others swear that Peter was assassinated after a drug deal went wrong, and that he and Free I had planned to launch a radio station in Jamaica, which the authorities feared might cause a popular uprising. He'd also been in dispute with his record company, and bragged about being owed millions of dollars, which may have attracted unwelcome attention. Whatever the truth, the police had never stopped harassing Tosh, who'd remained defiant as ever. In fact they'd nearly beaten him to death in retaliation for his outburst at the One Love Peace Concert – an incident that had coincided with the release of 'Bush Doctor,' the first of three albums he recorded for the Rolling Stones' own label. It says a lot about Peter's character that he would continue taunting and upsetting the Jamaican authorities, despite their reputation for brutal intervention. Challenging the status quo is what he lived for, as when recording 'Oh Bumbaclaat' – a term that's so derogatory, it caused even his staunchest supporters to blush. A year later, in 1982 he travelled to Africa for the first time. On his return to Jamaica he recorded 'Mama Africa,' and embarked on lengthy tours of Europe and the US.

He hadn't performed for over three years before his death and was rumoured to have become obsessed with the supernatural. He'd also become embroiled in drawn-out contractual disputes with EMI, thereby delaying completion of 'No Nuclear War,' which won him a posthumous Grammy and was arguably the most accomplished album of his career. Ironically, given his reputation as an iconoclast, his best-known hits would be covers of the Temptations' 'Don't Look Back,' shared with Mick Jagger, and Chuck Berry's 'Johnny B. Goode.'

He and Carly's murders would give rise to rumours that the Wailers were cursed in some way – a feeling strengthened by the death of Junior Braithwaite in June 1999. He also died at the hands of a Kingston gunman, just days after returning to Jamaica from a lengthy exile in the US.

With the exception of Rita and Vision, Bunny is the last Wailer left standing at the time of writing. The mantle of elder statesman suits him, which is not to say that he hasn't made puzzling decisions at times. Musically speaking, there have been grave disappointments to weigh against enduring highlights such as 'Blackheart Man,' 'Protest' and tracks compiled on 'Crucial Roots Classics' and 'Retrospective.' His live appearances, whilst sporadic, remain powerful expressions of the Rasta reggae idiom and yet they've sometimes been mired by controversy as a result of his homophobic outbursts and disputes with promoters. In-between recording new material and performing the occasional concert he's also notorious for making verbal (and sometimes legal) assaults on Chris Blackwell and the Marley Estate, whilst vigorously defending the validity of the original Wailers' line-up.

It's sometimes difficult to separate mythology from fact where Marley's concerned, despite the preponderance of archive material. Most books, films and documentaries reiterate Island Records' version of events and diminish the contributions of everyone else except Marley himself, including central characters like Aston "Family Man" Barrett. Present-day audiences and media commentators alike have been slow in questioning actions of the corporate entity that now controls Marley's name, image and story, and yet Bob wasn't alone when he stood under that tamarind tree at the corner of West Road and Third Street, dreaming of a singing career. The history of reggae music is rife with singers who've made similar journeys of discovery, but it was the Wailers that put reggae and Rastafari on the world map. Bob became a superstar but when he sang with Bunny and Peter, something magical happened. There's been no Jamaican act like them since and their harmonies can still make the hairs on the back of my neck stand up, even forty years later.

Thanks And Praise

A great many people helped in the writing of this book, whether by sharing recollections or invaluable time and resources. Their contributions made all the difference so thank you Dennis Alcapone, Richard Alderson, Esther Anderson, Bob Andy, Brian Atkinson, Theo Bafaloukus, Dave Barker, Elizabeth Barraclough, Hux Brown, Prince Buster, Charlie Organaire, Clive Chin, the late Leonard "Santic" Chin, Sebastian Clarke, Fikisha Cumbo, Martin Disney, Brinsley Forde, Winston Francis, Marcia Griffiths, Locksley Gichie of the Cimarons, Sidney "Junior Dan" Guissine, Bernard "Touter" Harvey, Ray Hurford, Lee Jaffe, Howard Johnson, Paul Khouri, Chuck Krall, Bunny "Striker" Lee, Roger and Ian Lewis, Earl "Wya" Lindo and family, Glen Lockley, Earl "Little Roy" Lowe, Larry McDonald, Jerry Neville, for his fabulous front cover illustration, the late Jimmy Norman, Niney The Observer, Lee "Scratch" Perry, John Reed, Sonia and Winston Rodney, Delroy Washington (whose calls were a constant source of knowledge and insight) and Don Williams.

Special thanks go out to the following, without whom this book probably wouldn't have got off the ground. Aston "Family Man" Barrett and Jennifer Miller, who started the ball rolling, and Roger and Mary Steffens for their enduring support and making me feel like a member of the family. Roger is a consummate reggae authority and he and Leroy Jodie Pierson's book 'Bob Marley and the Wailers: The Definite Discography' proved an invaluable research tool during the writing of 'Simmer Down.'

I should also like to thank Bunny Wailer, for his starring role in Jamaica's greatest-ever musical adventure; Catherine Gillo, for her editorial input and unstinting resolve when storm clouds gathered; Mike van der Linde, for his unbridled enthusiasm and treasures through the post; Echoes Magazine for keeping the home fires burning and the late Alan Douglas, whose friendship was a blessing I'll never forget. Thanks also, to those wonderful people at the Rototum festival and especially Sabrina, who unwittingly provided so much of the inspiration during my visit to Benacassim in 2011.

Sources

PART ONE

Chapter One: **Forward March**

Rachel Manley: Drumblair: Memories Of A Jamaican Childhood (Vintage Canada, 1997)
Rachel Manley: Slipstream: A Daughter Remembers (Ian Randle Publishers, 2000)
Peter J. Albert and Ronald Hoffman: We Shall Overcome: Martin Luther King And The Black Liberation Struggle (Da Capo, 1993)
Derrick Morgan, lyrics to Forward March.

Chapter Two: **Simmer Down**

Bunny Wailer, interview with Roger Steffens.
Steve Barrow and Peter Dalton: Reggae: The Rough Guide (Rough Guides 1997.)
J. F. Kennedy: Civil Rights Announcement, 1963.
Alvin "Seeco" Patterson, as told to Distant Drums.
Beverley Kelso, as told to Roger Steffens.
Bunny Wailer, interview with the author.
Leroy Jodie Pierson and Roger Steffens: Bob Marley & the Wailers: Destiny, Rare Ska Sides From Studio One (Heartbeat, 1999)

Chapter Three: **Keep On Pushin'**

Beverley Kelso, interview with Roger Steffens.
Joe Higgs, interview with Roger Steffens.
Bunny Wailer, interview with Roger Steffens.
Leroy Jodie Pierson and Roger Steffens: Bob Marley & the Wailers: Destiny, Rare Ska Sides From Studio One (Heartbeat, 1999)

Rachel Manley: Drumblair: Memories Of A Jamaican Childhood (Vintage Canada, 1997)
George Breitman: Malcolm X Speaks (Grove Press, 1965)
Terry Lacey: Violence And Politics In Jamaica 1960-70 (Frank Cass And Company, 1977)
Leroy Jodie Pierson, interview with Leonard Dillon.

Chapter Four: **Wantie Wantie**

Stokely Carmichael and Charles V. Hamilton: Black Power: The Politics Of Liberation In America (Pelican, 1967)
Walter Mosley: What Next: A Memoir Towards World Peace (Serpent's Tail, 2003)
Tony Uter, as told to Distant Drums.
Bob Andy, writing on the I-Anka website.
Bunny Wailer, interview with Roger Steffens.
Sebastian Clarke: Jah Music: The Evolution Of The Popular Jamaican Song (Heinnemann Educational Books, 1980)
Dwight Pinkney, as told to Distant Drums.
Beverley Kelso, as told to Roger Steffens.

Chapter Five: **Rasta Shook Them Up**

Hernando Calvo Ospina: Salsa! Havana Heat, Bronx Beat (Latin America Bureau 1995.)
Larry MacDonald, interview with the author.
Nathaniel Samuel Murrell, William David Spencer & Adrian Anthony McFarlane: Chanting Down Babylon: The Rastafari Reader (Temple University Press, 1998.)
Leroy Jodie Pierson and Roger Steffens: Bob Marley & the Wailers: Destiny, Rare Ska Sides From Studio One (Heartbeat, 1999)

PART TWO

Chapter Six: **Freedom Time**

Fikisha Cumbo: Get Up Stand Up: Diary Of A Reggaeophile (CACE International 2002.)
Bunny Wailer, interview with Roger Steffens.
Dennis Alcapone, interview with the author.
Prince Buster, interview with the author.
Thomas Hauser: Muhammad Ali: His Life And Times (Portico, 2004.)
Peter Stansill and David Zane Mairowitz: BAMN (By Any Means Necessary): Outlaw Manifestos and Ephemera 1965-70 (Penguin, 1971)
Stokely Carmichael with Ekwueme Michael Thelwell: Ready For Revolution: The Life And Struggles Of Stokely Carmichael (Kwame Toure) (Scribner, 2003)
Jackie Jackson, interview with Mark Gorney.

Chapter Seven: **Thinking Like Wolves**

Alton Ellis, interview with the author.
Burning Spear, interview with the author.
Bunny Wailer, interview with Roger Steffens.
Miriam Makeba with James Hall: Makeba: My Story (Bloomsbury, 1988)
Danny Sims, interview with Roger Steffens.
Toots Hibbert, as quoted in Kevin O' Brien Chang & Wayne Chen: Reggae Routes: The Story Of Jamaican Music (Ian Randle, 1998)
Ras Cardo: Reggae Jamaica: The Wailing Of A People (Xlibris, 2006)
Peter J. Albert and Ronald Hoffman: We Shall Overcome: Martin Luther King And The Black Liberation Struggle (Da Capo, 1993)
Sebastian Clarke: Jah Music: The Evolution Of The Popular Jamaican Song (Heinnemann Educational Books, 1980)

Chapter Eight: **Where It's At**

Paul Khouri, interview with the author.
Richard Alderson, interview with the author.
Danny Sims, interview with Roger Steffens.
Jimmy Norman, interview with the author.

Chapter Nine: **Black Power**

Walter Rodney: The Groundings With My Brothers (The Bogle L'Ouverture Publications, 1969)
Walter Rodney: Walter Rodney Speaks: The Making Of An African Intellectual (Africa World Press, 1990)
Andrew Salkey: Joey Tyson (The Bogle L'Ouverture Publications, 1974)

Chapter Ten: **Dream Awhile**

Richard Alderson, interview with the author.
Hugh Masekela and D. Michael Cheer: Still Grazing: The Musical Journey Of Hugh Masekela (Crown Publishers. New York, 2004)
Jimmy Norman, interview with the author.
Clive Chin, interview with the author.
Larry MacDonald, interview with the author.
Desmond Dekker, interview with Gordon Coxhill.

Chapter Eleven: **Nuggets For The Needy**

Dave Barker, interview with the author.
David Ritz: The Adventures Of Grandmaster Flash: My Life, My Beats (Crown, 2008.)
Hux Brown, interview with the author.
Aston "Family Man" Barrett, interview with the author.
Clive Chin, interview with the author.
Stokely Carmichael: Stokely Speaks: Black Power Back To Pan-Africanism (Random House, 1971)
Bunny Wailer, interview with Roger Steffens.

Chapter Twelve: **Living On Our Feet**

Bob Andy, interview with the author.
Aston "Family Man" Barrett, interview with the author.
James Brown with Bruce Tucker: The Godfather Of Soul (Fontana 1988.)
James Sullivan: The Hardest Working Man: How James Brown Saved The Soul Of America (Gotham Books 2008)
Bunny "Striker" Lee, interview with the author.
Dave Barker, interview with the author.
Clive Chin, interview with the author.
Bunny Wailer, interview with Roger Steffens.
Junior Dan, interview with the author.

Chapter Thirteen: **Shocks Of Mighty**

Dave Barker, interview with the author.
Little Roy, interview with the author.
Clive Chin, interview with the author.
Junior Dan, interview with the author.
Nathaniel Samuel Murrell, William David Spencer & Adrian Anthony McFarlane: Chanting Down Babylon: The Rastafari Reader (Temple University Press, 1998.)
Bunny Wailer, interview with Roger Steffens.
Aston "Family Man" Barrett, interview with the author.
David Brun-Lambert: Nina Simone, The Biography (Aurum Press, 2009.)

Chapter Fourteen: **King Street Shuffle**

Bunny "Striker" Lee, interview with the author.
Bunny Wailer, interview with Roger Steffens.
Lee "Scratch" Perry, interview with the author.
Roger Lewis of Inner Circle, interview with the author.
Bob Andy, interview with the author.

PART THREE

Chapter Fifteen: **One Eyed Jack And The Midnight Ravers**

Junior Dan, interview with the author.
Alan "Skill" Cole, interview with Roger Steffens.
Bunny "Striker" Lee, interview with the author.
Bob Andy, interview with the author.
Locksley Gichie, interview with the author.
Sebastian Clarke: Jah Music: The Evolution Of The Popular Jamaican Song (Heinnemann Educational Books, 1980)
Brinsley Forde, interview with the author.
Delroy Washington, interview with the author.
Fikisha Cumbo: Get Up Stand Up: Diary Of A Reggaeophile (CACE International 2002.)
Aston "Family Man" Barrett, interview with the author.
Danny Sims, interview with Roger Steffens.

Chapter Sixteen: **Island Hopping**

Aston "Family Man" Barrett, interview with the author.
Theo Bafaloukos, interview with the author.
Lee Jaffe with Roger Steffens: One Love: Life With Bob Marley And The Wailers (Norton 2003.)
Esther Anderson, interview with the author.
Al Anderson, interview with the author.

Chapter Seventeen: **Isms And Schisms**

Esther Anderson, interview with the author.
Bunny Wailer, interview with the author.
Nathaniel Samuel Murrell, William David Spencer & Adrian Anthony McFarlane: Chanting Down Babylon: The Rastafari Reader (Temple University Press, 1998.)
Lee Jaffe, interview with the author.
Fikisha Cumbo: Get Up Stand Up: Diary Of A Reggaeophile (CACE International 2002.)
Don Williams, interview with the author.

Chapter Eighteen: **Rockin' At Mr. B's**

Mick Wall: John Peel (Orion, 2012.)
Joe Venneri, interview with Roger Steffens.
Aston "Family Man" Barrett, interview with the author.
Laurie O' Leary, interview with Marco Virgona.
Jeff Griffin, interview with Distant Drums.

Chapter Nineteen: **Turn Me Loose**

Esther Anderson, interview with the author.
Peter Tosh, as quoted in Kevin O' Brien Chang & Wayne Chen: Reggae Routes: The Story Of Jamaican Music (Ian Randle, 1998)
James Brown with Bruce Tucker: The Godfather Of Soul (Fontana 1988.)
Lee Jaffe, interview with the author.
Rickey Vincent: Funk – The Music, The People And The Rhythm Of The One (St. Martin's Griffin, 1996.)
Joe Higgs, interview with Roger Steffens.
Chuck Krall, interview with the author.
Don Williams, interview with the author.
Peter Tosh, interview with Malika Lee Whitney.

Chapter Twenty: **Pass It On**

Esther Anderson, interview with the author.
Delroy Washington, interview with the author.
Hux Brown, interview with the author.
Aston "Family Man" Barrett, interview with the author.
Lee Jaffe, interview with the author.
Bunny Wailer, interview with the author.

21438806R00254

Printed in Great Britain
by Amazon